NERO
BUTCHER OF ROME

BY ERNST ECKSTEIN

ZEBRA BOOKS

KENSINGTON PUBLISHING CORP.

ZEBRA BOOKS

are published by

KENSINGTON PUBLISHING CORP.
21 East 40th Street
New York, N.Y. 10016

First Printing: June, 1978

Printed in the United States of America

THREE HUNDRED MARTYRS WERE TO BE
LIGHTED LIKE TORCHES BY THE SLAVES
AS SOON AS DARKNESS SET IN . . .

But the orgy had already begun. Nero lounged in
the arms of Poppaea; dozens of female slaves
passed wine to the emperor's guests; half-nude
boys, their shoulders covered by crimson robes
and panther skins, flashed through the crowd.

Directly in front of the imperial tribune, on a
long line extending from one end of the semi-circle of spectators to the other, stretched a row of
holes—perhaps three hundred in number—
spaced two feet apart. Into these holes the slaves
were planting posts, each of whose broad tops
supported a human form, wrapped to the
shoulders in hemp fiber. Stout iron wires fastened their bodies and limbs to the beams, and
the whole covering was saturated with wax,
pitch, tar, and oil.

The spectators could never be satisfied with
the mere hacking and mutilating of the gladiators' conflicts, and now the amphitheatre filled
with an almost tangible sexual tension as their
blood-thirsty longing rose to a feverish ecstasy in
anticipation of this new spectacle.

For soon the long-drawn note of a tuba would
be sounded as the signal, and the slaves, shrieking and brandishing their torches, would rush
upon the victims . . . .

INTRODUCTION

For many years after it was first published in 1889, Ernst Eckstein's *Nero* was a world-wide best seller—translated from the original German into every civilized language. Eckstein was a favorite author of American presidents from Grover Cleveland to Teddy Roosevelt, and there are those who say Kaiser Wilhelm used Eckstein's Nero, the leader, as a role model. We do know that Adolph Hitler, little known as a lover of literature, had a collection of Eckstein first editions at his summer home in Berchesgarten. There are elements of Nero's character, especially toward the end of his despotic career, which remind the reader of the late and unlamented Fuhrer.

Eckstein (1845-1901) was a lifelong and serious student of the Roman Empire, spending many years in Italy studying the original writings (in Latin, Greek and Hebrew) of Tacitus, Josephus, and Suetenius, to insure the authenticity of his plots, characters, and backgrounds. It takes a special writer to make history come alive, and its characters pulsate with life. As you are riveted to the story of Nero, you will realize that Eckstein doesn't create cardboard, one-dimensional characters. We first meet Nero as an art-loving young man, a dancer and musician. A boy with his own extensive library. A writer, himself. He is an avid student of the philosopher Seneca, who has taught his pupil that all men are created equal.

We watch with excitement and eventual horror as Nero's character changes from a loving emperor whose subjects throw roses in his path and swarm all over him to kiss his hand and toga, to the sybarite who, disguised as a peasant, visits brothels, frequents taverns, and with comrades of his mood, robs shops, insults women, and "practices lewdness," to the depraved monarch who let his city burn, and whose idea of great sport was to put Christians to death with exquisite cruelty.

All of this is in the novel *Nero*. We are present at love-feasts, where wife-swapping is winked at. We are privy to Nero's torture chambers, where innocent victims are made to confess to crimes they didn't commit. We learn what life in ancient Rome, at least among the patricians, was really like. Eckstein skillfully demonstrates the slow change of Nero's character (which, being Lord of the World, influenced the entire world of the time and, of course, our own history) through his relations with women.

First there is Agrippina, his mother. Almost as power-mad as Livia, the wife of Augustus, Agrippina was the last wife of the great Emperor Claudius. When it looked like Claudius would name his own son, Brittanicus, to succeed him, Agrippina had Brittanicus killed and served her husband poisoned mushrooms.

Claudius died, and Nero, Agrippina's son by Domitian, became Emperor. Agrippina did her best *not* to involve Nero in affairs of state; she ruled the roost, and with an iron hand.

By accident, after saving the life of a condemned Christian freedman from the headsman's axe, Nero met Acte, a Christian freedwoman. Agrippina had already betrothed Nero to Octavia, heiress to one of the most important families in Rome. But Nero fell deeply in love with Acte, though he agreed to marry Octavia for state reasons. Agrippina had Acte kidnapped and removed, and she ostensibly died at sea.

While mourning Acte, Nero begins to learn of his mother's many treacheries, and meets Poppaeia, the most beautiful woman in Rome, wife of a friend, Otho. Poppaeia rivals Agrippina for cunning and wickedness and sees her chance to become Empress. Both Agrippina and Octavia must be removed.

Meanwhile, many Roman nobles have been dissatisfied with the royal family's squandering of wealth, and many revolutions begin to simmer—acts of terrorism and treachery. Paul the Nazarene is preaching in Rome—his sect is being tolerated for the moment. Even Nicodemus, a friend of Seneca and a guest at court, is a Roman Christian.

It is against this background that the novel *Nero* takes place. Its major cast of characters, in alphabetical order, include:

ACTE—a beautiful, golden-haired freedwoman, who has come under the influence of Nicodemus, the Christian leader in Rome. She first attracts Nero's attention at the execution hill in Rome, where she pleads for a condemned man's life. Then, on one of Nero's expeditions into the heart of Rome, he meets her in an Egyptian magician's tent, and the meeting generates a series of events that change the history of the world, and the love of Acte and Nero remains one of the world's great tragic romances.

ARTEMIDORUS—a freedman foreman for an important Roman senator, he is in love with the entertainer Chloris. Artemidorus is a committed Christian and Chloris is a devotee of pleasure and pagan gods. Their relationship can only end in tragedy.

AGRIPPINA—the empress-mother of Rome, mother of Nero, and wielder of phenomenal power. Her spies are everywhere and to cross her is to face instant death. She loves her son Nero, but loves power—and, in her own words, Rome—even more.

BURRUS—Chief of the Praetorian guards, sworn to protect the royal family. A suspected lover of Agrippina.

CHLORIS—only in her teens, she is the greatest entertainer in Nero's Rome. Chloris is from the island of Rhodes, and a devotee of the goddess Aphrodite. Though she loves the Christian Artemidorus, she cannot understand any of the things he believes—until in one of the most heart-breaking scenes in literature—she understands it all.

NERO—the emperor, Lord of the World. He loves two women—one of them Acte, the Christian, is a pure and innocent love. The other, Poppaeia, helps turn him from a popular leader into one of history's ogres. The historian Tacitus calls Poppaeia one of "history's ugliest whores." Busts of Poppaeia, still in museums today, show her to be an unbelievably beautiful woman, even by modern standards.

NICODEMUS—leader of the Christian community in Rome, a friend of the philosopher Seneca, a guest and occasional companion of Nero. He trusted the emperor who proved to be a two-faced friend. Nicodemus felt that Acte's relationship with Nero could bring Christ to the court of Rome. He was wrong.

OCTAVIA—she loved Nero and wanted to be a good and faithful wife. She bore the transgressions of Nero silently, and preserved her own modesty and chastity among the stream of sexual license in which she had been forced to live since her birth. She proved to be an amazing friend to others in the cast, and her fate proved just how little justice there was in ancient Rome.

PALLUS—originally told Emperor Claudius to marry Agrippina. He was the slave of Claudius' mother, Antonia, set free because of his devotion to the family and his intelligence, and rose quickly to become the lieutenant of

Agrippina and a very powerful man in the court of Nero. Because of his closeness to Agrippina he was both feared and respected.

PHARAX—an ambitious Roman soldier who rose from man in the ranks to Centurian. Married to the slave, Hasdra, he spent too much time with the empress mother.

POPPAEIA—wife of Otho, friend of Nero. She hated her husband but played the "good wife" because of Otho's connections with the court. Considered one of history's great beauties, she seduced Nero, convinced him to divorce his wife, and proved to him that his mother was a villainess. She was an empress for a very short time.

SENECA—tutor to Nero and eventual senior advisor. An ally of both Agrippina and her son, he eventually supported a conspiracy against them.

TIGELLINUS—a Sicilian adventurer who became one of Nero's hangers-on. Nero trusted him, but Tigellinus was interested in two things—sleeping with as many beautiful women as was humanly possible, and power. Agrippina warned her son about keeping bad company, but Nero didn't listen.

BOOK I

CHAPTER I.

THREE of the Roman prefect's soldiers were dragging a prisoner along the Cyprian Way. He was a man of about four and twenty—condemned to death; he was to be beheaded by the common executioner, and then buried in the cemetery for criminals.

Wherever the armed men passed with their young captive, the people paused for a moment to gaze at him. The hapless victim's pale but calm features excited sympathy even among the indifferent Romans. These people, who saw thousands of gladiators bleed and die every year, fighting with men or wild beasts, and to whom the death-groans of a victim were delightful music, seemed struck with unwonted pity, the women especially—for Artemidorus was a handsome youth. His regular features, as sharply cut as if they were chiselled out of marble, his dark rapt eyes with long black lashes, his noble brow and fine thick hair were almost a match for those of Necho, the priest of Pthah, whose power over the noble ladies of Rome was due almost as much to his personal charms as to his art as a soothsayer.

Artemidorus, too, was of eastern birth. He was a native of far-off Damascus, had been bought as a slave at Jerusalem by the senator Flavius Scaevinus, and had come in his train to the City of the Seven Hills. Having soon afterwards obtained his freedom he had continued to serve his former owner as steward, reader, and librarian, nay, almost as a confidential friend, till a sudden turn of fortune had upset this peaceful and happy state of things, casting the once envied freedman into the hands of the authorities.

The nearer they approached their horrible destination, the slower and more reluctant was the young man's gait. The soldier in command of the little guard was forced to rouse him more than once with threats and warnings.

It was a glorious day in October; all Rome seemed to float in a golden haze. Ruddy-tinted vine wreaths, loaded with bunches of dark grapes, hung over the garden walls, or clung to the spreading boughs of the elm-trees; a breath of indescribable freshness and revival blew down the streets. The men seemed more erect, the women's faces more radiantly beautiful and attractive than usual. So it appeared to him at least—to the condemned wretch, who within a very brief time must bid farewell to this world of fair promise.

Where now was the confident courage to face death which a short while since had bounded through his veins like a breath of some better and superhuman life? As he noted the purple fruit swaying heavily overhead, he remembered a pretty Rhodian maid, whose blushing brows he once had wreathed with a garland of autumn vine-leaves as they sat in blissful solitude in the depths of his master's bowery park.

"Chloris! Chloris!" he sighed in a spasm of anguish.

What a cruel fatality that the image of his beloved should thus rise up before him at the very moment when he needed all his strength, and all his scorn of life, to keep him in mind that a disciple of the Carpenter's Son, the Nazarene, must follow his Master's example in hope and gladness!

Still, fight against it as he would, memory would paint the intoxicating joys of that past time in the most glowing colors. But a few weeks since he had seen Chloris for the first time, playing the nine-stringed cithara in the house of Caius

Calpurnius Piso, while she sang a Greek love-song. This had been her first appearance in the perilous ground of the capital—and her first triumph. Every one applauded her admirable skill and her glorious voice. Artemidorus, who was present in attendance on his master, was spellbound; from that instant he had been possessed with one idea: that she must be his.

And yet—yes, he had another and a higher purpose: he must save her soul. Ever since the never-to-be-forgotten moment when he first had kissed her lips, a passionate desire had filled his mind to rescue that lost lamb. For she was lost, in the opinion of the believing Nazarene, unless he could succeed in persuading her of the heavenly truths revealed in Christ Jesus. And with all the vehemence of his nature Artemidorus now strove for this, as he before had striven to win her heart.

It was all in vain. Chloris had seen nothing of life but its rosiest side. The world to her seemed a garden of pleasures and perfumes, formed only for happiness and unresisting enjoyment. Being a Greek she shrank from all that was harsh or gloomy; the doctrine of the Cross, with its sorrowful self-denial, could find no access to a nature so soaked in the sunshine of the Hellenic theology. The fair musician shrugged her shoulders; she explained to her lover that he bored her, and closed a long and vexatious discussion with a scornful: "Never!"

He had quitted her in fierce wrath after she had pronounced this: "Never!" He was not angry with *her* —for it was no fault of hers that evil demons should so wholly possess her foolish little heart; it was the malice of those old gods who, in spite of the Saviour's advent, still exercised great power over even the noblest and purest of mankind.— And then he committed the "crime" which led to his being accused of insulting the religion of the State, and condemned to a horrible death.

And was not his deep anguish a punishment perhaps, from the one and only true God? Was it not meet that he should be stricken to the very earth for his obstinacy in cherishing his love for Chloris, worshipper of pagan gods? All this passed through his mind in chaotic bewilderment, and he gasped as he steeled himself against the strange emotion which threatened to choke him. He tried to pray: "Blessed are they who suffer death for the Word's sake," he murmured with quivering lips. But he could say no more, the golden sunshine was falling full on the road.

Yea, the merciless God had chosen him out for the bitterest martyrdom on earth, the deepest despair. If only his dying eyes might once more have met those of his beloved, what a balm in that last fearful moment! But as it was—This was death in life.

"Parted from her. . . ." the words sounded in his ears. "Parted from her!" His knees gave way, and all was dark before his eyes.

"Do not stumble," said the soldier. "Since you must die, die like a man!"

Artemidorus pulled himself up. The paroxysm of fear was over. He took a deep breath and went onward, calm and determined. Presently, when the little escort, with the prisoner in their midst, turned off from the Via Cyprius to the south-east, so dense a crowd of men and women—for the most part very poorly clad—gathered round them that for a moment they were brought to a standstill.

"Artemidorus!" was shouted in every key. "Be steadfast, Artemidorus! Farewell, Artemidorus! Do not forget your friends; pray for us before the throne of the Almighty!"

Some grasped the young man's fettered hands and kissed them; others began to sing in a tone of solemn lamentation, and the name of Jesus, repeated again and again with a peculiar mode of melody, gave the dirge a character of its own.

A tall, spare man of fifty, whose large glittering gold ring showed that he belonged to the equestrian order, now made his way through the throng.

"Will you allow me," said he to the leader of the band,

"to embrace the prisoner once more before he goes to meet his fate?"

The soldier frowned. The number of those who sympathized with Artemidorus visibly disturbed him. Still, he could not repulse this sinister-looking personage, whose toga was flung over his shoulder with such haughty defiance, as he might have done a dependent on the bounty of the State.

"Then make it short!" he said stopping. "I am not made of stone and iron; but if it should come to the prefect's ears I should get into trouble."

"Nicodemus!" whispered Artemidorus, as his friend pressed a kiss on his brow in sign of blessing. "What an end! What a dreadful fate!"

"Courage, my son. Endure to the end! Though it was not wise to rush so madly into the breach, at any rate it was noble-hearted. Happy is youth, which does not dream how far more surely dull prudence wins the goal than scorn and vehemence!"

"You are right!" murmured Artemidorus. "I looked forward so hopefully to the future—and perhaps it ill-became me, one of the youngest. . . . But it was Chloris, whom I love and ought to hate—Chloris was to blame, with her horrible disbelief. I was like one mad; I had tried everything, every means: and in vain! And then when I reached home, when I saw their atrocious idols in the atrium, with their hideous, grinning. . . ."

"Silence! You have outraged Roman society, and that was rash folly. No one is persecuted here for his faith's sake. We may follow the path which lies plain before the soul of every disciple of the Gospel in perfect peace and security; but there must be no rebellion, no violence.—And you, dear Artemidorus, might perhaps have been a co-operator in the scheme I had so carefully planned.—I am inconsolable for your loss!"

The young man drew himself up.

"What!" he exclaimed. "You pity me? But is it not the

highest boon God's mercy can bestow on us to die and shed our blood for the doctrine of Nazareth?''

''And your witness will not be in vain, Artemidorus,'' Nicodemus whispered soothingly. ''Still, you might have lived, you might have. . . .''

But Nicodemus was interrupted in his speech by a sudden agitation among the people.

''Caesar!'' was spoken by a hundred tongues, and every eye was turned towards the Porta Querquetulana whence a magnificent litter with a purple baldachino slowly bore down on them. Eight stalwart, flaxen-haired Sicambri in scarlet tunics carried the lavishly-decorated couch on staves of cedar overlaid with gold. The ample curtains were drawn back.

On the pillows reclined a proud and majestic woman: Agrippina, the empress-mother; at her side was a youth of enchanting beauty, almost girlish in the expression of his large, enquiring eyes, his pouting lips sweet with a thousand gentle meanings, half-parted for kissing, half-breathing some melody.

At the sight of this train the captain of the guard was startled. He knew how Caesar disliked any incident that jarred on the unruffled serenity of his nature; especially how wrathful he could be with the decisions of the law and their terrible issues.

''Pharax, you are doomed to ill-luck!'' said the soldier to himself. ''If the prefect should hear of it, the centurion's vine-staff will dance over your ribs with Gaditanian grace! To be sure it is pure accident; but the prefect's servants are made to pay even for the vagaries of Fate. . . .''

''Caesar!'' Nicodemus, too, exclaimed. ''Then he will pass close to you in a moment!—Artemidorus, appeal to his clemency.''

Every one stood aside. Nicodemus seized the hand of a fair-haired girl whose eyes had been fixed in holy pity on the prisoner. She glanced up in wonder. Some important train of thought must have worked itself out in the tall man's brain, for a flash of sudden satisfaction lighted up his face, and an almost triumphant movement of his lips seemed to say: "This augurs success!"

He bent down to the girl and hastily whispered:

"Acte, do you see? Heaven itself opens a way. If you have ever for a moment doubted whether my scheme is pleasing in the sight of the Lord Jesus Christ this miraculous coincidence must convince you. Listen now to what I say to you. As soon as I nod, step forward, throw yourself at Caesar's feet, and pray that Artemidorus' life may be spared."

"That I will," cried Acte. "Do you pray that Caesar may be moved to grant the petition."

"I hope he will," murmured Nicodemus. "Only plead to him with the warmth and fervor you feel—or do you indeed feel no pity for this youth, who is doomed to die under the executioner's axe?"

Acte sighed and was mute. Then she looked fixedly but timidly at the imperial litter coming nearer to them.

"How handsome she is, and how childlike!" thought Nicodemus. "There is not her match in all Rome. . . . It must succeed! it must!"

"Hail Caesar!" The shout came nearer and nearer. The soldiers now joined the echoing cry, and the gaping crowd, including most of the Nazarenes. "Glory and honor to Caesar! Hail Claudius Nero, the joy of the human race!"

The emperor had signed to his bearers, and the litter stood still. The storm of greetings, to which Nero had responded with friendly waving of the hand, was succeeded by perfect silence.

"Some hapless wretch!" he said, turning to Agrippina. "You will allow me, dear mother, to enquire of the guard what his crime has been."

"Just as you please," replied the empress-mother. "It well beseems the Ruler of the World to interest himself in even the smallest thing that comes across his path."

"The smallest?" smiled Nero, looking in his mother's face. "A man loaded with chains, and in whose face grief and pain are so plainly written!—Nay, dearest mother, you do not

17

speak from your heart. Or does the dignity of Caesar require that he should take the woes of his subjects so lightly—as lightly as the fall of this rose of Paestum which is just dropping out of your hair?" And with a graceful movement he pushed the stem of the flower under the diadem of gems which confined Agrippina's flame-colored veil.

Then, addressing the chief of the guards, he said benevolently:

"Whom have you there, and what is his crime?"

"My lord," said the soldier, "he is a freedman of Flavius Scaevinus. . . ."

"What! of our friend the evergreen senator?"

"The very same."

Nero cast a searching glance at the young man, who kept his eyes fixed on the ground.

"To be sure; I know him—Artemidorus, who once read the works of Ennius to us in his master's park. Flavius Scaevinus was loud in your praises; he spoke of your trustworthiness, your discretion.—And now?—I do not understand it."

"My lord," the soldier put in, "the prisoner is punished under the law. A slave found him grossly insulting the household gods and finally throwing them down from their pedestals."

"Artemidorus," said Nero to the prisoner, "is this true?"

The young man raised his handsome pale face with a flashing look.

"Yes, my lord," he said in a firm voice.

"And did you know," the emperor went on with calm severity, "that by such an assault on the sanctuary of the household you were committing a crime worthy of death?"

"Worthy of death in the eye of the law—yes."

"And what prompted you to defy that law?"

"The love of the Truth."

"How so?"

"Your Roman gods are false gods. I believe in the true God, whom Jesus Christ has revealed to us."

"You are a Nazarene?"

"Yes, my lord."

"Does your noble patron Flavius Scaevinus know this?"

"Yes, my lord."

"Has he ever molested you for it?"

"No, my lord."

"Well then. Believe what you choose, and let others believe what *they* choose. Do you fail to perceive that this is plain sense and justice?"

"Jesus Christ has enjoined us to diffuse and teach his doctrine, and to fight against false gods."

"By all means. Fight away! But fight in the spirit. Do you expect to convince men by doubling your fists at them? Is abuse philosophical argument? In truth you have earned your fate, Artemidorus."

The leader of the guard made a disconsolate grimace. He had confidently hoped that Claudius Nero would put an end to the proceedings by an act of imperial despotism. And now, quite unexpectedly, Caesar declared that the sentence—which even he, Pharax, and his fellow-soldiers had thought barbarous and excessive—was deserving and equitable. What a disappointment!

But, meanwhile, Acte, in obedience to a sign from Nicodemus, had rushed forward from the ranks of the crowd. She fell on her knees on the street pavement, close in front of the imperial litter. She lifted up her blooming face with pathetic sweetness to Nero, and in a voice tremulous with the magical power of womanly pity, she cried: "Mercy, my lord! Mercy for my brother!"

The young despot's eye rested with pleased amazement on the slender creature who looked up at him with such fervent entreaty. Even the empress-mother could not help feeling a transient glow of sympathy, and a smile of unusual softness passed over her grave, proud features.

"I thought as much," said Nero with some feeling. "The man who has so sweet and gracious a sister may have sinned in error or from over zeal, but he cannot be wicked."

For a few minutes he seemed lost in contemplation of the fair apparition. Then, grasping Agrippina's hand, he went on in declamatory tones: "The day before yesterday was your birthday! I looked through the shops of every curiosity-dealer and jeweller in this city of two million souls, that I might have something made that should be worthy of you, and I could find nothing but that trumpery diadem. Costly as it is, it rests on your ambrosial head like a fillet of Corinthian metal. But now Fate has provided a nobler offering. To the honor of your best-beloved name, my dearest mother, I exercise my prerogative to pardon and release."

He commanded the soldiers to bring their prisoner close to the litter, while Acte withdrew with a bright glance of gratitude.

"You heard me," Nero said. "I pardon you!—Take him back to the house of Flavius Scaevinus, and explain what has happened to my noble friend. I only beg him to keep the criminal a prisoner for a week.—You, young man—I recommend you to be prudent and circumspect; and I say again: govern your tongue.

The reprieved victim's lips were twitching as though he longed to reply, in spite of the clemency shown to him. However, he suppressed his answer, crossed his hands over his breast, and murmured a hardly audible: "Thanks, my lord."

The prefect's servants, and foremost of all Pharax himself, removed his fetters; from that moment he was treated with polite consideration, and Pharax congratulated him with a powerful grip of the hand.

The returned victim was welcomed with enthusiasm in his master's house. The news of the emperor's act of clemency had reached home before him, and Scaevinus himself met him in the ostium. The slave who had so officiously reported Artemidorus' reckless proceedings had been given away some days since by the senator on whom he had brought so much distress of mind.

CHAPTER II.

THE imperial litter moved on amid the echoing accalama-
tions of the crowd. Nero and Agrippina had come from the
residence of Afranius Burrus, the commander-in-chief of the
praetorian body-guard. Burrus had for some days been
suffering from an attack of fever. The complaint was pronounced by the physician to be not serious, but a certain
degree of consideration and attention was nevertheless due to
so powerful an official. As the litter, with its military escort,
turned down the Vicus Cyprius the empress' thoughts
reverted to Burrus on his bed of sickness. Her mind was filled
with secret dissatisfaction. The more she saw the devotion of
the masses transferred to the son she had formerly idolized,
the more jealous she became of him as a dangerous rival, and
she sought escape from her burden of anxiety by dwelling
upon thoughts which restored her former confidence.

Burrus, the general of the praetorian guard, and Seneca,
Nero's former preceptor, had hitherto stood by her firmly
whenever it was needful to influence the young emperor in
carrying on the government to the empress' mind, or to
persuade her son that she, Agrippina, was the first person in
the empire, and he, by natural and filial duty, only the
second.

So long as Burrus was her sword and Lucius Annaeus

Seneca her buckler, what need she care for the murmurs or the acclamations of the populace? What mattered to her the muttered rumors of dark reports—for she was aware of them as a man may be aware of the unseen gaze of a hostile observer—which passed from lip to lip? Burrus, too, was the best prefect she could desire: keenly alive to her beauty, and deeply grateful for her slightest gracious smile, but even more deeply filled with a sense of his duty and the good of the commonwealth. He was wise enough to understand that an experienced and gifted woman was a better sovereign than a fanciful youth scarcely arrived at manhood.

"What are you thinking of, mother?" asked Nero in Greek. "You scarcely heed the greetings of the senators."

"Indeed—I did not observe. . . ."

"Thrasea Peatus passed us, followed by several clients. I nodded to him; but you took no notice of him; indeed you seemed to hide yourself intentionally behind the curtain."

"Did it strike you so?" replied Agrippina. "A mother is surely to be pardoned for such oversights, thinking incessantly as she must be of her son's welfare. I was thinking of your future; I confess that I am not altogether free from anxiety."

"Anxiety? On what grounds? Does not the earth lie blooming at my feet? Am I not Caesar? Aye, and by the glory of that ambrosial heaven, I can make men happy in the furthest ends of the world, as far as a Roman sail can navigate the seas! My people love me. But just now—this very minute—did you not hear? The grateful acclamations poured from a thousand throats like a Helvetian torrent: 'Hail Caesar! Long live Claudius Nero, the joy of mankind!'—Ah, mother, it falls on my ear like a festal hymn sung by the immortals."

Agrippina colored and slowly shook her stately head.

"And yet, my son, I am not easy. You seem to me too soft, too pliant for the terrible sovereignty of a Caesar. Your innocent eyes fail to see the hideous malice which lurks in the caves and hiding-places of abominable Envy. You must learn, while it is early, to rule with due severity. It is good to be loved; but it is better—and safer—to be feared. In this, as in many other critical matters, yield to my experience. Let me deal as I think best.—Do you believe that the senators who bend before your grandeur in seeming reverence are really imbued with a sense of that greatness? Ah, how little you know the aristocracy of Rome! They think: 'Nero is Caesar by our gracious permission.' If they should choose, and if the opportunity should offer, they would wreck *your* dominion as completely as they lately overthrew that of Cladius.''

"Of Claudius?'' asked the youth in surprise.

"Certainly—of your stepfather, my late husband. He was poisoned by the members of the senate.''

"Seneca told me a different story,'' said Nero.

Agrippina turned pale; but she at once replied with affected composure:

"You excite my curiosity. At the time, as you know, the senate prohibited all enquiry, and that circumstance alone. . . .''

"Enquiry would have been useless, as the poisoner was out of their reach. Have you really no suspicion. . . ?''

The empress was trembling.

"Not the smallest,'' she said, closing her eyes.

"Then it was to spare you,'' Nero went on. "It was Eutropius, the freedman, a personal enemy of Claudius, who did the deed.''

"Of course,'' muttered Agrippina. "But I fancied that he had only been the tool of others greater than himself.''

"No indeed. Claudius Caesar had threatened to bring him to justice for various thefts, and the criminal anticipated the judge. Then, before he could be seized, he vanished and left not a trace behind.—But let us talk no more of this horrible matter. If I had obeyed Seneca's injunctions, I should never have alluded to it.''

He drew the curtain, as though to screen a sensitive sufferer from the too-glaring sun; then, leaning his head fondly on his mother's shoulder, he drew a deep breath and suddenly asked her:

"What did you think of the fair girl who interceded for the life of Flavius Scaevinus' freedman?"

"I did not notice her."

"I thought her enchanting! Such an innocent face, and pathetic eyes!"

"That is an enthusiastic description! But unluckily you only speak in that tone when it is not quite suited to the subject. If only you would rave thus about your wife-to-be Octavia!"

"Mother, I have always been your willingly dutiful son; and I will obey you even in this, particularly as your late husband wished for this alliance. . . ."

"Obey? As if it were a punishment to hold out your hand to the noblest and most amiable girl in all Rome!"

"It might be inestimable happiness for some other man," said Caesar deliberately. "I do not dispute her merits; but I fail to appreciate them. The noble Octavia is perhaps too perfect for me."

"Are you going now to take up that very disputable position? Some flower-girl from Argiletum, or some butterfly creature like Chloris the cithara-player, whom you praised so extravagantly the other day, would perhaps be more to your taste? Small specks have a charm for you men, as Ennius said long ago."

"Do not let us quarrel, dearest mother! I will marry Octavia; I will esteem her and treat her worthily. But as to loving her, not even the immortal gods can force me to that. Eros will not come to order; he comes uninvited, and often with all the more violence where reason would forbid his entrance. Virtue and merit count for nothing in his eyes. A slave-girl has often been the object of greater passion than a sovereign princess—and in that case, Seneca assures me, the slave is in her rights."

"Folly!"

"Not folly at all, by your leave. In such a case the slave-girl represents the Will of Nature; and Nature is truer and

24

more trustworthy than human laws."

"So this is what Seneca teaches you!" said Agrippina with a spiteful laugh. "Very good! Then it would seem that his brilliant theories militate against my practice."

"You do him injustice. He only connects such reflections with the explanation and moral of a tragedy. He has never mentioned Octavia.—But seriously, mother, you have not the slightest ground for annoyance; my heart is free. Thanks to the teaching of my admirable master, I have learnt to control myself. The flirtations of my friends have never been anything to me but a matter of curiosity. I have never been in love; nay, I doubt whether I am capable of the feeling. Nevertheless, I repeat that I will meet Octavia with all the affection she can claim or expect as Caesar's wife. Are you satisfied, mother?"

"Not quite. Such cold-blooded indifference makes me uneasy. Octavia is really made for you; her clear, incorruptible judgment will be invaluable to you—a dreamer who runs daily risk of losing yourself in philosophical contemplation or in the whirlpool of artistic imaginings. You know my views. Art has its attractive side, but Caesar cannot become an artist. Think, but do not forget to live. Build theatres, protect poets, fling your gold like seed-corn to singers and flute-players, but do not write poems and declaim them yourself. Do not sing like a love-lorn girl; leave the cithara to professionals. The hand that wields a sceptre is not made to use an ivory plectrum.—That is my view of the case; and Octavia will influence you in precisely the right direction."

Nero smiled.

"You remind me of the time when you seized me so roughly by the ear because I was playing all sorts of mischief in the Subura with the baker's and the cook's sons."

"And do you, the son I have brought up, forbid me to find fault with you?" asked Agrippina angrily. "To whom do you owe your very existence? This world-shaking arm placed you on the throne. So long as you acknowledge that, your Genius will watch over you. If you rebel—well, I doubt whether you have strength enough to maintain yourself on this giddy height!''

"You are wroth without cause. Rebel? The shocking word was your alone. I know full well that it disgraces no man—not even Caesar—to follow his mother's advice. There is but one thing I should wish—and as we are on the subject I may say it— You cannot desire to have any one smile at Nero's undue submission to his mother.''

"I do not know how far you have any cause. . . ."the empress indignantly began.

"No, no, mother! I see you are taking the thing too seriously. We will drop the subject. It was perhaps foolish of me to mention it. In process of time matters would have settled themselves.''

"But you must see," she eagerly resumed, "how entirely free I am from all personal ambition. Should I otherwise be so anxious to see you married? This marriage will in the natural course of things weaken my influence. When Octavia is empress, she will play an important part—a part. . . .''

"I can quite imagine it," laughed Nero. She will insist on my praying to the divine Romulus every morning; on my hanging an amulet round my neck with the image of the she-wolf and the hungry twins; on my confirming her faith when, on every occasion, she sees the direct intervention of Jupiter and Juno!''

"And even if she did all this, what harm will it do you?"

"Harm?" Nero echoed. "Well, I know not your opinion of the divine origin of our ancestors. You never mentioned the tale to me in my boyhood. So I imagine that our views are the same.''

"What do you mean?"

"I have no faith in the fables that satisfy the mob.''

"Indeed? What then do you believe?"

"How can I put it into words on the spur of the moment?—I believe, like Seneca, in the existence of a powerful First Cause, an unseen Spirit which embraces everything and breathes into everything the breath of life. This First Cause dwells also in us; Its will is our will; Its feeling is our feeling. But the gods the people worship are just good enough to serve as a last bond to cement the crumbling virtues of our social system."

Agrippina was silent for some minutes.

"Do you know, my son," she said at length, "that you are on the high-road to become a state-criminal—very much after the pattern of that Artemidorus who has just had such a narrow escape?"

Nero smiled.

"You underestimate my tact. I can keep the emperor apart from the man. Before the senate, for instance, I should take good care not to make a display of the philosophical opinions which I cherish in my heart."

Agrippina shrugged her shoulders.

"It is one thing to worship Jupiter as the ruler of the universe, and another to accept these absurdities of the Greek popular poets as sterling coin."

"A true believer accepts even the absurdities," replied Nero. "If this were not the case he could only regard the representation of such foolish tales as blasphemous."

"I am afraid you are involving yourself in contradictions," said the empress. "However, I have to thank you for your candid confession. And, why should I deny it: in this you are your mother's son. To me, too, the gods are alien. I believe in nothing but Fate, and it is Fate that you marry Octavia."

"Octavia, the silent Octavia?"

"She is silent only when she knows that you are near. A girl of the smallest sensibility would at once perceive that you have no sympathy with her. She loves you with all her heart, but you, though you meet her as a friend, have never yet spoken to her in a tone which has had any ring of affection. It is this, my son, which makes her shy, which crushes her almost to the earth. If she did not dread embarrassing remarks—if she had no hope that, in spite of everything, she might at length succeed in overcoming your indifference, she

27

would long since have given it up."

"It would be best so," murmured Nero thoughtfully.

"It would be your ruin!" cried Agrippina in a fury. "I tell you frankly that I am sick and tired of the vapid nonsense you pour out when you are in Octavia's company—sick to death of it. I insist on your altering this! And since you yourself have no talent as a suitor. I myself will take care that you are at last united. You will perhaps learn to like her when she is indeed your own, and when you know her well."

"At any rate I may be allowed a year's respite?"

"That is too long."

"You gave me your word."

"I retract it. During the winter you may study philosophy or sketch Greek tragedies for aught I care; but as soon as spring comes on. . . ."

"My spring-time is to end," sighed Caesar. "Well, we will talk it over another time."

The litter paused at the door of the imperial residence. The empress-mother retired to her rooms in great dudgeon; Nero immediately forgot the dispute of the last few minutes. Seneca met him in the colonnade and invited him to walk with him till the next meal should be served.

Under the tall trees in the garden on the Palatine the brilliant teacher poured out to an eager listener all sorts of wonderful tales of the new social and religious movement which, though still covert and inconspicuous, was making great strides westward from the East, under the designation of the Nazarene Doctrine, and which in many of its principles had various unsuspected points of contact with the philosophy of the Palatium; it seemed especially worthy of impartial investigation by such men as Seneca and Nero.

CHAPTER III.

It was a week later. Breakfast was but just over in the Palatium.

Agrippina was reclining on a flowered divan under the trees in the xystus, and gossiping with a little party of select persons, among whom Lucius Annaeas Seneca, the government advisor and philosopher, was, as usual, prominent for his brilliancy and originality. By him stood Burrus, the captain of the body-guard. He was a visitor at the palace for the first time to-day since his illness, and was sunning himself in the presence of the empress like a worshipper of Mithras in the glory of the day-star. Lucanus, too, the young poet, Seneca's nephew, was one of this chosen circle; for the biting epigrams he could utter on this or that member of the Roman aristocracy had recommended him to the empress even more strongly than his uncle's eager praises.

While Agrippina thus held her own court—really charming all of her admirers who did not think her florid looks and haughty splendor too imperious and masculine, Nero, unmindful of his tutor's grave dissertations had quietly stolen away.

A struggle was gradually arising in the young ruler's nature; another Nero, in some sense the opposite to the artificially nurtured and wisely sententious Nero, occasionally gained the upper hand—a less sentimental Nero, who, under the guidance of his profligate adjutant Sophonius Tigellinus, laid timid plots for acquiring a practical knowledge of life and its various pleasures. Sophonius Tigellinus, a native of Agrigentum had first become known to Caesar in the Circus Maximus as the owner of a splendid team of horses which never failed to win. Nero sent for him to the imperial divan, congratulated him, and was so bewitched by the brilliant horseman's engaging amiability that they soon became fast friends. As Tigellimus had already risen to the rank of a supernumerary military tribune, Nero made him an officer of the praetorian guard and placed him in immediate attendance on his person. Seneca had at first raised objections, for the young officer of thirty was reputed to be one of the most irresistible ladykillers of the City of the Seven Hills, and inspired him on the whole with small confidence. Nero however insisted so strongly on the man's social and artistic talents that the minister soon withdrew his opposition, and only determined to watch with double caution over the emperor's weal and woe. It was Sophonius Tigellinus who had first stirred up Nero's adventurous instincts, and latterly had translated them into action, with inexhaustible and delightful humor.

Nero was especially liable from time to time to a vehement inquisitiveness as to small details: an obscure but exciting desire to mingle unrecognized with the common people, to make interesting observations, to witness new scenes, meet with adventures, and come into contact with genuine, unsophisticated human nature.

The emperor's wanderings seemed for a time perfectly innocent, and Sophonius Tigellinus took care not to figure too conspicuously as the tempter. It would have cost him too dear if, by any chance, Seneca should hear of it. But he firmly hoped that matters would come right in time. Things, which now seemed boyish and almost childish, must by degrees, and in spite of Seneca's warnings, degenerate into mad debauchery and frenzied pleasure-seeking—and then Tigellinus would be master of the situation. The teaching of the Stoa expelled by the jovial Epicurus; Seneca's philosophical wisdom felt an oppressive burthen; he—Tigellinus—hailed as the consoling preserver, bringing deliverance from the bog of satiety and ennui;—all this would constitute a foundation whence at one stride he might reach the highest power.

The wily Agrigentine of course let no one suspect these ambitious plans. He assumed the seeming of sharing all Caesar's youthful aspirations—he, who had already tasted every pleasure, who even as a boy had revelled in unbridled freedom! Nero did not perceive the difference between his own development and that of the Agrigentine; he believed in him, regarding the spoilt and dissipated debauchee as a guileless youth like himself. He forgot how joyless a life he had led after the death of his father Domitius Ahenobarbus, till Agrippina's second marriage with Claudius Caesar had lifted him out of obscurity. To Nero's artistic disposition it seemed, too, quite intelligible that the eye should crave for pictures, the mind for matter, the vivid imagination for experience.

The sun was still high over the long ridge of Janiculus when Nero and Tigellinus, wrapped in light cloaks, made their way to the Field of Mars which was thronged with people. The ten Germans of the body-guard with whom they had set out from the Palatium to obviate enquiry—were by this time sitting in one of the great taverns near the capitol, drinking to Caesar's health and that of his amiable adjutant in golden Falernian.

It was a beautiful day. The ample folds which Nero and Tigellinus had flung about their heads as though to protect them from the heat of the sun, hindered them from being recognized; and in Rome especially, where every citizen of any pretensions went about with a large following, not a soul would have guessed that these unattended pedestrians could be personages of the highest rank. Nero drank in the warm but refreshing air with long breaths. A deep blue sky bent over the tall trees, which here and there showed autumn coloring; the carefully-tended grassplots were sheets of brilliant green; the marble statues, the numberless gay booths, the colonnades and monuments seemed to bask in a purer light than usual. Up and down the main avenue moved an endless line of litters and foot-passengers. To the right and left fiery Cappadocian horses were prancing along the roads, with small-hoofed racers from the plain of Hispalis and snorting little ponies. Beyond, in the gaudily-decked promenade, between hedges of laurel and myrtle, a motley throng of mingled ranks was pressing: senators in togas bordered with purple, surrounded by clients and friends; grandees from Asia Minor in the gold-embroidered himation; black-haired Persians with tall tiaras and elaborately-wrought trousers; blooming Greek girls wearing the saffron-hued diploidion; Ethiops and Gauls, freedmen and slaves; fops and dependents on state bounty; school-masters with their pupils; sellers of vegetables and trinkets, alike recommending their wares in the shrillest tones; fortunetellers, seamen, soldiers of the city cohorts and invalided veterans.

"Do you not feel, best-beloved Caesar," Tigellinus began, "how good my advice is when I urge you to live as your spirit prompts you, and leave the weariful affairs of state to Seneca and Burrus? You, Caesar, are young. You must study the many-headed human creature whom you are called to govern, know it under its thousand aspects."

"You are right, Tigellinus," replied Caesar. "In fact—what should I be without Seneca and Burrus? Nay more—what should I be without you? By Hercules! You at any rate can release me for a few hours from the spell which the duties of my sovereignty casts upon me. I am Caesar—but before all I am a man, and I can say with the poet— "My heart burns ardently for all that is human."

They had now reached the shining marble precincts where the Roman populace held a perennial fair. Booths for wares

32

and shows of every kind displayed their temptations in gay confusion. Spaces for dicus-throwers and games of ball were cleared here and there among the crowd of cook's-stalls, wine-shops and fragrant heaps of fruit. Further on, on the bank of the Tiber, stood the wooden platforms whence those who swam races flung themselves into the rippling river; and scattered on all sides were spreading trees, tall shrubs, dazzling flower-beds, and statues of the gods in gleaming Parian marble.

Caesar and his companion stayed their steps in front of a tent with linen curtains and silver ropes where an Egyptian conjuror was plying his skill.

Cyrus—so the inscription over the opening gave them to understand—had arrived only a few days since from Alexandria, and he was already the centre of public interest.

The magician, a bearded figure, was reclining indolently at the entrance; he smiled loftily at the fast increasing crowd. Then suddenly starting to his feet, as if an idea had just flashed upon him, he set his child, a little creature of six or seven, on the magical tripod, as he called it, covered them both with a cone-shaped hat of Persian shape and as high as a man, touched the painted thing with his ivory wand and then remvoed it. To the unspeakable amazement of the mob the child had vanished.

The Egyptian now retired into the inner part of the tent while two black Africans removed the tripod and the paper cone, cutting all sorts of capers and antics. The bystanders shouted their applause; Nero, too, clapped his hands with the greatest eagerness.

"Wonderful!" he said in a low voice to Tigellinus. "A well-bred man of the world ought to be astonished at nothing; but I ask you: have you the faintest idea how that miracle was accomplished?"

Tigellinus shrugged his shoulders.

A herald in red and yellow now came out on the wooden platform and blew three blasts with all his might on a thundering tuba. He then proceeded to invite the noble

33

Quirites and their wives to hesitate no longer.

"Three sesterces!" he cried in shrill tones. "Only three sesterces for making you for an hour and a half the equal of the gods! Cyrus, my illustrious master, the star of the East, the master of Babylon, Susa, and Alexandria, the friend of many Asiatic kings, the favorite of every nation from sunrise to sunset, bids me greet you, and ask you whether any one ever made you such an offer before for three sesterces? 'No,' you will say. 'That none can do but Cyrus, the unique Cyrus.' So dip into the pouches of your tunics and buy the ivory ticket which will entitle you to breathe the air of Olympus for an hour and a half. When I blow this tuba for the second time the immortal Cyrus is about to begin."

The bystanders flocked in scores to the right, towards the table where three stalwart Frisians—also in incredible costumes—were selling the tickets. Nero and Tigellinus followed with the tide. The crush was so great that in a few minutes the emperor was parted from Tigellinus.

"My friend," called Nero in Greek over the head of the young girls who were pressing forward. "If we should be separated during the performance we will meet afterwards over there, by the maple tree of Agrippa."

"Very good," nodded the adjutant.

The Egyptian's tent was an unusually large one. Through an opening in the roof, as wide as a triclinium, plenty of light from above fell into the richly-fitted room. Spanish grass-mats lay on the floor. Hangings, which from a distance looked like Syrian, were suspended from cords in which silver threads were twisted. In the midst, on a stage-like erection, stood a large altar, divided off from the spectators by bronze chains.

Immediately behind it a heavy curtain of purple Tarentine wool now slowly parted. The magician stepped forth with majestic dignity from between the massive folds, while, outside, the herald sounded his tuba for the second time.

By degrees Nero had intentionally let Tigellinus get further from him. He was tolerably forward in the ranks, near the bronze chains, and he looked expectantly up into the tall Egyptian's flashing eyes.

The first performance was a trick which had found great approbation in Alexandria: The black Eurydice: so he chose to call the death and revival of a black pigeon, in allusion to the Greek legend.

As he apparently tore the poor little fluttering creature limb from limb, a faint "Ah!" of pity was audible quite close to the emperor.

He turned round. Just behind him stood none other than the sweet fair-haired girl who had besought his mercy for Artemidorus. The whole charm of that blooming face seemed to him but now to have dawned upon him. The lovely parted lips, revealing a dazzling and bewitching row of little teeth, breathed innocence, eagerness, and delight; the expression of amazement and pity lent the sweet, childlike face a look of maternal sorrow.

Ah, and her voice!

Her little cry had cast a spell of indescribable music over his senses; he longed vehemently to hear that voice prattle on, uninterrupted by all the magic arts of Babylon and Egypt. Very gently, that he might not startle her, he drew back a step or two and soon found others pressing to stand in front. He was now close by the young girl and whispered tremulously in her ear.

"Do you recognize me?"

"Yes, my lord!" she whispered back.

"Then do not betray me."

"At your command."

"Are you alone?"

She hesitated for a moment, and then timidly murmured: "Yes, I am alone, my lord."

"What is your name?" asked Caesar.

"My name is Acte."

"And do you live with your parents?—To what class do you belong?"

"My parents are dead. My father was a native of

Mediolanum, my mother was a Greek. They were both born in slavery."

"Impossible! You, a slave?"

"Freedwoman to Nicodemus."

"The man who sometimes studies philosophy with Seneca?"

"The very same."

A roar of applause at this moment went up from the spectators.

"Splendid, splendid. Hurrah for Cyrus, the favorite of the gods!"

The much-admired trick of "Eurydice" had been performed without Nero's being in the least aware of it. He stood motionless; his eyes fixed in admiration on the young girl's face, scanning its enchanting loveliness, like one in a dream. Which, of all the ladies of senatorial rank could compare with this brilliant beauty? Not one; not even Poppaea Sabina, Otho's fair young wife, though all Rome was raving over that flower of womanhood. . . . ! And as to Octavia, the future empress! True, from the point of view of a Greek sculptor, Octavia was perhaps a more perfect beauty, and there was a regal deliberateness in all her movements; but how cold, how insipid, how lifeless, in comparison with the budding fragrant grace of this low-born child!

"Impossible!" said Nero again. "*What* does Acte say she is?"

"A freed slave."

"A goddess!" he murmured, passionately pressing her hand. "Child, you have no idea how divinely lovely you are."

"My lord, you bewilder me.—I know full well that the great ones of the earth are apt to carry on their jests with the poor and unprotected. But I cannot and will not believe that you, who so nobly released Artemidorus, can intend to laugh at me. . . ."

"Laugh at you! I would shelter you in my arms like a

36

sister. I envy Artemidorus, as the dead envy the living! If you like, sweet little one, we will get out of this crowd and stand aside; there, at the entrance, no one will notice us—and I have much to say to you yet."

She followed him in silence.

"In truth, I cannot get rid of the idea," he went on in a tone that came fresh from his heart. "Artemidorus! How happy he who might change places with him!"

"But I think you are laughing at me all the same. You, the all-powerful monarch—and Artemidorus! What a yawning gulf!"

"Very true—but to my disadvantage! Artemidorus has the blissful right to kiss your brow, to clasp you in his arms. How glad and happy must he be when your lips, as sweet as spring blossoms, have touched his."

"I never kiss Artemidorus," said the girl positively.

"What? Not your own brother?"

"But he is not my brother, begging your pardon. You overlook the fact that Artemidorus is a native of Damascus, while my father was an Italian."

"But you besought mercy for your brother?"

"Yes, my lord; in the sense taught by the Nazarenes. According to their doctrine all who wear the semblance of humanity are brethren."

"Then in fact you almost cheated me. . . ."

"Nay indeed! You have only to ask one of the Nazarenes whether I deceived you. We Nazarenes, even in our daily intercourse, address each other as brother and sister, because we ignore every distinction which, in the eyes of the world might keep us apart. We call each other brethren though one may be a slave and another a knight; for we are all men alike by birth, and slaves, knights, or senators only by accident— unless it be by superior force or the injustice of our forefathers."

Caesar gazed into the pretty face with sparkling eyes.

"Child," he said, quite bewildered by her fascinating maidenhood, "you are but a spring-flower, and yet you talk

37

as wisely as a scholar. What you have just said is neither more nor less than the inmost kernel of the philosophy which Seneca instils into my mind. You put me to shame. I fancied that my views of the world raised me above the level of the best of my contemporaries, and now I find that a scarcely full-grown maiden feels as I do; nay, and expresses it more clearly and completely than my much-admired master! Am I dreaming? Have Plato and Socrates and the weighty Zeno been melted into one, and the divine trinity been born on earth once more in the form of a maiden?''

As he spoke the young emperor's face was fired with a rapt enthusiasm which lighted up his features and lent nobility to his gestures. His dilated pupils seemed to drink in the light of Acte's dark-blue eyes; his parted lips, where the first down was hardly visible, quivered with an impulse of passionate longing, so plainly betrayed that the most un-practised eye might understand it: the irrepressible and fervid confession of a first, idolizing love.

And those were not unpractised eyes which were watching him from amid the crowd—widely different as their trianing and experience had been. Sophonius Tigellinus, the wily and profligate Agrigentine, was observing this scene between Caesar and the blushing girl with the satisfaction which a tutor feels when he perceives that the seed he has sown has struck root. Claudius Nero was on the high-road to regarding the hawk-beaked philosopher as an ass, and to accepting the course which had hitherto been exceptional as the high-road of life.—That little girl, with her waving golden hair and kissable lips, was certainly a pretty creature. If Nero had not taken the bait with such unexpected readiness Sophonius Tigellinus himself might perhaps—by Hercules! he could imagine that a tete-a-tete drinking party—some wine of Cyprus and that rosebud—might have had its charms even for him. This, of course, was not to be thought of now; and after all, it mattered not, for Tigellinus might pick and choose among the highest and the fairest; he had only to hold out his hand and the most beautiful woman in Rome,

Poppaea Sabina, would snap her fingers at her husband. Yes, the splendid Tigellinus was quite sure of that, and he would think about it before long. For the present he had every reason to be satisfied with the results of this promenade in the Field of Mars, hugely satisfied, for Claudius Nero was plunging into the depths beyond all expectation—aye, by Epona! Beyond all expectation.

Another pair of eyes was watching the emperor and his rosy companion—those of Nicodemus. His spies had brought him information of how Nero and Tigellinus proposed to pass the time between breakfast and dinner. He at once had hastened with Acte to the Field of Mars and, as soon as he caught sight of Caesar, he stealthily drew back, leaving the rest to the young girl's mother-wit. Acte, who had only been in Rome a few weeks, having previously been in attendance on a relation of her master's at Ostia, was already noted in the Nazarene circle for the wonderful power and convincingness of her proselytism. The adherents she had won to the Christian faith might be counted by dozens. So Nicodemus, a feverish, restless soul, had resolved to strive for the stupendous end he aimed at, not by Seneca's aid but by means of his own; and to throw Acte the irresistible into immediate contact with the emperor. As a partner in an important firm of merchants, Nicodemus had become acquainted with the doctrine of the Nazarenes in the course of a voyage in the East; the death of a favorite son had confirmed his soul, when it was thirsting for comfort, in a conviction of the divine truth of Christianity; and when, through faith, he had lived down his grief for this loss, he burned with a really consuming zeal to promote the triumph of this saving Creed over the false religions of the Roman polity. He was well-versed in Seneca's philosophy, and had, in former days, been able to do the sage some important service in financial matters; he recognized gladly the intimate connection between the teaching of Jesus and that of the world-contemning Stoics, and built on them the daring hope that, by judicious treatment, Seneca's pupil might be converted into a disciple of the Carpenter's Son. Acte seemed to him made on purpose to be the instrument to this end, not merely by her warmhearted eloquence, but also—though he would not confess this to himself—as being the incarnation of feminine grace and sweetness. She would work on Nero's sensibilities, perhaps on his heart—and what harm could come of it if, for once in a way, faith in the Redeemer found an entrance on the wings of earthly and transitory love? Acte knew what was due herself.—At the last moment she would find strength to save her virtue from the surging waves and land it on the shore.

Thus Nicodemus argued with himself.

In reality, and as it were unconsciously, what he felt was this: "Even if this lamb should perish—the whole flock will be saved through her loss." The self-blinded man had forgotten that good can never come out of that which is evil and shameful; he had forfeited the faculty of unprejudiced judgment. At this moment he stood under cover watching the rapidly-growing intimacy of the pair with almost fiendish delight. Everything was going far better than he had ever dared to hope. The emperor's face betrayed none of that jesting frivolity which commonly characterizes a man's acquaintance with a beauty of humble birth; his manner was expressive rather of admiring sympathy, of almost timid respect. If Acte were but discreet, she might mould the heart of this nobly-disposed youth as though it were of wax from Hymettus.

The conversation between Caesar and the fair freed-woman had lasted for some time. Suddenly Nero, carried away by his feelings, seized both the girl's hands and pressed them passionately to his breast.

"Acte," he said, "the flute-like melody of your speech has undone me, and the heavenly sweetness and wisdom of your blue eyes. The things you so lightly allude to fill my mind with the most wonderful and amazing images! Let us be friends, Acte, true and faithful friends. Now I understand for the first time what I first read in a Saturnalia-poem by

Lucanus: that every revelation comes through woman. You, sweet Acte, have purity; I have power. I have only to raise my hand and everything in the world will change, as those little baubles are changed under Cyrus' magic wand. If we hold firmly together, you and I—Ah, how bewitching you are, how lovely, and how high-minded!"

He kissed her burning finger-tips with fervid tenderness. She gently drew them from his grasp—more by the influence of her beseeching eyes than by any exertion of strength. He touched her breasts . . . she pulled back with a faint smile.

"Come to see me at the Palatium," Nero went on. "Here, this ring will at any time secure your admission. I must make you acquainted with Seneca. You seem to me to have a deeper apprehension of the great problems of the Nazarene faith than Nicodemus.—Will you come, Acte?"

He had stealthily drawn off a signet ring, and now held it out to her, as a lover offers a rose.

"Thanks, my lord," Acte murmured in great confusion. "But an inner voice tells me that I may not accept the jewel; no more would it become me to cross the threshold of your imperial residence. . . ."

"Nonsense! When Caesar himself commands? You fear for your reputation? True, base slander is all the more venomously eager in proportion as the object of its malice is fresh and innocent. Come then with Nicodemus. . . ."

"Perhaps I may, my lord."

"Why will you not say, yes, without any reservation? Does it not look like destiny that we two should meet here for the second time, when you crossed my path but a few days since and filled my soul with sympathy?"

Acte colored violently and cast down her eyes, deeply abashed; but she said nothing.

"Then you will come?" Caesar repeated.

"I will see if I dare."

"What a blush, Acte! Do I look as if I meant you any harm? You are to be my sister, my heart's sister—if not, I shall die of longing. Consider, Acte: Nero offers you a

41

brother's hand—Nero, for whose favor kings grovel in the dust.''

"Oh, I know well the value of such favor!" replied she in full tones. There was a ring of strong and glad conviction in the vibrating girlish voice. Nero was as one intoxicated.

"Then it is settled, sweetest, dearest! What a happy thought of Tigellinus' to bring me this very day—this very hour, to the Field of Mars. All the treasures of the realm could not outweigh this moment! He is but a scatter-brain, who lives in the present only and hates thought—but for all that he has given me more than Seneca with all his worldly wisdom.''

Thunders of applause and a loud blast of trumpets announced the close of the performance.

"My lord," whispered Acte, as Nero was about to follow her out of the booth, "if you care for me at all you will now leave me. I might meet some acquaintance—and you cannot guess how cruelly and mercilessly I should be judged.''

"Very well; you see, Acte, I obey you already almost as a slave. But you will take the ring? I entreat you, with all my heart. . . .''

"Well then. . . .'' she murmured with some feeling. The heavy gold ring slipped on to her middle finger, which it fitted as if it had been made for it. A strange feeling thrilled through her, half ecstasy, half pain and anxious foreboding. She felt as though it were a bond from which no power on earth could ever free her.

CHAPTER IV.

ACTE made her way through the throng as quickly as possible, and got out of the tent before Nicodemus saw her escape.

She felt an unaccountable but irresistible need to be alone: her heart craved for solitude in which to reflect on the impressions of the past momentous hour. As she foresaw how strictly her master would catechise her and sift to the uttermost every word that Caesar had spoken she was filled with alarms. It was as though she were compelled to allow some sacrilegious and unfeeling hand to rummage through her dearest treasures. Before this ordeal she must for a short while be happy; she must taste in peace the bliss she had known, and so far collect herself as to be able to endure Nicodemus' questioning with tolerable equanimity.

For nearly half an hour she wandered about the least frequented part of the Field of Mars, now and then glancing timidly at the jewel she wore on her finger. She could have thought it all a dream; a ring with the imperial seal, given to her by the omnipotent sovereign himself! was it not like a tale of the prehistorical Pelasgian times? In those remote days the sons of Uranus, floating in the radiance of ether, had come down to the daughters of men and laid the thunderbolts of heaven at the feet of the shepherdesses of Oeta. But now and here, in actual, every-day Rome, alive with the very real clatter of the swords and lances of the praetorian guards—here on the shores of the Tiber, where everything looked so new and bright and living—it was incomprehensible!

Her gaze wandered away across the mighty city; a red haze hung over the southern horizon in spite of the clear October sunshine. Far off rose the sunlit temple of the capitol; to the right of these towered the Palatium, the home of the splendid youth who wielded the sceptre over that endless sea of houses, over Italy, over the world itself, and who yet had talked to her, a base-born girl, so kindly, so tenderly, with such indescribable confidence. She sighed.

"If he were only one of the miserable slaves who are toiling to drag the stones to build the hall yonder!" thought she sadly, "I would give everything I possess to purchase his freedom—I would labor and hoard for years to save as much as was needed—and then!—" She closed her eyes.

Suddenly she heard a voice softly calling her by name. Looking up she beheld a man of about forty in the dress of a man of rank. His keen grey eyes were evidently doing their best to express amiability and politeness.

"Acte," said he, "you are wandering as lonely as mourning Demeter. May an unknown friend be permitted to offer you his company?"

"But, my lord, you are a stranger."

"That disadvantage is easily remedied. My name will, I fancy, be less strange to you than my face. I am Pallas, the empress' trusted friend."

"Pallas!" she exclaimed in alarm, as if her knowledge of it were not favorable. "Your name, no doubt is well known and—feared."

"None have occasion to fear me but those who refuse my mistress the reverence due to her, who condemn her prudent course of action, who try to frustrate her glorious schemes, or are—in any way treasonable to her divine majesty. I am what I am by Agrippina's favor: Gratitude and fidelity are the most illustrious of the virtues!"

Acte stood as if wrapped in thought, gazing at the imperial ring. Then, suddenly pushing her fair hair from off her brow, she asked, almost defiantly:

"And how do you know me, and what do you want of me?"

"I observed you but just now, when Caesar condescended to speak with Flavius Scaevinus' freedwoman. I was at the head of the imperial escort."

"Indeed! I did not notice you."

"Not flattering! But you were so entirely absorbed that I am inclined to forgive you the oversight. Perhaps it was that very absorption in the emotions of the moment which fascinated me. You were a lovely, restful object in the midst of the turmoil of the scene. In short—you bewitched me. . . ."

"And why do you tell me this?"

"A strange question! Why does a man tell the amphora that he is thirsty? I love you, Acte, and entreat the gods to touch your heart that it may turn to me."

"Then you entreat in vain," retorted the girl. "I cannot love. I have neither sense nor heart for such folly."

"Folly, do you call it—the sweetest, the only flower of life! Acte, Acte, what are you saying? You cannot love? You, with those eyes that are soft with yearning, with your sweet, pouting lips which smile on the world in a perpetual kiss? You must try to deceive a duller wretch than I!"

"I cannot love," she repeated sadly. "And even if I could—do you think I would throw myself away?"

"Throw yourself away! Is the love of Pallas so poor and shameful a thing?"

"By no means—for a hundred other women. Believe me, I know the world and its sinfulness in spite of my youth. I know what Rome is apt to think of us freed slave-girls, and that your name is regarded as synonymous with dishonor and profligacy. Many, very many, would esteem themselves happy if they might share their sin with you, for you are powerful and rich, and something of the splendor of the imperial palace falls on the woman Pallas loves. But I scorn such elevation—which, in truth, is but degradation! I scorn it: in the first place because a horror of such misdoing is indelibly in my blood; and also because Jesus Christ of Nazareth, whose servant I am with my whole heart, preached virtue and purity in thought and deed."

Pallas was silent for a while; then he said hesitatingly: "You have told me nothing that I did not know, Acte. It was to be presumed that a young girl who begged for mercy towards a Nazarene must be his fellow-believer. Besides, I heard it from Nicodemus. I observed that you were both of his household, and I knew him from often meeting him at Seneca's—so you see, your haughty answer is no surprise to me. And yet it is a vain one."

"Why?"

"Because you are rejecting what you have not tested. Acte! This is the third time I have seen you. The day before yesterday at your master's house I had leisure to observe you; I was standing, without your noticing it, in the tablinum with the strange old man. You fled across the pavement like a young roe; you spoke to the slaves, and every one had a pleasant word for you; you watered the late-blooming roses; you threw grain and crumbs to the pigeons; you even shed a ray of the light that you bring with you into the heart of the old hound as he lay, half-paralyzed, by the tank, and he wagged his tail as he looked up in your face. I made up my mind: on the first opportunity I would tell you how much I envied the very beasts who enjoyed the blessing of your presence; I would tell you—but what ails you?"

"Nothing, nothing;" Acte stammered out. "A stupid fancy—a recollection. . . ."

She pressed her hand tightly over her eyes, as if she were giddy. Now, when she understood that Pallas was speaking the language of true and genuine love, her fancy suddenly called up an image so vivid, so tangible, that she could have screamed aloud: the image of Caesar at the moment when he had first told her how lovely he thought her. And with this vision came a convulsive chill, a sweet, intoxicating pang which almost made her faint and fall.

When she had recovered herself, Pallas went on with growing fervency.

"I cannot dare to hope that my words startled you so much. Was I too strong?—But at my age a man has not weeks and months to spend in wooing. So to be quite plain: Passa, Agrippina's intimate friend, Pallas the terrible as you yourself said, asks you to be his wife. Do you hear, Acte? His lawful wife—not his mistress.—Now, what is your answer?"

"That I thank him," whispered Acte, looking down, "and that I entreat him to forgive me when, in spite of everything, I say No."

"But are you delirious?"

"No indeed, my lord. It is because I am so clear in my mind that I find the courage to reject such an honor. A poor girl like me is no wife for a man of high degree. . . ."

He shook his head and laid his right hand on her shoulder. His flashing eye looked at her from head to foot, while the slender figure trembled at his touch.

"Am I to say that you are only too good for me? Must I thus humble myself? Do you not know that I am not free-born? Antonia, the mother of Claudius Caesar, gave me my freedom many years ago, and my own talents have raised me to be envied by all Rome: the divine Agrippina's confidential favorite."

"Yes, I knew it," said the girl. "Nevertheless the gulf cannot be bridged over. What a poor part should I be doomed to play in the splendid court-circle! It makes me dizzy only to think of it."

"You need not fear comparison with any one."

"No, no. The idea is odious to me.—Besides, my lord, you forget: I told you, I have only a soul and no heart. I do not love you, and to be your wife without loving you would be to cheat you."

Pallas knit his brow. He had not been at all prepared for this uncompromising refusal. His vanity was deeply wounded.

"Child," he said, after a pause, "you are behaving like a mad creature. I have clasped the daughters of senators in these arms—and without any punctilious ceremony—and you refuse to share my life and my position as my lawful wife? Your childish hesitancy is as crazy as my own extraordinary determination to marry you. But I cannot help myself: at the mere sight of you I was like one possessed; and now that you refuse to give me what you ought to have cast at my feet with tears of thankfulness—I feel more surely than ever that I cannot exist without you. Reconsider it, Acte. The empress' favorite is not a mere nobody, and those who do not gladly catch good fortune at the fountain-head may perhaps bewail for a whole life-time a single moment of wanton folly.—Now, farewell for the present. My followers are waiting for me over there on the road."

He nodded significantly; then he disappeared between the myrtle hedges.

Day was now drawing to a close. It was long past the hour of the evening meal. The crowds of litters and pedestrians which had flowed through the broad avenues had left behind them a certain deserted air which was enhanced by the glowing orange hues of sunset.

Acte now perceived that she had wandered on as far as the Aelian bridge. She involuntarily walked on, along the raised marble side-path as far as the middle, and there she paused, leaning over the parapet. From this spot—the summit of the middle arch—many hundreds flung themselves over, year by year, into the depths below: souls weary of life, to whom existence had lost all its savour, wretches worn out by the incessant struggle with the powers of Fate. . . . Down there the yellow tide was whirling and rushing like the uncanny whisper of a tempter. The foaming eddies circled on, swelling and sinking with the regularity of slow deep breathing; wave after wave twirled up between the towering piles of masonry, and wave after wave slipped through, down and away, spreading gradually in the distance till it was lost in the level surface of the wide river.

"That is comforting!" whispered Acte to herself, as she propped her forehead on the palm of her hand. "It comes and passes, and however wildly it may fret, it presently is calm again and flows peacefully to the sea."

Lost in thought she gazed a long time at the spot where the whirlpool foamed highest against the stonework, till at last she felt as though the bridge itself, with her and everything on it, was floating silently and smoothly down the stream. It was a strangely-pleasant sensation, an abandonment which refreshed her spirit after all her excitements, as sound slumber would have rested her body.

The sun had set when, at last, Acte, remembering her duties at home, turned to go. She hurried on in a southeasterly direction, and in about forty minutes reached the Vicus Longus—the long street—which parted the Viminal and the Quirinal hills. On the hardly-perceptible slope of the Viminal stood the handsome and well-built residence of Lucius Nicodemus, in all respects a thorough Roman, notwithstanding the fact that he was but fourth in descent from Lacedemonian ancestors.

Acte was much afraid lest she should be badly received by her hasty-tempered master, for she was late beyond all permission, and Nicodemus, with the pious severity of the Nazarenes, had but lately reproved her sharply for standing in the doorway at dusk with another of the maids of the house. Impatience, too, might have contributed to provoke him. Nicodemus, however, far from speaking a single reproachful word, beamed as she entered; he had been waiting for her in the atrium. He took possession of her as she came in, and led her away to the tablinum in the peristyle. Lamps were lighted on the supper-table. The family had finished their meal two hours ago: the master, the mistress, their daughter, and seven servants of both sexes, who had been all freed at once by their owner; for the doctrine of the Saviour was too positively antagonistic to slavery for a man of such rigid consistency as Nicodemus to accept the State institution on his own behalf. Besides, every member of his household had been converted and baptized under his roof; hence he could not suffer that bondage to endure which the sacrament had spiritually annulled.

"You must be hungry," he said, with almost tender anxiety. "Here comes Lesbia with your supper; she has kept something hot for you, Acte! Eat and drink, and then talk."

Acte seated herself on the end of the couch on which Nicodemus was wont to recline at meals.

"Eat, eat," he repeated kindly. "You must be half-dead! And your hands are as cold as ice! Here—this is good Vesuvian wine. I brought it up from the cellar on purpose for you; it will do you good, Acte—you are sadly over-tired."

"I really am," she said, hastily raising the brazen cup to her lips. "Forgive me for not returning home with you at once from the Egyptian's tent. . . ."

"Say nothing about it," said Nicodemus, with a smirk. "I am thankful, on the contrary, to see you take the holy task that is laid on you so seriously and zealously in hand. I saw Caesar standing face to face with you. If you are prudent, Nicodemus will have triumphed, and with him the Divine Galilean, before two moons have passed the full."

Acte, who had great difficulty in controlling her feelings, shook her head sadly.

"Nay, Master," she said gloomily. "Do not be angry with me—I implore you in Christ's name—but it is impossible."

"What is impossible?"

"That I—I should convert Claudius Nero."

"But you have converted him, if only you turn to account the advantage which fate has almost thrown into your lap. He was kindness and condescension itself. . . ."

"That is the very reason. He even took my hands and proposed to me to be his beloved sister. . . ."

"What?"

"Yes, indeed, those were his very words. And he invited me to the Palatium, and all I said, he declared, was the echo of his own thoughts. . . ."

"But this is simply a miraculous triumph, Acte! This is the

50

conquest of Rome, the Cross of Christ planted on the summit of the capitol. . . ."

"It is the death of all our plans," interrupted Acte. "I must crush the last hope in your breast. I will never see Caesar again."

"Are you mad, girl?"

"Thank God, I am not! I was never more in my right mind than at this moment. I will be frank and candid with you, for I owe you a debt of gratitude; you must not suppose that Acte could ever wilfully destroy a plan you had laid so wisely and with such honest purpose. I . . . I. . . ."

She hesitated. A burning flush turned her face scarlet, while Nicodemus sat pale and open-mouthed.

"I feel," she presently said, "that I am incapable of playing to the end the part you have assigned to me, without losing my own soul. You all of you declare that there is something in me which is more persuasive than the enthusiasm of the preacher. . . . I know not whether you deceive yourselves in this matter. But this I know: that Caesar looked at me with different eyes from those of any one else whom I have sought to win over to Christ. . . ."

"Well, and what of that?"

"Simply that I—that he will fall in love with me."

"So much the better!"

"Nay, not so much the better—for I shall love him too. . . . Yes, I love him!"

"This is going fast indeed!" cried the haggard old man, with an angry laugh. "And what then; what is the meaning of this monstrous confession? Love him as much as you like—but do your duty in propagating our divine faith."

"For that I have not the strength."

"Miserable girl!" exclaimed Nicodemus. "Has not Christ said that we are to put away earthly things to gain eternal life? Does not He command us to mortify the flesh and afflict the senses, when they would lead us away from the paths of righteousness and virtue?"

"Yea, and so I will," replied Acte. "If I followed my

impulses I should go at once, this minute—fly to him, to his arms, to his breast—for he is full of lofty feeling for what is noble and beautiful: that is the prompting of my sinful and rebellious will. But as I could only sink into shame and misery, if I yielded to it, my determination is firm: no power on earth shall move me to see the man again whose presence is sure to be so fatal to me."

"But supposing he himself commands your attendance?"

"Then I will die rather than obey him. Caesar has power over many things; but he can forbid no one to die who has the courage to face death."

Nicodemus sat silent for a while as if paralyzed. Then he stretched out his hand, which trembled convulsively, and said with a sob:

"Acte, in the name of the Saviour who shed His blood for us all, do not do this thing! Do not spoil my scheme—the grandest scheme since Christ left this earth! Do not ruin the whole future of the Nazarene religion, and the great and heavenly work of Redemption!"

"The world cannot be saved by sin."

"Acte! . . . By the grave of your mother, who died in happy trust in God's mercies. . . ."

"By the grave of my mother!" cried the agitated girl. "Your mention of that Saint is enough to make my determination immovable!"

"And you will not? In spite of my entreaties, Acte—in spite of my tears?"

"No—never, never!"

A change passed over the old man's face. A terrible curse seemed to hover on his lips, a fierce and awful cry of imprecation; his breath was labored, his lean, claw-like fingers were tightly clenched, and a flash of demoniacal hatred lighted up his reddened eyes. But he instantly controlled himself. Still trembling, he poured some wine into a cup that stood near him and swallowed it at a gulp like a man perishing of thirst.

"You will not?" he said hoarsely. "Ah, but Caesar *will*—

and Nicodemus *will;* and we shall see whether scattered pebbles can stick to the cliff when there is a thunder-storm in the valley. . . . You know me! . . . Now go to bed, you little fool. A new day may perhaps restore your common-sense."

Nicodemus' steps died away in the colonnade; she heard the faint creak of the doorhinges; then all was still.

Acte sat on, alone in the wine-smelling dining-hall. Her master's threat echoed with crushing distinctness in her brain. Yes, she knew him! Kind and just by nature, he was nevertheless capable of any violence when he was crossed and baffled in anything he believed to be judicious or necessary. Thinking, and still thinking, the foreboding sense of some imminent disaster weighed more and more heavily on her anxious heart.

Suddenly, as though a voice were calling to her from the dim recesses of the room, the words sounded in her ears: "Away, fly, or you are lost!"

She was seized with frenzied terror: "Caesar *will—*" "Nicodemus *will—*" Still, *she* could not, as surely as the Virgin's Son had said: "Blessed are the pure in heart!" No, she would not.—So she must fly; in no other way could she evade the struggle with that sinister power, with her own weakness, with Nicodemus' fury.

Very softly, like a guilty creature, she stole into her cubiculum. She was trembling in every limb. In great haste, as though her salvation hung on each moment as it flew, she collected a few necessaries. She fastened a gold chain, the last gift of her dying mother, about her neck as a talisman; then she wrapped herself up in a thick mantle, extinguished the lamp, and hurried to the back gateway.

Next morning the household shouted in alarm through the peristyle for: "Acte!" in vain. Her bed was untouched. A scrap of parchment was attached to the door with an ornamental pin, and bore these words: "Farewell, every one!" But there was not the faintest clue to show whither she had vanished.

Nicodemus, dubious and conscience-stricken, said nothing

of the events of the past day, and his unsuspicious household puzzled themselves vainly to find a reason for this sudden flight. All bewailed the loss of their favorite house-mate as a common misfortune. She was so gentle, so refreshing in her innocent mirthfulness; her sunny golden hair had brought a sort of heavenly brightness into the house; her rosy, flower-like grace, her voice, her song, as gay as a lark's—all henceforth would be lost to them; they would miss it as a blind man misses the glory of the sunlight.

Nicodemus tried to comfort his wife, who was almost in tears, muttered something about "a girl's whims," "over-wrought feelings," "soon come to her senses," and then took himself off to the prefect's official residence to give information of what had occurred.

Pharax, the soldier who had conducted the escort when Artemidorus was condemned to die, happened to be on duty in the writing-room of the department, to which Nicodemus proceeded for this purpose. The two men recognized each other. When Pharax heard what Nicodemus' business was he was all fire and flame. He led him at once to the prefect, spoke of the favor which Claudius Nero himself had shown the maiden, and remarked very significantly that it would greatly distress Caesar if any harm should come to the fugitive.

This prefect held out his hand to Nicodemus.

"My cohorts," said he, "are pretty-well trained, both those of the robe and those under arms. We shall soon hunt up the damsel, depend upon that. But indeed, I would bet my black stallion, that before we have seriously begun the search for her she will return of her own accord."

But neither did she return nor were the prefect's cohorts successful in their search. For fourteen days they sought her, even enlisting the services of regular slave-hunters—all in vain.

Nero, consumed by a secret passion, had set a considerable price on the finding of Acte, and ordered his praetorians to aid the prefect's cohorts, ostensibly as an act of graciousness to Nicodemus who was inconsolable—and Nero even was at last obliged to resign himself to the belief that Acte—lovely and enchanting Acte, who had filled his soul with such magic melody—had vanished utterly and for ever.

CHAPTER V.

WINTER was over and it was spring once more. The clear horizons of April shed their vivifying influence over the earth. Its lavish bloom had turned all the better quarters of the city to one vast flower-garden. The fountains of the Aqua Claudia and Aqua Marcia flowed with a fuller tide. The Forum and the Via Sacra looked as if fresh snow had fallen, so numerous were the white mantles of the street-idlers. The popular poets dreamed of new verses; the young men decked their fair ones with crimson roses; the maidens had visions of coming bliss.

Dejected and austere, in strange contrast to the happy multitudes he governed, Claudius Nero Caesar was walking one day in the pillared court of his palace. On his left hand was Seneca, his counsellor, erewhile his tutor. For ten minutes or more they went on in gloomy silence. Now and again, as they turned at the end of the marble-paved arcade, the minister stole a glance from under his lowered eye-lashes to read the emperor's inscrutable features. Strangely was the young monarch altered since the day when we saw him in the Egyptian juggler's tent with Tigellinus! His pale face bore the marks of struggles unseen by mortal eye, of an ever restless mind which must incessantly be analyzing, planning, devising, and yet never fructified in deeds. Perhaps, too, it was grief of heart which fettered his wings.

Nero, to whom Art had once seemed the fairest flower of life, had suddenly shut it out from him with bitter aversion. His favorite writers lay rolled up in the ivory coffers of his library; he no longer tried his skill in epic or lyric verse; his cithara hung forlorn among the bay wreaths presented to him by true admirers or false flatterers; not a song ever came from his once tuneful throat.

Since Acte's disappearance he had devoted himself wholly to philosophy, and a duteous contemplation of the aims which Nicodemus and Seneca alike esteemed as the highest calling of a truly great ruler. He had already made progress in this direction in many ways.

The remembrance of Acte seemed always to haunt his vacillating soul like an admonishing spirit. She had been an adherent of the Nazarene creed: could Nero then doubt it?

Nevertheless he did doubt. Less, perhaps, the saving power of the vast revolution to which he was being urged, than the possibility of accomplishing it. If, indeed, Acte had spoken to his soul—Acte herself, with her sweet persuasive voice—all hesitation would have melted away like snow before the airs of spring. But the mere remembrance of her could not effect this. It inspired him with that solemn piety we feel for the dead; but this pious emotion was inseparable from a gloomy torment of ever fresh regret which crushed him to the earth.

A wretched mystery!

What spiteful demon had snatched away the star of his existence? How, and why? He had found no answer to these queries; and Nicodemus, who knew the cause at any rate of the catastrophe, thought it prudent to be silent.

The footsteps of the two men rang almost weirdly through the empty peristyle. Not a slave ventured to be seen, not even a soldier of the guard. All felt that when a storm is gathering it is wise to seek a shelter.

"You seem out of all measure depressed, my lord," said Seneca at last, as Nero stared, more despondently each moment, at the ground.

"Possibly," replied Caesar.

"Then take the advice of an experienced man, who loves you and whose chief pride is in you."

Nero sighed. The world-worn expression of his young face was in singular contrast to the radiant peace and cheerfulness which lighted up the venerable features of his companion—a man sure alike of his powers and his aims.

"If you wish to be rid of your ill-humor," Seneca went on, "force your thoughts to the consideration of things as far as possible from those which haunt you."

"That is easily said," replied Caesar. "Ixion, when bound to the wheel, with all his philosophy could not think of anything but his torments."

"Are you suffering then, Caesar? I thought you would have succeeded better in what you promised me. Do you really pine so sorely for the fellowship of Tigellinus? For street adventures,—for midnight revels?"

"Even that is possible! Tigellinus was my intimate comrade and trusty friend. It is unfair in me to neglect him thus."

"You can show him favor now as of yore: but as an associate I own he is ill-suited to a sovereign whose schemes are so magnificent, so exalted. . . . My beloved son, I fully understand that youth must have certain rights. . . . Nevertheless the magnanimity of a monarch, however young and genial he may be, is best shown in his moderation. You make a sacrifice, no doubt, when you govern strictly according to the principles which I laid down and you approved; but this sacrifice is indispensable if you are to carry out the task you have set yourself; the Liberation of Mankind. No one can believe that you have a heart to feel for the sufferings of the populace if you revel in restless enjoyments. . . ."

"Have I done so?" asked Caesar bitterly.

"No, indeed! You have left that to the senators and the men who have risen to power, griming as they wallow in gold while the poor and wretched can scarcely cover their nakedness.''

"Well then—why do you accuse me?"

"I only meant to say: if you accept the task you must not be afraid of suffering; neither of frugality in your private life nor of the amazement of your former associates; neither of the reproaches of your wife Octavia, nor even of Agrippina's incessant complaints. . . .''

"Have I proved myself so weak in these respects?"

"You have done your duty as far as you were able. But in spite of all that, voices are to be heard declaring that it would be better for the commonwealth and more worthy of the Roman Emperor if he could only keep the empress-mother from interfering with state-affairs. . . .''

"And is it Seneca who tells me this—Seneca, who shared with Agrippina the conduct of my education?"

"Nay, pardon my boldness. But I cannot help myself. All the noblest of the empire share my views. So far everything has gone on fairly well, but I fear the time may come when Agrippina of all persons will most stand in our path. She is absolutely and entirely the incarnation of that un-philosophical view of life which we are trying to combat. Where we aim at equality and justice she works to widen the abyss between the rich and poor, the lofty and lowly, the free and the bondman; to dig a gulf that can never be filled up. Without any knowledge of the Nazarene faith, she is its fiercest opponent.''

Caesar stood still.

"Seneca," he presently said in a tone of singular constraint. "Do you think the times are ripe for the great scheme suggested by Nicodemus?"

"Ripe? Will ordinary men ever be ripe for a great historical transformation? It is only the thinking minority who toil at the evolution of the new order of ideas; the majority naturally rebels. But do you ask a sick child whether the healing draught is as sweet as honey? You must treat the selfishness of the senators with scorn, they know nothing of their common humanity with slaves and artisans. You must force the burning remedy between their teeth, though they should roar like Philoctetus."

"Yes, yes, that in itself would be a triumph," said Nero thoughtfully. "I hate the senators. . . ."

"With a few exceptions!—Flavius Scaevinus for instance. . . ."

"And Thrasea Paetus," added the emperor. "They are true men, and thinkers, whom I revere almost as I do you, my dear Annaeus."

"Do not revere me, only love me," said the old man. Nero silently pressed his hand.

"Those few," Seenca went on, "will stand by us in the struggle, and their influence will outweigh all the incapacity of their peers. Philosophy filling the throne—that is the grandest idea ever conceived by man. I, for my part, do not believe in the pious, dreamily-pathetic fables which Nicodemus repeats after the fantastic and imaginative natives of the East; but their core is sound, and as matters stand, they are at present the only possible means of making the sublimest part of the teaching of the Stoa, and of what we have discovered for ourselves, intelligible and accessible to the people."

Again Nero stood still.

"I doubt that," he said meditatively.

"What! After the account Nicodemus gave us but yesterday of the Christians in Palestine—of their contempt of suffering, the calmness, the fortitude they display in the contest with their opponents?"

"Yes, dear Annaeus. I was not unmoved by the impressive character of that report, but at the same time I was conscious of a painful oppression. How shall I describe it? I am grieved to the bottom of my soul by a view of the world which so utterly takes the savor out of this life, which treats all sweetness and beauty as an abomination, simply because it is feared that their temptations may divert the soul from things eternal, from a care for something beyond the grave. What have we to do—you and I—with this grey Nazarene creed,

61

since we do not believe in the heaven of the Nazarenes?"

Seneca bit his lips; then, suddenly assuming a majestic demeanor, he said deliberately:

"I do believe in it, my lord! Not, to be sure, as the trembling women believe who hide in the depths of the catacombs from the hatred of our priests and the rage of the insolent mob; but I do believe in it. Our spiritual part is immortal; we are a portion of the Eternal Godhead, condemned to individuality in this world, but vanishing as individuals when we die, lost in the great primeval source of light."

"When we die! But we are as yet alive! Must this fleeting existence be saddened to enable us to flow back to the Eternal? Was it needful that I should lose everything in order that, beyond the wood-pile on which my bones will be burnt, I may find nothing but a perpetuity of self-less unity?"

"What? . . . . What have you lost? Speak, my son. I have long observed that some sorrow was consuming you which lay outside the limits of our discussions. . . ."

Nero tried to smile.

"You are mistaken," he said with sufficient candor. "Nothing new has happened to me. Indeed, all we have done amply satisfies me; above all our edict as to foreign religions—which was *your* work, dear Annaeus."

"Nay, yours," said the senior in deprecation. "I only suggested, you carried it out; and how grandly! In spite of your mother, who at the prompting of her train-bearer Pallas, declared the whole thing to be a piece of plebeian idiotcy; in spite of the Pontifex Maximus, too, and of the priests of Jupiter, who declaimed at the growing audacity of the Oriental and Egyptian heresies; and in spite of your wife, who dreaded from hour to hour lest the thunder-bolts of Jove should be hurled down on the degenerate Palatium; in short, in spite of all the folly which rose up to oppose you from right and left, from above and below. No one living in the City of the Seven Hills, not even a slave, shall henceforth be punished for his creed's sake; no Roman bigotry shall compel him to sacrifice to the gods of the State! . . . . Is not this a glorious triumph for philosophy? And yet you are sorrowful?"

The emperor's brow cleared.

"You are right," said he, giving the minister his hand. "I ought to be content. We have done this and much more; though all this is but preparatory—tentative and preparatory—still it is well done and elevating. The reign of duty—the very word sounds like a divine trumpet-call, and lends encouragement to renunciation and self-denial. Yet I am but mortal, easily and often falling back into my natural weaknesses. . . . Sleeping or waking, it steals upon me continually: a burning, unsatisfied longing for happiness."

"Happiness consists in the fulfillment of the moral law," said Seneca sententiously.

"I do fulfil the moral law,—but no happiness dispels the cloud over my life."

"What in the wide world do you lack? You—Caesar, the philosopher, the husband of the fair and amiable Octavia, who would die for you, though she opposes you in some things. . . ."

"If it were only that! Opposes me! Do you think me so intolerant? As empress, and as my wife, she has every right to express her opinions. Certainly, I must confess that I feel a cold chill when at night I am condemned to listen to her admonitions as to the wrath of omnipotent Jupiter. But even were it otherwise—were she on the side of liberty, still I should find no rest. I know not what it is that drives me forth. Often I feel a kind of pity; then I look upon myself as a great criminal because I cannot be grateful to her for her ifinite kindness, and yet—well, it is my doom!"

"You do not love her," Seneca said sadly. Nero sighed.

"Love, love!—Love sweeps a man before it like a whirlwind—he is stunned by it, he is ready to die of the passion, and yet fire rushes through every vein! There is no room in his bursting heart for any thought but of her.— Her!—To possess her he would give all—everything—even a throne."

Caesar had uttered each word more vehemently, passionately, madly; he clenched his fist over his breast as though to still a wild storm raging within.

"You have known such love!" murmured his companion, enlightened by a sudden revelation.

"Yes. For once I will say it; I *have* loved! A fair-haired, lovely, heavenly maiden: Acte, Nicodemus' freed slave.— Woe is me! My happiness is as wrecked even before I had tasted it! That lovely, adored Acte—and I swear it by the grave of my never-to-be-forgotten father, Domitius—Acte should have been empress had not a barbarous and inscrutable fate cruelly torn us apart."

"What! A freedwoman on the throne of the empire?"

"You contradict the first principles of your philosophy," said Caesar, "when you ask the question in such a tone of amazement. I repeat it: I would have annulled Claudius Caesar's dispositions; Octavia would soon have found consolation, and Acte, the incomparable, would have been my wife. Clap your hands to applaud me, Seneca! A Nazarene on the throne!—that would have been a bold stride indeed towards the realization of your social revolution!"

"Indeed it would," said Seneca hesitating. "But I should be afraid. . . ."

"Alas, alas! You have nothing to fear," interrupted Nero. "The Empress of Rome bears the name of Octavia; Acte has vanished like a fallen meteor, and Nero has, happily, learnt to restrain his dreams.—Now let us end this momentous walk. For to-day I will forget that life is grave and be happy. When Flavius Scaevinus invites Caesar to be his guest, he has a right to expect a good-humored visitor."

"At your command! I will hasten to change my dress."

CHAPTER VI.

An hour and a half later a large crowd had collected in front of the imperial palace. It was with great difficulty that the soldiers of the body-guard, posted at the gates, spear in hand, were able to keep the inquisitive mob at a due distance. The steps and bases of the columns of the temple opposite were covered with men; half-grown lads had clambered up the gilt statues, and peering faces peeped between the columns of the vestibule.

"Here they come!" a clear boy's voice presently shouted. A murmur ran through the excited multitude as at the beginning of an anxiously looked-for performance. For the first time since their marriage Caesar was about to proceed through the streets of Rome in solemn state with the fair young Octavia. Flavius Scaevinus was giving a magnificent banquet in honor of the exalted couple.

Two military tribunes in silver armor rode first at a slow pace. Then came half a maniple of the praetorian guard, their flame-colored plumes nodding above their glittering helmets; next walked thirty slaves in gold-embroidered dresses, each pair bearing unlighted torches. The soldiers' spears and the slaves' torches were alike wreathed with roses.

"The empress-mother!" the words ran through the assembled multitudes. The amazement was universal.

"What! Even on such an occasion as this must Agrippina take the foremost place?"

"Incredible!"

"It was all very well so long as Caesar was unmarried. . . ."

"It is an insult to the noble Octavia!"

"Take care, Caius—and you above all, Sempronius! Spies are swarming all about us."

"Spies! What does that matter to us; we are only asserting Caesar's rights."

"And Roman custom!"

"The glorified Augustus would never have endured it."

"But Nero loves his mother. . . ."

"By Hercules, if he only knew. . . ."

"Be silent, do! Do you wish to lose your head?"

These, or to this effect, were the murmurs heard on all sides as the state litter appeared, borne steadily and smoothly on the shoulders of the well-known Sigambri. Leaning on the rich pillows by the side of the empress was her lady-in-waiting, Acerronia, a native of Hispania. This singular girl, though scarcely twenty years of age, seemed to unite the experience of a matron to the innocent naivete of a child. Her sea-green eyes at one moment had a look of most suspicious cunning; at another her wide sensual mouth could put on such a guileless pout that even a sceptic could not but believe in her simplicity. In her behavior to Agrippina she could change suddenly from the tone of a friend to that of the most abject slave; at the same time it was impossible to help feeling that she was not in earnest either as the friend or the slave. Her chief beauties were her waving red hair, her snowy complexion, and the brilliant teeth which, when she laughed, gave her little face the look of an amiable panther. The empress-mother delighted in her presence about her person: Acerronia was, perhaps, the only creature to whom her mistress had never spoken an ungracious word.

Agrippina, as she reclined on the cushions, supporting her pearl-crowned head on her hand, looked more dignified, more imperious, more self-confident than ever. Nero's desire for independence which, a few months since, had startled her so unpleasantly by the edict of toleration, seemed gradually to be dying away. For some time he had undertaken no important business without informing her of it, asking her advice and respecting her opinion almost as a command. That edict had evidently been no more than a passing whim; she would not raise the question again; any fresh attempt on her part would perhaps arouse his almost extinct antagonism. As matters now stood she had good reason to rest satisfied. Her son's veneration for her intellectual superiority was hardly shaken. Seneca himself seemed now to recognize the fact that no sound policy was possible excepting under the undisputed supremacy of the empress-mother, and she had at any rate, and above all, the commander of the praetorian guard on her side: the faithful Burrus, who could at need put in a decisive word. Burrus, in the course of time, had become more deeply entangled in her net; she fully believed that he was quite madly in love with his imperial mistress, although she granted him but short measure of the tokens of her graciousness.

Immediately behind the litter of the empress-mother walked Pallas, her private secretary and keeper of the purse, surrounded by a number of slaves. He wore about his neck a costly chain of honor, his imperial patroness' latest gift. Whatever this haughty and scornful woman might be accused of, ingratitude was not one of her sins.

It was Pallas who had originally advised Claudius Caesar, in his widowhood, to marry Agrippina. The timorous monarch, who was still smarting under the hideous licentiousness of his former wife Messalina—then but recently put to death—as a fresh and burning brand-mark, at first resisted with all his might. Pallas, however, would not give it up, for Agrippina, who at that time had seemed to be a model of strict virtue, really appeared to him to be the fittest consort for the vacillating emperor—besides which she had promised him such splendid rewards that he not only accomplished the marriage, but also the solemn adoption of her son by her first marriage: Nero, at that time a child playing in an infantine tunic.

She had never forgotten this service of love. Pallas, who was secretly despised by the aristocrats for not being free-born, and little liked by Nero himself, nevertheless, by the favor of Agrippina, played a leading part. The senate, to be sure, snarled with rage, but they submitted; more than once they paid signal honors to the powerful favorite: formal thanks for the services he had done the State, and even on one occasion, when he was ill, public prayers were commanded for his recovery. Agrippina herself bestowed on him all the richest treasures of her favor. She gave him estates, villas, palaces, slaves, jewels; and the chain which at this moment glittered on his sinewy throat was perhaps the kindest and most flattering of all her gifts, for every link of the splendid ornament bore a portrait of the donor, different on each.

Pallas passed for being one of the few men at the court of Rome whose life was fairly blameless. His intimacy with the empress-mother was free from even the superficial gallantries which Afranius Burrus made bold to show her. Long years ago Pallas had had a wife—a gentle, clinging Greek—but had early lost her by a terrible death. From that time he had lived solely for his vocation, which consisted in upholding the interests of the empress in every possible way.

An attempt on Agrippina's part to arrange a marriage between this faithful adherent and her maid of honor Acerronia failed more through his calm and deliberate indifference than through the vehement insolence of the red-haired tiger-cat, who, as the daughter of a knight from Cordova, looked down on a freedman and had the audacity to treat him with the utmost rudeness in the very presence of Agrippina.

And in other quarters, too, the empress' favorite seemed untouched by all who strove to win him; for Acerronia's views were not shared by all the young damsels of free birth.

On the contrary, there were some among the daughters of the senators who would have esteemed it an honor to become the wife of the man who had more influence than any one over the empress-mother and, through her, over Caesar. Pallas, however, had absolutely no wish to form any such new tie. The memory of his gentle Andromeda rose up in too sharp a contrast to the shrewd and calculating damsels of Rome. This was his state of mind until, one afternoon, he first set eyes on fair-haired, rosy Acte. Then, suddenly, the successor whom he had deemed it impossible to meet with was found. All at once the heart of three and forty was aware of a strong revival of the rapture which had seized it once, so long ago, when he had first beheld the lovely form of the fair Greek on the seashore at Stabiae. "Now or never!" said he to himself. He remembered the old Etruscan legend of the briar which had long been in despair, and yet at length bore roses. Nor did he smile over this poetic transformation, but confessed that never, until now, had he truly understood the meaning of that oft-sung ballad.

Then he saw Acte again,—at the house of Nicodemus—without her knowing that an admirer was at hand; and subsequently, among the laurel hedges on the field of Mars, he gave utterance to his feelings. And suddenly she vanished, like Proserpina snatched away by the ruler of darkness.

Her refusal had been amply explicit. Pallas could only assume that she had fled on account of his suit. "The terrible!" she had called him at the very first; and that she was afraid of him, foolishly afraid, her flight sufficiently proved. And his soul was full of bitterness.

He, the all-powerful Pallas, vanquished by the womanly dignity of her appearance, had offered this incredible little fool his hand and heart in honorable bonds, instead of merely sueing for her favor, as she herself had expected; and his handsome proposals had so stirred her aversion that she had taken refuge in flight, as though he were plague-stricken. She had fled from him, leaving everything behind, because she was afraid he might have recourse to violence!

What a miserable defeat! odious, intolerable humiliation!

The thought of this catastrophe had weighed on his mind for weeks. To lose that rosy, radiant girl—and to lose her thus! it was beyond all endurance.

Of Acte's real motives he had not the faintest suspicion. He regarded Caesar's zealous search for her as a mark of his regard for Nicodemus, who was known to be on friendly terms with Seneca. If Pallas had but known the truth, he would have raged like Ajax when the gods darkened his mind.

Now, as he marched behind his sovereign lady's litter, surrounded by the gorgeous array of palace slaves, the object of secret envy to thousands, Pallas had schooled himself to his disappointment. He held his expressive and determined head high; he felt himself altogether the creator of the dynasty of Agrippina and Nero. Still, he looked somewhat aged. When a man of ability, who for years had defied all sentiment but a desire for the fruition of his labors, suddenly falls a prey to an irresistible passion and immediately after suffers the pang of seeing every hope vanish, his scars are deeper than those left by the more stormy griefs of youth.

The magnificent train of the empress-mother was immediately followed by the gilt litter in which Nero and his wife Octavia were borne. This, too, was escorted by thirty torch-bearers, and half a maniple of the body-guard under the command of the amiable Agrigentine, Sophonius Tigellinus. This brilliant horseman was riding his fine black Cappadocian close by the side of the young empress. The acclamations of the crowd made his steed rather restive, but this only gave him a favorable opportunity of displaying in the best light his exceptional mastery as a rider, while now and again he glanced from under his long black lashes at Octavia as, blushing a little, she bowed right and left in greeting to the enthusiastic populace.

"She is handsome!" thought the Sicilian ladykiller.—"As handsome as Diana, but also, I fear, no less austere.—And you do not love her, my omnipotent Nero! Amazing, perfectly absurd! I believe that if, at the beginning of my career, I had met with such a woman as Octavia, I should never have become the insatiable sinner who is now sitting his horse in such style!''

The young empress was indeed such a beauty as could not fail to influence the susceptible Agrigentine. As a girl she had been naturally gay and mirth-loving, but now her expression was singularly grave and reserved, in marked contrast to her soft and gentle features. A shade of sorrow lay over the long, brown lashes which were generally downcast; she reclined in silence by her husband's side, and his face, as pale as marble, seemed to strangely reflect her inmost and secret soul.

The statusque stillness of a imperial pair, and the strange atmosphere of moral alienation which surrounded them, could not fail to produce a painful impression on any eye that looked beneath the surface. It was plain that fate had here bound together two hearts, each noble in itself, but which were antagonistic in thought and feeling. How should Nero, with his imaginative nature and ardent thirst to live, whose utmost effervescence had only been repressed by the practice of the arts—Nero the septic, the man of inward storms and struggles—how should he match with Octavia, clearly confident and pious, her nature satisfied with the faith of her forefathers, who answered her husband's every doubt with a sigh of pity, or a smile of assurance and hope?

When Claudius Nero had come to a serious decision, shown magnanimity, or achieved any victory over himself Octavia merely took it for granted. How could any one hesitate when a matter was so clear and plain? An honest man could find his way even in the dark . . .

To Nero such speeches from his wife brought a mixture of contending feelings: vexation, admiration and shame, but, above all, a defiant discontent which now and then assumed the darker hue of a germ of hatred.

''Hail, Caesar, hail!'' was shouted anew by the crowd. ''Hail to the empress, our beloved Octavia!''

Nero, drawing a long breath, looked at his youthful wife;

71

he tried to smile—she looked up for a second and then cast down her weary, dreamy eyes with a sigh. In fact she seemed appallingly indifferent—and so she always was, thought Caesar. Not even on her wedding-day had she shown that sweet agitation which transfigures even the plainest maiden as a bride. She had remained rigid and silent: Pygmalion's statue before it was inspired with life by Aphrodite.

How different was Nero! By Zeus! he had never indeed loved her, and yet, when they had found themselves alone within closed doors, and he saw before him his blooming young bride under the warm, magic light of the hanging lamps, he felt as though his former indifference were but a fable: she seemed more sweet and lovable than even Helen to Alexandros. He sat down on the gilt seat with lion's paws for legs, tenderly drew her to him, and whispered ardently: "We will be happy, sweet Octavia, happy all our lives!" And he rained kisses on her blushing face, her scented hair, her snowy shoulders. While she—who, as he had been repeatedly assured by her confidential attendant Rabonia, a freed-woman, was dying for love of him—she—the "stag-eyed, tender bride" listened to all his intoxicated raptures from first to last, as if she were a marble statue. If she had but rebelled! but she made no resistance, she was not shy; she submitted to his caresses without emotion, without the faintest gleam of joy. Thus, from the first, Nero ceased to believe in her love for him. At best she seemed to feel for him a sister's affection. He was not hypocrite enough to conceal from her for any length of time that he, on his part, felt even less. The breach was past healing. Appearances only were kept up for the outside world.

Among the escort with the imperial pair was Phaon, Caesar's favorite and most trusted slave. A suspicion of audacity, almost of impudence, that played on his lips, gave the stalwart man of six-and-thirty a boyish appearance. Phaon did not look as if he took a too gloomy view of the great problems of existence. His philosophy was perhaps that of Horace: "Pluck the joys of to-day, and hope for as little as

72

possible from the future!"

By his side walked five or six others, carrying little coffers of citrus-wood inlaid with pearl. In these were a variety of precious objects—Caesar's gifts to his host's wife and daughters.

Seneca's litter closed the procession. He was surrounded by a little knot of court functionaries and praetorians. With him in the litter was the captain of the guard, Afranius Burrus.

The multitide greeted these two popular men with shouts of welcome.

"Hail, the Dioscuri of the Empire!" went up from a thousand throats.

"Seneca is smiling!" said a grey-haired client. "Look, he is smiling like a man borne in triumph! No doubt he has good news from the frontiers. His statecraft has reduced the Chatti who could not be quelled by the sword."

"Never think it!" replied a flaxen-haired Hun. "The Chatti are as shrewd in council as they are brave in battle. But they wish to keep friends with Rome and to be at peace, so we are about to send the highest-born of our nobles to greet Caesar, and treat with him in the name of all the tribes."

"But even that is a triumph!" said the Roman. "I was sure of it from Seneca's smiling. Ah! he is the flower of all philosophy! Verily the toga is mightier than the sword!"

"Do you think so?" said the German. "Burrus, to judge by his looks, is of the contrary opinion."

The two men with their characteristic heads—the invincible thinker, and the vigorous, determined warrior—were in fact a riddle for a thoughtful bystander. Seneca—pale and calm, his lofty forehead bald and deeply lined; Burrus— red-faced as if he had drunk a score of glasses of wine, muscular, almost coarse: which of the two held the fate of the empire in his hand? Seneca, who aimed at the overthrow of the institutions of secular antiquity—or Burrus, who as the empress-mother's ally, was bound to support them? Or was it perhaps written in the stars that neither of these should turn the scale in the progress of things? To any man capable of foreseeing this, the self-conscious assurance, the air of ruling history worn by both faces, otherwise so unlike, would have been indescribably comic.

The festal train moved slowly and solemnly along the Via Sacra towards the Porta Querquetulana. There was a flowery fragrance in the air, a breath of spring; as though Jupiter himself vouchsafed to do homage to the earthly representative of his infinite omnipotence.

CHAPTER VII.

FLAVIUS SCAVINUS stood in his vestibule to receive the imperial family and their suite with all due respect.

While Agrippina descended from her litter with great dignity, leaning on the arm, covered by a mantle, of her lady-in-waiting, the stalwart praetorians marched slowly in at the gate. But for the garlands of roses twined round their helmets and spears, which lent a poetic softness to the scene, the proceedings would have borne the aspect of an invasion.

The grey headed senator looked on in astonishment at the unusual proceeding, and the empress said with a smile:

"Our warriors will add splendor to the festival you have prepared for us; nothing is to me more delightful or impressive than the clang of Ares' arms amid the blossoms of spring. I beg of you dispose of the men as you think fit. Let them mingle with the slaves; set them in groups round the festive sports; place them as a body-guard to your guests—or to such of them as you wish to honor—just as you please. The men have been instructed to obey unhesitatingly."

Flavius Scaevinus, to some extent deceived by Agrippina's masterly powers of dissimulation, tried to persuade himself that she had, in fact, intended to pay him a signal mark of attention.

This illusion however, was soon dispelled. A scarcely

perceptible twitch played about the empress' full chin, a gleam of irony; and Flavius was sure of what he might have suspected from the first: Agrippina, who had numerous spies at her command, knew that Flavius Scaevinus was an uncompromising foe to her supremacy; nay, that on various occasions he had discussed with the other senators: Barea Soranus, Piso, and Thrasea Paetus, the ways and means of checking her too-preponderating influence. As she herself would assuredly not hesitate at any crime in defence of her position—her past career, which was no secret to any one but Cladius Nero and his wife, was guarantee for that—she was prepared for the same promptness of decision on the part of her opponents. If, then, she must walk into the den of the lion, Flavius Scaevinus, she was anxious to secure her safe return.

Agrippina now turned to Metella, her host's wife, and with the majestic condescension of which she was mistress, enquired after her health, while Flavius was receiving Nero and the youthful empress.

It was the custom on such occasions that the Roman Emperor should kiss the senators. Nero knew how to give this empty form an air of genuine feeling which seemed to proclaim to all the world "I regard this man as a son." Flavius kissed Octavia's hand; and his eyes sparkled, as with a slight blush, she spoke a few polite words. Octavia had always been a favorite with him; he did not guess that she was suffering; he supposed her union with Nero to be the ideal of silent happiness. Agrippina was exasperated to perceive that Flavius Scaevinus seemed unable to tear himself away from the young couple, while Metalla was saying to her: "My sovereign mistress Agrippina, if you please we will go in."

In spite of Flavius' known disaffection, Agrippina had taken it for granted that the master of the house would devote himself to her, and not leave her to Metella—a bony creature, old before her time—a merchant's daughter—(in point of fact she was descended from one of the most respected families of Ostia)—a plebeian who, as a child, had worked at patching old sails, and now carried her head as high as if her husband's purple-hemmed toga had been promised her in her cradle. However, Agrippina swallowed down her displeasure, tried to smile, and marched very haughtily through the door-way.

The spacious Corinthian atrium was already filled with a crowd of illustrious guests. Senators with their wives and daughters; knights who had distinguished themselves in the service of the State or as legal authorities; the Pontifex Maximus; the priests of the three great divinities; the prefect of the city; several owners of large estates in southern Italy; a few clients of privileged rank—all forming a gay assembly in the half-roofed hall.

At a few paces within stood a man of middle height, with a peculiarly clear and firm expression. His intelligent eye resembled Seneca's; but his face and manner alike betrayed an inflexible will even more plainly than those of the prime minister. This striking-looking man was Thrasea Paetus, Agrippina's relentless judge, the fervid patriot who had set all his hopes on Nero's accession to the throne, and who was now destined to learn that the ambitious empress could govern the state to all intents after her own fashion, in spite of open and secret opposition, that she winked at corruption and depravity on all sides, gave the most important posts to her most worthless favorites, and only endured Seneca himself because the narrow scope of his philosophy unfitted the young emperor for the exertion of any really practical powers.

Thrasea Paetus scarcely bowed as the empress-mother came in; but he hastened to meet the young couple even more earerly than Flavius himself, clasped Nero's Apollo-like figure in a long embrace, and kissed him three times solemnly on the brow.

Octavia seemed deeply struck by the appearance of this noblest of all the Romans. Her bosom rose and fell with agitation as though she had lost all self-control, and her eyes rested for an instant with rapt melancholy on her husband's face: never had he seemed so handsome, so incomparable as at this moment. She could have cried out to him: "I would give up all the splendors of earth if only, at the age of fifty, you could look back on such a life as that of Thrasea Paetus!"

When the imperial party had exchanged a few words here and there with the most privileged guests, a sprightly trumpet-call gave the signal for the banquet to begin. The company proceeded in pairs to the cavaedium, where the steward had superintended the laying of two long tables under the deep-blue sky. All round the Doric arcade torches, of man's height, were burning in sockets of beaten brass, and their perfumed smoke curled softly up in the growing dusk; smaller lights were fixed along the ridge of the roof.

With all this illumination the tables did not need the usual number of bronze lamps, but they were lavishly decked with flowers. Wreaths of roses and violets crowned the silver jars of wine and water, the precious murrhine vases, and the artistic ornamental vessels. Three hundred thick chaplets lay ready for the heads of the guests. Rose leaves and stemless narcissus flowers strewed the floor as far as the eye could reach; every column was twined round with ivy and acanthus leaves.

It did not take long to assign places to the guests, thanks to the good management of the head slaves and their assistants. A soft melody—a song of southern Hispania, "Art thou sleeping?" was its name—was sung in the garden, and meanwhile slaves and maidens poured golden Vesuvian wine out of Etruscan ewers into the dimly-gleaming goblets.

The place of honor at the head of the left-hand table—looking from the atrium—was given to the empress-mother. On her right reclined Burrus, captain of the body-guard; on her left the master of the house.

Nero filled the corresponding place at the head of the other table, between Octavia and his host's wife. There was no table across to connect these two, which was the usual arrangement. Only the outer side of the tables had couches drawn up to them and the inner, as was customary in Rome, was left open, so Flavius and his wife had no one on that side of them, and the row of guests was continued onward from Burrus on one hand, and from Octavia on the other.

Next to Octavia came Thrasea Paetus the stoic; then a wealthy Egyptian lady, Epicharis by name; next to her Annaeus Seneca the prime minister, and on his left a senator's young wife of fourteen.

From the very beginning of the banquet, at which oysters from the Lucrine lake and Asiatic sea-urchins were first served, Thrasea Paetus devoted himself to the young empress. Octavia had only addressed a trivial remark to him—a polite question as to a recent incident in the games in the circus, which was keeping Rome in a state of excitement: it was not yet finally decided whether Tigillinus' swift horse "Fulgur," or Anicetus' "Flava" had been the winner. A commission had been appointed to settle this all-important dispute; witnesses were examined as though it were a question of a suit for extorting a tax. As yet Anicetus had the strongest supporters, which annoyed the partisans of Tigellinus all the more, because their opponent had, strictly speaking, no business on land at all. Anicetus was a naval officer. Not long since he had been in command of the fleet off Cape Misenum, and he was only in Rome for a while on private affairs when he had disputed the prize with the long-victorious Agrigentine.

Thrasea Paetus smiled, incredulous that her interest in the matter could be genuine. He answered her in just such a tone as he might have used to say: "Yes, Madam, the weather is indeed lovely."

Octavia nodded absently, and asked a second question which presently led to an inexhaustible subject: Augustus Caesar and his magnificent achievements for the extension of the empire.

Nero himself, and Thrasea's Egyptian neighbor, Epicharis, frequently took part in this conversation, and even Annaeus

Seneca released himself from his partner's vacuous chatter to put in a weighty word now and then. The flow of this discussion became so grave and solemn indeed, that Nero could almost fancy himself in his study at the palace, where the gifted philosopher had, especially during the last few weeks, incessantly insisted that life meant self-denial, self-control, and duty.

These memories, in the midst of this gay and noisy meeting, suddenly filled the young monarch with a painful sense of its utter vanity. In truth was a startling contrast, and could not fail to appeal to Nero's artist-soul.

While, at this upper end of the table, the conversation had taken a turn so grave as to be worthy of the Stoa, at the bottom the laughing and talking came bubbling up like the sound of a prattling spring in the clefts of Tibur. Handsome youths turned with polite speeches to their fair neighbors, while the winged god sat invisible between the happy couples, sharpening his darts. Older men were enjoying a talk over past days, telling many a merry tale of their experience when on duty in Sicilia or Asia Minor, emptying goblet after goblet, and quoting in self-defence the words of the Greek drinking-song "Now is the time to drink."

Ah, and there was Otho, the jealous and devoted slave of his bewitching wife Poppaea Sabina, ever kept his watchful eye on her. She, far enough from him at the other table, was reclining next to that dangerous man Tigellinus!

By Hercules! She was a charming woman, with her soft liquid eyes and her fascinating manners, bending her flower-crowned head over her right shoulder. Otho could not but rejoice in the possession of such a prize, and his satisfaction accounted for his jealousy. The more precious the jewel, the more reasonable it was that he should take care to preserve it.—Sophonius Tigellinus must have whispered some highly-spiced remark in her ear; Poppaea's eyes twinkled under their lashes like those of a roguish fawn, and after a short struggle with herself she laughed so heartily, showing her pearly teeth, that her tortured husband felt the blood mounting to his temples.

Nero had been watching the pretty, laughing creature as if half-asleep; now his eye rested more thoughtfully on her sweet face: Twenty years hence Poppaea Sabina's rosebud lips would be deeply set in wrinkles, her flashing eyes reddened, her blooming cheeks sunk and pale—almost as withered as those of the philosopher and minister. . . . But then she could say: "I have enjoyed all that this transitory life has to offer. I drank to the bottom of the cup before a spiteful fate upset it! I have gone through no suffering for the sake of a mere Idea!"

It seemed as though these reflections in Caesar's mind had by some emanation communicated themselves to Poppaea's. Till this moment she had been under the spell of Tigillinus, but she now suddenly looked up at Claudius Nero and her eyes met his melancholy, meditative gaze. The color that flamed into her cheeks was deeper than that which had just suffused her husband's. Her face, her throat, her very shoulders glowed as if dipped in crimson dye. Then, reflecting that Caesar would notice this blush, she became so much confused that Tigellinus murmured: "What ails the fair Poppaea? Do you not feel well?"

She recovered herself immediately.

"Laughing so incessantly has gone to my head," she said lightly.

"I understand the reproof," replied Tigellinus. "But you see, noble Poppaea, my duties are by degrees becoming so onerous, so tragical, so important, that I must now and then relax. In Caesar's presence a laugh has of late been quite a curiosity. If things go on like ths much longer, I shall be swallowed up in the abyss of melancholy.

"That sounds remarkably comical."

"Do you think so? . . . . But I am quite in earnest. I feel my soul ossifying. So when good-fortune gives me the opportunity, I take all possible advantage of it to lend a helping hand to so charming an Epicurean as Poppaea in practising her delightful philosophy."

"An Epicurean! I? . . . Well, if you like. . . . And why not? Is not this life all too short? What use is there in hanging our heads? or in painting misery blacker? It is pity that your Caesar should allow himself to be thus driven into the desert by Seneca, so young as he is and formed for happiness! Look at him—with those eyes as black as night! Are they not quite heavenly?"

"What enthusiasm! If you thought half so highly of me. . . . By Zeus, I should go crazy with ecstasy!"

"Do not be a hypocrite," said Poppaea. "You, the conqueror of all hearts, who can count up a dozen or more pleasant reminiscences in this group alone! You, whose adventurous good fortunes are famous to the furthest ends of Hispania and Lusitania—famous? or shall I say infamous? . . . . But to turn from this too delicate subject: follow the advice of a friend—for I am your friend, in spite of everything and everybody!"

"I am your most obliged! Well, and what is your advice?"

"Do your utmost to undermine the prime minister and his philosophical nonsense."

"And how am I to set to work?"

"Absurd! Make Caesar understand clearly that it is possible to be a great ruler, a powerful thinker, a glorious benefactor to his empire, and at the same time a rational creature! Look again. The same strange shroud of melancholy I have many times noticed before is passing over his face. Really, if it were not for manners' sake and an insane regard for the presence of others, I would get up without more ado, and softly lay my hands on his shoulders—and—and try to comfort him!"

"Indeed! And what would you say to him?"

" 'Caesar,' I would say, 'what makes you so sad at heart? Why do you never laugh? Why do you pucker up your brows? Look about you! Youth, grace, and beauty smile upon you. Enjoy what the fleeting hour has to give; be a man among men!' . . . . That is what I would say, soothingly and from the bottom of my heart; and when he heard me it might perhaps occur to him that it would be wiser to strew the path to eternal darkness with flowers, than to attend to the commonplaces of his minister and listen to such delightful music with the expression of a condemned wretch!''

The Agrigentine laughed.

"That would be a real stroke of genius, worthy of our amiable Poppaea! Show your contempt of society and its foolish prejudices. Go and try!''

"That is easier said than done. You are not taking my husband's anger into account. Otho would crucify me!—In fact, golden youth, let me beg you not to bend your scented locks too often in my direction! I just caught a Balearic war-glance from Salvius Otho's eyes—you understand me? A look as heavy as a Balearic leaden sling-stone. The other day, too, at Piso's house, he thought you gazed too deeply into my eyes. And you know very well that I only permitted you to esteem me as a friend—as a brother.''

Tigellinus frowned.

"I remember now,'' he said ironically. "Forgive me for having forgotten it at the moment. You were so eager as you spoke of Claudius Nero. Of course you would allow greater freedom to Caesar, the philosophical monarch whom you desire to convert, than to a Sicilian nobody.—That I quite understand: every man according to his rank and merit.''

"Indeed! And what right have you to make such an insinuation? Guard your tongue, you quintessence of audacity. You are unfortuantely licensed to say much—but not everything!''

Again she looke dup half timidly at Nero, sighed, and then went on enthusiastically, as if speaking to herself.

"This is the difference between innocence and degeneracy. Caesar has spoken to me three or four times in his life; but if he had been on intimate terms with me ten times as long as this horrid Tigellinus, he would never, I am certain, venture to assume so ill-bred a tone. He has respect, and feeling; he understands. He is as a god where all others are mere frail dust-eaten mortals!''

Nero had meanwhile grown more silent and gloomy every minute. He no longer heard a word of Octavia's dignified conversation with Thrasea Paetus. There was only a dull murmur in his ear without sense or connection, like waves of sound rising and falling—empty, voiceless, as if infinitely remote. His thoughts had gone back to the day when he had pardoned Artemidorus. In fancy he beheld the lovely Acte with her glorious fair hair and clear blue eyes: he could hear her now, imploring his mercy in her moving tones. It was she—the one incomparable maiden: she was kneeling before the imperial litter and raising her white arms—he saw her—he could have painted her!—Then suddenly the lovely vision vanished; another and a more exquisite moment rose before him—the only moment when he had ever been truly happy. He was standing in the Egyptian magician's booth, Acte opposite to him—and her voice again sank more deeply, more seductively into his passionately throbbing heart.

Acte! Loved beyond words! Why did you vanish as you came? As fleeting as a spring-blossom, a floating breeze which is gone almost before it has fanned the fevered brow?

It was strange, but at this instant he felt as if he had now for the first time solved the riddle. She had fled from *him*—for love of him, and of no other. She had felt that he, too, idolized her; she desired to escape the catastrophe she foresaw, the fearful struggle.

He looked across at the other table where his mother filled the place of honor. Yes, the inexorable Agrippina would have crushed his very heart. A freedwoman, a girl who had been a slave! Hardly would she have allowed him to keep such a low-born creature as a mistress; much less as his wife!

Acte, to be sure, could not know *what* he would have dared for her sake, or that no sacrifice would have been too great, no breach too cruel, if only she had been the prize to be won.

Foolish child! Why, why had she vanished, leaving only that oracular greeting: "Farewell, every one!" One line of explanation, one single frank word, and all might have been well.

He thought it over again and again, and then remained in strange doubt. Nicodemus, the inquisitive Nazarene, had assured him that Acte was a perfect sphinx to him, with her motiveless flight. And if he did not see clearly in the matter—he who had known her from the first—it was, and must remain, a mysteriously oppressive marvel to the melancholy emperor. One thing alone he knew: that the whole wide world besides was as nothing to him, that he cared only for that one memory of pain and joy.

What a dismal fate, what a broken life! If Acte were but at his side, in the place of the woman who was so utterly unsympathetic to him, who with all her kind-heartedness wounded his deepest susceptibilities, how gloriously his task of governing would proceed. With what mighty deeds would not love and happiness have inspired him—deeds which, as it was, he could only strive to accomplish in weariness and grief by the aid of Seneca's cold precepts and Nicodemus' fantastic theories. Yes! he might have triumphed! He might have been the immortal creator of a glorious era of human freedom and fraternity. The Heaven of the Nazarene, with its peaceful and beautiful pardon, had seemed a reality in fair Acte's eyes.

Claudius Nero pressed his hand to his eyes. He, the first man in Rome, the sovereign ruler of the whole mighty empire, from the Pillars of Hercules to furthest Mesopotamia—he, adored by his subjects, wealthier than the Lydian King, full of eager vitality, of a desire for all that was good and lofty and beautiful—he was alone and poverty-stricken on the throne of his splendid dominion! Alone, and desolate unto heart-breaking!

A sudden silence startled him out of his gloomy meditations. The cheerful clatter which had filled the flower-decked cavaedium all at once ceased. Flavius Scaevinus, raising a cup wreathed with roses high in his right hand, pledged Nero the well-beloved, the exalted, the fortunate. With ingenious politeness he included the names of Octavia and Agrippina in the toast, and then reverting to the sublime person of the emperor, he invoked every blessing the gods could bestow on that beloved and radiantly youthful head.

This masterpiece of oratory was hailed with a storm of applause. More especially had a sentence struck fire in which he had said "Nero, Octavia, and *after them* the noble mother who has brought up a prince full of such admirable qualities,"—this "after them" had seemed to Flavius' adherents, who were all hostile to the empress-mother, quite a stroke of genius. It was a scarcely-veiled hint to the assembled guests, and to all Rome as listening with their ears, that they should support Agrippina's foes, and strive to release Nero from the overweening influence of his ambitious and tyrannical parent. At the same time it was the first distinct suggestion given after a long time, to the elder empress that she should abdicate of her own free will, and no longer exact from the Roman people what seemed unendurable.

This hint had just now a peculiar significance. An important political discussion was to take place in the senate in the course of the next week. It was to deal with a dispute with the Chatti, a German tribe close to the borders. The quarrel might possibly end in a declaration of war, although the Roman general in charge of the fortress of Moguntia, had strained every point to meet the reasonable demands of the Chatti to the utmost. It was hoped therefore that Agrippina would understand that Flavius' frank suggestion conveyed a wish that Caesar should appear alone at the council, and free from her guardianship.

The toast was drunk, the cries of Ave! had died away Agrippina smiled with the utmost self-command: her eyes sparkled with a sinister light—but she smiled.

Each of the guests now proceeded to make a solemn libation by spilling a few drops of the fragrant Samian, and again a shout arose of: "Hail Caesar! Hail Claudius Nero! Hail to the well beloved, the fortunate monarch!"

Nero slowly rose. He thanked the asembly by waving his

hand, without uttering a word: it seemed as though his emotion at the heartiness of this homage were too much for him. But what had really brought the tears to his eyes was a thought far indeed from the noisy mirth of the festival; it was the feeling which clung with rigid tenacity of a dead hope to the fair image of a rosy girl, and the adored name of her who was lost for ever.

CHAPTER VIII.

THE banquet in the torch-lighted cavaedium was ended. Metella and the imperial pair led the way, and the whole assembly passed out through the open ante-chamber into the park. The forum-like space immediately behind the house was lighted up by numberless lamps behind red glass transparencies. Higher up on the slope the grand avenues of trees, with their undergrowth of acanthus, anemones, and laurel, were seen in a dreamy half-obscurity.

For a while the guests stood about in easy groups, friends who had overlooked each other exchanging greetings and cooling their hot faces in the delicious breeze which came in scented gusts over the flower beds. Every one seemed the happier for being released from the constraint of the table, breathed more freely, and refreshed himself for further enjoyment of what might be yet to come.

Poppaea Sabina, the beautiful wife of Otho, rested her round arm on the shoulder of her Phoenician companion Hasdra and walked a few steps towards the park.

"It was high time that our host should release us," said she with a sigh. "What a lovely night!"

"As lovely as a dream!" murmured the sentimental Hasdra.

"What ails you, child? You are trembling."

"I have seen him again."

"Whom? Your praetorian?"

"My godlike Pharax! while we were eating he passed twice through the hall."

Poppaea laughed.

"Then you really mean it?" she asked in amazement; "my pretty little doll, my tiny, clinging Phoenician, has fallen in love with a soldier? And with such a colossus! By Eros! I should have given you credit for better taste, Hasdra."

"And I, madam, swear to you by Melkar the god of my fathers, that no living mortal ever could compare for nobility of appearance with my splendid Pharax."

"You are in love—so it would be folly to run down your Pharax; and I see very plainly that you would marry him if he were a slave or an executioner. When once you have taken a thing into your head. . . ."

"Aye, madam, so it is. I am a foolish thing—and I almost wonder you have patience always with my shortcomings and follies."

"Pooh! And I take good care that the little Barbarian shall not get into mischief behind my back. Besides, I like your vehement nature which, on occasion, can creep so meekly into a shell of gentleness and submission. I know you are attached to me—and if need should arise, I could count on you in all confidence."

"To the very death!" Hasdra declared.

"Thank you! But now just tell me—have you any proof that your godlike Pharax returns your liking?"

"Yes—for lately when we met, by accident. . . ."

"He stared at you as a Briton stares at the capitol. I know that. But I do not think that a sufficient guarantee."

"Nor I either. But he looked at me so hard today. . . ."

"Like three Britons," laughed Poppaea.

"Nay, more than that; he sent me a scrap of papyrus by one of the slaves. . . ."

"Impudent rascal!"

"True love is often audacious," said the Phoenician.

"Here, noble Poppaea, read this—and give me your honest opinion."

Poppaea took the note, and by the light of a girandole she deciphered it, as follows:

"Pharax, the praetorian, sends humble and respectful greeting to Hasdra the Phoenician.

"I hope that Hasdra will look favorably on Pharax, one of the body-guard of the empress-mother, for it is a post of great honor. We praetorians are not like common soldiers, who are sent into Gallia Narbonensis or Asia, on the contrary, we are chosen men, and our chief, Afranius Burrus, says so too. So if I venture to speak to you of my love, oh charming Hasdra, it is not as if a common soldier paid you his addresses—quite the contrary.—I love you dearly; I have seen you five times, and as you are as sweet as a rose that is enough for me. I may also tell you, without wishing to flatter myself, that I stand high in the good graces of the Empress Agrippina. Only the day before yesterday her highness told me that, if I went on as I had begun, I should soon be a centurion. Now a centurion is very near being a military tribune. I must express my reverence and love to you this very day, and ask you whether I am too far beneath you. A girl's heart is often so strange. Answer me soon. I love you passionately, and greet you in the gladdest hope."

"Well, what do you say to it?" murmured Hasdra.

"An offer of marriage," said Poppaea with indifference.

"Do you think he means it honestly?"

"Undoubtedly!—And if you like him you have only to say yes. At the same time I think that pretty little Hasdra, Poppaea's favorite, should reflect before accepting such a plebeian husband."

"Not for an instant!" cried Hasdra, putting the note into her bosom. "To-day rather than to-morrow!—A plebeian! What do I care for his birth when he speaks to my heart?"

The simple force of her nature jarred painfully on Poppaea's cold temperament.

"Romantic little simpleton!" she said with a sneer.

"I am as the gods made me," Hasdra retorted. "Indeed, I do not understand how Poppaea can speak thus, for she, too, knows what love is. To be sure. . . ."

"Well, finish."

"I am afraid you will be angry with me. . . ."

"Have you ever found me so petty? Speak."

"Well then: I meant to say that I, Hasdra, understand by love a different thing from what you do. You love Otho your husband—but you let Tigellinus say all sorts of pretty things, and Caius, and Lucius, and Titus and Taitus. . . . You see, noble Poppaea, that would go against my feelings. I can love but one—all the rest are no more to me than so many dummies."

"You can love but one!" Poppaea muttered sadly. "Hasdra, my child, I know not whether to pity or to envy you. I love not one—no, not one; not even Caesar whom I mean to captivate."

"How am I to understand that?

"You must know it—for I may soon have need of you—sooner perhaps than you think. Hasdra, I care for only one thing: power. Among women I must be the loveliest, the most admired. And so I am; all Rome is at my feet. I grudge no pains or trouble to enhance and preserve the charms bestowed on me by nature. . . ."

"That I know," Hasdra put in. "Your precious salves, your baths of milk. . . . And I know, too, that you are the fairest of the fair. Only Octavia perhaps might compare with you, if she were not always pale, and so grave and silent."

"Octavia! Do not speak to me of Octavia! Do you know why I married Salvius Otho? For love? Oh you innocent child. Through Otho, as Caesar's friend, I hoped to be brought near to Caesar, to win his heart, to depose that pale ghost Octavia from her place at his side.—Hush! There goes Sophonius Tigellinus, stealing away with Acerronia!—You shall hear more to-morrow. I need not enjoin the strictest silence on discreet little Hasdra."

They retraced their steps towards the house as if they were

tired, while the Agrigentine passed them in another direction.

"Will you at length speak out?" said Acerronia with some ill-humor. "What? Follow you here into the elm grove? Not for all the treasure of Croesus. Agrippina will be wondering as it is. . . ."

"Agrippina is deep in conversation with Seneca. When he once has got any one into his philosophical clutches. . . ."

"Better his philosophical clutches than those of a robber. You are a perfect vulture, Sophonius. I do not trust you for an instant. Now, confess: the wonderful secret you were to tell me was a mere subterfuge."

"Nay, listen and judge. Pallas, your Pallas. . . ."

"*My* Pallas? I advise you to keep such a form of speech for those who may like it better; Poppaea Sabina for instance. . . ."

"Aha! you are jealous then."

"I? You deserve that Jupiter should hurl his thungerbolts at your silly head!—I, jealous? And of you, every woman's lover, who can never let a stola pass unmolested? You really are as inane as Malkus in an Atellan farce.—Well, and what about Pallas— though he is no more to me than he is to you."

"Indeed! Pallas is nothing to the red-haired Acerronia? Innocent creature! As if all Italy, including the islands, did not know that you were secretly bethrothed!"

"It is a bare-faced lie! Who says so? Tell me the slanderer's name, and I will drag him to justice."

"But you will not disprove it."

"Tell me the villain's name," she insisted wrathfully.

"He himself. . . ."

"What? He himself?" she interrupted. In her excitement she overlooked the fact that she had gone slowly on with the wily Sicilian far into the avenue of trees—and without gaining the treasures of Lydia.

"He himself," Tigellinus went on, suddenly throwing his arm around her with irresistible force, "had not, to be sure, any experience of kissing the red-haired tiger-cat's lips—but your excellent friend Tigellinus has a mind for once to try for himself.—You need not struggle, sweet one. I know very well that Acerronia is dying of love for me."

"Then come away into the thicket at any rate," she said submissively. "This then was the beginning and end of your discourse! And the story about Pallas. . . ."

"Was a mere excuse," whispered Tigellinus. "Come, and make no noise. One more kiss, my pretty pigeon—can anything be sweeter than such a dear little bill? That is right— how I thank you, bewitching darling! And now tell me that you will be mine—speak, enchanting little tiger-cat! May this brief happiness lead to more enduring joys? I love you passionately!"

"Yes," murmured Acerronia. "It shall lead to something more. . . ."

"You make me so happy!" said the Agrigentine.

He held her glowing face in both hands and bent over her again with seductive tenderness; but at that moment he felt the soundest box on the ear that ever made the most shameless gallant's cheek tingle. Acerronia was free and flying as nimbly as a weasel, back to the illuminated garden.

"The little vermin!" laughed Tigellinus. "So distinct a language of the fingers as this might have saved Lucretia from suicide. Quite shameful! I have not had the taste of such a slap on the chops since I left school. But never mind— she shall learn better! She has entirely bewitched me by this— and, if her kisses were only false ones their coloring was strangely like the real thing."

He hummed a Greek drinking-song, and slowly followed in the tracks of his singular companion.

Acerronia had gone at random to mix with a group of guest of whom Anicetus, the captain of the Misenum fleet, was the centre. The conversation had naturally turned on the race between the steed "Fulgur," belonging to Tigellinus, and the naval officer's fine thorough-bred. In her rage against Tigellinus Acerronia began: "Anicetus. . . .," and she would have gone on to say "I have made a solemn vow to the

94

gods if only they will decide the quarrel in favor of your splendid horse Flava. . . ." But the words died on her lips; she only uttered his name, and then, when Anicetus looked at her enquiringly, she could only gasp out: "Has the verdict been given yet?"

They all smiled, even Artemidorus, who stood aside with Milichus the slave, a humble listener. The vehement's girl's air and manner were too funny; they all understood at once that in the very act of speaking she had changed what she meant to say. The meanest slave in the City of the Seven Hills was acquainted with every detail of such a matter as the rivalry between the two horses, and a feverish interest in the decision was so widely spread that quick-witted Acerronia at once perceived how completely she had betrayed herself. Either she would be regarded as "far from Urbane"*—a favorite phrase with Tigellinus—or her blunder would be ascribed to some very compromising cause.

But no one, in fact, could suspect what had so scared her wits.

A strange, a mysterious expression had come over the face of Anicetus, which, added to her confusion, produced a feeling of alarm in Acerronia, usually so courageous. The naval commander was leaning against a statue of Pomona. As she pronounced his name, she fancied that she saw him with his eyes shut, like a corpse—water was streaming, green and gleaming, over his thick hair. His wide nose and half-open mouth looked rigid in a last gasp; and Pomona, standing majestically above, had the features of Agrippina.

Acerronia started back. In a moment the goblin illusion has vanished. Still the impression it had left on her mind was so deep that she went off quickly as possible to Epicharis, who was reputed to have great skill as a soothsayer.

"I see nothing alarming in it," said Epicharis with a smile. "You will take a sea-voyage in the course of the year, with your Mistress Agrippina, in which Anicetus will play the part

* Urbane from Urbs a town.

of Poseidon with his trident, will guide and protect you, and bring you happily to port. The waves may toss you perhaps— but, as you yourself saw, their fury was not able to overthrow Pomona the proud goddess—the empress-mother who refreshes us with all her benefits."

"Thank you," said Agrippina's maid of honor with a pretty gesture of her hand. "Still, I cannot shake off some remains of uneasiness. That dreadful Anicetus. . . ."

"He is a most intelligent man," Epicharis put in. "Who knows, Acerronia, how it all came about. Love is a strange visionary."

"Love?"

"Yes, to be sure. He loves you ardently, passionately. . . . It is the talk of every one at this moment— and now-a-days men are not wont to give their love unless they are tolerably sure of being loved in return."

"Now may all the gods of Latium defend me! I—me—No, it is incredible! Here am I, wedged in between two of the greatest rascals! On one hand, Tigellinus, on the other Anicetus; the first a quickly-consoled widower, the second a married man! The first as impudent as a beggar at the circus; the second artful, crafty,—with a nose as wide as an Ethiopian's! Is this your world of fashion—Rome, the incomparable?—I would sooner marry a soldier of the bodyguard—him, for example, who at this moment is carrying a bisellium to that odious Hasdra!. . . ."

"Really, that one?" said the Egyptian, smiling.

"Why not? He is at the utmost half as great a liar as an average Roman patrician, and not one thousandth part so insipid."

"Do you know him then?"

"As it happens I do. His name is Pharax, and he is in conspicuous favor with the empress."

"Octavia?"

"Nonsense!—When I speak of the empress I always mean Agrippina." A smile of subtle irony curled the noble Egyptian's lips.

Suddenly a loud flourish of horns was sounded, announcing the performance of a Sicilian dance.

"Let us find our places," she said.

Under the escort of the prime minister, who happened to be near them, they made their way to the oval, sand-strewn arena. The banquet in the cavaedium had not been a very long affair. The convivium or comissatio, as it is called, the drinking party, enlivened as usual by conversation, was to take place out here in a less ceremonious but all the more elegant style. At the foot of a famous plane-tree, a century and a half old, Flavius Scaevinus had erected a tribune for the imperial party, the front hung with purple Indian tissue, gold cords and tassels.

To the right and left of this magnificent dais, in imitation of the emperor's tribune in the circus, extended two large semicircles of cushioned seats for the rest of the spectators. On the opposite side, where the two rows almost met, towards the middle walk—light bronze seats with red leather cushions, S-shaped sofas and luxurious divans were placed for those restless spirits who preferred to wander among the spring-scents of the park, and to look on for only a few minutes at some especially interesting performance. In front of each seat, on an elegant monopodium with an ivory base, stood drinking-cups mounted in gold, fresh garlands, little baskets of cakes from Picentum and graceful grass mats with Ionian figs and almonds from Campania. Slaves in bright colors moved noiselessly about, filling the wine-cups and anticipating the wishes of each guest with obsequious haste.

A file of praetorians stood as a guard of honor on each side of the imperial tribune; among them Pharax, whose shrewd features were conspicuous among the commonplace faces of his comrades. The rest of the soldiers had modestly taken their places among the spectators, apparently without design, or remained indoors in the triclinium, where Milichus, the head slave of the house, served them with Nomentine wine.

Five or six minutes elapsed and then Chloris, the beautiful

cithara-player, came out of a tent near the back gate, and standing in the middle of the circle struck a full chord and began to play a Hellenic hymn. Still the company lent a careless ear; a very small number had taken their seats, but among those were the empress-mother and Octavia, as grave as ever. Even they seemed absent-minded. The young empress looked enquiringly at her husband, who was standing apart, leaning against a pine-tree and talking to Tigellinus without showing the smallest wish as yet to take the seat assigned to him between his mother and his wife.

It had struck Octavia, too, that during the last few days Nero had seemed more than ever dejected, nay positively melancholy, and tormented by conflicting thoughts. If he would but open his heart fully and candidly to her who loved him so well.—But he gave her not the smallest insight into his anxieties, and when, without any suspicion of what troubled him, she piously bid him turn to the gods, Caesar's brow was knit with increased pain and his lips curled with suppressed but bitter scorn, or even with hatred and vehement disgust.

Was he indeed the enemy of the gods? Or was it only that she was so unhappy as to rouse his personal aversion by her well-meant hints? Was it indeed she herself that weighed on him like lead, and hindered the young eagle in his flight to the utmost heights of happiness?

The tears started to her eyes. Wholly absorbed in her own evil fate, she failed to observe that Agrippina, as pale as death, was sitting with her head resting on her hand and silently muttering. Flavius' speech was fermenting in that ambitious soul, torturing it like a scorpion gone mad. But the deeply-aggrieved sovereign had already planned her revenge; the smile with which her nostrils quivered now and then already bore the character of an odious triumph.

At this moment Burrus came up to her, and her face cleared at once. She was a mistress of the arts of dissimulation; Burrus, captain of the praetorians, must not suspect what her thoughts had been.

"You were right," she said graciously. "This girl had

98

wonderful talent. I was quite absorbed in the flow of her tones.—There, the hymn is ended. . . .''

Chloris was rapturously applauded; she bowed gratefully but did not withdraw to the tent.

The seats now rapidly filled; only about forty persons remained, walking alone or in couples through the alleys, or sitting outside the festive amphitheatre in eager conversation. Among these, however, was Otho, holding his beautiful wife's hands, half in tenderness and half in pride, while he reproached her for her over-graciousness to a man of such ill-repute as Sophonius Tigellinus.

"You know that I trust you, though confidence is perhaps a folly, for a woman's heart is like a cloud before a south-east wind—it may go any way at any moment. And you, sweet Poppaea, have such a look, so soft, so distracting, that a man straightway loses his senses—and so I am fool enough to trust your immovable truth. . . .''

"And do you, my beloved Otho, think yourself a fool for that?'' said she roguishly. Such an irrisistible glance fell on him from her flashing eyes that he could hardly resist the impulse to snatch her in his arms.

"Ah, you beautiful, blooming rose,'' he murmured passionately, "are we not mad to spend this splendid evening here amid this throng of people instead of in the blissful silence of our home? Poppaea, I never look at your smiling lips, your slender figure, your snowy skin without thinking of Helen who raised a storm of passion wherever she appeared.''

"An ugly suggestion! Helen was a profligate creature.''

"You are right. It was a stupid mistake. I ought to have said you are as fair as Helen and as faithful as Penelope! But for that very reason, my dearest, avoid the very appearance of ill. I cannot bear to see a man of such a bad character as this Sicilian meet your eyes with such a familiar look. I know he is agreeable; he knows how to flatter while he makes a show of that respect which beguiles a woman's pride. All the more readily will people conclude that you are entangled with him.

Now, to please me, you will do as I ask you and avoid this seducer? You would do better to exercise your charms on Nero Caesar.''

"Do you think so?" asked Poppaea taken aback.

"In all earnest. Try to cheer him, make him take pleasure in trifles; oust the dreadful Seneca! That would indeed be an achievement.''

The young woman colored deeply but shook her head. Then she cast down her clear grey eyes.

"Poppaea will not force her way," she said lost in reverie. "If Caesar should condescend to find half as much pleasure in my society as in yours, why should I not value the distinction? But as it is—shall I flutter about him like a moth round a light? No, my dearest Otho, I am too proud for that, and—I do not care enough.''

"But you forget that I have always been one of his intimate friends, that I knew him as a boy. . . .''

"Hark!''

The silver strings of Chloris' cithara were again heard, and the full tones of her voice now rose in harmony with the instrument. Every sound was hushed. She sang exquisitely— this Greek in her saffron-colored drapery: the Rhodian nightingale, as she was called by the gilded youth of the vast metropolis. And how nobly she stood there, in her right hand the plectrum, in her left and nine-stringed instrument supported by a pale yellow ribbon, pale yellow roses in her beautiful, waving black hair: a figure from Homer's days.

In contrast with the ringing hymn she had just played, a melancholy lament now flowed from her lips, a yearning melody as of one mourning for the lost, whose tears have turned to song. It was strange how the beauty of the purely-pitched tones struck to the hearts of this assembly of whom the larger half were utterly depraved by the profligacy of the age; which, but now, had laughed so recklessly, toyed so stealthily, jested and feasted so arrogantly.

The rouged coquette, who had smiled assent to four lovers' vows that day, struggled hard to maintain her feigned indifference to the soft melting tones which sang of the loftiest and deepest emotions that stir the human heart.

The insolent, blasé youths who knew far more of damsels of light repute than of the members of their own family circles, who held aloof from courts of law but never missed the performance of a pantomime or the orgies of frail and fashionable hostesses, involuntarily assumed a less foppish air and ceased the bold whispers in which they had criticised the young Rhodian's charms.

The artist's triumph was complete. Never had she sung so splendidly, so feelingly, since she had been on Italian soil, and when at the end of the song, Artemidorus, by his master's orders, knelt at her feet and presented her with a coronet of gold, the enthusiasm of the audience could hardly find expression in clapping and shouts of applause.

"Sweetest Chloris," whispered Artemidorus, in a tone audible to none but the blushing girl, "take this—and tell me: which is dearer to you, this precious crown or my bursting heart?"

"Your heart—you know it!" murmured she. And as she took the gift, she pressed his hand; he was trembling with happiness.

"What infinite joy to be so loved!" he replied, as he rose with supple dignity. "In less than a year she will be mine. And so lately I thought I must die, away from her—away from her! Away from her—that was more horrible than death itself."

"That Artemidorus is a handsome fellow," whispered a senator's young wife to a companion of equal station. "What a pity that he is not free-born!"

"Why?"

"Well, the reason seems no mystery to me."

"Nonsense. For my part—if I could choose between him and the famous Sophonius Tigellinus, I should infinitely prefer Artemidorus."

"Do you think so?"

"Of course. That is—you understand what I mean? As a

husband, or even as a permanent—friend, I should prefer Tigellinus. But just as a chance whim...."

And both women laughed.

But Chloris, happy in the consciousness of her artistic triumph, and still happier in the certainty of being loved by Artemidorus whom she had so nearly lost, bowed thrice on all sides, greeted the empress-mother, who had applauded her with special warmth, in Greek with a heartfelt: "Zeus protect the Mother of the Empire!" and then vanished into the tent, making way for a stalwart pair of athletes who were to have a wrestling-match.

Before the thundering music which was to perform during the contest had struck up, Nero had turned away from Tigellinus, leaving him alone. The Greek girl's song had wrung the depths of his wounded soul. With a wave of his hand he dismissed two young men of his acquaintance who were about to follow him.

"Extraordinary!" said one to the other. "Even here, in this festally-decorated garden, he seems lost in thought. By Epona! It is high time to put a spoke in the wheels of that dismal Seneca.—Just twenty, and as wise and cold as Zeno. It is not to be endured! What metaphysical riddle is the dreamer puzzling over now that we, his most faithful friends, are a vexation to him?"

Yes, it was a metaphysical riddle indeed that was occupying Caesar—only a practical one and not theoretical— the metaphysical riddle of a true and heartfelt love, which could find no answer when Reason asked: "Why do you cling with every fibre of your being to one, scarcely seen and then for ever lost—while others no less fair, or even fairer, are blooming all round you like roses only waiting for the gardener? Why does your yearning claim none but the freed slave, while Octavia, whose noble profile is pronounced divine by every sculptor in Rome, is your life's partner?"

Even Chloris the Rhodian, whose voice had shaken his soul to its foundations, was, strictly speaking, more beautiful than Acte. And yet Caesar had no eye for her. The magic power of her art had only been the lever which had brought to light, with tenfold vividness, every detail of those painfully sweet memories.

Nero felt that he could not help it—that he must fly from the glitter and turmoil of the crowd; must lay the fierce tempest which had arisen in his heart this night with terrific force.

Every one would have seen it; they would have seen the tears which were now silently trickling down his cheeks,—and this must not be. He was Caesar: and he must show a firm front, not only to the Parthians and the Chatti, but also to his own inmost self in its ardent, distracting throes.

The wind whispered softly through the tree-tops; it sounded like a cradle song. The tossing waves must sleep which were raging in his bosom like the surges raised by a hurricane.

Come, sacred, peace-bestowing night! Cast thy shadowy mantle over thy favorite's woe! Grant him peace, even if joy may not be his!

CHAPTER IX.

BEFORE he perceived it Nero was wandering alone through the dusky wood. . . . The moon, in its first quarter, poured its dim silver light on the pebble-strewn path, for here the primeval trees opened out to form a wider way. Suddenly he started. Close behind the laurel hedge by which he was dreamily waking something moved; and as he stood still to listen there was a rustle of steps making a way through the underwood.

Nero was unarmed, and a monarch—even the best—has always secret foes who hate him from the bottom of their hearts, and hesitate at no means of attacking him. Nevertheless the imperial youth, strong in the consciousness of good-will to all, and even more perhaps in the sense of his manly growth and vigor, felt no sort of fear.

"Halt!" he cried in a low but threatening voice, and his right hand grasped the silver stylus of his writing-tablets. "Whoever you may be, come out on to the path; I command you!—I, Caesar!"

But the laurel bushes were still.

"Do you hear?" Nero said. "Do not disobey me. One single cry for aid, and the soldiers of the guard will hunt you down like a wild beast in a snare!"

"All-powerful Caesar," whispered a tremulous girl's

voice. "Do not be angry if I hesitated. . . ."

"Acte! You—you!" cried the young man in a tone of wild rapture—"You here? living—in the flesh?"

The slim figure crept cautiously forth from the thicket; in the next instant Caesar had clasped her in a passionate embrace. He kissed her quivering lips, as if in one moment of rapture to make amends for all the suffering of the past.

"Acte!" he repeated, "heaven-sent Acte! It is indeed you?"

His voice trembled with ecstasy, and yet with anxiety, as though he feared that this might be the fleeting trickery of a dream, to vanish in an instant. For some moments she suffered the vehement torrent of his caresses as in a silent and delicious trance. She had lost all power of resistance. But presently she blushingly turned away her face, though even yet she was not capable of freeing herself from his arms. Her head still rested against the shoulder of this one and only beloved of her heart, whose image she had carried in her soul with inextinguishable yearning, even as he had hers.

His lips rested on her sweet waving hair which shone in the moon-light like a fine tangle of silver and gold. He felt as though he had at last, after wandering in despair through a desert, found a blossom whose perfume was intoxication, but whose dew-filled cup had brought him healing.

Suddenly she started back.

"My lord, you are degrading yourself!" she murmured, almost beside herself. "Do you know what you have done? You, the monarch of the earth, have kissed one who was once a slave!"

"Yes, yes,—I have kissed Acte! I would fain proclaim it to the world from the capitol. I have been happy for the first time since I drew breath!"

"Happy!—is it true?" she asked, with sparkling eyes. "Oh, how glorious that sounds! But what matter—for even though you *were* happy, you were in disgrace and sin: In disgrace, because I am but a freedwoman and unworthy of you; in sin, because Claudius Nero has a noble, high-souled wife; whose heart will be broken if she learns that her faithless husband has so cruelly betrayed her."

"Octavia!" cried Nero, with indescribable bitterness. "She was not my choice; I was a foolish victim to the welfare of the state and the desires of my advisers. But listen: I swear to you that never, while I lived, would I have consented—not even if my imperial mother, Agrippina herself, had gone on her knees to me—if I had but known where I could find the only idol of my heart! . . . . Acte, how indefatigably I have sought you! How incessantly have my confidential servants searched all Rome to get some tidings of you! How often have I asked your friend Artemidorus about you.—All in vain! Tell me, where have you been? Why have you left the man who loved you to lose all hope, and sacrifice himself idiotically to a fate which is now immutable?"

"Caesar, I obeyed the voice of my conscience. I had hardly looked into your eyes when I felt that you had bereft me of sense and soul. But I knew, too, what folly it is in the humble flower of the field to gaze up at the sun floating unapproachable in the ether. I loved you—fearfully, beyond all utterance. . . ."

Again she hid her face on his shoulder. Then, drawing herself up with dignity, she went on:

"You know, my lord, that I am a Christian. You have heard from Nicodemus and from Seneca what our doctrines are, and the duties they enjoin. As a Christian, then, I was forced to fly from you, for we pray daily to the God whom the Saviour has revealed to us: 'Lead us not into temptation.' Nicodemus gave me a perilous part to play in the work of conversion which our Church had planned. The Brethren and Sisters, it is said, find me more lovable than any one else among them; my ways are engaging, my speech is eloquent. So I was chosen to appeal to unbelieving Caesar, and open a way in his heart for the balm of Faith, since he might perhaps keep it closed against the reproving counsel of men. But oh, my lord, I had from the first a feeling that this was the wrong course, and that Nicodemus, when he mingled the things of earth with those of Heaven, was acting in opposition to the spirit of the divine Redeemer. When, to crown all, I perceived what an overpowering charm you yourself possessed, one thought was ever present in my mind, as though spoken by a prophet: Fly, whether to life or to death.—That one blissful hour in the magician's tent was enough to make it clear to me that I should be lost—so I fled, far away from the city and the suburb, northwards to Falerii, where I found shelter and employment with some worthy husbandmen."

Nero looked pensively in her face, on which the moon was beaming.

"And how came you here?" he asked after a pause. Acte's eyes fell.

"My lord, you put me to shame; but this, too, I must confess. I have been in Rome these eight days. A lady of rank, who saw me by chance as she was travelling through the quiet country of Falerii, took a fancy to me—and I had been longing to get away from that monotonous existence, so I thankfully accepted the rich Sicilian's offers and became her companion and reader. I came with her to Rome, where she had various business to attend to. Early to-morrow we start for Capua by the Appian Way. . . ."

"But all this does not explain to me why I find you here, in this park?"

"So you not yet guess?" whispered Acte shyly.

"I heard from Artemidorous that you, my lord, were to be Flavius Scaevinus' guest to-day. Artemidorous let me in by the little gate leading into the grounds at the top of the hill. I have been hanging about for an hour or more, hiding or coming out, for I wanted to see the face of my sovereign lord once more, before going forth for ever into the cold and darkness."

"Then Artemidorous knew where you were?" said Caesar in surprise.

"Yes, my lord. He is an old friend of mine. His master, Flavius Scaevinus, has twice passed the hot season by the sea at Ostia, where Nicodemus, too, has a residence. I knew that

Artemidorous would be troubled by my sudden disappearance—more so than the others. So I wrote to tell him that all was well with me; and once, when he had some business to transact at Cures for his master, he made a round by Falerii and came to see me."

"And this is how he rewards me for having spared his life!" cried Nero furiously. "I have asked him again and again: Where is Acte?, and each time he had declared that he knew nothing, absolutely nothing."

"He had sworn not to tell of me—aye, and he knew my reasons."

"He is a villain! He was bound to tell the truth to Caesar, who had released him!—When I think of what I have lost through him and his lies I could throttle him with my own hands!"

The young monarch stood tall in his wrath. Storm-flashes seemed to play on his ruddy lips. All the torture of the past few weeks, the grief of his wrecked love, the aching misery of his lot in having to play the despot when he was in subjection to men and principles, and secretly to promote a creed which, as incarnate to him in the person of Nicodemus, he now almost loathed—all this raged and surged in his panting breast like the tumult of rebellion. What sort of a pious community was this which heaped burden after burden on his shoulders and, with contemptible trickery, chose such a creature as Acte to be the instrument of its base intrigues? He knew nothing of those obscure and humble Christians who gathered round their elders to be instructed in the word and life of the Crucified Jesus: how He had healed the blind and comforted the sorrowing; what He had said in the Sermon on the Mount, or as a youth among the scribes in the Temple.— Caesar was thinking only of the sly, hollow-eyed fanatics, who seemed to preach the doctrine that everything, however atrocious, was justified by the sublime end. So cruelly was his soul divided that he blamed with equal vehemence on the one hand Artemidorus for his brotherly devotion to the girl, and on the other Nicodemus for so recklessly imperilling her.

He pushed his fingers through his thick hair till the fading rose garland fell from his head into the dewy grass.

Suddenly he seized Acte's slim soft hand with tender passion.

"Let us forget all we have suffered!" he said with a deep-drawn breath. "You came here to see me once more; you love me to-day as you did then; and, by all that is sacred, Fate may do her worst with me, if I lose sight of you again after I have found you! Do you not perceive, Acte, that it is, as you would say, Providence itself—who has brought us together again at this moment of all others, just before the journey which you really thought possible—you sweet little simpleton? Let yourself be caught—for you are the only creature living who can give peace to my soul. Act, ever-beloved Acte, will you be mine, my own, body and soul? If you will, I swear to be true to you till death. I will live with you, and die with you. I will kneel by your side, and lift up my hands to your God. I will believe—so far as I can believe, that Christ died for the salvation of mankind. I will raise the symbol of that faith wherever Caesar's arm has power to overthrow the altars of Jupiter and the rabble of gods. The whole empire, shall follow me in obeying the Galilaean, and you, as the Caesar's chosen love, shall sit enthroned high above the unnumbered hosts of your people in such glory and splendor as no woman ever knew before you or ever shall after."

Acte sadly shook her head in the moonlight.

"No, my lord," she said tremulously. "Good never yet came out of evil. The Church of the most high God does not stand on a foundation of wrong-doing, but on the immovable faith of its members. It will conquer—and without me, even without the support of emperors—simply by the power of its truth!"

"Is this the language of love? Sweetest, heavenly Acte. . . ."

"Remember Octavia!"

"I do—and I feel no pang of conscience. Octavia cannot lose what she never possessed. My heart was yours long before I was cheated into this marriage by the craft of those about me, the authority of a mother for whom I had a childish reverence, ah! and the infinite desolation of my heart. Acte, if you leave me again it will be my death! If you bid me, adored one, I will this very day speak to Octavia and insist on a separation. . . .''

"Never!"

"You will not be mine in the face of the whole world? You dread the storm that would be raised if Caesar were to part from his imperial consort?—Well then; your will is my law. Let it be enough that, as Caesar, I fulfil the duties which bind me to the miserable routine of the palace, and shed the joy of your love on Nero—the man. Yes, you are right to set aside all the promises I made to the Christian, for I ought to have appealed only to the woman. I do not want to bribe my adorable Acte by the favors of an emperor, but to win her heart as a free gift, from her own beloved and loving hands!''

His voice shook with such overpowering passion that Acte trembled from head to foot.

At a few paces further, where the ancient plane-trees mingled their boughs to case a deep shade, there stood a bench covered with a rug of Tarentine wool.

Nero drew the scarcely-resisting girl with soft caresses to sit down by his side. A tide of bliss beyond words welled up in her long-desolate breast. Clinging to him closely, she shed softly-flowing tears of joy and exquisite rapture. Then she was silent.

When they presently rose to go they stood looking at each other for a minute without speaking. Acte pushed her tumbled hair off her brow, and fastened it with the pins and ribband which had fallen into disorder, looking into her lover's eyes with delicious confusion. There was no trace of repentance in her blushing face; nothing but unutterable love and devotion.

"Then you remain?" Nero whispered, once more clasping her fondly in his arms. "Yes? You promise? Acte, Acte, how am I to thank you for all this kindness and love. Farewell, my darling, my only real and sweetest bride!—I must hasten back to join the company again: I am afraid my absence will have been noticed already.—I see you still wear my ring. Show it to Tigellinus' door-keeper. You will be treated there like a princess, and have a room given you where you may sleep quietly in the consciousness of the infinite happiness we have before us. Artemidorus may go to inform your mistress that she must look elsewhere for a companion. Acte was born to a higher destiny than to the waiting-maid of an old lady from the provinces. Write what is needful here, on this wax tablet; I will see that the lad carries it to its destination very early to-morrow.—Where is your Sicilian staying?"

"At the house of her friend Epicharis, the Egyptian."

"The one who is here this evening?"

"The same. Artemidorus told me about it. Indeed, if we had not been starting so early to-morrow, my mistress, too, would have been among the guests."

"Then Epicharis may carry home your message to her at once," said Caesar.

Acte wrote.

"Now," whispered Nero as he slipped the tablets into his tunic, "go, my sweetest, dearest girl. How happy you have made me, happy beyond words! My heart overflows with joy—I could embrace all mankind. Go,—but take this burning kiss to tell you how wholly and completely my heart is yours." Once more he pressed his lips to hers. Then she went away towards the little park-gate, while Caesar, wrapping himself in his toga, hurried back to the festive scene whence the bewildering noise rose louder as he approached.

CHAPTER X.

As Claudius Nero reappeared on the scene a fight between gladiators, which had excited the heated spirits of the audience to the highest pitch, was drawing to a close. One of the combatants had fallen on his knees, bleeding from many wounds; his sword, broken short, lay in the sand a few paces away. The conqueror looked round enquiringly and then fixed his gaze on the tribune of the imperial party, to catch, from the lips of the empress-mother the verdict which would seal the fate, for life or death, of his disarmed antagonist.

Agrippina, although Acerronia was whispering hints in her ear, evaded the decision referred to her; for she was no more than a guest like the others. With calm dignity she waved her hand to the gladiator, indicating the rest of the company.

The profligate and enervated youths and heartless coquettes were anxious to taste the cup of this sanguinary performance to the dregs. On all sides they sat with eager eyes and thumbs turned down. This, being interpreted, meant "Spare Flavius Scaevinus the expense of a surgeon. Go on—Deal the death-blow!"

A moment's hesitancy: then the victor's blade plunged straight into the victim's breast. A dark stream of blood gushed up to heaven. . . .

Suddenly, in the midst of the echoing thunders of applause, Caesar appeared. He mounted the steps of the tribune with the august air of an Apollo, and took his seat between Agrippina and Octavia.

"You should have prevented this," he said, turning to his mother. "Or you, at any rate, noble Octavia, whom men call gentle. To be sure, as being every inch a Roman, even you are steeled against the horrors of death! I understand that, and I submit. But to-day—only to-day—I know not why—the feast has been so delightful, so harmonious.—You should have made an effort to prevent so happy a day being desecrated by a murder."

"A murder?" said Agrippina amazed.

"Yes, a murder," Caesar repeated, "for though it may be legalized, it is still a cowardly murder. Have you never heard Seneca's opinion of it? Flavius Scaevinus is merely doing his customary duty as a host, and not obeying his own feelings, though he seems to approve of the horrible taste of the day. In his heart he shares the views of my immortal teacher."

"Combats of gladiators are a tradition from our forefathers," said Octavia. "Cicero himself, though he was as good a philosopher as Seneca, looked upon them as the best school for manly courage. How should it ever have occurred to me to resist the will and the customs of the people of Rome?"

"So it seemed to me," said the empress-mother emphatically. Her mood was positively ferocious. Now that she heard Flavius Scaevinus openly praised as a pattern of ethical conduct, her wrath at his bold toast made her blood boil more hotly than ever.

"Mother," said Nero again, while two slaves carried away the dying Thracian, "tell me, what ails you? Were you displeased at what I said to Octavia?—But it is my most sacred conviction.—You look gloomy and vexed. And I am so content, so happy, bathed in such a tide of festal joy and young life that I could spurn death in my path!—Mother, I know that our host's speech wounded you. The point was fine, but it contained a subtle poison. . . . You see, Mother, a considerable number of the senators, and the greater portion of the Roman people desire that I alone should wield the sceptre; still, Nero knows full well to whom he owes the throne. You shall remain empress of the realm, if only you rule with perfect clemency and do not offend against the laws of the empire. You need only give way to me in trifles, only in sport, while in all grave matters you shall rule supreme. I am not ambitious; I will not suffer myself to be led astray by the admonitions of those who want to expel you."

But before Agrippina could answer, a loud cry for help rang out from the great avenue of pines, just behind the arena. Every one started from his seat, and rushed, the praetorians leading the way, into the wide walk where Flavius Scaevinus was discerned slowly tottering forward, leaning on the arm of the fair Poppaea Sabina.

"Murder, murder!" Poppaea was shouting in her deep-pitched tones. "What an age is this! A host is not safe in his own house!"

In a moment Nero was at the senator's side, and put his right arm round his body as though to protect him. He thus lightly touched Poppaea's arm, and, in spite of the excitement of the moment, she started at the contact. It seemed as though she wished to make Caesar feel how strongly he influenced her.

"Tell me what happened," said Nero anxiously. "But first—how are you feeling?"

"For this once affairs seem to have turned out tolerably well," said Flavius jestingly. "I was walking here with Otho's wife, and neglecting my duties as host while I listened to her delightful conversation, when suddenly I heard a rustle in the shrubs. I thought it was a night-bird; but before I had time to consider the matter I felt a blow here, on my shoulder. 'Oho!' cried I, and turned round. But there was no one to be seen; I only felt the warm blood trickling down my back."

"Praetorians, surround the park and the house," cried

Agrippina. "The wall is high, every entrance is closed. The wretch shall not escape with a whole skin!"

"Bring torches!" shouted Tigellinus, while Nero and Poppaea helped Flavius, who was covered with blood, to reach his sleeping-room.

"Lost pains!" said the wounded man, with a meaning glance at Agrippina. "These assassins are wily, wonderfully wily; and they are lucky, too, in that our vengeance always seeks them in the wrong direction."

When they had reached the cubiculum Nero turned to Artemidorus, who stood there in great alarm.

"Help me," he said, "to lift your master on to his bed."

"Sovereign Caesar," said the freedman, "here are plenty of people, and the physician among them—Scaevinus would never forgive me if I allowed. . . ."

"Silence," Scaevinus put in roughly. "Do as Nero our emperor bids you. He is the ruler; to him alone do you owe obedience, even if he commanded you to . . . . to lay hands on his own mother."

Claudius and Poppaea exchanged a glance of amazement, which, on her part, at once became a languishing gaze of admiration. Then Caesar, with hardly any apparent effort, raised the body of his robust friend, while Artemidorus lifted his knees, and so shared with the sovereign of the world the labor of a sick-nurse, laying the patient on his brazen couch. As he drew back Nero perceived that his snow-white toga was soaked through and through with blood. A strange feeling came over him. Blood on the day which had brought his beloved Acte back to his arms!—this boded evil. But he refused to give way to the feeling.

"Folly!" he said to himself. "Nero can no more believe in the old wives' tales of the soothsayers than in the love adventures of Jupiter. I myself will be Jupiter with my enchanting Acte by my side, and will leave the dominion of the earth to the blinded creatures who find the joys of this brief life in the struggle for supremacy."

Flavius Scaevinus' wound did not seem to be dangerous.

The dagger, which had been thrust in mad haste, had gone too far to the left. It was skilfully bandaged by Polyhymnius, and he prepared a kind of lemonade of ice-cold water and syrup for the exhausted man which evidently revived him.

Flavius was then able to thank Caesar again, with expressions of deep feeling. "That is the truly royal nature," he added, thoughtfully, "which is always ready to exert itself when there is misfortune to be alleviated, wrong to be punished, or a noble deed to be rewarded. Nero, who helps his friends like a brother, may count on us in the hour of greatest peril."

Then he turned to Poppaea: "Give me your hand, most lovable of Roman women. Were I but twenty years younger, I might envy your fortunate Otho. You are as lovely as the divine Aphrodite, and as gentle as Eos. Promise me that you will come to see me to-morrow. I must hear the end of the delightful story you were telling me."

"If a servant might be permitted to express himself freely," the physician interposed, "and to take proper care of his master, I would venture to suggest that the divine Caesar and noble Poppaea should at once withdraw. The fever, which must presently set in, might otherwise rage alarmingly."

"You speak wisely," replied Caesar. "Come, Poppaea. Your devoted Otho will be nearly dead of jealousy by this time."

"Leave him alone, my Lord," said Poppaea mischievously. "Jealousy is the oil which feeds the flame of love!— Besides," she added in a low tone, "Jealousy of Flavius Scaevinus!—You over-estimate his talents."

She gave him a bewitching look as they walked on, through the large central hall, into the garden once more.

Here prevailed the wildest excitement. Caesar's body-guard was dispersed in knots of three and four, throughout the grounds as far as the outer ring fence, searching the endless avenues and thick undergrowth. A torch-bearer was with each party. The boldest of the senators and knights, arming themselves with swords provided by Milichus, the chief slave of the household, joined them so far as their condition permitted. But most of them, and particularly the younger ones, had applied themselves so vigorously to their host's wine that they tumbled about like votaries of Dionysus. These indefatigable drinkers, after a few fruitless efforts, sank back on the cushioned seats. Even Tigellinus, hardened as he was by practice, could only get himself fairly in motion with the greatest difficulty. Those of the women and young girls who had not fallen asleep on the couches, had taken refuge in the cavaedium. Only Agrippina and Octavia, who looked very grave, remained sitting proudly erect in their places, under the bright and equable light of the unflickering candelabra, as majestic and calm as statutes.

Nero had drawn his sword. He himself was bent on avenging the cowardly crime which some spiteful and cunning foe had committed against Flavius Scaevinus. Poppaea Sabina, snatching a torch out of its brazen stand, hurried after him; for Otho, her jealous husband, was nowhere to be seen—or his wife knew how to avoid him.

Poppaea, throwing a light on the tangle of brushwood, suddenly started and stopped. Close to the path, in the little ditch which carried off the water to the valley below, she caught sight of a glittering dagger. She picked it up without a word, and Nero, in his haste, had not seen her stoop.

The blue-gleaming blade had three edges; the traces of blood upon it were not many, but fresh enough to leave no doubts as to the importance of this unexpected find.

Nero was now rushing on far ahead, and Poppaea took advantage of the propitious moment to wipe the poniard on the dewy grass, and then carefully hide it under her girdle.

She understood everything now. She had happened, by a singular accident, to observe this weapon in the empress' room quite lately; it was an inconspicuous stiletto, not likely to betray its imperial owner.

The incident had been simple enough, and yet it had come about like the ingeniously-constructed plot of a tragic poet.

118

Poppaea could see it all: the luxurious sleeping-room, and Agrippina, who had been ailing. Poppaea had brought a garland of flowers as a "greeting to the illustrious sufferer"—in point of fact to ingratiate herself with an eye to Nero, and Agrippina had been unusually gracious; the yellow roses had won her heart for the moment. She desired that Poppaea should be admitted, and thanked her in person. There was no one else in the room but Acerronia—the red-haired tiger cat.

Suddenly Agrippina sank fainting. The perfume of the roses had perhaps too strongly affected her overwrought nerves. Acerronia carefully held her up, rubbed her brow and cheeks, and cried out to Poppaea, who was much alarmed: "The essence, I entreat you, the essence; in the closet to the right, behind the ebony cabinet.—A little phial with the words "Never too much."

Poppaea searched. In her agitation she could not immediately find the ivory button that opened the closet; she felt and pressed, till one of the silver panels of the wainscot suddenly sprang out.

The array of crystal bottles, well-known in Rome as containing the poisons mixed by Locusta, sufficiently betrayed the fact that she had seen what she was never intended to see. Here, too, lay ten or a dozen daggers with "three sharp angles" and copper handles.—She saw it all at a glance and but for a moment; but her memory was good. She noiselessly closed the silver panel again and found the handle of the closet, seized the little phial, and hastened with it to Acerronia.

No one had noticed anything. And now no one should know how strangely important the discovery she had then made had become.

Agrippina must not guess that Poppaea Sabina carried about her person the proof that the empress-mother had instigated the murderous assault on Flavius Scaevinus, or that one word from her would unmask the criminal to her unsuspicious and confiding son. Thus the young beauty

119

would remain mistress of the situation. For the present, complete silence!—but, when circumstances might require it, then, by Jupiter, Nero should acknowledge how exactly this stiletto matched the others which lay with Locusta's phials.

All this passed through her mind like a lightning-flash. She ran on, full of triumphant satisfaction.

She soon overtook Caesar still hunting indefatigably.

"Here come the foremost of them back again," she said with a sigh. "Their search would seem to have been as vain as ours."

"Nothing, dear Caesar, nothing at all," Tigellinus stuttered from afar. "And the tribunes of the praetorians, whom I crossed in the track, have not found the slightest trace. By Hercules! They have thrust their lances through every laurel and myrtle bush; any rascal hiding there must have been spitted to a certainty."

"Then the criminal must have climed over the wall," said Caesar.

"It is hardly possible, unless he had a ladder; but then we must have come upon marks made by the ladder in the soft ground, even if the mean villain had pulled it up after him. Besides, there are praetorians outside, and the men of the city-watch who were attracted by the noise."

"Very well; then the murderer is among us."

Tigellinus shrugged his shoulders.

"Which of all this company could be such a vile coward and ruffianly scoundrel? Besides: who could be the enemy of our worthy Scaevinus? He is universally beloved, a pleasant genial boon companion. His slaves, too, are devoted to him. Perhaps Artemidorus. . . ."

"Artemidorus was in the house when we heard the cry for help."

"Well, well. But he ran away from him, a few months since."

"That was from fear, not from hatred."

"But who could it be then?" said the Agrigentine, tottering a little. "You cannot believe that any passionate adorer of Poppaea bore malice against a man of sixty because they took a walk in the park together?''

"At present I believe nothing," said Caesar. "But you will allow that the dagger cannot have flown by itself, like Melinno's pigeon. I shall therefore simply do my duty in the matter. Find Burrus; desire him to collect his praetorians. The town cohort may keep watch outside in case the assassin should have taken refuge in the top of some thick tree. As matters now stand, I can trust no one. Every one, from the senators to the meanest slave, must be searched. Men shall know that in Nero's realm such foul play meets with immediate retribution."

Five minutes later the roll of drums was heard. The guards came trooping in from all sides, and in a very short time all the guests, too, had assembled.

"Come and sit on the dais with us," said Caesar to Poppaea Sabina. "You, as the companion of Flavius Scaevinus at the moment of the shameful attack, may represent, as it were, the public conscience. Your distress and beauty may rouse some remorse and shame in the guilty, and so facilitate discovery. Besides you, Poppaea, who were with him are the only person altogether above suspicion—you and we, the imperial family."

As Poppaea took her stand on Caesar's left hand, Agrippina eyed her with a singular expression, which the audacious dame met with calm civility. Of what use would it be now to provoke Agrippina? No, no. Poppaea was too cunning to be precipitate with her far-reaching schemes.

"Who can the imperial criminal have bribed so promptly?" said Poppaea to herself. "Burrus is said to be in favor— but I do not think him capable of it: it shows too base a nature! Perhaps Ubius the centurion, who is getting promotion so fast.—But why should I trouble my head about it? Since I know the fountain-head of the villainy, I know enough."

In her heart she could not help laughing to think how quickly and easily—thanks to Agrippina's fainting fit—she had seen through the game, and so gained an advantage which, in all probability, would sooner or later be valuable to her. But, in spite of her triumphant glow, she controlled herself and so maintained due dignity when Nero, his eyes flaming with indignation, addressed the assembled guests:

"A crime has been committed—a crime unequalled for baseness! Help me to unmask the criminal. Let none who are conscious of innocence think it unnecessary to prove it; for not a soul shall quit this spot till he has made it clear where he has been all the evening, and that he neither has any concealed weapon, nor any stain of the blood so foully shed. You, gallant praetorians, the upholders of the Empire and of law, you, above all, must make it your business to discover the wretch. Imagine the intolerable disgrace if he should be found in your ranks! Away with him! Away from the noble troop of chosen warriors! He is unworthy to meet his death at the hands even of the executioner."

A murmur of approval rose from the crowd.

"Then begin with me," said the empress-mother, holding out her arms as if to deliver herself over to a dishonoring doom. As she did so the point of silver nail, sticking up through the hanging over the balustrade, tore her hand. The blood dropped on the armor of Ubius, the centurion standing at her right hand, and, as she started back with a little cry of pain, on her own white dress.

"Mother!" exclaimed Caesar in horror, "what are you doing? Blood again, on this day which began so gloriously and promised to end so serenely?"

"This blood is a trivial accident, my son; still, the will of the Immortals is often revealed to us by accidents. They perhaps desire to warn you, your favorite, that you are insulting the guests of Flavius Scaevinus by holding a criminal enquiry here; as if this scene of festivity, and a senator's park, were the crowded basilica where practised lawyers vie with each other in splitting hairs!"

Nero clasped his forehead in bewilderment. Was he still the boy of ten or twelve, whom his mother would punish when he came home with a torn tunic, pulling his hair in the rough and ready Oscan fashion? He was on the point of replying—with perfect moderation but very decisively—that the safety of his citizens was of more importance in his eyes than any regard for social properties. Burrus, however, was beforehand.

"Potent Agrippina," he said firmly, "my duty requires me to proceed at once to obey Caesar's orders. If the ladies are offended by it, I cannot help it: Caesar's mother will be ready to acknowledge that, as an old, if ill-bred, soldier, I am doing my duty."

Agrippina shrugged her shoulders. If the general of the praetorians took Caesar's part, what could she do? But she secretly promised herself that she would forthwith bind the bear with chains of roses, and in such a way as that she could for the future suppress such unexpected outbreaks of his sense of duty.

Burrus now called by name eight of his men on whose fidelity he could implicitly rely, and ordered them to search first their comrades, and then all the men in the company who could not prove where they had been during the commission of the crime; finally every slave in the place. The ladies, young and old, who might not be able to exculpate themselves at once were to retire to the atrium under the escort of a few praetorians.

None of the ladies rose. The whole business was over sooner than could have been expected. Every one had at least two or three witnesses who could assert on oath that he or she had been far from the scene of the murder. No one had any kind of dagger, and the shape of the wound left no doubt that it had been inflicted by a stiletto. The upshot of the enquiry was in every respect nul.

"I said so," cried Agrippina. "We must beg your forgiveness, noble guests of Flavius, if our beloved son's very creditable zeal for justice has carried him rather too far."

Nero said nothing. His soul was full of other thoughts. He rose in silence and contrived to give Artemidorus Acte's letter to the Sicilian lady, without being observed.

The imperial train returned to the Palatium in the same order as when it had come to the senator's house. Metella, wife of the unlucky Scaevinus, accompanied her illustrious guests to the vestibule.

"I hope he will soon recover," Agrippina murmured, kindly kissing the lady's brow.

"I hope so, too," cried Nero, pressing Metella's hand three times to his lips.

"And may the monster who has thus troubled your peace be discovered, in spite of the cunning he has shown," said Octavia, as she affectionately embraced the weeping wife. "Be comforted, dear Metella. Polyhyminius is an excellent physician, and the wound is slight."

Then they set out.

Neither Nero nor Octavia spoke a word. Not a sound was to be heard but the even step of the bearers, the torch-carriers, and the soldiers of the escort.

Nero's eye was fixed on a sun of glory, which he had seen that evening for a moment only, but which would rise to-morrow to shine on his whole, happy life. Octavia, without knowing anything of this, had, on the contrary, a gloomy feeling that it would never be day again.

Her husband's calm and contented silence was strangely eloquent. His eye was beaming, his lips wore a smile like that of a child dreaming on the eve of its birthday of the doll that has been promised it. It was evident that one thing alone could have put him into such a happy frame of mind and shed this youthful radiance over his face: the Rose of Babylon, which so many seek in vain—happiness. Poor Octavia! She felt with deep and heart-rending pain that she had no share in this feeling; that the Rose of Babylon in *his* hands, meant for her perpetual anguish, self-sacrifice, and misery.

"To thy protection I commend my life and being, All-merciful Jupiter!" she murmured inaudibly. She wrung her hands and sighed as though her heart would break, but as noiselessly as the young Spartan who let the fox he had taken gnaw at his vitals.

Claudius Nero, who was smiling so blissfully at the star-lighted April night, should never know how infinitely wretched she was.

CHAPTER XI.

Six weeks had elapsed.

In the verdurous xystus of one of the most delightful villas outside the arch of Drusus, Acte was sitting on a marble seat covered with rugs, and watching the shadow on a sundial with expectant longing. Suppertime was past. Nero was supping this evening with Anicetus, the commander of the fleet. He was a guest therefore, and not the host, as in the Palatium; so he could come away when he pleased. He would feel that he must hurry to her as soon as possible, for he loved her more than the splendor of his throne, or the finest discourses of his learned prime-minister.

The young sovereign was ready enough now to yield to the influence of all the magnates of the capitol. He allowed his mother and Octavia to interfere in matters which, even in Agrippina's opinion, were the special prerogative of the emperor. Flavius Scaevinus' toast seemed to have left no mark whatever.

Nero assented to everything that Seneca—not unfrequently prompted by Tigellinus—submitted to him. By their combined advice he doubled the pay of the praetorian guard for the month of December in which hie birthday fell; and, strangely enough, in all the fourteen regions of the capital, it was currently reported that this politically significant step had been hatched in the brain of the Sicilian. Caesar was always present when court ceremonial or the business of the state required it. But he did all this in the manner of a man who performs his daily task with cheerful resignation, but looks for happiness only in his hours of freedom.

In fact the thought of Acte filled his brain from early dawn till evening fell. The whole world was to him but a setting for that one precious image which he kept as a secret treasure, a few hundred paces away from the turmoil of the Appian Way.

No one knew of this as yet, excepting Tigellinus to whom he had confessed everything in an effervescence of rapture. He felt as if he must suffocate under the excess of happiness, and Tigellinus, who had always been his friend, had sworn solemnly, by the manes of his mother, not to betray him by a word.

Acte sat with her little feet crossed, in their red-ribboned sandals, waiting for her idol. He might cross the threshold at any moment. This retired spot, with the marble seat among the rose-bushes, was his favorite nook, and she was accustomed to await him here. The shadow on the sun-dial moved swiftly onward. Acte, confident in the certainty that he would come, sat musing on her lot, and thought herself enviable above all mortals. The six weeks just past were as one long balmy dream. She had shaken off everything that would link the present to the past. Now and then indeed she thought of the miserable days of separation, but her heart only beat with higher rapture.

Nor did her conscience give her a moment's pang. She knew, indeed, that, as a believing Nazarene, she was living in sin, in loving a man who was another woman's husband, not only according to the law of Christ, but by that of his own heathen gods. She knew it; but—she did not feel it. At any rate, not when she thought of him whom she worshipped beyond all earthly limitations. One look of his heart-enthralling eyes was enough to send the last remnant of self-accusation to the four winds.

And had she not done all in her power to avoid Caesar? Had she not fully intended to fly to Sicily, where not a gleam of his radiant divinity could ever have reached her? She had only wished to bid farwell to that enchanting and beautiful face which to her was a foretaste of highest heaven; and it was mere chance, or the finger of destiny, which had bound him forever to her existence, in the very hour of parting.— Yes, for ever! Such love as theirs could have no end; death alone could tear asunder what no other power on earth could divide.

Besides: had she really robbed his cold-hearted wife of him? Had not his whole being belonged to her from the first—to *her,* though born a slave? Had Octavia ever understood him half as well as she?

Particularly during these last weeks—a fortnight perhaps. It was about so long since an increasing asperity had been evident in the demeanor of the young empress; her manner to her husband had become almost hostile. Under the pretext of sleeplessness and constant headache she had entirely withdrawn from the emperor's apartments. Yes, that pale-faced, heartless Octavia might share the throne of Claudius Nero, and the external honors of majesty; she always appeared by her husband's side when formality and custom required her presence; beyond that she could call no part of him hers—none.

Acte could not know what Octavia had suffered. If she could have divined it, she would have hesitated to call the young empress heartless and cold.

Just thirteen days since, Tigellinus had requested a private audience of Octavia. He made a pretence of important state affairs to beg her to dismiss Rabonia and the two slaves in attendance, and then, with courtly deference, he began:

"Madam, I feel that it is my duty to lay at your feet a terrible communication, which unfortunately lacks nothing of completeness but the name of the guilty accomplice, which I have sworn by a sacred oath not to divulge."

"What can it be?" said Octavia.

"A commonplace thing enough, and yet a sorrow for the Empress of Rome—a misfortune which it is impossible to speak of."

"You seem much agitated. Have I done you any wrong?"

"A wrong, Madam, which strikes to the very bottom of my soul—the wrong which many do me who do not know the real, true, honest Tigellinus, but only the social mask which bears the name. Swear to me, Madam, that you will keep the secret—swear that. . . ."

"I swear."

"Then you must know that your lord and husband loves another woman, a young, lovely, and enchanting creature—but not worthy to plait your beautiful fair hair. His warmer feelings are lost to you for ever; she has bewitched him as Circe bewitched the companions of the long-suffering Odysseus.—You totter? You are faint?—Take courage and trust me. Here is a heart which will gladly face death for the adored and ever-beloved Octavia."

She had sunk, half stunned, into his arms. Intoxicated by her grace and sweetness, he pressed her passionately to his heart.

She thrust him away.

"Wretch!" she said, and her lips quivered. "If he were six hundred times worse and more faithless than you say—at least I will be true to him till my last breath!—What insolence is this? Only your blood could wash out the stain of your touch!—but I do not want blood. Jupiter in his sovereign justice will punish you duly."

"Madam. . . ." Tigellinus gasped out.

"Leave me!"

"And there can be no hope for me? Not even if I were to prove that Nero is false to you with barefaced publicity?"

"If you do not go quickly I will call for help," said Octavia, drawing herself up with all the dignity of youthful majesty. "Have the women who have dwelt within these walls been so vile that such a one as you should dare. . . ."

"I go, Octavia," hissed Tigellinus, as pale as death. "I

go—till we meet again!"

Acte knew nothing of this overwhelming incident. To her Octavia was only a poor creature whom God had never intended to understand and satisfy Caesar's heart. And that she, a base-born girl, could so amply do this, she regarded as an unmerited grace from Heaven. She felt dizzy as she contemplated her own measureless bliss; tears started to her eyes.

"God of mercy!" she murmured. "Forgive me for being so happy! or, if indeed Thou canst not pardon, let me pay for every day of rapture here by a hundred years of pain in the next world—of torture—so that at last, at last I may be united to him once more. I will never weary of whispering in his ear that Thou didst come down from Heaven in the person of a servant among men to redeem us from the burden of our sins! I will save his soul—alas! out of selfishness; for what would Heaven and all its glory be to me without the only one I love—more than anything in the wide and infinite universe."

A sunny smile lighted up her face. She felt as though the Christ-God had heard her; her heart was full of such sacred emotion, such divine peace. She started up. In the peristyle she heard Phaon's step—Phaon, the faithful slave, to whom Claudius Nero had entrusted the stewardship of the little villa. She knew what this meant. Phaon, watching from the roof of the upper room, had spied the well-known litter whose silken curtains hid the Apollo-like form of the young emperor. The four Lusitanian bearers were dressed in inconspicuous grey tunics and were perfectly silent; no one paid any heed when this litter came through the ostium into the half-roofed court-yard.

Acte went forward through the peristyle as far as the corridor. Here she waited with a beating heart while her lover, in a flowered tunic and carrying his white toga over his arm, got out of the litter, and made his way to the delightful room where a five-branched candelabrum by this time threw its softened light over the pannelled walls and magnificent furniture.

The hot blood rose to her cheeks. It was delicious to sit out there, under the evergreen oaks, among the rose-hedges by the fountain, hand clasped in hand as they talked, repeating for the thousandth time how madly they loved—beyond all telling. But here, in this quiet room, where whispered love sounded so mysterious, so subdued, here heart and soul were more irresistibly intoxicated; nor was there any fear that the eye of any prying maid should dare to intrude on the sanctity of their happiness.

The heavy door closed upon them. The lamp, hanging from a crimson cord, shed a clear calm light like the pale disk of the full moon. On a table of polished citrus-wood, in front of the window screened with flowers, stood a silver-mounted jar of Greek wine, two goblets, with snakes for stems, and two opalescent murrhine drinking cups. By the rose-hued cushioned couch, close to the divan, was another monopodium with fragrant fruits and a shallow saucer of crisp lemoncakes.

Nero seated himself on the corner of the couch, threw a strong arm round his lovely companion, and pressed her to his heart.

"At last, at last, I have you once more," he said tenderly, and he kissed her blushing face, her white shoulders and her beautiful hair which fell in waves over her neck. She clung to him fondly, stroking his hair and throwing her arms in eager gladness round his neck.

This was the charm which so bewitched him in Acte, this girlish shyness, and virginal confession, blended with the fervent strength of boundless love.

Then he asked the ever-recurring question with pressing fervency: "Do you love me? Have you thought of me very often?"

"Incessantly, every instant," whispered Acte. "But you, out in the grand world, where handsome women and beautiful girls are as plentiful as flowers, where homage surrounds you at every step, and admiration casts a

132

thousands snares in your way. . . .?"

"My divine Acte, you over-rate these things.—I tell you truly if the beauty of all the women from Tanais to the furthest ocean were concentrated in one enchanting creature, I would scorn her and cry to divine Aphrodite: 'All your masterpieces are mere bungling compared with Acte—the fair-haired treasure whose large eyes look so deeply into mine, and smile up at me as much as to say: Here, Caesar, is your home.' "

"Yes, that is what my face would say to you! I love you from the bottom of my heart—noblest, dearest of men! I am yours, now and for ever, even if I were to perish eternally. Crush me, Nero, crush me. It would be a happy death!" How lovely she looked amid her blushes as the ardor of a guileless heart seemed to bear her soul aloft on wings.

She closed her eyes as though the supernatural radiance of her imperial lover dazzled her. Her eyelashes quivered and glistened with moisture. She breathed more heavily till presently she was asleep, a living image of happiness and infinite contentment.

Nero took up the wine-jar and filled one of the snake-footed drinking-cups. He stood, holding up the fragrant Cyprian in his right hand and gazing at the sweet, sleeping girl, who, as she lay with her arm gracefully bent over her head, reminded him of the beautiful statue of Ariadne in his room at the palace. He watched the beautiful flushed face, the lips half parted as if to bestow a kiss, revealing the dazzling teeth, and a breath came over him of that poetical inspiration which had so often been strongest under the strangest circumstances that his enemies had inpugned what was a genuinely artistic impulse as an actor's artifice. He raised the wine-cup to his lips, half emptied it, and then, murmuring to himself, he wrote the following lines on his tablets:

"Yea, by Zeus the Immortal, thou art the true Ariadne!
Wrung by consuming torment, wearily threading the endless

Mazes of knowledge, my spirit found no hope of issue,
Goal, nor clue to all its unendurable travel.—
Thee and thy beauty I pledge, drinking this gift from
Bacchus!
Trust me, I never, like Theseus faithless, can leave thee and
live,—
Woe to thee, hapless Fool, blinded by hideous delusion,
Woe! That thou could'st madly abandon thy self-given
treasure.
Darkly the halls of thy gloomy dwelling-place lower around
thee,
Ruthless to him who could scorn Love and its peaceful
delights.''

The rhythmical and well-balanced strophe, which was not
amiss for an impromptu, filled the heart of the young
sovereign with a sort of transcendental rapture. He sat down
again on the edge of the couch, and looked meditatively at
the pretty enigma which lay smiling before him in the sweet
figure he could never sufficiently admire. Her abundant
golden hair, which alone would have sufficed to shed the
light of poetry on a world wrapped in gloom, her rounded
arm, her throat as white as the blossom-snows of April—by
all the gods, it was like a heavenly dream! He held his breath
in a sort of sacred ecstasy, not to wake her—the picture was
so ineffably lovely.

And how she loved him! How wholly she was devoted to
him; her touching self-abandonment had no equal in all his
empire!

Suddenly he felt sad. Was it not a pity that he should be
forced to hide this jewel as if his love for Acte, which was the
joy of his life, were a sin? What though there was a conscience in man's breast, which approved what was good and
condemned what was evil: Well,—his conscience had never
felt clearer than at this moment; the supreme divinity could
wish for nothing more perfect or righteous than this deep and
heartfelt affection. He tried to conjure up the image of

134

Octavia, and so put it to the test whether any voice in his soul could still make itself heard on behalf of his unhappy wife. But all was silence.

Acte was his dream and his life, and since he loved her he acknowledged but one duty: to be happy in her, and to make her happy.

He once more sat for a while lost in thought. How lovely she was—like a hardly-opened spring-rose! How young!—But alas, only the gods of the Greek mythology could have perpetual youth! This sweet child, so like a blossom, breathing, as it were, the very ether of Olympus, could not, with all her charms, resist the gnawing tooth of Time. Those blooming cheeks must gradually fade, the whole enchanting form wither and shrivel—and at the end of the hideous course of decay stood a pale and hollow-eyed spectre—Death.

"Woe is me, Death!" Nero murmured. "Then I will taste of life with the greater avidity so long as it shines upon me!—Acte, enviable creature! You believe that death is but a passage to a better life, that the corruption of the body is like the change of a caterpillar which is presently to flutter a brilliant butterfly in undying glory. Ah, if I could but believe it too! Nicodemus your former master has often tried to prove to me what alas, alas, does not admit of proof: the hope of eternal joy in the ambrosial halls of a world beyond the grave. When I met him with doubts he would raise one finger like a Sibyl, and say in prophetic tones: 'My Lord, you must have faith!' He cannot see that there is no sense in it. It is as though he were to say to a sick man: You must have health!—He disgusted me with his want of logic!—Acte might say the same thing and rejoice my heart, for in her I should not feel the contradiction of ideas, only the depth of her belief.—To die—to die.—To go away for ever with all that one has ever felt, or thought, or dreamed, or loved!—It is strange how the idea possesses me.—I used to understand what Seneca meant when he proved to me that to perish and lose oneself was no evil. Since I have had Acte I could wish to live for ever; yes, for ever, for her sake."

He bent over the sleeping girl and kissed her wildly. She opened her eyes, held out her hands with a blissful smile, and clasped him fondly. Then she, too, drank some of the wine he offered her—drank as if she were dying of thirst—and repaid her lover with a kiss, bid him sit down by her side and, leaning on her elbow, gazed into his face.

"Acte," said he, stroking her golden hair, "my star, my jewel, are you happy?"

"Infinitely happy."

"Have you a wish that you keep from me?"

"No."

"Ah! You are blushing. Tell me the truth."

"Well I was thinking that it would be very delightful if I might go with you sometimes—to the Field of Mars for instance. Do you remember that hour we spent in the magician's tent? But it is out of the question. . . ."

Nero rested his handsome young head on his hand.

"Out of the question?" he said, and he stroked her soft chin. "And who, sweet Acte, is to forbid it?"

"Your mother, Octavia, the Senate—how can I tell?"

"I will prove to you how much you are mistaken. I am master: the Praetorium and the worthy commonfolk will obey me.—To-morrow,—to-morrow I cannot; I dine with Thrasea Paetus. But the day after I will find some pretext. At four after noon I will take you out in the grand avenues of the Campus Martius."

"Oh, how delightful!" and she clapped her hands. She had in fact been sometimes very lonely in the seclusion of her country home, though Phaon, her head slave, had been instructing her diligently in history and natural science, and with excellent success.

"Now I see that you will dare something for my sake," she cried, enchanted. "But I will take no unfair advantage of your goodness. Discretion is the mother of wisdom, they say. So far as in me lies none of the odious gaping idlers that crowd the street shall recognize me. I will wear a veil. . . ."

"Do as you please. But now, we have time only for a

quarter of an hour more of our sweet, world-forgetting chatter. The hours when I may be happy are always as swift as an eight-winged Hermes!''

"Ah! Nero! My King . . . . my God."

"Acte—my Acte!''

CHAPTER XII.

Two days after this, Caesar again, and in the best possible humor, made his way to the villa where Acte waited and longed for him. The sun was still high, but a delicious breeze had been blowing since early in the day from over the Tyrrhenian sea; it breathed soft refreshment through the tall cypresses, and wafted the perfume of the damask roses, like a wanton child, into every nook of the garden. A handsome litter, with eight Lusitanian bearers in violet livery, and slave attendants in splendid dress, was a gift from Caesar to his beloved Acte. This he told her when they were both seated in it, and the violet-colored curtains were so closely drawn that no one could look in without considerable trouble and difficulty.

She thanked him with a kiss, but yet in such a way as to make him feel that the magnificent present was as nothing in her eyes compared with the happiness of sitting by his side and being sure of his love. Suddenly she clung blushing to his side and stroking his cheek murmured softly:

"It is just as if we were married—truly married in the eyes of God and His law. Ah! Nero, that would be heavenly indeed.—I, in public, at your side, in the heart of Rome! It makes me giddy only to think of it.—Let me open the curtain just a finger-breadth. My veil is thick enough; no one can know me."

"Just as you like," said Caesar. "I listen to your voice as to the voice of Fate."

"We can see so much better—this splendid Rome and the magnificent palaces, and the citizens in their white togas.—There, almost in front of us, is the Aventine with the temple of Diana; and out there, to the left, the long ridge of Janiculus. How beautiful the blue-black shadows are against the light!—Tell me, shall we cross the Forum? I want to see your imperial residence, and try to persuade myself that I have a right to cross the threshold of the Palatium."

"And so you have, Acte. . . ."

She put her hand on his lips.

"Do not speak," she said caressingly. "It is enough that I should have expelled poor Octavia from her place in your heart. Enough, and more than enough! But I would die sooner than give it up. . . . No. The Palatium is the home of the guiltless, and rather than pursue her into her own sanctuary, I would die the most horrible death at her feet."

"Do not talk so madly! Suppose that she herself thought of deserting the sanctuary, and without a regret? That she should fly, and leave me standing alone in the midst of all this splendor?"

"But she will not.—Now we are turning a corner; this is the Via Sacra—there, guarded by the Temple of the Dioscuri, is the venerable Palace of the Caesars, towering to the sky. My own beloved Nero's palace. . . ." But she suddenly drew back. "How annoying!" she exclaimed.

"What is the matter?" asked Caesar.

"It was Pallas, the empress-mother's favorite. He passed quite close to the litter; and he recognized me."

"But you are as thickly-veiled as an Egyptian oracle."

"Not quite—and Pallas has sharp eyes. I told you. . . ."

"Yes, you told me that he had dared to lift his eyes to the divine Acte. He must indeed be unhappy; I pity him from the bottom of my heart."

"But he recognized me, and I am afraid. . . ."

"Of what, my timid fawn?"

"That he will try to do us an injury. . . ."

"Am I not Caesar?"

"No doubt. But just because you are Caesar you have foes enough already, so it seems unnecessary to raise up enemies in your private life, and particularly so sinister a foe as this ominous-looking Pallas."

"You over-rate him. Besides, even if he recognized you, could he know at once who was with you? Depend upon it when he asserted that I was in love with a freedwoman of Nicodemus' it was no more than a passing guess. He will look elsewhere for a rival; and Claudius Nero will find means to hinder his hurting so much as a hair of your golden locks."

"You are right," murmured Act. "Courage and Trust: let that be our motto!—Merciful Heaven, how beautiful that is: the whole Campus Martius is one flower-strewn garden. And the plane-trees—the evergreen oaks—the blaze of flowers between the grass-plots! And then the box-shrubbery with the trees all cut into shapes!"

"Do you see the huge C. N. C. in front of the marble pillars of the portico?"

"They stand for Claudius Nero Caesar!" cried Acte in delight. "All the beauty and splendor of the world seem created only to do you homage, my own dear love!"

"And yet, amid all this splendor you are the only pearl that really gives me joy."

She looked up in his face.

"Is that quite true?" she said saucily.

"As true as that the May sun is shining overhead and perennial spring in our hearts. Acte, words cannot tell how utterly I am a different man since you have loved me! I understand nature now and myself; the eternal yearning which goes on throughout the universe is no longer a puzzle to me. And I firmly believe that the yearning, the craving, the will to be happy is the only genuine core of our life. To live is to love, to love is to demand.—And do not the Nazarenes

141

teach this, though they postpone the demand till beyond death, and hope for an eternal will, an eternal life?''

Acte, thrilled with unspeakable gladness, leaned her head with its ribband-bound curls against his shoulder.

''There is the Egyptian's tent,'' said Nero in an altered voice. ''When I think of the way in which that cunning Nicodemus dealt with your happiness! Shameful! His justice and wisdom had only left out of his calculations the fact that a maiden's pure heart is not a piece of goods to be bargained away, but a treasure which she alone can bestow of her own free will. . . .''

''Nay; not of her own free will, but because love lays an inevitable yoke upon her. Oh, I loved you madly. If you had but taken me by the hand, I should have followed you blindfold to the end of the world!''

''Yes, I lost an opportunity,'' Nero muttered sadly. Then, rousing himself, he went on: ''For shame foolish youth! You have everything you care for and you are singing elegies and dirges! Let us be gay, Acte. Let us enjoy the present lavishly and to the utmost. Melancholy thoughts are foolish indeed when love meets love. There is the tent to be sure, but I can laugh at the sight. Am I not a thousand times happier than I was last autumn? Do I not know now what I then could not even guess: that you love me.''

''I like you best in this mood!—How bright and sunny it all is here among the avenues of trees! And my love resplendent on all sides—in marble, in bronze, in silver, in gold—and everywhere the same glorious and adorable hero. You have the most bewitching mouth I have ever beheld. Lips that seem created for kisses, song, and eloquence. My head will be turned with elation and pride. To the uttermost ends of the inhabited earth your name is heard, your heavenly and beautiful name. . . . 'Nero,'—The Lusitanian murmurs 'Nero,' and reverently bends the knee before your image. 'Nero,' is repeated in Asia and Africa; 'Nero,' in Gallia and to the furthest limits of Germania. . . .''

''Where they certainly do *not* bend the knee before the

image of Caesar.''

"No? and why not?''

"Because they are a free people and lend no adherents to the Roman eagles.''

"But you showed me from our upper chamber, a noble chief of the Chatti in Roman armor.''

"That was Giso, the son of Lollarius. Giso serves with us in order to learn the Roman language and the science of warfare, in order to make use of his experience in his native land.''

"And you allow it?''

"Why not? If I were to forbid it, would it not look as though the Roman Empire were afraid of the German tribes on the frontier?''

"You are right. I had not thought of that.''

"Besides, that brave young chieftain has honorably repaid us for what we have done for him; in the East, against the revolted Parthians, and further north, against two Sarmatian tribes who showed no respect for the Roman authorities.''

"Ah!'' sighed the girl. "How happy should I be if I could but share all these cares with you.''

"Do you not see that I myself have ceased to take them seriously? You and the beauty of Nature, the ever youthful mother, who betrays an ineffectual attempt to vie with you in loveliness—that is my world: my present and my future!— Look how the light has suddenly flashed out from the pediment of the temple of Minerva. The sun is sinking to the west, and it is as though the Goddess of Wisdom were signifying her approval of me by the brightness of her night-scaring lamp.''

"Aye, the Present and the Future! We will drink to them this evening in Cyprian wine as long and as deeply as you please.—But tell me, who is that magnificent woman in a litter with a slender Oriental at her side—that light red litter with bearers in yellowish brown?—She is handsome, but there is something in the fire of her eyes that frightens me.''

"Did you never hear of Poppaea Sabina, the wife of

Otho—my childhood's playmate. . . ."

"Yes, yes.—But look how she gazes at you! She must have recognized you from afar. What rage in her proud face!"

"What are you doing?"

"Holding the curtains closed till we have passed her."

"To make her observe us more particularly?"

"To prevent her casting an evil eye upon you.—Tell me, Nero, do you often come into contact with her?"

"Very seldom. Besides, I am as surely protected against the evil eye as though I wore an amulet round my neck."

"We Nazarenes do not believe in the magical power of such charms. But if you would cut off a lock of my hair and always wear it about you—that, I should think, must bring you good luck."

"I will steal that lock this very day. It will preserve me when all around me falls in ruins."

"Tell me, who was the black-haired girl by Poppaea's side. She, too, had a look in her eyes.—The pair were a match, I think."

"Do you think so? It was Hasdra, Poppaea Sabina's companion—They say she is over head and ears in love with Pharax. . . ."

"Pharax?"

"The newly-made centurion of the body-guard."

"That man? But no; he was till lately only a soldier in the city-cohort."

"Yes, the very same; he was one of those in charge of Artemidorus that day.—Those who enjoy the favor of Agrippina make rapid progress on the way to dignity. . . ."

"Well, I wish Hasdra joy of Pharax, and Pharax of Hasdra. Do you know, Nero, I should like to see everyone happy and glad to their heart's content. Ah! if I were ruler of the world there should be no more grief and no more sorrow; nothing but bright joy, ambrosial rejoicing. . . ."

"Then stay the hand of Death when he mows down the blooming child, snatching it from its mother, or the noble son from his father. Then exterminate mad hopes, and

144

sickness, and age eating into our bones. . . . !"

These were the last serious words they spoke—How richly leafy were the boughs which the elms, the pines and the maples extended over the deliciously shaded road! At each turn taken by their bearers, enchanting vistas opened before them, either to the five peaks of Soracte, to the heights of Albanum or the long and picturesquely dented ridge of the Sabine hills. The tower of Maecenas stood out proudly against the blue distance, and around them, as far as the eye could reach, were flowers without end, luxuriant spring-verdure—a world made for dreamy delight.

But before the sun had touched the summit of Janiculum the happy couple were at home again, in the villa outside the arch of Drusus.

That evening Nero supped with Acte. She was beside herself with delight on so joyful an occasion. Her cook had provided a dainty meal; with her own hand she poured out the finest wines for the man she loved—noble Campanian, made in the year when Claudius had ascended the throne; then a vintage of the time of Augustus; and finally, to crown the merry feast, Falernian named after the last consul but two of the Republic.

"What a happy day!" said Acte joyfully. "All hail to the present and the future! This is just as we planned it in the litter!"

He emptied the goblet to the bottom and set it down noisily among the dishes of fruit.

"Come!" he said with a sigh, and pressed a burning kiss on her cheek.

They went into the adjoining room—they felt as though they had but just left it. The five-branched lamp was alight; only milk as cool as snow was standing on the table instead of wine. She threw her arms round his neck; then everything seemed the same as it had been yesterday. Suddenly there was a knock at the door—a low, modest knock; but decided, too, as given by some one who felt he had a right to be there.

Caesar started up in anger.

"What is the meaning of that?" he said quivering with rage.

"I have no idea. None of the maids would dare—Phaon perhaps. . . . ?"

"Phaon," replied Nero, "knows that I have strictly forbidden. . . ."

"Then something extraordinary must have happened to induce him to disobey. . . ."

"Shall I open the door to him?"

"Only go to the door—ask. . . ."

She had turned pale at the sudden and ominous sound which had fallen on the silence of this peaceful solitude like the blare of a war-trumpet.

"My heart is beating so!" she said tremulously.

"You dear little simpleton," he said, tenderly stroking her long hair. "What are you afraid of? What on earth can come to harm you while you are as good and sweet as you have always been, and while Caesar protects you with his arm?"

He calmly went to the door, thrust back the bolt, and asked through a chink: "Is that you, Phaon?"

"Yes, my lord," was whispered back. "Pardon me for neglecting your commands in the hurry of excitement. But it was indeed a singular accident."

"Wait a moment." Then turning to Acte he went on: "It is Phaon. May he come in?"

She had thrown a creamy white palla over her shoulders.

"Certainly, so far as I am concerned," she replied, half curious, though she still felt the shock of the alarm in every limb. The slave came in and bowed respectfully.

"Speak on," said Claudius Nero.

"The story is shorter to tell than the fable of the dying lion. As I was standing just now in the vestibule, and looking out at the rosy evening sky, thinking of nothing, or of very little up came a stranger—some Pacuvius or Lucillus—with the hood of his paenula pulled half over his face, and asked me as roughly and uncivilly as a street porter whether Acte, the freedwoman of Nicodemus, lived here."

146

"And what answer did you give him?"

"I told him shortly and plainly that he was an insolent lout."

"Well, Phaon, it must be admitted you dispense with all circumlocution as bluntly as a propraetor. But the lout himself—how did he swallow such a hard morsel?"

"He rushed at me with some violence, seized me by my clothes, took a few blows of my fist and then bellowed out furiously: 'Do you mean to pretend offence, you rascal? I am here in the name of a high authority which can crush you utterly."—'Another word and I will see you five or six fathoms deep in the earth!' cried I, for I was angry. So then he saw that I was not a man to submit to being bullied, and he was rather more polite. After a little discussion he handed me a wax tabled with two seals: 'The business is most pressing,' her said solemnly. 'The life and happiness of Caesar himself may perhaps depend on its prompt delivery, so fly—and step out like a hero!"—Pardon me—so then I hurried here in spite of your commands, for I thought that perhaps there really was need of haste and that Fate required it."

Phaon retired.

Caesar took up a silver fruit-knife and divided the silken string which held the tablets closed. Then he read as follows, in a low satirical tone:

"Acte, formerly a slave, but enfranchised, to her own ruin, by Lucius Nicodemus, Knight of Rome, is hereby required immediately to break off her connection with the exalted sovereign of the Empire, to restore the divine Caesar without delay to his illustrious wife, who bewails him in despair.

"I swear by Jupiter that Octavia herself knows nothing of this proceeding! On the contrary, it is from a sense of justice—or rather the prudence of true patriotism, which leads me to treat on terms of business with the seductive traitress.

"If the said freedwoman, Acte, will express her readiness to quit her house and the vicinity of Rome within three days, never to return, the adherents of the young empress will exercise leniency towards the said freedwoman, and neither trouble her any further nor report her to the Aediles for condign punishment; on the contrary, on the day of her departure a sum of money shall be paid over to her, sufficient to secure her a comfortable income for the remainder of her days. If Acte should refuse, the most terrible consequences will be relentlessly visited upon her.

"He who sends you these tablets has both the will and the power to execute his threats.

"Acte is required to announce her decision finally this very day: at the beginning of the second watch she is to go up to the roof, and call out in a distinct tone: 'Yes, I will go,' as the messenger who conveys these tablets shall pass the house followed by a torchbearer. His mark of identity is a flame-colored scarf over his *paenula,* and he will say in a loud voice: 'She repents!' "

As Nero ended, Acte sank stricken on to a bronze stool. Scalding tears fell from her half-closed eyes. Nero laid the tablets on the table, quietly but with some internal trepidation. Then, turning to Acte, he said:

"My darling! . . . . But I know the handwriting, carefully as it is disguised."

The sobbing girl looked up eagerly and Nero wiped the tears from her cheeks with the corner of her dress.

"It is my mother's hand, the Empress Agrippina's," he said gravely. "She has guided the stylus with the utmost caution, and here and there traced a character intended to mislead me. But I should know it, even if she wrote with her left hand. Look at her A, and this S, almost like a Greek S.— Besides, who else in Rome would be so bold as to address such an outrage to Caesar's bride."

Acte sighed.

"Certainly I have more cause to fear your mother than your wife!"

"Octavia is serious and deliberate," replied Nero "Her love has long been dying of a decline. So far you are right.

Sooner than Octavia I should suspect certain State officials—disaffected senators and knights. There are many persons who detest Agrippina's overweening arrogance and who might possibly write such a threatening letter as this with a view to exciting our suspicions of her. There are senators' wives, too, who may have remarked with displeasure that ever since our happy meeting at the house of Scaevinus I have avoided all festivities.—But all these possibilities are mere fancy; I am sure of the fact: I recognize the empress-mother's despotic tone in numerous phrases; she who never expresses a wish but she sees it instantly fulfilled."

"What a grievous blow!" moaned the girl.

"Grievous! Why? Who is sovereign and ruler of Rome—I or Agrippina?"

"But she is your mother."

"You mean to say I am her slave because I have hitherto submitted to her practical co-operation in affairs of State? But you are mistaken, Acte! What I have permitted until now I permitted only because it suited my ends. I am not an Asaitic monarch whose chief pleasure is to make his unlimited power felt to the remotest limits of his kingdom. I have no enthusiastic love of the ceremonial machinery of official life, the petty litigation of the citizen classes, or the trumpery ambitions of the military. Whatever I have done of this kind has been done out of mere duty. Between Seneca on one side, and Lucius Nicodemus on the other, I have gone on along the beaten path; but the more I have been relieved by others of the wearisome burden, the better have I been pleased. I am a man, Acte, devoted to all that is noble and beautiful, an artist, a poet. Ah! and above all a tender and passionate lover, to whom one hour in your arms is dearer than a hundred victories over the Parthians. Since I could call you mine I have left care to others. Agrippina and Seneca wield the sceptre, hardly have I kept up communications with Burrus and my zealous adherent Tigellinus, who now and then reminds the bodyguard of my existence at the cost of a handsome largesse. But now—now

149

when they want to rob me of the one thing I have kept to myself—now they shall learn that it is my favor which has lent them importance; that I am the lord over all, and that I will defend my happiness to the last drop of my blood!"

"You will bring yourself to ruin!" said Acte piteously. "Do not row against the tide; do not be so mad as to struggle against such overwhelming odds! Nero, my beloved, you deceive yourself. Believe me, you cannot in a moment recover your grasp of the reins you have so nearly relinquished, and before you can seize them over Acte will be lying crushed and maimed under the horses' hoofs!"

He snatched her to him in a frenzy with his left arm round her waist he lifted up his right hand and swore a mighty oath that he would shelter and protect her to his last dying breath. Acte clung round his neck and kissed him, happy once more, sweetly, coaxingly, with her own delicious childlike mixture of girlish simplicity and fervid womanhood.

"Nero, what am I to do then?" she murmured tenderly. "You have only to speak. I will obey you blindly, even if I knew it would be my death!"

"You are to stay quietly where you are," said Nero with a smile and a kiss. "Our faithful Phaon must put double bolts to the ostium and posticum.* I will send a dozen of my servants to guard you. If the stranger should be insolent or violent when you refuse to answer, just desire him to be off; and if he does not then withdraw without delay, order his capture.—One more kiss, Acte. What a delightful spring fragrance is shed by your hair! Narcissus and rose!—Now, be of good courage, my adored love, my precious sweetheart!"

"Farewell," murmured Acte. "All joys attend you!"

"I will take possession of these tablets," said Nero with a business-like air. "This very evening I will speak to Agrippina. She will not deny that it is her doing. And at any rate the Palatium shall know how Nero will take it if any mortal hand is raised against Acte!"

*Front and back sales.

He threw his toga over his shoulders, and with a last look of infinite tenderness at Acte, left the room.

"Quickly, men!" he cried to his muscular Lusitanians, who were resting on the marble floor between the slender Corinthian columns. They sprang to their feet in all haste and put the bearing-straps over their shoulders.

Nero settled himself on the cushions; Phaon stood by the litter and the head slave of the atrium with a few slave women pressed forward officiously.

Caesar flung a handful of gold pieces among them, nodded farewell in the customary fashion of Roman magnates, and then said decidedly: "To the Palatium."

CHAPTER XIII.

THE four Lusitanians had lighted their horn lanterns in the ostium; a few slaves followed with tall slender torches.

The endless length of the Via Appia which they reached in about a hundred paces, lay silent in the enchanted twilight. White, fleecy clouds, silvered at the edge by the moonlight, floated in the vault of heaven. On both sides of the road the tombs stood up in front of the country villas—gloomy warnings of the transitoriness of all that is fair, of the claims of pleasure, the indefeasible claims of passion. Far away, beyond the Tiber rose the hill Janiculus, standing forth, proud and defiant in its sublime solitude, above the weird pathos of the dim moonlighted scene; like a lonely wreck in a petrified sea which gleamed on all sides as Caesar made his nocturnal journey.

On the right, as they turned into the Via Sacra, they found the guard which Caesar had commanded should be placed there at the beginning of the first watch. The praetorians silently followed the litter.

Ten minutes later the imperial train was standing in front of the torch-lighted vestibule of the palace.

Seneca, who had been expecting his lord that evening for an important discussion, hurried out to meet him. Nero impatiently waved him aside.

"All grave talk must wait till to-morrow. I must attend now to some more frivolous private affairs.—Where is Octavia—and the empress-mother?"

Seneca wrapped his toga round him with dignity.

"Caesar's wife," he said stiffly and ceremoniously, "is, I presume, in the oecus with the empress-mother. Does Caesar desire to speak with the two illustrious ladies?—It is already late, and I fear that Agrippina is much fatigued. It was only at the request of Octavia, who seems unusually excited this evening, that she remained up a few hours later than she is wont."

"Most reverend Master," murmured Nero deeply annoyed, "be so good as to impress on your memory the fact that there can never be anything extraordinary in Caesar's keeping any one waiting. It has happened two or three times before, and it will often happen again, without my choosing to listen to covert reproaches, even from you whom I esteem so highly. By Hercules! I am amazed to find what I have come to. May Claudius Nero allow himself no greater freedom than the son of some upstart whose money is his only title to a place in the Senate?"

This vehement retort was spoken in Greek, out of respect to the venerable philosopher and prime minister.

"My Lord—Caesar. . . ." stammered Seneca also in Greek, "you will pardon me. . . ."

"Have done with words, my worthy friend. If you desire my gratitude, arrange for my immediate admission; I wish to speak with both the ladies and, in fact, with both at once. So Octavia may perhaps condescend not, at any rate, to vanish through a side door, as has of late been her habit, as soon as her husband comes into the house."

Seneca bowed and made his way at once through the dimly-lighted atrium, his left hand wrapped in the folds of his toga, while his right still clenched the book-rolls.

"I shall expect you presently in my study," said Caesar to Seneca, as the old man returned from his errand, quite furious at the part given him to play. "I am in great agitation, my dear Master, very great agitation. Pardon me if I addressed you more abruptly than my reverence for your laurel-crowned brows demands. Do you know what has happened?"

Seneca shrugged his shoulders.

"I can guess," he said, "but I assure you that *I* have had no hand in the matter. I know that it is folly to argue with passion, but it may be suggested that it should show some consideration. That you should remain away so long on your bethrothal-day, of all days, is, in my opinion, overstepping those limits which even Caesar should respect."

"Our bethrothal-day!" cried Nero in a tone of genuine amazement. "I did not know it—nor did she say a word of the matter. Not that I care!—Well, I will presently submit to be lectured—we meet again!" and with these words he went out into the ladies' spacious sitting-room.

Octavia was seated in her silver arm-chair as pale as a waxen image. Her eyes were riveted on the mosaic flowers of the paved floor. Even when Nero paused in enquiry in the middle of the room she did not look up.

Agrippina, on the other hand, rose with truly imperial dignity from the deep pillows of an ottoman on which she had been reclining, and went forward to meet her son. She was on the point of addressing him in the categorical tone she was wont to adopt, when Nero, with an ominous glance, held out the open tablets, and said in a low voice:

"Empress Agrippina, answer Caesar. What is the meaning of this extraordinary missive?"

Agrippina involuntarily shrank back a step or two as she saw her son drawn up to his full height, his youthful face pale and dignified, and full of such grave and splendid manliness.

"Mother," he went on, "do you deny having written it?—I see that Octavia, too, knows of the matter; otherwise she would greet me instead of sitting rooted to the ground like a recalcitrant Daphne. So I need not hesitate to discuss it in her presence.—Again I ask you: who wrote these lines on the wax

I hold?"

"I did," replied Agrippina, calmly folding her arms.

"Then allow me to point out to you that you have assumed a tone which I am neither accustomed nor disposed to hear."

"Are they any concern of yours then?" said his mother ironically. "How could I guess that these tablets would fall into Caesar's hands?"

"Of course you could not. But I thank Fate that I was on the spot at the right moment. The poor child would have allowed herself to be brow-beaten. I would have you to know, Mother, that your secret messenger will never hear the words you so eagerly hope for: 'I will go.'—I, Caesar, have given orders that if the fellow should prove insolent he shall be shown the way back in a manner which the law allows to every Roman citizen—nay to every stranger. . . ."

"You dared?"

"I dared, Mother. And to make an end of the matter once for all I speak to you, too, Octavia! For a long time you have been my wife only in name. How then can it wound you if I devote to a fair and charming creature that which the proud Octavia disdains:—the fervor of a heart thirsting for love? Every mark of the respect I owe to the empress I do not fail to pay you. My intimates are discretion itself. I visit the quiet house where I dare be happy—without any pomp or display, unspeakably happy—while here I meet only rigid formality, cold indifference, comfortless vacancy. I do not reproach you, admirable Octavia. You are as heaven made you. But I now implore you, let me, too, be such as nature made me! Let me love, while you can only think of doing your duty and serving your gods."

"Unhappy man!" exclaimed the empress-mother, while Octavia turned away without even moving an eye-lash: "Is this my reward for all I have done for you and your future prospects?"

She seized him by the right wrist and dragged him away with the fury of a maenad to the furthest corner of the room.

156

"And do you think," she went on in a whisper, for she wished to spare her fellow-conspirator Octavia, "do you think it was for my pleasure that I married Octavia's father? Claudius was a scarecrow, do you hear, a perfect scarecrow; a poring student full of literary absurdities, a dolt who sat inventing new letters of the alphabet while his wife made him the laughing-stock for the whole world. I married that man after Messalina's death; I became empress,—my heart was full of loathing; one thought alone upheld me: my son would one day rule the Empire. . . ."

"Mother!"

"Silence! It is the truth. . . .! And then—what did I do? Year after year I dinned it into Claudius' ears that he must cut off Britannicus from the succession, and I never rested till the stiff-necked emperor gave way, and passing over his own son, proclaimed you, his step-son, as his successor!"

"But, mother, I beg of you—why all this long tale now?"

". . . . On one condition; that you should marry his daughter Octavia. We struck the bargain,—for never was a daughter so little like her parents. Her beauty at most she may inherit from the wretched Messalina. In all else—by Jupiter! there is not a woman in Rome to compare with your Octavia in virtue, high-mindedness and purity of life; and her father's imbecility has left no trace in her. After Claudius' death, if the bond had seemed to you quite unendurable you could have broken off the betrothal. But now Octavia is your wife. She loves you; she is descended from one of the noblest patrician families;—and the long and short of the matter is that you disgrace yourself when you so grossly insult her for the sake of a miserable, hypocritical hussy!"

"Your language is gross!" cried Nero, wrenching himself free. "You may thank the gods that you are the mother of the man whose sweetheart you abuse in such unmeasured terms."

"I have a right to abuse her! Or are you free to disculpate yourself?

"Yes, mother; in two words: I cannot live without Acte."

"Then you are a fool and a villain! I say again: have you forgotten everything—my sacrifices and efforts, my incessant anxiety. . . .?"

"I have long known that the zeal with which you have striven for the mastery is for your own sake chiefly. To be Caesar's mother, to govern in his name, to keep him in leading-strings like an incapable infant—that was the dream that flattered your hopes."

"Who says so?" she cried furiously.

"Men who are incapable of falsehood. I myself can detect the effects of that dream.—Nevertheless, you are my mother, and for that reason I have submitted in all things, often against my better judgment. I have repressed every innocent impulse towards independence the moment I perceived that it would cause you pain. But now Agrippina's domineering interferes in a matter in which Nero alone is master, in which no reproaches can check him and no respect restrain him."

"You speak like a madman."

"It may seem so, but I know what I mean. I mean, once for all, to break the bonds you have flung round my neck! Even the unhappy Octavia suffers under the terrific despotism of your iron will. Your despotism brought about our marriage, but it cannot compel us to feel any love for each other, nor even to affect it. . . ."

"Boy, what are you saying?."

"You must make your choice, mother. Either swear to me by Jupiter, the avenger of perjury, that you will leave my darling treasure—the freed slave, as you call her—in peace henceforth, or else this day is the last of your arbitrary interference in the concerns of State. I will no longer suffer you to hold council with Seneca as to the fate of the Rhine-provinces, or with Burrus over what takes place in the barracks of the praetorian guard. If you defy me, I have men at my call whose vote in the senate, or whose good sword in the highway, is on my side."

"Folly!" said Agrippina, with a forced smile of composure. But she had turned pale to her son's unwonted tone, and needed all her self-control not to betray how deeply she was moved.

"Once more I say: make your choice," said Nero firmly.

Agrippina had recovered herself quickly; she went close to him, stroked his tingling cheeks with a soothing hand, and said with the gently-reproachful glance of a grieved parent:

"How you excite yourself, and talk really perfect nonsense. What would Nero be without a mother who has raised him to his supremacy? Just consider: Burrus and his praetorians are blindly devoted to me. . . ."

"What?" cried Nero.

"Absolutely and blindly," she repeated positively.

Nero shrugged his shoulders. "How little you know the Roman people and the soldiers of the guard! So long as Nero seemed to be your docile son—well and good! All Rome knew how I clung to you, so that obeying me was obeying *you*. But if a breach were to divide us—which Fate forsend—do you hear me Empress Agrippina?—The men would remember then to whom they had sworn fidelity. Was it to you or to me?"

"Do not let us quarrel," said Octavia, speaking for the first time. "I am waiting here, not for threats or fine phrases; simply for a plain and decisive answer. Have you no feeling of the horrible disgrace you are bringing on us? Nero—Caesar—Octavia's husband, intriguing with a low-born wench. . . ."

"I can tell you one thing," said Caesar in bitter scorn. "This low-born wench knows one thing, at any rate, of which many a lady of senatorial rank is ignorant: how to love, and to make those she loves happy. . . ."

Octavia could listen no longer. She rose and left the room, going to her bed-chamber where she broke down completely, quite worn out with the indescribable agitations of the past week.

"It is well that she has left us," Agrippina began once more. "What I have to say to you is, in fact, hardly to be uttered in her presence."

"You excite my curiosity."

"I will be frank with you and go straight to the point. You must know, my son, that I regard your infidelity as less disgraceful than your amazing blundering in your manner of behaving here. Possibly we were mistaken in our anticipations of our gentle Octavia's character; possibly you two could never have pitched your lives in the same key, even with the utmost effort.—And for all I care, you are free to seek indemnity for the mistake you then made. Only do not transform a passing fancy into a public bond. You will admit that it was shameful to show yourself on the Campus Martius with this. . . . Acte."

"Mother!" cried Nero furiously.

"Hear me out! I will go further still: Had you fallen in love with Septimia or any lady of high rank I would overlook it. After all, Caesar is Caesar, and thousands of other men who have not the prerogative of sovereignty, do the same thing. But that you should perform this vulgar idyll with Nicodemus' freed slave, sing tender songs to her, crouch at her feet, and make yourself the object of unbounded ridicule to every man of taste—that is indeed unworthy of you. Aye, by Jupiter, and even more unworthy of me!"

"Mother, if you could but see her, if you could note the pure and lofty soul that beams through her eyes, if you could hear her speak—so wisely, so sensibly. . . ."

"It is maddening!" interrupted his mother. "I tell you once more, if she is ever so enchanting you have behaved like an idiotic schoolboy! A bewitching blossom! Well then, gather it, as any wayfarer plucks a wild rose. Then it would be regarded as mere pastime, a caprice like the whims of Jupiter who sometimes descended from Olympus to win a mortal. But before one can turn round you have established her in a regular home, given her slaves as if she were accustomed to order a household, and think and do nothing but what happens to please her; you shower fresh roses and violets on her every day; in short, behave like some fanatical priest of Isis worshiping the statue of his omnipotent divinity.

So no doubt, a conceited doll, is very well pleased to find herself so suddenly on a tide of wealth and splendor. . . ."

"Stop!" Nero broke in. "At least cast no suspicion on the disinterestedness of her love. She would gladly have accepted shelter in the humblest hut of the slaves' quarters, but I forced all this upon her because I am of opinion that nothing in the world is too good for her; and moreover, because the woman whom Caesar adores ought to be lodged like an empress. . . ."

It was partly rebelliousness and partly boastful defiance that prompted his speech; for, in fact, Acte's villa, though charmingly pretty, was by no means opulent—at most an artistically arranged residence.

"Whom Caesar adores!" echoed Agrippina bitterly.

"His chosen bride, if that suits you better. I regard her in that light, though the unhappy state of affairs does not allow of my raising her to the rank of my wife."

"Boy, are you out of your mind?"

"Not to my knowledge. But I swear to you that if I were not fettered, so to speak, to Octavia by the most solemn form of which has come down to us from our forefathers, this divine Acte should be my empress consort, in spite of all the nobility of imperial Rome!" Agrippina laughed—a despairing laugh. Crossing her arms with convulsive energy she marched up and down the room, gasping for breath.

"A hussy on the throne of Augustus!" She suddenly broke out, wringing her hands. "The mere thought is a crime against the State—a villanious blow in your own mother's face!"

"Compose yourself. For the present there is no prospect of such an issue. But, if it ever should happen, do not challenge me to answer the question: What empress of her predecessors has ever been more worthy to wear the crown than the one divine and incomparable Acte?"

"A slave-girl," groaned Agrippina.

"What do you mean by that? Are you still in such darkness that you are unconscious of the mighty wind, the spiritual spring-gale, which is making itself felt throughout the world from Syria to Lusitania? Or do I alone stand high enough for the heaven-sent and portentous breeze to fan me?—Not in vain has Seneca instilled the doctrine into my heart that all men are by nature equal; that the distinction between high and low is an artificial one; that the supposed rights of the great reside only in their defiant and arbitrary power.''

Agrippina was foaming.

''When has Seneca ever preached such madness?''

''Every day of his life since I first knew him.''

''Then he must be removed. A reprobate monster! I believed his teaching to be sound, as he made you a dutiful and affectionate son. But now—away with the juggling sophist!''

''Mother,'' Nero began after a long pause, ''if Seneca has incurred your wrath, I will discharge him from his office. He is philosopher enough to dispense with the palace. Have you any other wish—it is a command to me. Only one thing you must not expect: I will not abandon Acte. If I discern the smallest symptom of hostility, I will provide her with a German bodyguard of her own!''

Agrippina started. It seems as though an idea had flashed across her brain which promised her the victory. For some time she stood with her sensual but expressive eyes fixed on the ground. Then she said in a softened tone:

''Answer me, dear boy: is all this a mere outbreak of the obstinacy you have inherited from your father, Domitius Ahenobarbus, and which you have hitherto restrained, or do you really love this girl?''

''I love her more than any earthly thing.''

''Well then, love her. But I implore you let it be in secret. I will see what I can do to console the hapless Octavia.''

''Mother, you make me so happy!'' cried Nero in passionate accents; he flung his arms round the empress and kissed her burning cheeks.

''You foolish child,'' she said affectionately. ''But do not for a moment fancy that I approve of what I submit to out of too great weakness. I believe—and that is my only comfort—that time by degrees will bring you to your senses."

"Believe what you like—and dream of all that pleases you best. I am dreadfully tired. Good-night!"

Nero hastened away beaming with contentment. The slaves were awaiting him in the atrium to conduct him to his bedroom.

"Foolish, simple boy!" murmured Agrippina to herself, as the curtain fell behind Caesar. "To think that you can override me—me! How his eyes flashed fire as he threatened me! But I thank the gods the world is so ordered that the waters cannot drown out the mountain!"

CHAPTER XIV.

AGRIPPINA at once quitted the oecus and hurried to Octavia's dimly-lighted room. The young wife had flung herself sobbing on to her bed, and a flood of tears bedewed her arm and the deep feather-pillows.

"Do not weep," said the empress-mother, half sharply and half in pity. "If you had set to work a little more cunningly, the fledged bird would not have escaped you. She is but half a woman in my opinion who, though young and fair, cannot bind a man whose heart she has once possessed."

Octavia slowly lifted her tear-stained face; her lips moved as though she would fain have remonstrated.

"That is enough," Agrippina went on. "I did not come to reproach or to criticise you. Of what use indeed would that be? What is done cannot be undone by all the cries of the wailing-women.—On the contrary, I have come to assure you that you shall ere long triumph over your rival."

"Triumph?" echoed Octavia, with the dejection of despair.

"Yes. My resolution is taken. He declared defiantly that nothing but death could sever his tie to Acte. For that death I will provide!—It is necessary."

Octavia hid her face, trembling.

"Do not let it trouble you," said Agrippina, consolingly.

"Decency, virtue, and the honor of Caesar's dignity demand it. We are in a position where there is no choice, so all means are lawful. Did not Mucius Scaevola, who is famed in history as one of its noblest heroes, steal like a paid assassin into Porsena's tent? Did not Brutus condemn his own sons to death for the sake of his country, and of the dignity of the consulate? And Caesar's throne stands higher and shines more splendidly than anything else under the sun.—In short: I give him three weeks to think better of it. If by that time he has not got rid of that reprobate hussy, her fate is sealed. I will have her killed!"

"Almighty Jupiter!" gasped Octavia, starting up in horror. "You will not do that . . . . Caesar's mother!"

"And why not?"

"Because . . . . because. . . ."

"There is a limit," Agrippina went on, "beyond which good nature is simply monstrous. When history shall judge me it will fling many a hard word at my character; for how many of all the commonplace men of the future will be capable of understanding me, and my motives? And all that I can scorn as trifling and nonsense. One thing only: the curse of being laughed at—that would madden me! I represent the law, and the honor of the imperial family; it is my part, as head of that family, to protect its ancient honor, and to send the guilty creature who has stained it out of the world!"

Octavia went up to her.

"Dear mother," she said in moving accents, "I, of all women, should be the last to take her part. But my conscience tells me that it is only my regret for the love I have lost forever that makes me so implacable in judging her,—and it would be a murder all the same."

"Well and good, call it murder! But when a thief comes into my sheltered home to rob the treasury, I have a right to commit murder."

"Mother," sobbed Octavia, "Acte has not robbed me of the jewel of his love, for it never lay in my treasury. I would thank the gods daily on my knees, and spend my last coin on

166

sacrifices and offerings of incense, if, after years of striving, I could win his heart—aye, if for no more than one short week!—But in this way—by cruel, merciless force—no, mother, it is of no avail! It would only embitter him more deeply; he would suspect me of plotting his loss;—he would hate me, whereas now he is but indifferent."

"Have no fear of that," replied Agrippina. "A man can live down any sorrow—especially when he is Caesar. If he really loves her—well he will mourn for her a short time, and then with all the more eagerness seek to replace her. Then it will be your part to be fair and tender, to take advantage of the memories which will now and then rise up. He cannot possibly suspect you of anything that may happen to Acte. He knows how deeply you revere the gods, how timid and dutiful you are. At the worst I would come forward frankly and tell him in so many words: 'I, your mother, freed you from Acte! Octavia's little finger is prettier than that girl's whole body; behave better, and let by-gones be by-gones.'—Now, go to bed, Octavia, you must be as tired as I am!"

"No, no; I will not let you go!" cried Octavia. She had gently laid her hands on Agrippina's shoulder as she turned to leave the room. "Indeed you mistake him. Do not persuade yourself that he will be easy to deal with. If he really loves her—and I fear he does—he will take up the challenge for her sake with all the powers on earth. And if you do not defy him openly, if you snatch her from him by foul means, then may Jupiter preserve us all! You, I, all Rome will be crushed in the excess of his fury and anguish. The short time since he became my husband has been long enough for me to see into the dread-inspiring abysses of his soul. In it everything lies crowded in confusion: good and evil spirits, happiness and ill-fortune, the Divinity and the destroying monster. I should have been happy above the lot of women if Fate had but granted me the task of encouraging all that is noble and splendid in him, of banning the demons of darkness. This the unsearchable decrees of the gods have denied me—and have granted it, it would seem, to this Acte.

Leave me then to my agonized wretchedness, so long as *he* is happy, so long as the germ of immortal achievement thrives and blossoms in him!''

Agrippina stared her in the face with an expression of non-comprehension—as though she had spoken Gothic or Sarmatic.

''I do not understand you,'' she said at length, with a shrug of despair.

''If you loved him as I do you would understand. You might have stopped his mouth at once, you might have led him away—under any plausible pretext—and have spared me all this. Oh, what I have suffered! What misery, when he could so plainly insist on your explaining yourself, and so utterly despise me, his wife, as to fight the battle for his sweetheart in my presence!''

''There! You see how she is injuring you—the wretched viper! That is just what I want to do away with. You are really so bewildered. . . .''

''No, indeed, I see it all quite clearly. What I last said was but the incontrollable outcry of my tortured soul. Acte tortures me, yes, to madness—and yet you must not kill her! Swear that you will not, by all you hold most sacred! Or else I shall never have another moment's peace; or else I will go straight to him and betray your scheme to him!''

A flush of frenzied rage flamed up in the elder woman's face:

''You have a slave's nature!'' she exclaimed furiously. ''He who lies down in the dust of the highway like a beggar, must not be surprised if he is ridden over.''

''I will go to him now,'' Octavia panted. She drew her tunic together over her bosom with trembling fingers and took up her white palla.

''Well then,'' said the empress-mother, seeing that Octavia was in earnest, ''I promise you. . . .''

''By the highest and holiest between earth and heaven,'' Octavia dictated.

''By my sovereign power over this vast empire,'' Agrippina

amended it, with the mien of an autocratic Niobe. "The girl for whom you intercede shall come to no harm. But you will, I hope, allow me at the same time to make every effort to dissolve this connection by any other means in my power. If it is a matter of such indifference to you—well! But to me, as Caesar's mother, it is an abomination and I shall act as my pride dictates."

She marched out of the room without a word of farewell, and the Syrian hanging slowly fell back over the door.

Octavia dropped on her knees, quite worn out, and prayed.

"All-merciful mother of heaven!" broke from her quivering lips. "Juno, Protectress of women, have pity on me! I have loved him as my highest treasure from the very first, and I was dumb and cold out of self-suppression, because I wanted to kill hope in my aching breast. And then came that short and blissful dream when at each moment I could have cried out to him: 'Do not believe that I am cold; I am almost dying of passionate, unspeakable longing. It is only because I am bashful, because I have so long despaired that, in spite of all my joy, there is still a weight like lead on my heart though it throbs with gladness'—And perhaps if I had then mastered the agitation that raged in my breast— Fearful thought!" She bowed her head; her light brown hair fell in abundant waves over her white brow, covering her face and bosom.

"Juno" she murmured again, "Protectress of women and full of grace, forgive me if in my foolish inexperience I have neglected anything. Have mercy on me! Heal this heart, wounded unto death; cure it of its fervent love; let the flame be extinguished like a taper in a draught, or lend me some magic charm to win back Claudius Nero! For I cannot long endure thus. All night I bedew my deserted bed with tears, and when morning dawns I ask 'what good shall another day do me, since it brings me no change?' Have mercy on me, save me from this consuming wretchedness, and so shall I praise thee, supreme Matronalis, all my life long!" Then she rose, somewhat comforted. "Oh, the might of Nature!" she murmured as if in a dream. "What was it he said to me about the might of Nature and her mysterious purposes? Jupiter does not hurl his thunderbolts, nor Cupid shoot his darts, yet there is something divine hidden under every outward semblance, and Love is the most active and powerful of all deities. When a husband and wife ardently love it is in the name of the secret power and for the fulfilment of its infinite purposes."

Slowly, as if lost in thought, she pushed back the wealth of hair that fell over her forehead.

"Yes, yes, that was what he said, or something like it. The man loves in the woman he worships, not herself alone, but his unborn child."

She covered her face with her hands, moaning:

"Alas! Alas! Had I made him the happy father of a son like himself, then indeed. . . ."

After a short pause she cried shrilly:

"Oh, no. My child would not be the fulfilment of his hopes. If Acte. . . . Oh, I am the most wretched woman living."

She sank fainting into a chair.

Presently some one knocked twice at the door of the cubiculum. Octavia knowing it for her two confidential women, Rabonia, a freed slave, and Phyllis, bid them come in.

Rabonia, a woman past the bloom of youth, allowed herself to glance enquiringly at Octavia, who answered with a slight nod. Rabonia proceeded to undress the empress, lightly and noiselessly, while Phyllis loosened her sandals, removed her bracelets, and took the few remaining gold pins from her hair which now fell like a mantle over her shoulders. Rabonia twisted it into a knot, and could not refrain from remarking on the matchless beauty of the fragrant brown mass.

"You kind soul," said the young empress, "do you think to give me pleasure by your simple flattery? I thank you for your good intention.''

When Octavia had taken her bath as usual in the adjoining room, Phyllis disappeared with a humble obeisance, which at the same time betrayed that she was attached to her mistress. Rabonis helped the empress to bed, and then lay down herself on a mattress covered with rugs, to keep watch and guard over this fair flower of womanhood.

The blue-shaded lamp shed its melancholy but soothing light on the pale, sorrowful face; she lay there with closed eyes indeed, but was still awake long after Rabonia was sound asleep.

CHAPTER XV.

A FORTNIGHT later, six persons were sitting in subdued discussion in Flavius Scaevinus' study: the master himself; Metella, his wife; Barea Soranus; Paetus Thrasea; Epicharis, the wealthy Egyptian lady; and Annaeus Seneca, the prime minister. Seneca had fallen so greatly out of favor with the empress-mother through his determined opposition to any measure adverse to his imperial master's favorite that Agrippina was doing her utmost to expel him from his influential post at court. In point of fact—and not-withstanding his theory of the supremacy of the Will of Nature which, in the case of love, expresses itself all the more decisively in proportion as the passion seems to be most perverse—the philosopher regarded Caesar's infatuation as a passing intoxication which would work itself off without injury to his mental development if only they gave it time; while, if they did not, it might entail the most serious consequences.

Agrippina as yet feared to proceed to extremities—that is to say to hoodwink Seneca and carry out her plans with a high hand—for Nero's attitude, on the whole a most reasonable one since that last painful discussion, had inspired her with a certain respect. The hapless Octavia's words, too, had perhaps left their mark behind.

However, the prime minister thought the hour was fast drawing near when it would be said: "Barriers—and strong ones—must be set to Agrippina's encroachments."

"Friends," said Paetus Thrasea in his moving tones, "I am of opinion that if Nero is not to be induced to take some decided step at once, we must proceed independently—though as considerately as possible. The lamentable incident at our host's garden-festival sufficiently proves that the murderess of Claudius Caesar and Britannicus has not forgotten her atrocious art. If our friend Annaeus Seneca, who knew of these dark deeds from the first, has not long since plotted to break the power of this daring criminal it has been solely out of regard—a too submissive regard perhaps—for a dutiful son, unsuspicious of his mother's guilt. But Nero seems to withdraw more and more from all share in the concerns of State. Agrippina is to all intents sole monarch of the Empire; and though she has promulgated some few wise and useful decrees, she exercises the most atrocious tyranny, when she thinks it to her immediate or possible advantage."

"True, true!" cried Metella and Epicharis both at once.

Thrasea Paetus went on! "Her abominable crime against Flavius Scaevinus has especially roused my wrath. I was silent—for I say nothing when speech seems out of season; but I was at once convinced that that dagger-thrust was Agrippina's reply to our noble friend's toast. For many weeks he lay in great suffering. Now, at last, thanks to the skill of his honest physician Polyhymnius, he is well again. With his consent I have invited you to meet in this room, for it appears to me to be due alike to friendship and patriotism that we should give so shocking an incident our most serious consideration."

"You think then that there is no doubt as to the author of the crime?" said Barea Soranus, turning to the speaker.

"It is universally rumoured that Agrippina was guilty of it."

"And what proof have we of her instigation? I hate the wretched woman—but I love justice. And what Thrasea

174

Paetus has said so far has not entirely convinced me."

"How is that?" asked Paetus.

"Well, I see very clearly why Agrippina wanted to clear Claudius, for instance, out of her way. Personally she loathed the poor fool; his pedantic crotchets constantly crossed her path; and if they were in fact poisoned mushrooms which she finished him off with, I, for my part, take it in proof of the old saying ascribed to her: 'Mushrooms are a food which make gods of mortals'—Yes, I understand that, though I think it base and low. Then, subsequently, she poured some poisoned water into the noble Britannicus' mulled wine. Here, too, I must admit that the criminal's motives were intelligible; that, from the stand-point of an ambitious and ruthless woman, her proceedings were natural and logical. But when in revenge for a few words—which, after all, were only intended to convey to Caesar's mind that he was no longer a child—when, I say, she proceeds to be revenged for that innocent speech by immediate assassination, I am at a loss to account for it. We do not shoot larks and thrushes with a catapult."

There was a pause.

"Paetus," said Flavius Scaevinus, "you have already thrown out several hints to me, but the physicians would only allow you to visit me that once in my room. I was to be perfectly restored, they said, before I might shake my faithful old friend's hand again. I suspect that you know more than Barea Soranus thinks. So now will you fill up those hints, that all here present—and especially the prime minister—may hear all you know."

"Willingly," replied Paetus. "I was on the point of doing so when our friend Barea gave such rhetorical utterance to his doubts. Seneca will not be astonished, for he knows the empress' morals, and her unbridled and ignoble nature."

"It is true," said Seneca, "and her audacity grows more dangerous every day. I have forgiven her past career for Nero's sake, and because I am of opinion that it becomes the true philosopher to be stern towards himself but lenient to others. Now, however, this raging stream must meet a check, otherwise it will drown out the empire—and the hue of its waters will be a reeking red!"

"And this is what our hopes have come to!" sighed Flavius Scaevinus.

"To this!—under the rule of the humanitarian Nero, the inspired enthusiast for art, who has indeed, perhaps, but one fault; that he devotes himself only too passionately to everything that fires his fancy."

"This is quite beside the question," observed Barea—a gloomy-looking man—"Thrasea Paetus will perhaps tell us what he has observed."

"Well then, my dear Flavius Scaevinus," Thrasea began, "the attack on you plotted by the empress-mother was only half political; as such it was indeed highly injudicious and premature, for it led to our contemplating the danger which hangs over our heads with firmness and composure, and elaborating our plans with renewed energy. She inferred from your speech that even you, whom she regarded as half-converted to her side, would in fact be a stone in the wall which the ancient State of Rome, as yet scathless, intends to raise against her encroachments. She cried in her sudden fury: 'Down with every obstacle—and the sooner the better!' At the same time, her wrath would have been less vehement if Otho had not smiled with satisfaction while you were speaking. Only a few days before she had offered him her patronage and he had responded with mere polite speeches and a courtier's excuses;—it was Poppaea who told me this.— That smile turned the scale."

"Pooh" interrupted Barea. "Who knew what he was grinning at. At his wife's pretty red lips, perhaps, or at Acerronia's saucy face."

"Do not heat yourself, worthy Soranus," Paetus said. "Whatever Otho was smiling at, it matters not. The fact remains that he smiled—or, if you prefer it, grinned; that the empress saw the grin, and ascribed it to her own unpleasant position. I myself saw unmistakably that she suddenly turned pale at that much-discussed smile, though the most cutting words you spoke had long been uttered. Her wrath as an insulted and offended woman was boiling within her; she longed to show Otho, whom she has not yet quite given up, what awaits the man who dares to defy the handsomest woman in Rome—for so she thinks herself."

"Hm," muttered Soranus.

After a pause Thrasea Paetus resumed: "I at once perceived that she was plotting something. Possibly, too, she hoped to impress Otho by the swiftness of her vengeance—for she has not given him up in spite of his devotion to Poppaea. In short, she took the first opportunity to give her favorite officer an order which he carried out with frightful exactitude—though with insufficient skill, the gods be praised!"

"I, too, observed the empress' brief dialogue with one of the centurions," said Metella. "I thought it a breach of good manners, but I supposed it to refer to some confidential matter. For, as we know through Poppaea, Agrippina has no prejudices in the choice of her favorites."

"Still she keeps such affairs very secret," replied the wealthy Egyptian. "I, at least, hear much of what is going on, and nothing has ever come to my ears regarding any such favoritism."

"Well, people are of course cautious in making such remarks," said Paetus with a laugh. "But at one time it was an open secret that the centurion Gallienus was master of her favors and to this day he is said to be under the illusion that he—a mere nobody—rules the sovereign who rules Rome."

"All this proves nothing!" exclaimed Barea Soranus. "I can assure you that up to the very moment when we heard Scaevinus call for help, the centurion had never left his mistress' side."

"Very good," replied Paetus. "But it was quite possible to give sufficient instructions, and to hand over a dagger to the ruffian who was to do the deed, within the ten minutes that elapsed between the short conversation with Agrippina and the assembling of the body-guard—this, I suppose, is not self-evident to my critical friend Soranus; but I may add that I myself saw the transaction between Gallienus and one of the praetorians.''

"That certainly is weighty evidence," replied Soranus. "But I nevertheless must persist in doubting as long as there is the smallest possibility of any other explanation. Must events which succeed each other in time be necessarily connected as cause and effect?—Nay, do not be impatient, Thrasea Paetus. I am only putting forward my arguments. But, in fact, without any special modesty on my part, I would trust to your clear-sightedness rather than to my own.''

"And even if you did not trust my clear-sightedness, as you call it, you would still believe my words as being those of a truthful man. I do not merely suspect, I know that Agrippina is the criminal. I know it from the lips of a woman who was present at the banquet, and who is intimate enough with Agrippina to know her well—any, who found the dagger with which the deed was done, and recognized it as belonging to the empress-mother.''

"By Hercules!" exclaimed Soranus, "then I say no more!"

"Who is the lady?" they all asked in chorus.

"That I may not tell you.''

"That is a pity," Flavius Scaevinus observed.

"But I can guess," said Metella.

"And so can I," added Epicharis.

"But where did the nameless witness find the dagger?" asked Soranus. To which Seneca replied:

"Evidently on the spot where the deed was done; the criminal flung it from him. But if I may offer you my advice it is this: Let us turn our minds to the consideration of what is to come, and not of what is past. Agrippina has constituted herself an outlaw—that is beyond a doubt. But if she were as pure as the pious Iphigenia, the welfare of the State would require that she should be deposed. I say deposed, for no one here knows better than I how really she is the sovereign, while Nero, my divinely-gifted disciple, is ruler only in name.

At first that may have been a good thing; but now the soul of every high-minded Roman revolts against the disgraceful fact that such a woman governs the glorious realm of Augustus. Every week that we let pass, without dragging her dominion to the dust is an added danger to the empire.—Do you wish to see Agrippina, in the devouring rage of her ambition, dispose of her own son as she did of her step-son Britannicus? To see her imprison or murder Caesar, that she may suck the juices of the Roman people, like a bloated and poisonous spider? I see her now, in my mind's eye, and she really is like a monstrous spider. The centre whence she extends the rays of her web is the Palatium; every thread of it, to the very frontiers of the empire, is beset with soldiers bought over with the wealth of our provinces. Always and unceasingly do I repent having been too yielding to her at first; in my confident expectation that Nero would prove a fully-fledged eagle quite soon enough, I meanwhile found excuses for that detestable woman's growing influence!"

He broke off suddenly. The famous orator had never spoken with such hearty conviction or such striking energy of gesture and expression. At the same time it must be confessed that a care for his own safety had essentially contributed to the inspiration of his eloquence. A listener had reported to him how bitterly Agrippina had expressed herself concerning him, and his conduct with regard to Nero. The essential thing now was to steal a march on the empress-mother if they hoped to win the day.

This tale-bearer, a Greek slave whom he had once protected by his gentle intervention from one of Agrippina's fits of fury, further betrayed to him all that had passed between the young emperor and his mother, as to Acte; and Seneca, on his part, had also endeavored to dissuade Nero from keeping up this connection with her. In the event of Claudius Nero showing such self-discipline Thrasea Paetus and his coadjutors would find him a powerful ally. Unfortunately, however, as it proved, they could not count at all on the love-sick youth's co-operation. The revolution in the palace was thus deprived of its most powerful lever, which would have removed a thousand obstacles from the path with the greatest ease. If the youthful monarch had been inspired with a real love of active government, with his help everything could have been done without any disturbance, or, very probably under the semblance of a voluntary abdiction on Agrippina's part. But, as matters stood, it seemed very likely that they would be compelled to have recourse to force.

To point out the easiest way of applying that force was the task which Seneca had set himself in the remainder of his speech.

He began by enlarging on the necessity for winning Burrus, the captain of the praetorians, over to their side, and then securing the sympathies of the men themselves. Up to the present time Nero had hitherto paid the bounty to the guard with great regularity, and occasionally doubled or trebled the sum. In her anxiety to consolidate her dominion, the empress-mother had frequently distributed this money with her own hand, and added special marks of honor for the military tribunes and centurions.

Burrus, without being exceptionally vain, was very much under the spell of the empress-mother's charms; she knew exactly how to manage him, and it did not seem particularly easy to break that spell. Seneca, however, believed that he could solve both these problems in spite of their difficulty.

The soldiers were to be dealt with through a few of the centurions, who were to be provided with unlimited supplies of money. As to Burrus himself, this rough bear, on whom gallantry sat so ill, was above all things a soldier. He would consider it more to his honor to serve under Caesar independent, than to prolong the present situation, which made him look more like Hercules turning Agrippina's spinning-wheel than at all suited with his character.

As soon as Burrus was gained over, an easily managed intrigue must be carried out: Seneca would request Burrus to have all the praetorians in readiness in the great barracks.

The prime minister would then conduct Caesar thither, with a large following of senators and priests, and persuade him to declare, in a short speech to the soldiers, that, for reasons of state, Agrippina's dominion was at an end. A sum of money would then be distributed to the men, exceeding all Agrippina's largesses by one-twelfth. Meanwhile Julius Vindex, a military tribune who had long been in their confidence, would stand prepared, in case of need, with a troop of young men of senatorial rank, who would incite the populace to rebel against the supremacy of the palla, (petticoat government.) There were weapons enough and to spare in the huge vaulted cellars of Epicharis. The Romans, in their partisanship for Nero, could be trusted, in spite of the degeneracy of a too luxurious age, to draw the sword once more and prove that the spirit of the glorious Fabii was not yet quite extinct. In the senate, which the prime minister would at once convene, Thrasea Paetus would use all the power of his eloquence and personal influence to bring about the overthrow of Agrippina's train-bearers; and he was at the same time to propose that all that had been done should be ratified as legal, and that the solemn thanks of the liberated should be offered to the conspirators.

The little assembly drew a deep breath when Seneca ended his glowing address. And, in fact, no one had any suggestion to add. The parts were so judiciously assigned, the several wheels of the whole intrigue so precisely fitted together, that no criticism seemed possible.

"So be it!" Barea Soranus exclaimed at length: "And when all this is successfully achieved, accuse the empress-mother publicly as a murderess, before the State-tribunal of the Patres Conscripti, and banish her under safe guardianship to Pandataria where she will have time to reflect that a love of political power, though becoming in men, but ill-beseems a woman!"

CHAPTER XVI.

ALL through the following week heavy clouds overcast the sky, in spite of the advanced season of the year. On the evening of the twenty-fourth of May the rain fell on the city of the Seven Hills as steadily and quietly as though the weather-god were holding his dreary December-orgy.

The empress-mother was staying at the country villa on the Alban Hills, where she seemed to have forgotten everything that usually occupied her restless spirit in the spring beauties of luxuriant nature.

Strange rumors passed from lip to lip, under the seal of strict secrecy: Pharax had been suddenly promoted to the rank of military tribune. He had availed himself of a few days leave to secure the affections of Hasdra, Poppaea's clinging little companion. They exchanged promises, after a zealous correspondence, and nothing was wanting to complete the affair but the ratification of the empress.

It was strange, but Agrippina hesitated to give her all-important consent. On the other hand, Pharax was often seen, wandering with the beautiful sovereign in the farthest recesses of the park; nay once she had clasped his brawny fingers with both dainty hands.

Yet the consent to his marriage with Hasdra was still delayed.

Octavia had also quitted the capital, and withdrawn to her villa at Antium.

Nero was alone at the Palatium, and would dream away the hours of the forenoon in the retirement of his museum, while Burrus and Seneca were briefly disposing of the affairs of State—not just now very momentous, despatching couriers to the empress-mother, and considering the proximity of the summer holidays when the hour of respite should strike even for them—the two hardest toilers in the universe.

Nero now supped with Acte almost every day. He rarely returned before midnight, and when he found himself alone in his magnificent but solitary chamber, he often lay awake till the fourth watch, seriously engaged in considering the immediate future. His beloved Acte could not of course remain in Rome, if he left the capital to stay for a time at one of his delightful country houses in Campania.

What he would have preferred would have been to take some villa on the shores of Lake Benacus in northern Italy, and represent himself as being a knight of Mutina or of Verona, and Acte as his wife. But he at once saw that this was out of the question. If Caesar were to disappear for a whole summer, if not even Octavia or Agrippina could give information as to his retreat and the reason of his disappearance, it must inevitably lead to discussions which he would prefer to avoid. Firm as he was in his determination to defy Agrippina on that one vital point, he was clearly conscious of a secret qualm when he pictured the high side of her wrath. He could guess that a spirit dwelt in that woman's breast which, when once unfettered, would wreck everything in its way. So he thought that it would be best to linger yet awhile in Rome and meanwhile employ his confidential ally, Sophonius Tigellinus, in finding a suitable residence for Acte at Baiae, a populous town where Nero himself had a magnificent residence. There he could dwell alone, so far as the world was concerned, and would not offend by neglecting the outward respect he owed to his wife. He could gaze unobserved into his Acte's eyes as long and as often as he wished—and, for a few months at any rate, the main problem of his life seemed to have found a happy solution.

It was at just the hour when Nero, in his cubiculum, had come to this determination, and stretched himself on his bed in full contentment, when a troop of horsemen came dashing down the Appian Way from the Alban Hills. The men were protected against the fury of the story by large leathern cloaks and from beneath these the blades of their broadswords peeped out. In spite of the steady rain, the night was dimly light; the moon was visible above the slowly-drifting clouds and mist. The cavalcade was headed by Pallas, Agrippina's trusted ally, his face carefully concealed. He it was who had watched for the time and opportunity, who had followed up Acte, discovered where she lived, and spurred Agrippina on. And he was now bent on carrying out a project which was more akin to his inmost desire than to that of his imperial mistress.

His very bones tingled with torturing jealousy and consuming rate against the happy pair, who were enjoying the spring dream of their first love here in this peaceful villa. So unjustly had Fate dispensed joy and suffering, blessings and curses!

How she must adore that boy if she could prefer to be his mistress while he, Pallas, had offered her honorable marriage. What was Nero, in spite of his illustrious birth, more than Pallas—the freedman, who has risén from nothing to be everything, who had made his own way, and who could often do more with the empress by his influence than Seneca's disciple and his tutor to boot?. . . .

Only three days after the painful scene between Caesar and his mother, Pallas had ventured on some gentle hints, had been encouraged, and finally had been commissioned to cut the inextricable knot by a bold stroke, after the manner of Alexander of Macedon.

The lava pavement of the Via Appia echoed under the hoofs of the armed horsemen; before they started, every man had been required to swear, in the temple of Mavors at

Albanum, that whatever that night's expedition might lead to, he would keep it eternally secret, and above all, under pain of death, would never let it be suspected even that the much-dreaded Pallas had been their leader.

On and on, down the great street of tombs.—All around seemed dead at this hour. The lights were out in the tall and lordly houses. The owners were already gone to their quiet country villas, and the stewards left in charge had long since retired to their pillows.

After riding on for half a mile the cavalcade turned to the left.—About three hundred paces further—and Pallas bid his men dismount. He then left two of them in charge of the horses, and with the remainder he went forward to the ostium of the villa where Acte lay in happy slumbers, gave three thundering blows with the panther-headed knocker on the iron-studded oak door, and when the ostiarius was heard coming through the inner doors, shouted in a feigned voice: "Open the gate."

"Who is there?" asked the slave within.

"Do you not know my voice?"

The door-keeper was silent for a moment.

"No," he then said coolly. "And be you who you may, what can induce you to ask admittance here at so late an hour?"

"That I will tell you when you have let me in."

"I cannot and will not, till you have told me."

"Idiot!" cried Pallas. "Do you want to lose your head?"

"I do not see what danger threatens my head."

"Open! I command you in the name of the Empress Agrippina."

"Agrippina is merely Caesar's mother. I refuse to open—in the name of Caesar."

"Then I shall use force."

"Force against the emperor?"

"As I say. I give you just three minutes to think better of it."

"I will take advantage of them to raise the alarm. There

are twenty of us here, and twelve of them are German fighting men."

"What can they do against sixty, who have surrounded you on all sides? Besides, as you know, the mercenaries are all devoted to Agrippina. And on my finger glitters a signet ring, which will prove to you that I act under the orders of the powerful mistress in whose name I summons you. I have a document too. . . ."

"Very good,—then wait a moment."

The echoing tramp of horses, and now this vociferous parley between Pallas and the ostiarius, had roused most of the inhabitants of the house from their slumbers. Acte herself, a snowy mantle flung over her shoulders, now made her appearance in the atrium. Torches and pine brands were lighted. Acte's slaves and freedmen came rushing in from the rooms to the right and left, armed with swords and lances, while the body-guard especially selected by Caesar for his fair-haired mistress, marched in from the peristyle in military order. Their chief now went to the great door with the ostiarius, and asked, in a tone which for an instant gave pause to Pallas:

"What is the meaning of this untimely disturbance? I am centurion of the imperial guard, and in this place I am the representative, with full powers, of the Ruler of the World!"

After a short pause for reflection, Pallas answered him as he had answered the ostiarius.

"You bear Agrippina's signet?" replied the centurion. "Then you may know that our mistress bears that of the divine Caesar. You can draw the inference for yourself."

"I draw no inferences—I act. The empress-mother has commanded me to carry Acte, Nicodemus' freed slave, to her Alban villa without delay."

"At this time of night?" laughed the soldier. "Are you mad, my lord? Take yourself off quietly with your armed men, and do not disturb our night's rest any further. We are under Caesar's orders to refuse admission to any one who may seem to us suspicious—even by day, and much more by night, when criminals and robbers ply their business."

"I am very sorry!" said Pallas ironically. "But we cannot possibly return without having fulfilled our orders. I pledge my honor by all I have and am, that Agrippina will not utter a single hard word to Caesar's fair sweetheart."

"As to what you have—that you might afterwards take back;—what you are I do not know. Nothing of much repute I should think, or you would not accept such a hangman's duty. Besides, a man who has observed your party from the roof tells me that you wear hoods and have half-hidden your faces. If you take my advice you will pack yourselves off as quickly as possible, before the city guard can lay hands on you; if not, the prefect, who is a stern judge, may possibly have you all crucified."

"You refuse then?"

"I refuse."

"Then on your own head be it! Come on, men! Break the door open!"

"I will fell the first man who comes through the breach!" cried the centurion. "We can defend this pass, I should think!"

Three of Pallas's men stepped forward. They swung their heavy axes with ominous vigor and the blows echoed with a dull roll like the thunder bolts of Jove.

The broad iron plates resisted the attack stoutly for some little time. But at the sixth onset they began to grow loose and to rattle; the wood cracked at every seam; a hinge started, and the next minute the whole door fell with a crash; even the heavy iron bolts were wrenched from their sockets.

The axeman stood aside, panting, and the soldiers rushed in, sword in hand. But the fair Acte's bodyguard, and even her slaves, male and female, were standing prepared to give their assailants a warm reception. The four leaders fell like stricken beasts on the long swords planted to meet them. One man who tried to make his way through by crouching low, received his death blow from Phaon, Caesar's faithful house-slave.

188

Still, those behind pushed forward over the dead and wounded with irresistible force. Covering their bodies with their bucklers they forced a passage through the narrow opening into the atrium, where a battle now began, which the fury of the two parties engaged promised to render a fearful struggle.

Suddenly a shrill whistle was heard: the disguised intruders hastily turned to escape. As they were on the point of gaining the victory Acte's astonished garison allowed them to retire unimpeded, not even disputing their right to carry off their dead. Even the centurion, who had stood the brunt of many fights, thought it only prudent to facilitate their retreat.

The last man had but just quitted the ostium and the worthy door-keeper was devising ways and means of patching up the half ruined door, when a slave girl, Erotion, came running and shrieking out of the peristyle into the court-yard.

"Woe on us all!" she cried, her voice choked with tears. "Caesar will throw us all for food to his muraenae! She is gone, stolen—Acte, our sweet, lovely mistress!"

"Impossible!" Phaon declared.

"Yes indeed, indeed—"

"Then you played traitor!"

"I?" wailed the girl, beside herself with genuine sorrow. "She was kindness and goodness itself, as gentle as a sister to us all! I—I betray my Acte! For shame, Phaon—but you do not really think it!—But listen how it happened. She knew at once what they had come for; and she wished to spare all bloodshed, so she made up her mind to escape by the posticum. We opened it softly—very softly—and she was just about to run off to the right down the Vicus Alienus, when two of the ruffians pounced upon her. One snatched her up on his horse, and before I could cry out: Jupiter save us! the wretch had vanished in the darkness."

"Jupiter save us indeed!" cried the centurion. "When Caesar hears how badly we have guarded his treasure—"

"Pooh!" said another girl. "It will not be so bad as you

189

fancy. All his rage will fall on Agrippina."

"Who knows," said Erotion, "whether it may not be a punishment sent by the gods. Caesar loves his charming Acte ardently—but Octavia is his wife."

"Nonsense," muttered the Oscan slave who swept the courtyard. "Otho, Poppaea's husband did not even ask whether I was married or not when he bought me of Flavius Scaevinus. The immortals have too much to do to trouble themselves about every love affair."

"Goose! Do you still fancy that Otho cared for you. Just look in a mirror! But it's a shame for us to fool away our time so. . . ."

"Fellow soldiers," said the centurion, for Phaon's words had given him a shock, "I am very uneasy. Shall we stay here to allow Caesar to pour out his wrath and despair on our heads? Or shall we be off at once to the Alban villa and commend ourselves to the good graces of the empress-mother?"

"That is a good idea!" said one of the mercenaries.

"I serve Caesar," said another, "and I hate women's government."

"Aye aye—and so do I!" cried three men in chorus.

"Very good, then we will stay here," said the centurion. "Our Caesar will understand that it is no fault of ours."

"And he will need faithful adherents in this quarrel with his mother!"

"Cursed creatures, all these rascally men!" grumbled a slave woman as she came in with brushes and mats of soft grass. "Crucify me, if the whole atrium is not a pool of blood!"

The other women and girls had meanwhile rendered aid to the wounded. The victims of the fray were carried back to the beds they had scarcely quitted, bandaged as well as circumstances allowed, and refreshed with drink cooled with snow.

Phaon was unhurt. At first he had thought it might be possible to pursue the robbers; but he at once gave up that

190

idea. It was indeed absurd—and for this reason: that there was not a horse belonging to the household. He paced the peristyle, lost in thought. The rain had ceased, but the wind howled lamentably through the deserted colonnade, as if it were bewailing a sad and inevitable disaster.

CHAPTER XVII.

WHEN they had ridden about a thousand paces to the eastward the party of horsemen divided.

The larger number went off at a gallop along the Via Latina, towards the moonlit hills, carrying with them the dead and wounded; the rain-clouds were fast clearing off. The others, with Pallas at their head, made their way by the Via Appia at a smart pace, till they reached the little town of Bovillae where they made a halt.

The burly landlord of the smoky little gate-tavern was roused from his sleep: for after the exertions of the last few hours they needed some refreshment.

Pallas left his eight or ten horsemen in the tap-room while he conducted Acte, as pale as death, into the sitting-room which the tavern keeper reserved for distinguished guests; Pallas had taken charge of the girl on his own horse, as soon as they had left the last houses behind them on the Via Appia.

A Samnite slave-girl, with tousled, blue-black hair hanging over her eyes, jumped barefoot on to the table to light the corcodile-headed lamp which now shed a dismal light from its smouldering wick.

Pallas bid Acte be seated and uncovered his face. Then, crossing his arms over his chest, he went close up to her and asked her in an uncertain voice:

"Do you know me?"

"Yes, and better than ever."

"What do you mean by that?"

"That formerly I used to regard the empress' friend as an upright and brave man; but now I know him for a scoundrel."

His hand involuntarily sought his sword; but he controlled himself.

"Acte," he said, "let us discuss the position of affairs with perfect equanimity. I have cautiously refrained from speaking throughout our ride; you can understand my motives. What we have to say is not intended for the ears of my followers."

"Speak on," she said coldly.

"Acte! wretched and ill-omened girl, I have loved you out of all measure. I have offered you what even a freeborn woman might have accepted: my hand, my home, and my heart! Acte, you might have been the honorable wife of an honorable man; you have preferred to be Caesar's mistress—a bane to the imperial family—a criminal, so far as Octavia's happiness is concerned. Every one is indignant with you, the people point their finger at you;—I have come to you by the command of the empress-mother, and you dare to call me a scoundrel! Miserable girl, ask yourself whether such audacity does not deserve death!"

Acte rested her head in her hand, a shadow of compunction passed over her pensive face. Then she colored suddenly; raising her lovely lashes she fixed a defiant gaze on Agrippina's emissary. The more harsh and severe his speech, and the more she felt him justified from the standpoint of Octavia and the empress-mother, the more surely did she feel, in the obscure depths of her strong nature, that by virtue of a still higher law she had a better right to the man she loved than any other woman. Some friendly monitor of the Nazarene creed who could have knocked at the door of her heart with words of gentleness, who could have pointed out to her that a true Christian must make a sacrifice when the joy of her heart is opposed to the laws of the Divine Saviour, might very likely have guided her agitated spirit into the right way. But Pallas, speaking in the name of Agrippina and outraged society, while in fact he was only obeying the impulse of his own passion, was not the man to confirm her respect for prescriptive right and the empress-mother's will.

She looked up at him and replied quite calmly:

"No, I am not what you call me. I tell you to your face—and why should I be ashamed to own it since it is the very essence of my being. . . . Never till I loved Nero did I know what life meant! Aye, Pallas! I love him more than anything in the whole world. I was as a wife to him, and I see no evil in it. It was his own irresistible need of me that brought him to me. And he was not my lover, as you understand the word when you use it in the same sense as Publius Ovidius, but my true husband. He shared with me every feeling that stirs his heart—and if it were not for Octavia—and she is noble and good, though she cannot satisfy the deepest cravings of his soul—he would simply and boldly have placed me on the throne."

"In that you lie!" exclaimed Pallas.

"I do not lie. He has sworn it to me a hundred times, as he has knelt in adoration at my feet. But then I have replied: 'Never mind, my own true love, I do not ask the splendor of the Palatium, no, not even for the honor of being called your wife in the face of the world. I want nothing but yourself, Nero, if you were the meanest slave!' "

"Words—mere words!"

"It is the truth! And he loves me as fervently as I love him! The empress-mother knows that only too well; hence her frenzied wrath. But she cannot alter the thing; his love is unbounded, as deep as the surging sea which can never be emptied if you toil for a thousand years! And as for you—Pah! I despise you. Why, you are betraying the mistress you pretend to serve! Not justice, but hatred and mean jealousy are your guiding stars!"

195

"Call it what you will. One thing is certain, and that you shall shortly understand: You are in my power."

"In your power?" laughed the girl. "At first I was bewildered by your attack; it overwhelmed me like despair: it seemed so strange, so impossible.—But now I say to you: I laugh at your low cunning. At this very hour Nero is probably on his way to rescue his Acte. Caesar's arm reaches farther than you fancy. When you are pining in chains—well, I will speak a good word for you out of gratitude for your not having been brutal to me while I lay across your saddle. Yes, you shall be forgiven everything—through my intercession! How glad and proud shall I be when he says to you: 'You may go free, for Acte, my fair-haired darling, has desired it!'"

Pallas stared in dumb amazement at the enchanting creature, who seemed to grow taller with the exaltation of her feelings.

"Girl," he said, "will you listen to me?"

"Willingly," she replied with a smile. "If you regret what you have done, I will forgive you all—all. Only take me back to my happy home, and you shall moreover be splendidly rewarded. Shame will then perhaps make you the most faithful adherent of the man you meant to betray."

He seized her hand with a bitter laugh. "You forget," he said, "that I love you. Never, never, shall you return to him alive. I know that Caesar's arm reaches far, but the ruler of Rome is Agrippina. In a few hours we shall be at Antium. A boat awaits us in the harbor which will carry us on board a swift bireme. Your fate is already settled:—I am to take you to Sardinia and sell you there as a slave to the head manager of the imperial mines who has for years been wholly devoted to the empress-mother. Once there, my pretty bird, you will be narrowly watched. If you should be refractory—well, it might happen that one day you would find yourself spending a short time underground, in the caves and galleries where the ore is found by convict-laborers. No one will ever know what has become of the fascinating Acte. The men who attacked your villa are all, without exception, picked soldiers of the empress' guard; they were all disguised; not a dead man whose face might have betrayed us was left behind in your atrium. So you may at once abandon all hope. Agrippina's plot has been perfectly successful.—Acte is blotted out of the book of the living!"

She sat gazing in his face in dismay.

"Is this true?" she said hoarsely. "Or are you merely tormenting me out of revenge, because I refused you that day? Do not do that, Pallas! Was it any fault of mine? Can any mortal help what he feels? Do not make me suffer now, I implore you, for what was the decree of Fate.—You only meant to frighten me, I am sure? Sardinia! what a fearful thought! I knew a young Ligurian who spent two years of imprisonment in the depths of those mines, and he came home greyhaired.—Speak, Pallas; your silence is more terrible than your anger. Agrippina—the mother of my beloved Nero—cannot be so cruel—or, if indeed she were, you would have had no hand in such a crime."

"How pretty you look in your beseeching alarm," murmured Pallas. "But it is as I say. I call all the gods to witness. The empress has commanded it and I have no mind to lose the imperial lady's favor, so I must obey. Thus but one way, only one. . . ."

"Name it! no sacrifice will be too hard for me if it only restores me to Nero."

"That is not the point. I was only speaking of the misery of imprisonment. Listen then. I will save you at the risk of my own life; I will send my men back from Antium, and embark with you, you poor, terrified child, on a ship that is to sail for Alexandria at sunrise. I only ask one thing: that you should teach yourself to forget Claudius Nero. In the swarming crowd of the Egyptian sea-port an individual is as completely lost as a grain of sand by the sea-shore. Do not look up at me so indignantly; I am the same now that I always was. You shall be my wife, my lawful wife—not my mistress—I will condone all that has happened, though the mere thought of it sends the blood to my head!—Consider well, Acte. Do not answer in haste. We still have half-an-hour before us.—Meanwhile drink a little of this wine and eat a few mouthfuls of bread.—I love you, Acte, ardently and deeply. What to you seems cruelty is only the irresistible impulse of my nature."

He filled a metal cup out of an earthenware jar which the tavern keeper had just set on a table near the door, and offered it her with knightly grace, while the waiting-maid brought in a few slices of barley-bread.

Acte very slowly emptied the cup—drank it to the dregs. Pallas stood aside and gulped down a few drops of the dark-hued country vintage with a frenzied air. His face was burning; the hand which raised the cup to his lips trembled as if he had an ague.

About twenty minutes elapsed; then Pallas again went up to Acte.

"What is your decision?" he enquired hoarsely.

"Can you doubt? I confess that the constancy of your attachment moves me; but if you ever for a moment could think that I would be unfaithful to Caesar—whose I am, body and soul, till I die—and for your sake!—"

"Not for my sake," interrupted Pallas, "but for your own sake. . . ."

"It is all the same. If you ever thought that I could be faithless to the star of my life merely to prolong my existence, you are simply mad. I, go with you? I, be your wife? Would not every moment that remains to me in the future be full of inconsolable longing and miserable self-contempt? No; rather will I face the worst that can befall me!—Indeed, indeed I do not say this to insult your honor. Any other man, were he the noblest of youthful senators, would be no less odious to me. Am I a chattel to be bought and sold? Or did not Nicodemus give me my freedom that I might enjoy its rights? Horses and dogs may change owners, weapons and pictures, rings and necklaces, and lose nothing of their value; but a woman's heart—? Pallas, confess: you yourself would feel how unutterably low I should fall if I yielded to your entreaties."

"Yes, if it were of your own free will. But as it is, you would yield to necessity—"

"I will not! I tell you plainly and finally: I would rather kill myself than pay any heed to your proposals. Take me back to Rome. Do not sin against the sovereign who can reward or can crush you."

"And this is your last word?"

"My very last."

"Then your fate is sealed. In a few hours you will be afloat on the high seas, and Sardinia will swallow you up for ever."

"Poor weak mortal!" cried Acte, starting to her feet. "How can you pretend to foretell what shall happen to-morrow? Can you determine how long your breath will come and go, or how soon Agrippina may cast you into outer darkness? Do not boast of the victory, for you do not yet know how many your foes are.

"Claudius Nero will search the whole world through, and he will find me—for this time I mean to be found! Woe then to you and all who have plotted my ruin!"

"You speak confidently!" said Pallas furiously.

"I do, and I bow my head bravely to this penance, for I know that I have sinned. The hand of God Almighty, in punishing me, shall absolve me! But I shall see my loved one again. A foreboding that cannot deceive me, tells me that my lips shall still tenderly kiss his brow when the hapless Octavia shall have long quitted this earth, and Agrippina, and you yourself, her crafty, contemptible tool!"

"Silence, or I will have you fettered!" cried Pallas trembling in every limb. "I am your gaoler—nay, at need, your executioner; so do not provoke a man who can annihilate you. Besides, you must learn that Pallas has invincible determination. You will submit to me yet—and before we reach Sardinia, if it costs me my life!"

Acte lightly clasped her hands, and her lips murmured a prayer. Pallas went to the door and bid his men prepare to start. Then, turning to Acte, he said:

"At the first cry of alarm you attempt to utter, I stab you with this stiletto," and he held the weapon close to her eyes.

Five minutes later they were on their way, riding through the dusky night.

CHAPTER XVIII.

PALLAS had taken Acte, shuddering at his touch, before him on horseback again. His brain was in a turmoil. Now he felt a tide of fury, a craving to kill, like that of a madman; now a softer impulse of that Nazarene virtue which repays evil with good.

"Fear nothing," he whispered in a sudden impulse of soft-heartedness. "My last threats were foolish. Lean on my arm without a fear, or you will be tired. If you can, try to sleep; my Hispanian has a particularly easy pace. Be comforted, Acte! The future rests in the councils of gods. Who knows: perhaps all may yet be well."

And Acte, worn out with fatigue, followed his advice like a docile child. Her head rested trustfully on her enemy's shoulder, for she felt in the depths of her heart that no evil could befall her so long as she was faithful to Nero.

They turned off to the left just before reaching Antium. They must avoid passing through the seaport where the population began to stir betimes. Day soon began to break. The sea came in sight, and a stately bireme which was riding at anchor at a few thousand paces from the shore.

Pallas looked with unutterable melancholy at the fair face of the slumbering maiden. As the air grew sharper, he drew the cloak from his own shoulders and laid it over his prisoner's slender form.

Two large tears fell from his eyes—on Acte's hand, which twitched a little; and he angrily rubbed his eyes with his fist, as if he were ashamed of this weakness. But the hot tide of feeling swelled more strongly in his soul—a lava-stream of all-conquering magnanimity. Yes, he felt that there was a kind of self denial which might make a man sacrifice his most ardent wishes, which could resign everything to gain one sole end: the happiness of the one he loved.

For a minute he was possessed by the idea of turning back, of carrying the stolen girl back to Rome, in spite of Agrippina, and of throwing himself at Caesar's feet. Whether the monarch proved clement, or thrust a sword through his heart, he cared not: Acte, at any rate, would have gained her heart's desire.

But then the terrible thought of the intoxicating bliss which would begin again in the embowered villa flashed on his mind—it seeme to clutch at his throat with tiger's claws and choke him. He spurred his horse and flew on ahead of his companions, as though he were afraid that the temptation he had so vehemently repelled might return.

Acte in Nero's triumphant embrace! Rather would he endure the eternal reproach of having destroyed her! She might perish miserably in consuming torments, but Caesar's burning kisses should never more be pressed on her exquisite lips—or Pallas must go mad. Ah, that lovely mouth, which, even in this hour of terror, was parted in so bewitching a smile. Ah, that fragrant, heart-bewildering flower of girlhood! If a god would but have granted him only once to call her his and then, in the consciousness of that bliss, to be swallowed up for ever, he would not have hesitated for a second.

As they reached the broad shore-road leading from Antium to Astura and Clostra, the sleeping girl woke up. She looked about her in alarm. It was but a dream then that had cheated her soul so sweetly and yet with such painful oppression. She was not lying on the velvet lawn of her own

202

little garden, not by the dancing fountain, not by the side of her adored lover—singing, in his soothing voice, the old song of Eros in fetters; the fearful reality which she had scarcely forgotten held her still in a merciless grip.

She woke fancying that her distress was caused by the last words Claudius Nero had spoken to her in her dream: "Farewell, Acte; this is my last song; break the cithara!"— Now she knew that it was the much dreaded Pallas and his nocturnal seizure that had disturbed the delicious and tuneful vision. She might not be happy in her love even in her dreams.

The eastern sky was growing lighter every moment. A fresh breeze blew from the Tyrrhenian sea over the spreading green plain. Rich meadows, overgrown with acanthus, fields of tall wheat, already turning gold-color in places, sparkled with morning dew. Curls of pale blue smoke rose from the scattered huts and houses, telling of fires where the inhabitants were cooking wheat-porridge, the traditional Roman breakfast dish.

And there it lay—rose-tinted in the sunrise, as though it were some innocent pleasure-boat—the terrible bireme! The two banks of long oars hung idle and motionless in the blue water. The tall mainmast, the yards with the sails close-reefed, the whole maze of rigging at this distance looked hazy, and was picturesque rather than imposing—and yet Acte trembled in every limb. She now perceived behind the swaying reeds on the bank, a boat which was to take her on board. . . .

Merciful Saviour! was there no rescue then from the misery?

Pallas had not failed to note the shock to Acte, produced by the sight of the open sea and the vessel. He was prompted to take advantage of this mood for a last attempt at persuasion.

"Reflect once more!" he said with some agitation. "There lies the bireme which may carry you either to slavery or to freedom. I will forget everything, everything. May the wrath of the immortals descend on me if I ever speak a word that can recall the past! I will shelter and cherish you as my most sacred treasure. Your wounded heart, which now aches so sorely, will gradually be healed; you will be happy, and learn some day to thank me for not having desisted from my suit.— Do you hear? Why do you not answer? Here we are at our journey's end. . . ." He sprang from the saddle and let the girl slip gently to the ground. One of his followers now joined them; the rest turned back with the horses, after hastily placing the various saddle-packs in the boat that was awaiting them.

A sunburnt, sinewy boatman, wearing a Phrygian cap, took the oars.—The little boat shot straight across the wide and glittering waters, playfully defying the foaming wave-crests. In the distance Antium lay rosy-red in the sunrise glow, and to the south-east, about equally remote, the little town of Astura was visible. Solitary fishing boats were already making their way out to sea from both ports—white or yellow specks of light against the deep, transparent blue.

Pallas had seated himself by the side of Acte, who spoke not a word. They were fast nearing the bireme. They could already distinguish the eagle's head at the prow, painted bright scarlet, the name of the ship: "Cygnus," and the figures of the galley-slaves, ranged in two rows of seats and peeping curiously through the round oar-holes. Every man of them was to Acte an executioner, and she fixed a rigid gaze of horror on the object of her terror.

"Well?" said Pallas, touching her left hand under the folds of his horseman's cloak. She started violently, but made no reply.

"Acte!" he began again after a pause, but in Greek. "Speak to me in the language of your lost mother, if you are afraid of being heard by my men and the pilot. This is earnest, Acte, bitter earnest. In five minutes we shall be on board—and I swear to you solemnly by my father's grave, when once I have given instructions to the captain, it will be too late!"

Still she spoke not.

Suddenly she looked up at him calmly and resolutely, and said in her soft Ionian tongue: "Sit a little father off."

"Why?"

"That I may give you my final answer. It bewilders me to have you so close to me."

"As you wish."

"Now," she went on in a low voice, "now if I chose, I could easily prove to you by my own act what I think of your hateful proposals. Before you could prevent it I could slip over the gunwale, down into the infinite sea, and be free for ever from your plotting and guile, from your hatred and your love as you please to call it. . . ." Pallas was about to start up. She put out her hand to re-assure him: "I could," she said, "but I will not. Stay where you are, and be easy!—My faith in God's Almighty Will forbids me to do it. Yes, and even more than that, hope, sweet and irresistible hope, prevents me. I shall see him again, the noblest, dearest, only one I love—more than anything in Heaven or on Earth, I shall see him again! I am sure of it; for an inner voice tells me so, a voice of assurance which can never deceive. By the blood of the Saviour, shed for us all for the forgiveness of sins, I shall see him again!—Take me where you will! Obey the wicked orders of your mistress like a docile slave! I would scorn all the treasures of earth at the price of faithlessness to him; much more mere freedom—and with *you!*"

"Wretch!" snarled Pallas, furious.

"Silence! Or when we reach the bireme I will tell every one how you, Agrippina's devoted servant, were ready to betray your sovereign for the sake of a 'wretch.' "

"You dare! I would punish you for the lie as you deserve: I would extinguish the hope of which you boast; I would put your eyes out! with this dagger,—do you see?—I would put out those eyes, those accursed, sunny, blue eyes which led Caesar to his ruin!"

"That you would not!" she replied defiantly. "It is the

business of Caesar's slaves to protect what belongs to Caesar, not to injure it.''

"No, I will not. But only because I scorn to do it. You are beneath my anger. You shall see; and you shall live, that you may feel your misery still more deeply. Pine in helpless anguish, writhe like a trodden snake, groan, despair!—but accuse no one of causing your woes but yourself, your own childish folly, which let you dare to dream of wielding the sceptre of Rome!''

She only shrugged her shoulders as if in pity.

In a few minutes Pallas and his prisoner were standing on the deck of the bireme. The sailors were in the very act of hoisting sail; the creaking of the tackle was like the sinister croaking of ravens.

The soldiers remained in the little boat.

Pallas put on an ominous frown and took the captain aside, while two of the sailors held the girl by her hands.

"I have brought you a condemned prisoner," Pallas whispered; and he proceeded to read in a low voice a document on parchment, signed and sealed by the empress-mother. He emphasized certain passages so strongly that the captain cast a side long look at him of timid enquiry. When he had read it to the end Pallas placed this important document in the captain's hands, with instructions to take great care of it and act on its contents to the letter.

"Agrippina," he added, "rewards royally, but she also punishes as ruthlessly as the judges of Hades. Take that little hussy safely to her destination, and do not forget to put her in fetters when you conduct her to the director of the mines. She is as agile as a Cappadocian filly, and capable of anything. During the voyage keep her between decks, and watch her like a jewel!''

"Very good, my lord! Everything shall be done exactly to order."

"So much the better for you. Take this purse of gold as earnest money. As soon as we have trustworthy news of her arrival from the director of the State-mines, you shall have three times as much paid to you at Savona, which is your next destination, and an equal sum for distribution among your men. But, absolute secrecy, or you are lost men, every one of you!"

"Be quite easy, my lord."

"Farewell; Aphrodite Euploia send you a fair passage!"

As he spoke a screaming sea-mew shot across the bows from the left.

"May that be no ill-omen!" exclaimed the captain—for this was a Roman superstition.

"No, no ill-omen!" echoed Pallas. And he went down the ship's side into the boat again.

When he and his followers had reached land once more, he rode off straight to Antium. The short journey was soon accomplished, and without being recognised they reached the residence of one of Agrippina's adherents, where they were refreshed after the fatigues of this exciting night by a plentiful breakfast and a long, comfortable sleep.

CHAPTER XIX.

WITHIN a quarter of an hour of the disappearance of Acte and her cunning captors, Phaon hurried off with a few torch-bearers to the Palatium, to which he had free access by day or by night. The guards posted in the vestibule enquired with astonishment what Caesar's confidential servant could want at such an unusual hour.

"That I will tell his Highness himself," replied Phaon. "He must be roused at once; lead me to his bed-chamber."

Phaon's excited haste was more eloquent than words. So one of the praetorians conducted him to the imperial ante-room and informed the slaves who kept watch there of his demand.

"Go in yourself then and wake him," said the head slave.

Meanwhile, however, Claudius Nero, haunted by anxious dreams, had started up wide awake. He heard subdued but excited voices, rubbed his eyes, as if in doubt whether he were not still dreaming, and then called out with a sigh:

"Cassius, what is the matter?"

"My lord," replied Phaon instead of the slave, "I bring disastrous news! May I come in?"

"Phaon! You? I dread the worst misfortune. Come in quickly, and speak."

Nero was sitting up on his bed.

"A stratagem, an unheard-of plot!" murmured Phaon as he went in. "Acte, the wife of your heart, has been just now carried off." And he briefly related the events of the night.

Nero started up, both feet at once on the lion-skin which lay on the moasic floor by the side of his bronze couch. In the dim light of the pale-blue hanging-lamp he looked like a wax image in the moonlight.

"Cassius!" he shouted in a voice of dull thunder, "come and dress me. You, Elpenor, order out saddle-horses—ten, twenty, thirty. The picked men of the cohorts are to be mustered immediately in the Via Sacra!—Phaon, give me a cup of water."

After he had drunk it, while hurrying his clothes on, he went on in Greek:

"Then you defended yourselves, Phaon? Fought bravely?"

"Yes, my lord! There was not a man there so mean that he would not have given his life for his emperor. For my part, I swore by my mother's head to die rather than let the vile ravishers reach Acte's cubiculum. . . . Perhaps we might have triumphed, in spite of superior numbers. . . ."

"My good friend," said Claudius Nero, deeply moved, "from this moment you are free. And to the end that you may fully enjoy your freedom I endow you with two knights' portions and my country-house at Eirene. You are as faithful and just as the Abu!"

Then, turning to his body-slave, he went on:

"Cassius, make it your business to see that the necessary documents are prepared this very day by my private secretary."

Phaon bowed low and kissed Caesar's hand.

"It was not for the sake of a reward, but because I love you, that I tried to protect your treasure—in vain, alas!"

"Were the men who attacked you praetorians?"

"My lord, I suspect it—in spite of their wearing cloaks, and hoods pulled down over their faces. The ostiarius knew their leader. That is to say he did not know his name, but he recognized his figure and voice as familiar, as soon as the man handed him the wax tablets signed by the empress-mother."

"I only wonder that none of the neighbors came to the rescue. It was well known that Caesar's mistress dwelt in the villa. . . ."

"Illustrious Caesar, you know the cautious habits of the Romans. A night alarm keeps them all within doors—and such disturbances are common enough, after all."

"Have you any idea whither the audacious ravishers have escaped?" asked Caesar.

"They galloped off by the Via Appia."

"Then there is still a hope! Agrippina will not dare to hurt a hair of my Acte's head. She knows too well that if she kills her, she kills me. Cassius, my sword! Phaon, follow me."

He stood there with the weapon girt about his hips, like a young god of war. But suddenly he frowned.

"By Hercules!" he exclaimed. "And who gave you leave to come here, unannounced?"

The question was addressed to the prime minister, whose rooms adjoined the first cavaedium. Seneca, though excessively startled by the rough reception, calmly replied: "My duty, my lord."

"Indeed?"

"I heard a commotion in the Palatium at an unusual hour: consequently I inferred, by the rules of logic, that something unusual was going forward."

Nero had drawn his sword. He seized the speaker by the front of his tunic, looking like a man in a frenzy.

"It is well that you should have come!" he said, grinding his teeth in fury. "And I see you know why. Confess this instant where you have taken her, or by my honor as Caesar I will run you through as the cook spits a thrush!"

"Nero," said the philosopher, "you are beside yourself. Dare not to lay hands on the man who has to this hour been your truest friend. Or nay—rather kill me than insult me so grossly in the presence of your slaves."

Nero drew back somewhat abashed, but still holding the

211

bare sword in his right hand.

"Forgive me," he said, controlling himself with difficulty. "But appearances are against you."

"How?"

"During the last few weeks you and Agrippina have conducted the affairs of state almost at your pleasure,—and the trick my loving mother has just played me is so cursedly akin to all her other schemes, so like her notions of right and law, that I feel inclined to suspect you had had a hand. . . ."

"Had a hand. . . . ? What are you talking about?"

"My happiness is destroyed! Acte is in Agrippina's power. Ah! You understand now? And are not even surprised! By Zeus, you were the first to blame my love for her!—Then you are indeed the empress' accomplice!" And he raised his weapon in wild excitement.

Seneca quietly reasserted his innocence.

"Be silent!" cried Nero. "I believe you. I should be a wretch indeed if I did not. No human being could descend to such baseness as to speak to me of kindness, and plot in his heart to make me so miserable!—Now, come on! Agrippina shall surrender her! She shall and she must, or the earth shall yawn between her and her desperate son!—What do you want?"

"I am going with you," said the minister.

"What for?"

"My place is at Caesar's side, now and at all times—even in his revolt against Agrippina's encroachments. We will undo what is done at any cost."

"Are you in earnest? You, an aged, gloomy-looking man; you, who have told me a thousand times that the sovereign of the world might have but one love; the State. . . ."

"I am in earnest, for I have become convinced that Nero as the lover of that incomparable mistress will prove a better ruler than if she is reft from him."

The horses were by this time pawing the pavement of the Via Sacra.

Seneca called for his cloak.

In a few minutes Caesar and his escort were in their gold-embroidered saddles. Ten enormous torches threw an unsteady flare on the deserted Forum, lighting up the very battlements of the Capitol. The columns of the temple of Saturn, and the dark walls of the Mamertine prison stood out in the ruddy gleam against the cloudy sky. Nero himself, with his glittering armor and the *sagum* flowing from his shoulders, looked spectral and sinister in the glare; he was hardly recognizable as the gentle, harmonious creature of an hour since, as the gracious emperor solemnly mounting the steps of the senate house, or bowing his thanks to the crowd who shouted: "Ave Caesar!"

The little troop set out, preceded by a dozen praetorians. They turned off to the right, between the Caelian and Palatine hills, and under the gloomy vault of the arch of Drusus, coming out of the endless line of the Appian Way. Out there, to the west, beyond the statelier houses of the main road, lay the villa—the abode of bliss—where Nero had been so happy; where, lying on Acte's bosom he had forgotten the world with its splendors and its vexations; where the large, expressive pupils of her blue eyes had smilingly solved the problem of existence which till then had filled him with secret and shrinking dread.

He ground his teeth with rage. If it should be too late? If Agrippina's fierce hatred should already have overstepped the bounds of all he dared conceive of? . . . .

Only yesterday he had found a note lying among the book-rolls and pen-stands in his study—a note of inexplicable purport, to which he had paid no heed, so wholly was he absorbed in the image of his beloved. But now, as he remembered the strange missive, scales seemed to fall from his eyes.

"She who once protected you," so the words ran on the sage-green strip of papyrus, "now is compassing your ruin. Do you know the old fable of the Lioness? The young lion whom she had suckled presently grew bigger than herself, so she killed him as he lay asleep. Beware, Lion! These are the

213

words of those who warn you: The manes of Claudius Caesar and the hapless Britannicus.''

Seneca, who was still vigorous and active, in spite of advancing years, was riding on close at Caesar's side. He had his own thoughts on the subject. He had that very day been with Flavius Scaevinus. The conspiracy seemed to be prospering; but greater difficulties had arisen than they had anticipated. Now, beyond all expectation, this incident had occurred. Could any god have shaken the dice to better purpose? Even if things should, to all appearance, return to their former state, a gulf had opened for ever between Nero and Agrippina. One thing Seneca knew full well: Nero, would never forget the anguish of this night of horror,—he was looking distracted, and as pale as the dead. Till this hour Seneca had done his utmost to screen the crimes of the empress-mother from her son's ken. But now, when matters were so entirely altered, he might at any rate give a hint now and then.

And so Seneca's thoughts and Caesar's reached the same issue at almost the same instant. Nero began by repeating to his companion the contents of the mysterious note.

''My slaves shall all be put to the torture,'' he went on wrathfully, ''unless you can reveal to me who has dared to play such a trick on Caesar!''

''My lord,'' replied the minister with secret satisfaction, ''Cyrus the Egyptian—as you are aware—disseminates such warnings, asked or unasked.''

''Cyrus, the light-fingered juggler of the field of Mars?''

''The very same.''

''Bah! How could he get into the Palatium. He is known to everybody; the men on guard would have seized him.''

''Remember his amazing skill. Did you not see, yourself, how he raised the dead to life? The man who daily works the miracle of the 'Eurydice' trick without being detected could also make his way into the Palatium.—And certainly this warning seems to me to have come from outside.''

''The lioness—the young lion,'' Nero murmured. ''By

214

Hercules, it is clear to me! Misfortune is an efficient schoolmaster."

He was silent for a time.

"Seneca!" he suddenly exclaimed.

"My lord."

"The young lion will show fight."

"He will do well."

"Do you say so? He will not be doing wrong by resisting his mother?"

"When she attacks him? No.—But, believe me, all will go better and more smoothly than you imagine. As soon as the lioness sees that her powerful son is shaking his mane in earnest she will yield."

"One thing more," asked Nero after a pause. "What is meant by: 'The manes of Claudius Caesar and the hapless Britannicus?' and why should Claudius and Britannicus be those to warn me?"

Seneca shrugged his shoulders.

"By your leave, my lord, I postpone the explanation for a few days."

"Why?"

"I may be mistaken. . . ."

"Mistaken?—Why do you look at me thus, Seneca: so anxiously and ominously, and yet as if in defiance? Speak! By Hercules, I am sick of perpetually feeling my way in the dark. If I had been better informed, I should have had time to prepare myself more thoroughly.—What is this about Claudius and Britannicus?

"My lord, you may have me run through by your soldiers, for the power lies in your hands; but you will never be able to force me to speak when prudence commands me to be silent.—I must be silent, Caesar, for your sake. See first what terms you can make with Agrippina. It must depend on that, whether I answer you or not. To the best of my power, I am Nero's friend and adviser, not the slave of his caprice."

Caesar frowned; a bitter answer hovered on his lips. At last he said with perfect self-command:

"Very well; I rely on you. Nay, I beg your forgiveness! In the madness of despair I fell upon you like a brutal mastiff; I am ashamed of it.—I know dear Seneca, what I owe you, I know what you are to the Roman Empire and to the world at large. Henceforth you shall exercise even larger powers than hitherto. You shall command and act just as seems best to you; for all I care you may erect temples to the God of the Nazarenes, and give them liberty to fill every office, if only I find my Acte once more! My adored Acte! I ask for neither glory nor power. Leave me to happiness and peaceful retirement. If I am robbed of her, everything else is mere vapor; the whole universe will not fill the hideous void."

Seneca nodded, as though he were but now beginning to understand the all-consuming fire of this passion.

"Do not misunderstand me," Nero went on. "I do not mean to be unfaithful to my calling as sovereign. I will do my duty—but without ambition or care for dominion. I will be the foremost and most zealous servant of the State—only I must have Acte, otherwise everything may go to rack and ruin!—Tell my mother this; your persuasive eloquence will do more than I can do to open her darkened eyes."

"I will do what I can," said the minister decidedly. "You know—indeed you just now said so—that from the first I have been averse to Acte's influence and your connection with her. The first duty of a monarch is to obey the law. But I now see that the fault was ours in allying you with the luckless Octavia. Eros is perverse; he yields not to reason. I will therefore seek some way of releasing you from your union with Octavia."

"Releasing me!" cried Nero in a tone of rapture. "What joy!—and for her, too. Released! Free!—and Acte? Will it then be possible. . . ."

"My young friend," said Seneca with emotion: "Exceptional men call for exceptional measures. The welfare of the empire is paramount—but an unhappy ruler is a bad ruler."

"Dearest, wisest of men, I thank you! Yes, the empire

shall flourish like a garden in spring time, if only you bring about the thing I so ardently long for.''

He was now silent for a long time. The Alban range rose higher and nearer in front of them as they rode on through the night—a spectral and ravined wall. The road seemed never-ending.

"About twenty minutes more," said Phaon the faithful, as Nero gave utterance to his growing impatience, to the dreamy moon.

On and on; at last the steaming horses stopped at the door of the vestibulum, Phaon knocked, the door-keeper's head appeared peering through the bars.

"It is Caesar," said Nero imperiously.

The door turned on its hinges, and the old ostiarius fell on his knees.

"My mother?" said Nero in growing excitement. "Take me to the empress-mother—this very moment!"

The door-keeper's boy ventured on a timid excuse.

"Away with the wretch to the headsman!" Nero shouted in rage. "Let me to her or you die."

A few soldiers of the body-guard now came forward. Seeing Caesar, they greeted him with a respectful "Ave!"

Nero repeated his desire to speak with Agrippina immediately, addressed them as his faithful adherents, and threw them some gold.

"My lord," said the captain of the watch, "if you will swear to us by the gods that you are plotting no evil against the empress. . . . You have a numerous escort, perhaps one of Burrus' cohorts."

Nero turned pale.

"Evil! I—her son—against my mother? Are you out of your senses?"

The soldier shrugged his shoulders.

"Pardon, my lord—but it was said. . . ."

"Who said?"

"I you put me to torture I could not tell you. One of our men perhaps, or some slave. It was but a chance word that I happened to overhear. . . ."

Caesar drew a deep breath. It had come to this then! Agrippina lived in dread of her own son. What a hideous perversion of all natural good-feeling. It might indeed have been said of her: "She who fears evil is capable of evil; she who talks of enmity is plotting enmity in her own heart. . . ." And had not Nero ample proof of it? At this very time, in the snare laid for Acte—?

"I will take care that your insolent speech shall be punished," he said to the soldier. Then, turning to the others he added: "I will await the empress-mother here, in the oecus, alone with the prime minister. Remain outside the vestibule till I rejoin you."

"What a noise!" said the calm voice of Agrippina who at this moment came into the atrium accompanied by Acerronia, before Caesar had gone forward into the oecus. "Is it you, my dear son? Embrace me.—What brings you here at such an early hour? Has anything gone wrong? I entreat you, speak!"

"Not before your mercenaries," said Nero.

"Then come with me.—Acerronia, my trusted friend, may be present no doubt?"

Nero's expression was anything rather than flattering to the red-haired tiger-cat.

"For aught I care!" he answered scornfully. He suspected her of having formented Agrippina's wrath and disgust against Acte.

The pretty kitten face, with its tiny freckles and sea-green eyes, which sparkled and twinkled so uncannily in the torch-light, would, under any other circumstances, have retorted even on Caesar with a similar grimace; but for once the red-haired harpy was strangely indifferent. There was even a peculiar smile about the corners of her mouth; it really looked as though she were more in the mood for kissing than for biting. Agrippina, who was tired of Pharax, the stalwart tribune, had yesteready, for the first time, hinted to the fair Hispanian that she might hope to find a lover in this dashing warrior. Pharax, one of the most intelligent officers of the guard, of free birth—nay, had it not recently been proved that he was the son of a man of knightly rank?—had respectfully explained to the empress his secret wishes with regard to Acerronia and besought her to support his suit; to this she of course had acceded, since she was aware that her lady-in-waiting had an unconfessed liking for Pharax.

The truth was that Agrippina had promised her cast-off favorite a handsome dowry, if he would but consent to marry Acerronia. This would enable him, if he chose, to retire from the service and live at ease with the bewitching damsel. The "firebrand," usually so quick-witted, had not the faintest suspicion of this compact; she firmly believed in the disinterested devotion of the military tribune; she was as happy as a blooming girl, just conscious of a first kiss.

Agrippina led the way into a small room furnished with Persian luxury; at a sign from her one of the guards had lighted it up. Nero followed, arm and arm with Seneca; behind them came Acerronia, smiling at her own thoughts.

"Where is Acte?" asked Caesar, going close up to Agrippina.

"What concern of mine can Acte be?" replied the empress coolly.

"You have had her carried off. Your bandits seized her by night."

"My son, I do not know what you are talking about."

The blood rushed in a hot tide to the young man's face. The veins in his forehead swelled like ominous snakes.

"You shall learn to know," he thundered out at her. "But I must control myself or mischief may come of it. Seneca, do you speak instead of me."

The minister briefly stated what Agrippina already knew, and added a warning that it was not wise to draw the bow too tightly. He put forth all his eloquence, all his philosophy to appeal to Agrippina.—In vain.

"Mother," cried Nero, convulsively clenching both his fists: "Do not lie to me. I shall scorn you as if you were the meanest hussy in Rome if you are too cowardly to tell the truth!''

"Very well," she said, turning as pale as the statues in the niches round the room. "You have guessed rightly. Acte has been removed, and by my orders, for the welfare of the empire. I have banished her—and never shall you know where she is hidden. Never!"

"You have killed her!" groaned Nero suddenly staggering back a pace or two.

"No," said Agrippina in a firm voice. "By all the holiest feelings I have known, by my love for you whom I once nursed on my knees, I have taken every care that she shall suffer neither injury nor want. Now, do you believe me?"

"Yes. But of what use is this miserable admission? The fact that we are parted is injury and want enough!—I will have her back, cost what it may. Where is she? You must and shall tell me."

"Never!"

"Never? And if I die of it?"

"Then at least Nero will die unstained, on the pinnacle of his magnificent empire, and not dishonored by a life-long devotion to a low and worthless slave girl."

"Mother!" He had raised his fist, a shudder ran through his fevered frame. "Know this, not another human creature than you would have outlived this moment," he went on, as his arm fell by his side. "Farewell.—I will find her. By almighty Jupiter, I know the lioness now who seizes her sleeping cub by the throat! Beware, mother, and think better of it. Do not sacrifice me to your vanity, to your insane pride, or else—"

"Well, what? or else—?"

"Farewell!" And Caesar rushed away as if bereft of his senses.

CHAPTER XX.

THE horses flew down the valley again in mad haste; but presently the party halted: the horses were ready to drop. They were refreshed with bread and water and rubbed down with elm-leaves. After resting for about half-an-hour they started again at a more moderate pace.

The vast capital lay before them in the light of dawn like a giant awakening from sleep. The grey mist floated and undulated over the temples and theatres, the palaces and thermae, like a mysterious sheet under which the sleepy limbs were beginning to stir.

At last they reached the arch of Drusus. Caesar, perfectly pale and with a fixed stare, galloped through the busy Forum, without paying any heed to the acclamations which greeted him louder than ever. On all sides excited groups had gathered, talking with eager vehemence of the latest extraordinary news: Caesar's nocturnal excursion. They had already heard the details, for the slave-women from Acte's villa, and especially Erotion, had rushed to the Subura as soon as they had got over their first alarm to relate the events of this fearful night, with much lamentation and wailing, to the venders of vegetables and bread.

Though no one had a word to say against Octavia, the people were on the whole disposed to take Caesar's side; for

Octavia with her calm dignity was thought to be cold to her husband, while Acte's name was seen through a halo of womanly tenderness and love.

"I have seen Nicodemus's fair freed-woman myself," said a hungry-looking client as he came out of his patron's door. "She is an exquisite creature, and I can quite imagine how Caesar must fume and rage at losing her."

"Very true, Lucius," said another who walked by his side. "Compared with Acte's glowing flame, Octavia's good graces are like the smoky wine of Massilia compared with the richest Cyprian. The wife was forced upon him. . . ."

"It would all have gone on very smoothly," the client went on. "But the empress-mother is said to have persecuted Octavia till at last she consented.—Now we have this scandal! Between you and me, Agrippina seems to have been more jealous and violent than Octavia herself."

"To be sure. She was afraid lest Acte should gain too much influence,—over the government of the empire even. . . ."

"Not a doubt of it. So she swooped down, like a country boy robbing a nest. But I fear that her rash attack may bring worse upon us."

"How so?"

"Well, you saw him ride past? Caesar I mean: he looked like Achilles in his rage, about to take revenge on Patroclus. Never did I see such a spectral fire under his eye-lids. I trembled as I beheld him."

And they walked on, past other folks who were discussing the same subject in subdued voices.

Meanwhile, the man whose name was on every lip in Rome this early morning, had flung himself, quite tired out, on his bed, where he instantly fell asleep. No dreams disturbed his refreshing slumber. It seemed as though beneficent Fate were granting him complete restoration of the powers he would need for the impending struggle.

He woke towards noon; he called for a cooling drink, but sullenly and briefly refused all solid food.

He thought and schemed. For hours he remained alone in his private room. Slaves and freedmen stole past the barred door on tip-toe; no one ventured to beg admittance. Even when Seneca timidly knocked, about the dinner hour, he was answered with a half-imperious, half desperate: "Leave me in peace."

It was not till long after darkness had once more closed in that Nero went to the door and bid his slave Cassius to bring a light, and some bread and Samian wine. The court officials and guests in the house were to go to supper when it might suit the head-cook's convenience. The prime minister would worthily represent Nero himself.

Then he desired the attendance of Phaon. When his trusted servant made his appearance, Caesar put into his hands an order on the keeper of the treasury.

"Spend and spare not," he said grasping the freedman's arm. "Send out ten thousand spies and messengers—twenty thousand—as many as you like, and each one with the pay of a military tribune. Bid them search as though it were a matter of life and death. Whoever finds her may have any reward he asks—the throne itself for aught I care! But find her—go, I have delayed too long. No, no; I will listen to nothing—I cannot endure your presence. You have the face and form of man!"

Phaon, deeply moved, withdrew; Nero sank again into inconsolable brooding.

"It is in vain," he groaned. "I have gone through it all before—search is fruitless—I feel it, I know it!"

The next day brought the same torments.

He left his bedroom before sunrise and crept timidly, like a returned fugitive, to the museum, where Cassius, had already prepared some breakfast for him. But Nero, though he must have been hungry, would not at first take a mouthful. He sat at his writing table in gloomy meditation, playing with his reed pen or with the yellow-tinted strips of papyrus which lay before him in neat packets. Then he sprang up, paced the room stealthily like a tiger in a cage, clenched his fists, or clutched his hands about his throat. Presently he uttered a yell like some beast of prey, threw himself in anguish on the sculptured brass couch and clasped his hands over his face. There he lay for a quarter of an hour, either quite motionless or twitching in every limb, like a man in an epileptic fit.

At last he rose, and went back to his inlaid writing table— the table where he had so often invoked the muse, in Greek or latin—where he had written this verse:

> What sweet delight to sit by the waterfall
> When Acte's tresses veil her in lovelines,
>> And when her smiles like May day sunshine,
>> Ravish even soulless nature.

Ah! that happy time!

He now seated himself, took up one of the yellow sheets, dipped the reed pen, and wrote as follows:

"Claudius Nero to his illustrious Mother, the most potent Agrippina.

"I am hovering between life and death. Mother, if you ever loved me, solve this terrible riddle.

"I have sent out thousands of messengers; but I foresee that they will return without having found the slightest trace of my beloved Acte. You are too great, too powerful. No one may hope to conquer whom you defy.

"Mother, I will cherish you as long as I live if you will but give me the smallest clue to her fate. I already almost despair of her still being alive. Ah, and I loved her so—beyond all measure, out of all reason. Mother, give her back to me. I implore you by the ashes of my dearly loved father Domitius.

"Can you not feel for me at all, when I tell you that I love her? The answer I crave will be brought to me by Cassius, my slave, as quickly as he can come; do not delay for mercy's sake, I beseech you! Give him a fresh horse; tell me that I may hope.

"Jupiter preserve you!"

When he had tied and sealed this letter, he was a little calmer. He called the slave, gave him the necessary instructions, and then ate a little of the meal, which consisted merely of milk, new bread, and a dish of tunny-fish. But nothing tasted well; his throat seemed to have closed up.

He then dropped into a luxurious arm-chair. He counted the flowers in a Syrian rug at his feet, or sat staring at the handsome coffered ceiling, as though unconscious of himself or his surroundings. The time till Cassius could return seemed eternity.

And still there was the corroding anxiety about Acte. This was the third day since he had kissed that mouth, which at every meeting had so much to say to him that was kind and loving. Her last divinely sweet embrace!—If any god had whispered to him what would happen within a few hours!—Perhaps it was for the last time on earth!—and an unearthly presentiment seemed to murmur in his ear: "Yea—the last. Never, never more would he be so glad, so rich, so blest!"

Cruel horror! What to him was all the wide world if Acte did not fill it with her radiance? Even the newly-awakened spring had brought him joy for her sake alone. The roses had been so fragrant only because Acte had enjoyed their perfume; the flames of sunset, which had uplifted his heart to the realms of poetic dreaming, had seemed so divine only because he could look from the blazing splendor of the sky into Acte's black pupils, where the crimson glory of the clouds was so exquisitely mirrored. Then when she sang one of her melting songs: "Uranus, Father of the Universe—" or "Helios now drops the reins and descends to Oceanus—" he, too, had made music and struck the cithara. Their voices had combined in sweetest harmony—the earth had been so lovely in its spring verdure—the Palatium, with its worldly grandeur and functions, had seemed so far away, that Nero had felt as though he must die in that delicious enthralment—die as a wave dies that is lost in the ocean. Yes—that was love, that had been happiness—and now? He got up and went to a cabinet of ebony in which the rolls of his chosen library lay side by side on bronze shelves. He carefully took out an elegant written copy with red edges, of his favorite Greek poet.

How often had he and Acte, shoulder to shoulder, read the immortal epic of the home-coming of the long-suffering Odysseus, and allowed themselves to be carried away on the stream of that incomparable melody!—Now, what a grievous change! The verse which then had filled his soul with a thrill of delight and admiration,now lay before his eyes empty, dreary, dead.

And Cassius was not yet returned. He read on and on to deaden his impatience. Then it suddenly came upon him to feel as though there were in all the world but one way of easing his heart of the anguish of his loss: the sword! Yes. If he, like the heroes of the crisp-haired Achaians, could overwhelm a host of foes, if he could raze an Ilion to the ground, then perhaps he might forget the bright dreams of his youth and resign himself to eternal night!

The sun was high in the heavens when Cassius came back from the villa on the Alban hills. He brought a letter on Alexandrian parchment, fastened with three ties. Caesar's fingers trembled as he loosed the silver-wrought cord. The letter was as follows:

"Agrippina, to her beloved son Claudius Nero, happiness and blessing. I willingly give you a truthful answer.

"When, just now, you stormed at me in a way which Caesar's mother can not submit to if she herself has any respect for the exalted dignity of the sovereign, I treated you with greater roughness than I ought perhaps to have shown.

"I must now inform you that the immortals themselves have effected an eternal separation between you and that unhappy girl.

"Acte, by my orders, was conveyed to Antium, and there carried on board ship. I meant no evil: what I did was done out of the purest and deepest love for you. I intended to banish her, without hurting her, for a few months to Sardinia, that Nero meanwhile might forget his folly. However, the bireme which was steering westward with Acte on board, was run into in the most inexplicable manner, when only a few thousand paces from the shore, by a large Hispanian merchant-ship making for Ostia. As the bireme sank almost immediately, only a very small part of the crew escaped, especially as the sea was running rather high. All the rest, and among them Acte, were drowned. Bow yourself, my beloved son, to the stern decree of Fate. All your sighing will not bring the poor girl to life again. I, for my part, will cherish and care for you with redoubled tenderness, and support you in the fulfilment of the really divine task to which you are called: the government of the Roman people.

Farewell."

As Nero dropped this letter and clutched with trembling fingers at the back of his chair, Phaon timidly came into the room. For a half a minute he paused, doubting, at the door out of which Cassius softly made his escape like a dog that is scared by a lion. At last Nero started up.

"It is a lie!" he cried in heartrending tones. "She lies! Acte drowned? It is a contemptible falsehood, this collision with a Hispanian merchantman!—There, Phaon, read it, and tell me that the letter is a tissue of lies."

Phaon, breathless with agitation, hastily glanced at the parchment, then he said, speaking with difficulty:

"My lord, I would lay down my life if I could prove the empress a liar. But I myself have just come from Antium. . . ."

"Miserable wretch. . . ." stammered Nero.

"Most noble Caesar, bow to the will of immortal gods. Agrippina tells you the truth. All the Quirites know it for a fact. The bireme sank, and all on board excepting the steersman and three sailors, found a watery grave."

"Prove it, prove it!" cried Nero desperately. "You are lying, too. Agrippina has bribed you! Prove it—do you hear?

or your head shall be flung at your feet."

"Claudius Nero may be inconsolable; but he can never doubt the truth of his faithful Phaon. The proofs are easily given. The merchant-ship is at this moment in the harbor; it was seriously damaged in its collision with the bireme, and if it had not been for the extraordinary exertions of all the oarsmen it must have gone to the bottom. The harbor authorities, whose honesty is well known, have already examined the crew of the Hispanian vessel, as well as two sailors picked up from the bireme, both freeborn. . . ."

"Then return at once to Antium!" cried Caesar breathlessly. "The harbor-master must put the Hispanians in chains. Bring them here—every man of them. They shall be cast to the wild beasts and slowly bleed to death in the clutches of ravening tigers—the heartless villians, who dared to send Caesar's dearest treasure to perish in the deep!"

"Even in his sorrow Caesar will be just," Phaon murmured. "The Hispanians are innocent. The man who is answerable for the catastrophe is the steersman of the bireme, who did not get out of the way in time."

"Then bring me the steersman. No torture is too cruel for that wretch, no torment that man can invent. I will strangle him with my own hands, tear him limb from limb, flay him. . . . so—so—"

He ground his teeth and held out his hands clutching with his fingers like claws, as if possessed with the bloodthirsty rage of a Gaetulian lion; suddenly he staggered; overcome by grief and despair he fell into the arms of his faithful attendant, who carefully laid him on the cusions of the divan. Beneficient unconsciousness shrouded his heart-sick and storm-tossed spirit.

Phaon stood with clasped hands, wondering what was to be done and gazing at his master's pallid face. Perhaps he was glad to allow the hapless man these few minutes of self-forgetfulness; perhaps he had a presentiment that it would be well for Caesar and for the Roman people if the miserable youth should never awake to life again.

When Nero opened his eyes again he called for a cup of the strongest wine, drank it off at a gulp, and then bid Phaon to leave him. With forced composure he once more read his mother's letter; then he sank into a state of brooding lethargy.

"Dead, dead!" he murmured from time to time, and then sat in silence for half-an-hour, staring at the floor. He saw nothing, heard nothing. Evening came: still a dull oppression weighed upon his brain, a shroud which concealed from him how miserable he was.

Suddenly the veil was rent. Claudius Nero started up, terrified at himself, and fell on his knees. The sweat stood on his brow; he wrung his hands like a penitent in prayer wrestling with the divinity for mercy.

"It is all over!" he groaned in a suffocated voice. "Never, never more in this life shall I say: 'Acte—my heart's darling!' Never, never! Ye gods—whether there be gods or no—I adjure you! Is the thought to be endured? All over! Ruined, gone for ever! If I might but once again look into her heavenly eyes, now closed in eternal night, I would gladly let my whole forlorn and miserable life flow away in one reeking stream of blood. Ah! if at my last gasp I might but hear her voice once more, her sweet, pure, appealing tones. What a world is this in which such a crime against Beauty and Goodness is possible! Acte—my own love—dead! And these senseless walls stand as they stood yesterday—and will stand, in scorn, for perhaps a thousand years. This swarming city rejoices, as it did before, in its childish, pleasure-seeking existence. The senators assemble in the capitol as though nothing were changed. The vestal maidens offer their sacrifices, the praetorians mount guard, revellers feast and drink, vagabonds thieve, the Nazarenes sing and pray—all as if to-day were as calm and happy as all the days that perceded it!—A curse on the wretched mob that do not mourn at home when Caesar's heart is breaking—Caesar who rules them all. Loyalty indeed!—But no! I forgive them; they are guiltless! What have I to look for from the people, when my own mother lays a ruthless hand on her son's happiness! Acte, Acte!''

He sprang to his feet.

"I have only reaped what I had sown," he went on with intense bitterness. "I have been a fool, a contemptible slave! Why did I let things go so far? My kind mother! She is so anxious to do me honor, to share the cares of government with me! Do not deceive yourself, woman—destroyer of my life! Half the dominion is not enough to heal such wounds as mine: The world henceforth shall know who fills the throne of Augustus—You, or I!''

"Phaon!" he called in a voice of thunder. It sounded as if he had fought down his stupendous sorrow with a giant's strength, and now gave a shout of triumph. The freedman appeared at the door in some trepidation.

"Go and desire the prime minister to come to me," said Caesar, without looking at him.

"I hear and obey."

"Stay, Phaon. Does no one know who the robbers were who carried off my Acte?"

"No, my lord. All enquiry has proved fruitless. 'Agrippina's slaves,' says one. 'Praetorians,' says another.''

"Hush! My question was a foolish one. Even if I knew—they were but tools in Agrippina's hand.—Good; the prime minister.''

Seneca came into the presence with grave, almost melancholy dignity.

"My friend," Nero began with iron firmness, "do not fear that I shall wail and lament over her who is for ever lost. What I have to discuss with you concerns the great future." He proceeded to explain his views in brief but cogent terms.

"Now you are indeed Caesar after my own heart!" exclaimed Seneca clasping him in a solemn embrace. "All that lies in my power and in that of my friends. . . .''

"Yes, I know you will support me with your counsel, and when needful with your sacred sword. Act, Seneca, plan, calculate! My tortured brain is still on fire. . . .''

"You are not to relapse into the weakness you have but just conquered. By Zeus, I will not allow it!—This very day I will speak with Tigellinus. Our first onslaught against Agrippina's domineering arrogance must amply prove to the Roman people that Nero now recognizes his duty as filling a place in the world's history."

"You were to tell me something about Agrippina. . . .; concerning Claudius and Britannicus."

"Not yet, if you will take my advice as a friend. You will stand forth more great and noble, if you act solely on your responsibility as the sovereign, and not on the ground of certain rumors which, after all, are perhaps. . . . only rumors."

Nero bowed assent. "I trust to you," he said with a sigh. "Protect me from myself. Give me an omnipotent magic wand to lay the ghosts of a by-gone time which whirl around me—so fair and yet so appalling!"

"That wand is the sceptre. Wield it like a hero. . . ."

"Aye, or like a fiend if you will!"

CHAPTER XXI.

BY dawn on the sixth day after those events the atrium of the imperial residence was splendid with festal decorations.

The marble podium at the entrance to the chamber of archives was covered with costly carpets, and here two thrones with lion-clawed legs and had been placed under a golden canopy. An abundance of the most beautiful flowers, intermixed with luxuriant greenery, hung in garlands between the columns, were strewn on the floor, and arranged in vases along the colonnade. The most gorgeous hangings clung, wherever it was possible, to the sheeny marble. The walls of the chamber of archives were positively dazzling with these splendid textiles; the statues in the colonnade were covered with them; even from the roof hung heavy tassels and fringes which blazed more richly with scarlet and crimson as the sun mounted higher.

This day, at the second hour, Caesar was to give ceremonial audience to a deputation from the Chatti. The great family residence—the Palatium—had been chosen for the occasion rather than the senate house, in order to give the proceedings a less political aspect, and perhaps a more splendid and warmer color. If this long-expected diplomatic ceremonial had not been in prospect, Seneca would probably have asked leave of absence some days since. The heat of the last week of May was sultry and summer like in the city; some cases of fever had already been reported from the narrow Subura. As it was he was forced to endure the discomfort, for this was the first grand opportunity for dealing a home-thrust to Agrippina's ambition, not only before the assembled Fathers, but in the presence of a foreign embassy. Now, at last, she could not fail to understand that a new era was dawning on the government of the Roman empire. The tribe of the Chatti, though the least barbarous of all the German stock, and Rome's immediate neighbors on the northern frontier, having been provoked by various incursions of the Roman soldiery to assume a threatening attitude during the past year, had associated themselves with the Sicambri in various plots against the rule of Rome. If the propraetor, who represented Caesar's sovereignty in the northern provinces, might believe his informants, an invasion of the Roman empire was meditated by the whole of the unsubdued Germanic races. Still, the Sicambri were the only tribe of them all in whom the notion of national unity had as yet struck root. All the others, as far north as the Guttones and Rugii, wasted their best strength in internecine quarrels, in spite of the great memories of the time of Varus, and remained indifferent to the new idea for which perhaps they were as yet unready. Even among the chiefs of the Chatti indeed, there had quite recently been fierce family struggles.

Under these circumstances, Caesar's wily plenipotentiary had found no difficulty in inducing the Chatti by various diplomatic wiles—certain concessions and especially the payment of an indemnity—to change sides. He painted an alliance with the mighty Roman empire as so splendid an end that, after brief facillation, they resolved to send twelve of their greatest chiefs to Rome under the guidance of Lollarius, the imperial general, to offer gifts to Caesar and to submit proposals of neighborly peace. The chiefs were to supplement these ostensible proceedings by others of a more serious character, and the settlement of certain matters which the propraetor did not think proper to deal with on his own responsibility.

Agrippina had, some days ago, expressed the quite superfluous, and, from the point of view of the Roman people, no less arrogant and insolent intention of coming from her Alban villa to assist Caesar in the reception of the twelve emissaries and to preside, in the most literal sense, over the whole ceremony. This, then, was the point where the prime minister purposed to insert the lever wherewith to overthrow the empress-mother, gently—but in the sight of all the world.

Since the day when Nero had sent for him, and had told him that he meant to indemnify himself for the cruel loss brought upon him by Agrippina and adverse fate, by the magnificence of his undivided empire, Annaeus Seneca had not been idle.

"Be calm," said Seneca very coldly. "It is not the first time in the history of the world, that a noble tree, after bearing noble fruit, has suddenly become corrupt. Indeed, it has lately been rumored—but forgive me; I cannot bring myself to utter it."

"Do you think that you ought to spare my feelings?" said Caesar with a laugh. And after a short pause, Seneca went on:

"There is no help for it; you must hear it all! For the question at stake is: 'You or she.' There is an ominous ferment in every grade of the population: The senate murmurs secretly; the knights, the small merchants, the artisans, nay, the very slaves are seething with fury at seeing the state trodden under foot at the caprice of a worthless woman. Burrus—I tried to shut my eyes to the fact, but I have lately been assured—Burrus is not alone. . . ."

"It is a lie!" cried Nero starting up. "She might forget herself, and stoop to dishonor, but never would she belie her stupendous pride!"

"I may be exaggerating," Seneca muttered. "But do, yourself, as you have done before. Disguise yourself and mingle with the populace in the suburbs. Visit the taverns, the eating-houses, the barbers' shops. There you will hear all sorts of things rumored concerning a certain military tribune named Pharax.''

Nero groaned aloud.

"And is this all true?'' he asked after a long silence.

"So true, Caesar, that you may bury me alive in the field of criminals if I lie! Why are you trembling, Claudius Nero? What I have told you is mere human weakness, discreditable—in my opinion degrading—but still not unpardonable. Do not look down in dejection. By the great Spirit that rules the universe, what grief awaits you then, if I tell you what *worse* deeds than these she has done!''

"Speak,'' cried Nero desperately. "I am prepared for the worst now. Nay, it will be a sort of agonizing joy to know the very worst.''

"I say once more, all this is but human,'' said the prime minister. "A hot-blooded woman accustomed all her life to command, unbridled by any man, and, in spite of advancing years, as fair and youthful-looking as summer fruit—such a woman must always be the prey of her insatiable instincts and impulses. But,'' and his voice rose like thunder coming nearer, "she need not therefore be a murderess.''

A smile as vacuous as that of an idiot passed over the wretched emperor's features.

"Do you know,'' Seneca went on, "how your much to be pitied step-father Claudius met his death?—I will be just: I will admit the folly of the victim. Claudius was no fit husband for Agrippina. Domitius Ahenobarbus could keep her in order with his iron fist; Claudius, Messalina's widower, was a lost man before he began the contest. And yet, did he not love her devotedly? Was he ever guilty of a fault, much less of a crime? He governed or, to be accurate, he let others govern. The crime he committed in the eyes of his loving Agrippina was that he did not place the empire in *her* hands, and that he would not banish or kill his own son Britannicus, even though he had already disinherited him in your favor.—Then, when she began laying all sorts of plots to enable her to seize the helm, Claudius perceived what she was aiming at. He made up his mind to divorce her and to reinstate Britannicus in his rights as heir to the throne. What should Agrippina do? Two courses were open to her: to conciliate her husband by gentleness, submission, and kindness, or to get rid of him by foul means before his determination should take the form of action. At that time the poisonous elixirs of Locusta, were her favorite means of death. That accursed woman gave her a tasteless and senseless fluid, which had the inestimable advantage of poisoning the victim slowly but all the more surely. As it happened a stew of mushrooms, the emperor's favorite dish, was served at the family table, and Agrippina made one of the cooks select a fine specimen into which enough poison was dropped to insure the fatal result. The dish was served. With the attentive care of a dutiful wife she pushed the poisoned mushroom towards him: 'It looks excellent,' she said—'fresh and tempting.'—And she herself ate of the others. When Claudius presently grew drowsy it was supposed that he had drunk too much. In the course of the night, however, he gradually lost his sight, his hearing and his power of moving; and he died in fearful torment.''

He had hailed Nero's sudden revolt with such enthusiasm as to suggest to Caesar that a step which he had felt merely as a craving was in fact a merit.

That same evening Seneca had visited Flavius Scaevinus, and had informed him that if Caesar's decisive energy should only endure he himself might be counted on as a conspirator against his mother. They might therefore safely delay the execution of their plot to overthrow Agrippina, as it would undoubtedly produce a far better impression on the senate, as well as on the populace, if Claudius Nero himself took the initiative.

After discussing this with Flavius, Seneca nevertheless made the necessary preparations to protect himself against any possible violence, on the part of the empress-mother. Burrus, who knew nothing of the conspiracy, was easily persuaded to entrust the command of the half-cohort which was on guard in the palace, to Tigellinus; particularly as he had of late been less blindly devoted to Agrippina. It had come to his ears that Pharax was high in Agrippina's good graces; and the rumors which supplemented this report, though vague, were unmistakable in their purport, and offended his soldier's pride. Not, indeed, that he felt any disposition to rebel against the empress-mother; but he wished that she should see that he was not the facile toy in her hands that she evidently thought him.

Tigellinus was no sooner placed in command of the guard then he distributed whole sacks full of gold among the soldiers, while Nero, in obedience to his minister's hint, kept himself in the background.

This morning, very early, when Agrippina had taken her seat in her carruca, drawn by four foaming Cappadocian steeds, to be conveyed from her country house to the city, Seneca had thought the moment arrived when it would be well to revive Nero's embittered rage against his mother by divulging the secret he had postponed.

While Caesar's slaves were robing him for the great ceremony, Seneca was sitting with his arms folded in the emperor's private study, and carefully working up his momentous revelation. Cassius had already informed the monarch that his minister wished to speak with him before the arrival of the senators and on matters of importance. Nero was impatiently urging his attendants to haste.

Seneca met him with a mien of unwonted gravity when at length he made his appearance in his purple-edged toga.

"Come, my beloved son," said the minister confidentially. "We have still half an hour before us. Here, sit down and listen to me."

After briefly recapitulating a few fundamental principles of the Augustan state-craft, and especially insisting that it was sometimes good policy to regard half-forgotten crimes as though they had never been committed, he went on to exonerate himself from the reproach of ever having in any way condoned Agrippina's acts.

"Believe me," he said with emotion, "a hundred times has the voice of the inward divinity urged me vehemently to declare to all people that they would be justified in thinking no good of Agrippina. One thing alone has withheld me: my anxious regard for you, the blameless son of a guilty woman. I knew how deeply you revered your mother; that you alone, in all Rome, wore a bandage over your eyes, and never guessed the things which often enough brought the blush of shame and rage to our brows."

Nero was listening in breathless anxiety and convulsively gripped his companion's wrist, while Seneca went on:

"No, beloved Caesar, I am not raving; what I am saying is not the outcome of a disordered brain. Ask Tigellinus; ask even Burrus, if you please,—Burrus, who forgives her crimes only because, rough as he is on the surface, he has a softer heart than a young poet. . . ."

"What am I to understand by that?"

Seneca, dropping each word with leaden emphasis, replied:

"Well—he is in love with Agrippina:—and her lover."

"You dare to say this to me!" cried Nero in a piercing and terrible voice. "Burrus her lover? Caesar's mother loves that rough soldier!"

Seneca ceased. Caesar sat with a fixed stare.

"What a monster!" he stammered out at last. "But who will pledge his word—even if it were, like you, a philosopher who knew what man can be—that this history is anything more than a foolish tale invented by her enemies, and circulated by the credulous job?"

"If you will but promise her a free pardon, Locusta herself will readily confess the truth; for in every case in which poison played a part she was the accomplice of our imperial criminal."

"Seneca, my friend and teacher, I would take your word for it though my spirit should wither with shame and grief! But, woe is me! What can I do?" And he sank back in his chair as if utterly exhausted.

The minister, taking no notice of the young emperor's despair, went on:

"And do you know how your half brother Britannicus came by his death?—I was not one of those who lamented his exclusion from the throne. Britannicus, though a noble youth, was not to be compared with Agrippina's son. The empire gained by his disinheritance. But why need Agrippina trample that promising young life in the dust? Britannicus was unselfish; he would have been your friend, your best adviser. His cool, clear judgment would have supplemented your glowing imagination. Posterity would have spoken of you as of Damon and Pythias, of Pylades and Orestes. . . ."

"Nay, do not speak of Orestes." Nero murmured with a shudder.

"Why not?"

"It makes me shiver! Orestes. . . . killed his mother."

"And very rightly; for his mother and her paramour had killed his beloved father." Nero's gesture was one of deprecation.

"Well, as to Britannicus," Seneca began again. "Agrippina murdered him, too—and with such indescribable cunning, such base perfidy, that one may doubt whether history can show another such example.

"Britannicus was forewarned: nothing would he eat or drink till a slave had first tasted it in his presence. But your mother contrived to poison that which nature supplies purer and less contaminated than any other earthly thing. She desired that his spiced wine should be served to him so hot that he should ask for water to cool it. His *praegustator* had already tasted the steaming fluid in the murrhine cup, and the liquor was harmless. But no sooner had Britannicus poured in some of the poisoned water and swallowed a mouthful than he fell back, a corpse."

"What?" cried Nero. "But I was witness to the frightful occurrence. They said it was a fainting fit; he did not die of the stroke till some days later."

"That was what we were told—we and the world; for the meal could not be interrupted. But, believe me, my beloved son, I have proofs of this crime, too."

Nero flung himself forward across the table, thrusting his trembling fingers through his hair. Seneca went up to him gently and laid a hand on his shoulder, whispering as though moved to compassion:

"Let me tell you no more. Only one thing you yet must hear: the attempt to assassinate Flavius Scaevinus was again a plot of Agrippina's vengeance. His speech stung her to the quick. . . ."

"Leave me, leave me," groaned Caesar, in heart-rending tones of anguish. "I know enough!"

At this moment they heard in the atrium the watchman's voice announcing the hour.

"It is time," said Seneca. "Control yourself, my dear young friend! Nero the son is no more! Heaven grant that Nero the Emperor may shine all the more glorious from the summit of his undivided empire!—Nay, my boy, no tears. Look out on the world with the bold glance of an eagle as he soars towards the sun. Show these northern barbarians that you are the very incarnation of the glory and splendor of the Roman name—you, the beloved of your people! Be a man, an Augustus!"

Claudius Nero slowly rose. This hour of horror had indeed steeled and hardened him. With lofty dignity he stood in front of his old tutor, who also seemed at once to have forgotten what had so moved and shaken him. He looked enquiringly into the young sovereign's face: it was like a marble statue of an Apollo, radiant not only with beneficient glory, but with destroying lightnings. Those blooming lips, which for many weeks had worn only a blissful smile and parted only for kisses, were now set in calm determination. Yes indeed, the rebellious Chatti, as they looked on this brilliant young Nero might well say: "Woe to the nations when Nero Caesar is their Foe!"

He went out into the oecus, where his escort had been waiting a quarter of an hour.

BOOK II

CHAPTER I.

THE senators had meanwhile assembled in the atrium in surprising numbers; though a large proportion of them had already left the city for their summer quarters, they had come into Rome for this occasion, in obedience to the empress-mother's commands. Epaphroditus, Caesar's private secretary, had received them, and led them with due reverence to the cushioned seats which had been placed in curved lines between the pillars of the colonnade on each side.

The morning sun now cast a band of light as broad as a man's height on the wall of the chamber of archives. The mass of flowers sprinkled by slaves with a fine spray of fresh water, glistened like a spring garden bright with dew, and the gorgeous carpets blazed in more vivid hues as the sun rose higher. Seneca had all his life made it a point of honor that such ceremonials as this reception of the Chatti envoys should be perfect down to the smallest details.

Caesar came forth, surrounded by his splendid suite, and after greeting the assembled senators in a distinct voice: "My lords I bid you welcome!" was making his way towards the dais; and, almost at the same instant, Seneca made his appearance outside the vestibule and offered his hand to the stalwart, grey-bearded leader of the German chiefs. They had dismounted from their long-maned chargers.

Nero responded to the senators' cry of: "Hail Caeser!" with a gracious wave of the hand; then he seated himself on one of the thrones under the canopy. On his right hand stood Burrus and a few military tribunes. On his left were Sophonius Tigellinus; Otho, husband of the fair Poppaea; Lucanus, a young poet whom during the past few months Seneca had done his utmost to protect and push; Epaphroditus, the private secretary; and a few more state or court officials with their most distinguished adherents.

Beyond these, on both sides, there were detachments of praetorians in gilded armor, with tall scarlet horse-tail plumes on their shining helmets, their swords at their sides and their long lances held upright, like men on guard. At the head of the rows of senators, to the right and left, sat the consuls in office whose functions, since the new constitution of the government was merely nominal; still, the appointment was not the less eagerly contested.

The prime minister had provided the German deputation with a praetorian guard of honor, which now marched in through the ostium and took up a position in ranks on the left of the entrance. Next came Seneca, walking with the chief of the Chatti, Lollarius by name. The rest—all finely-grown men of from thirty to forty years of age, and all blue-eyed and fair, excepting two whose hair had a darker, southern hue—followed close behind Lollarius, but stopped when they reached the middle of the atrium, while their leader was courteously conducted to the podium by Seneca.

"All powerful Caesar" the minister said, "this brave and illustrious man, who with his noble comrades has come to the Palatium as a friend of the Roman Empire, is Lollarius, prince of a province, and foremost in the council of the Chatti; a famous captain in the field, and perfectly acquainted with our speech, our laws, and our customs."

Having spoken Seneca stood aside, close to Sophonius

Tigellinus, who gazed with surprise and curiosity at the German chief's brawny proportions.

Nero rose, went down to the lowest step of the podium, and held out his hand to the envoy with a winning smile.

"You are welcome—you and yours—to our sacred City of the Seven Hills. Uprightness and courage shine in your eyes. That I like. I offer you our honorable friendship, in the name of the assembled Fathers and of the free and independent Roman people. For it was to seek such friendship that you came to Rome—as we are informed by our propraetor, your neighbor by the Rhine."

"As thou sayest, omnipotent Caesar," replied Lollarius in excellent Latin. For he had some years since paid a visit to the capital of the world,—as his son was now doing—to study the statecraft and arts of war of the Romans. "When thy representative had granted our requests, I could not see why we Chatti should quarrel with Rome—though I deeply deplore the fact that the imperial legions have by degrees made Roman soil of many a German territory."

"Why deplore it?" asked Caesar.

"Because we Northmen, whom the Romans still regard as separate tribes, are far more closely allied than the Italians and the Hispanians; because we might form a single and mighty empire of one race and nation, were it not that Rome alienates some and that others are crippled by miserable dissensions. We alone, with the noble Sicambri, truly understand the close connection of all the German races,the supremacy of the idea of a State which you Romans have so grandly worked out—the idea,in short, of the Fatherland."

Nero now went up the steps again and slowly reseated himself; two slaves, at a glance from the prime minister, placed a gilt chair on the podium.

"That I understand," said Caesar benevolently."I beg you to be seated in that chair. An ambassadors's person is as sacred to the laws of nations as to those of hospitality, and it is not seemly that he should be kept standing when the formalities of greeting are ended."

For a moment Lollarius hesitated. Then he went up the steps with perfect self-possession, as though conscious that his race were destined at a later day to feel themselves as much at home in this palace as the imperious despot now before him.

"Lollarius," Nero began again when the envoy was seated, "you see; the mere fact of our meeting has been enough to settle the matter we purposed to treat of: So long as open and honorable war is not declared between us, not a Roman shall henceforth dare to cross your frontier on an unlawful errand. You must pledge yourself to us to the same effect.—And in all other particulars we will live in amity. Your people shall sell to us your products of fishing, their handsome furs, delicious game, and the salmon from their river Logana. From us you may obtain tools, Tarentine woollen goods, milk-white robes for your wives and maidens, girdles and pins, and above all our great Roman wines. For, as I learn, the cheering grape does not thrive with you; its place is taken by a strange brew of wheat and barley with which, wonderful to say, you make a certain imitation of our wines of Italy."

"My lord," replied Lollarius, smiling as he stroked his thick, grizzled beard, "we have two kinds of liquor: a sweet and a bitter. The former we call mead, and the other beer; and verily, when the mead-bowl goes round, while a war-song is sung in chorus, and juicy slices of the deer's haunch or of bear ham smoke before us, even thou, oh Caesar, wouldst admit, in spite of Roman splendor, that we Germans know how to live."

"I do not doubt it," replied Nero. "Every custom has its justification, every way of life has its advantages.—Well, we are agreed then! Give me your hand: Peace and friendship.—Merely for form's sake my secretary Epaphroditus shall draw up a proper document; not because there can be any doubt in the matter, but to be preserved among our archives. For you, too, of course, have some official building or sanctuary where your important deeds are preserved."

"Our priests and chiefs are not ignorant of letters," said Lollarius.

"Then to-morrow you shall have the documents to sign," replied Nero. "But now that this is settled, let me ask you to tell us something of yourself and your companions. Who are the men who came with you? You might have brought them in here."

Lollarius rose; but Caesar detained him.

"Begin with yourself," he said graciously. "Your name is Lollarius. It sounds almost Latin."

"It is modified into Latin for your benefit, for you would be less able to master the rough northern sound. In German my name is Lautharto, which being interpreted is Great Heart. The castle of my father stands on the banks of the Lahn, or as you call it Logana, not far from the spot where the beautiful Wisacha flows into it. Further off rises the wooded Vogelsberg, or Bird mountain, so called by reason of its innumerable wild-fowl whose crowing rings through the dim forest like the weird croaking of Wotan's ravens. Oh! our land is a splendid one!"

"It is strange," observed Nero, "but we Romans love neither forest ranges nor rocky gorges. We crave for broad and flowery meads, for laurel-groves, and above all for the sea-shore. Have you no sea, no lake even in your neighborhood?"

"No, Caesar. The Lahn and the Wisacha must suffice us. Your beating surges are to us a thing unknown. But yet, to be exact, at about a hundred paces from my dwelling, the Wisacha tumbles over a pile of boulders so suddenly, and from such a height, that its roar is not unlike the thunder ot the Tyrrhenian sea. This fall is called by the people 'Der Guss,' or 'Die Giessen.' * and my castle is called the fortress by the Giessen."

For a while Nero sat chatting with the bearded chief of the Chatti, as though the ruler of the Roman empire were almost inclined to make his appearance, during the coming summer-months, as a guest among the forests of the Logana. Meanwhile he now and then glanced at Seneca, who each time replied, hardly moving his lips: "You still have time, my lord."

At last Lollarius descended the steps and fetched in the three noblest chiefs of his following. One of these, a golden-haired, ruddy-faced young man named Heilo, was charged to offer to Caesar a magnificent gift: twelve living aruochs, which had been brought in vans, constructed for the purpose, along the great highway on the left bank of the Rhine as far as Vesontio, and from thence to Massilia, where they were shipped for Ostia. The vessel conveying the huge beasts was now lying at anchor under the Aventine, and Heilo besought the emperor to vouchsafe at his earliest convenience to receive this token of friendship sent by the Chatti.

Nero expressed his thanks, and as Seneca still stood calm, he desired that the rest of the deputation should be admitted. After talking to each in turn, he raised his right hand. At this signal twelve servants in scarlet tunics came forward from the colonnade, and gave to each of the twelve envoys a costly sword with a gold hilt and sheath, as a return gift from the emperor.

Those senators who at first had secretly demurred to Caesar's too great affability, thought it judicious to join in the shout of applause which was now set up by Flavius Scaevinus, and some other members of their illustrious body. This applause was not without a purpose; some of Agrippina's declared adherents could scarcely control themselves. As the minutes went on their dismayed countenances expressed more clearly their impatient wonder: "Where is Agrippina? Why is she not here to take her place by the side of her son whom she made Caesar?"

Agrippina was still on the clattering high-road in the carruca with its wide awning.

The prime minister had enquired of her majesty in due form at what hour the reception of the Chatti was to take

*The pouring.

place and received her reply. Agrippina had allowed ample time for the journey. And was it Seneca's fault, when Caesar suddenly gave his orders that the ceremony was to take place just half an hour earlier than the empress-mother had wished?

She reclined without a suspicion by the side of her companion, the green-eyed tiger-cat, and laughed to think how absurdly easy it was to tighten the reins when a refractory boy thought he had the bit between his teeth. She believed herself entirely mistress of the situation, and silently applauded her own signal statesmanship, which could so skilfully second the dispensations of chance. Yes, indeed; for that girl Acte might have been dangerous to Agrippina's love of power; in the course of a prolonged connection with Nero she might gradually have attained to a degree of insight which would have enabled her to perceive how little science was needed for governing the world. That passionate love-dream was only the prelude. In the course of a few months other feelings, other desires and hopes would have matured in her soul. . . . If, for instance she should have presented her Caesar with a child—a son! What a stimulus would that have been to the mother to strive for influence and dominion!— Fate had here achieved a master-stroke; Agrippina might rest content. A gracious smile hovered on her lips.

"Well, Acerronia?" she said, at the conclusion of these pleasing reflections. "You seem very dull and indifferent to-day. Not once have your looked out of the carriage window, though Pharax, handsome Pharax himself, leads our armed escort. But lately you were all joy and triumph, like a hundred thousand larks thirsting for love, and now, on a sudden, so reserved? Has anything come between you? What is it?"

"No," replied Acerronia with strange asperity. From any other mortal, half as rough a reply as this "No" would have meant loss of favor for ever. But Acerronia enjoyed exceptional immunity. Agrippina took her hand.

"What has vexed you, my sweet?" she asked in motherly

tones. "I noticed when we started that there was a shadow on your face."

"That Pharax!" exclaimed Acerronia contemptuously.

"He is bethrothed to you, and unless the gods interfere, he will be your husband before the autumn. I was forced to promise. . . ."

"Forced?" said Acerronia, "who could force you?"

"Well, he implored, he entreated me. . . ."

"And how many entreat without being heard?"

"I do not understand you," said Agrippina. "Have you changed your mind? But you liked Pharax from the first time you met."

"Yes, I liked him very well, and still like him. But one thing I do not like—and that is that *you* should have liked him so well."

"You little fool," said Agrippina laughing. "Are you dreaming, or have you been drinking? Why should it vex you that the husband I have chosen for you should be a man I approve of? Would you like it better if I thought him odious?"

"Perhaps—for I sometimes suspect. . . ."

"Well?"

"Dare I speak out?"

"Certainly."

"Well then, I believe that you yourself are over head and ears in love with him."

Agrippina looked extremely grave.

"You may thank the gods that Caesar did not hear you say that. He would have had you crucified."

"And so he may!" Acerronia muttered. She bit her lips and frowned.

"Let us have no more nonsense!" said the empress severely.

"Well then, tell the slaves to repeat to you the things. . . . the. . . . the. . . ."

"You ought to sink into the earth for shame! you, the daughter of a knight of Corduba, can listen to the low prattle of slaves! Now, indeed, I understand you!—Then you must know, Acerronia, that I myself overheard what two such husseys said to each other as they were trimming the hedges in the park at Albanum. They dared to speak evil of their empress; for such low-born creatures do not know how to distinguish the condescension of the sovereign for political reasons from the tenderness of the woman. I speak out, without reserve, for it disgusts me to find you in this foul mire. At a sign from me those slaves would die. But Agrippina esteems her immortal name too highly to feel herself insulted by disgusting slaves.

The empress spoke with such dignity and solemnity that she triumphed over Acerronia's doubts.

"Forgive me," the girl sobbed, hiding her face on her mistress's shoulder as though seeking protection from herself. Then suddenly sitting up, and clenching her fingers like claws, she went on: "But I am no sovereign of high birth; I may condescend to punish such vile, lying lips if I ever again hear them talking such scandal. I swear by Jupiter. . . ."

"Gently, my child," said Agrippina interrupting her. "Look, we are already among the bustle of the houses. Dry your tears; you have a part to play. This is the first time you have appeared in public before the senate."

"Why did not Pallas come, too?"

"He is ill of fever. He sent me word that he was ill last night."

"I confess to you, madam, that for my part I have no wish at all to stand to be stared at by those solemn dolts the senators."

"You use such expressions! Solemn dolts, indeed! And what are you thinking of? Today, at such an important ceremonial. . . .!"

"My red hair is even more important. You yourself say it is beautiful—almost as beautiful as your own raven-black tresses; and the older men are the greater fools they are!"

The hoofs of the horses were now thundering on the

251

pavement of the Via Sacra.

Tigellinus had by this time been informed of the approach of the travelling carriage and its glittering escort. While Caesar was still talking to the Chatti, the Agrigentine stole away to receive the empress-mother and her suite in the vestibule.

"Madam," he said, "make haste, I beg. This way, if you please, through the side-door. The seats of the envoys stop the way into the ostium."

"What? already?" cried the empress and a flush of anger dyed her cheeks.

"Yes, already. You are rather behind time, to the great regret of Caesar and the assembled Fathers."

"I? How so? We are as punctual as soldiers relieving guard. What is the meaning of this?"

Tigillinus, affecting the deepest submission, shrugged his shoulders.

"Our Lord and Sovereign willed it. I represented to him—but he thought that the Chatti, having come with so good an end in view, ought not to be kept waiting. But there is still plenty of time. Your presence will give the crowning sanction to this great historical compact."

Agrippina's blood was boiling. Without waiting for Acerronia and her attendants, she majestically walked forward through the end door on the left hand side. The senators rose. Agrippina turned to the dais. At this, Nero, strongly controlling all the abhorrence which surged up in him, calmly descended from the throne, hastened to meet his mother, and greeted her with the usual ceremonial kiss.

"What a delightful surprise!" he exclaimed—for this was the part Seneca had advised him to play. "Our affairs of state are settled; we can now enjoy with double satisfaction the intimacy of the family circle."

The murmur of applause which rose from the majority of the senators made the empress-mother aware of the completeness of her downfall. She felt that she must become nothing less than ridiculous if she did not put a good face on a bad business, and the perfection of her self-command was a real triumph.

"I have to thank you," she said, kissing her son on the brow, "for having dealt so quickly and successfully with this complicated and difficult matter.—It seems to me that this noble assembly, Romans and Chatti alike, are only waiting for Caesar to dismiss them. But before you do so, pray express to them my heartfelt interest in the conclusion of our treaty of friendship, and then follow us to breakfast in the smaller oecus."

She bowed with dignity and left the throne room; but her indignant soul was hot with rage and consuming hatred.

"This is Seneca's doing!" she snarled between her teeth as she rejoined Acerronia. "I have for some time observed that the wretch was distant and perfidious. The history of this affair will be the talk of the city—of the whole Latin country—of all the provinces! My position is irrecoverably shaken! It will everywhere be rumored that Agrippina has abdicated.— Abdicated? Never! Time will show!—Patience and caution! But be silent, Acerronia. Not a man under Jupiter's heaven, and least of all that ungrateful boy, must ever suspect how deeply this blow has entered into my soul, or the mob would shout for joy.—Patience, and yet patience! I can quietly win back all he has wrenched from me. Oh! I quite understand; this is his revenge for Acte! I am glad indeed that her accursed body became food for the fishes!"

CHAPTER II.

The pilot and two sailors who had escaped alive from the dreadful shipwreck could give no information as to the fate of Acte. Everyone supposed that she had been drowned with the rest of the persons on board the ill-fated vessel. When sturdy Gauls and muscular Iberians were conquered in the struggle with the hostile waves, how could a frail young girl have won the victory?

But they were mistaken. Before the ship had sunk, Acte, throwing her arms round a plank split off the stern, had flung herself overboard. She was unhurt and in full possession of her senses, and she presently came to the surface, still clinging to the plank, but out of reach of the sailors, who one and all sank after a short and ineffectual struggle; for seamen by profession are notoriously unable to swim.

The girl alone held out. Accustomed as she was to float for half an hour at a time on the heaving element, it needed but a small effort of her supple limbs, aided by the supporting plank, to keep her head above water. She made no attempt to progress; any idea of reaching the shore at such a distance would have been madness. A fishing boat, or a trading vessel might perhaps come within hail: that was her only hope of rescue. So what she must aim at was to save her strength, and not lose courage and her presence of mind.

Her trembling spirit went through all the phases of fear which, as the minutes went on, threatened to chill the pulses of her throbbing heart. She told herself that her blissful dream of love could not be fated to end so horribly. She tried to summon up the steadfast self-confidence she had been able to display to Pallas, and to believe that Nero's love hovered, like a guardian spirit, even over the endless waste of waters. In spite of the sacred fervor of her feelings she could not resist the conclusion that her situation was a desperate one.

Meanwhile the spring breeze had covered the waves with white crests, as far as the eye could reach. The unhappy girl could not hope to be seen from any vessel, unless it chanced to pass quite close to her; for her pale form, her light-colored dress, and fair hair mingled indistinguishably with the snowy sheets of foam. Up and down, up and down; the waves rose and fell with the regularity of mighty breathing. Now Acte was on the trembling crest; then she found herself sliding helplessly, as if she were part of the heaving flood, down into the dark blue hollow, only to be lifted to the top once more. The roar and rush quite drowned the sound of her repeated shouts for help, and her clear voice sounded thin and dull— or was it her deadly and increasing terror which deprived it of its clear silvery ring?

Out there, on the western horizon, she could see the huge merchant ships making for Panormus and looking like pale, fleeting ghosts; but not one of them came out of its course to rescue her. The fishing boats of Antium did not venture so far out to sea in such a wind. The vessels sailing to Ostia from Gaul or Spain took a more northerly course. On which side could quaking anguish look for help?

The wind was rising, and Neptune's horses tossed their flying manes higher and higher. Surge after surge broke and fell over the trembling creature; a stream of water from her front hair incessantly drenched her white face so that she could scarcely open her smarting eyes.

In this agony her heart turned to the Omnipotent God as

256

revealed in the land of Judaea by the Carpenter's Son of Nazareth. "Oh, Jesus," she cried, and then prayed with silent fervor for deliverance. She offered her stricken heart as a sacrifice to the Redeemer. "Take everything," she groaned in her anguish. "My life henceforth shall be devoted to the Faith; I will wander from place to place, from village to village, like the holy Apostles, to carry Thy teaching even to the eternal ice of the Goths and Skandri. . . ."

And behold! the Saviour of the world seemed to smile upon her. New strength revived her fainting soul; the strength of hope.

But then the form of the young lover whom only yesterday she had cradled so fondly in her arms rose, flashing like a meteor, between her and the image of the gentle, tender Galilaean. The Redeemer's features grew sterner and graver, and He turned away His face.—No, she could not pray. She had sinned a deadly sin before the God of the Christians.—She was a renegade, a betrayer!

The priest had often, indeed, spoken of the grace of an Almighty God, of how He is ready to receive the sinner back into the fold of the saints, if only a true craving for light and forgiveness, and repentance for past sin were to be found in the soul of the erring lamb.

But Acte did not repent. Repentance would have been a negation of her very existence, the utter annihilation of her self.

No, she did not repent! So there could be no rescue for the impenitent sinner from this fearful hour of death.—Acte shuddered.

And then—mysteriously, stealthily—a breath of strange memories came over her. Had she not once known other gods; less austere and even more human in thought and feeling than the God of the Nazarenes? Had she not in her tenderest years raised her eyes in faith to the throne of golden Aphrodite? Aphrodite had risen from the billows of the sea. She, then, was familiar with the raging element. She would be gracious and still the storm that tossed it, if only Acte besought her devoutly—Acte, the love-stricken! For love meant sacrifice to the goddess, humbly laid on her altars, and world-forgetting kisses!—Such kisses as Nero's lips could give were no abomination in her sight, but a good work and pleasing to her divinity.

Acte trembled with three-fold horror to find how persistently this memory of her childhood haunted her. The white roofs of Corinth rose before her mind's eye: she heard the great Apostle's solemn admonitions, she saw his solemn, impressive face and the reverent assembly of the faithful.— That had been at a time when Nicodemus had spent three months at the isthmus, and had been baptized there. Paul's tones of thunder had sunk into her heart like the trump of the judgment day. Eternal torment, the pains of hell, and utter damnation—these were the lot of the reprobate who, having once known the grace of the Lord, should slide back into the snare of unbelief.

"Oh God, the only true God, forgive my deadly sin!" she groaned. "Save me, oh save me for Thy beloved Son's sake. Amen."

But nothing happened.

All round her lay the comfortless raving waste, the myriad throats yawning to swallow her, and no gleam of promise, no immortal hand put forth to help her in her misery.

The old gods had lost their power; they were but shades, vain phantoms. And the true God, who had sent the Saviour on earth, thrust her out to perish without pity.

"Nero, I die loving you!" she murmured once more.

She felt herself sinking. A blue-green twilight was all she saw, a chaotic murmur of waters filled her ears, fantastic monsters, swimming amid pale lightnings, were rushing and snorting about her. Then all was silence.—

When Acte opened her eyes once more she was lying in a handsomely furnished bed-room. Her aching head was resting on a pillow covered with Cordovan linen. The coverlet was of the finest purple Tarentine wool, mixed with threads of gold.

On her left a half-grown girl was kneeling by her side and busy rubbing her listless hand with some perfumed spirit. An older woman, was leaning over her and laying a handkerchief dipped in snow water on her forehead.

At the foot of the bed she saw a pale and beautiful young woman, standing as if chiselled out of marble; she had brown, stag-like eyes which seemed to flinch a little as they met Acte's enquiring gaze.

"Where am I?" asked Acte.

"Among people who mean well toward you," replied the older woman, smoothing the wet compress with her wrinkled hand.

"Oh, what infinite happiness!"

"Yes indeed, you poor child."

"And how did I get here?"

"By the aid of the gods, and of a kind-hearted sea-farer."

"But I sank—deeper and deeper—and I thought all was at an end. . . ."

"You might well think so. Even that good Abyssus, who saved you from the waves, thought at first that all trouble would be in vain."

"Abyssus? I never heard that name before."

"He is an Egyptian, and pilot of our mistress's pleasure barge."

"And he saved me?"

"Yes, my child."

"But how was it possible? All round, far. far away, there was not a sail to be seen—no, not one! And I had prayed so earnestly. . . . ; oh!it is coming over me again—I am sinking—help, help, for Christ's sake!"

She shut her eyes and for a minute of two lay senseless. Then she looked up again more brightly than before.

"It is nothing," she said, with a smile, to the old woman, who bent anxiously over her. "But tell me how it all happened."

The attendant glanced enquiringly at the tall lady, who

was still standing motionless at the foot of the bed and seemed to be collecting her thoughts with an effort. As her mistress made no objection, the good woman briefly gave Acte the information she asked for:

"We went out at dawn this morning rowing far out to sea. Our mistress could not sleep, and the fresh air might do her good. As the sun rose the wind rose too; it had only just gone down a little, and now it blew three times as strongly. We turned round at once, and made straight for the harbor. Well, that was how it happened. Out in the middle of the waves we saw the pretty creature who is now lying on the pillows here. You were clinging convulsively to a piece of wood. Our Abyssus spied you and did not take long to consider; he leapt overboard like an arrow, and at the very moment when your hands were losing their hold, he seized you by your floating hair. The boat was dancing like a mad thing, the rowers did not know what to do; I prayed to Father Neptune in despair. Twice they shouted from the helm: 'Save yourself Abyssus and leave the drowned thing to her fate!'— But our mistress gave her orders, and Abyssus is dauntless, so whining was of no use.—At last he caught the rope, and tied it to your body. So you were drawn up. Then he came himself—he is a brave swimmer; he was half-stunned, but delighted to have won the victory. The mistress gave him her hand and said nothing,—not a word; but we saw that it went to his heart. I believe he wiped away his tears—and now he watches you as if you were his own child."

"Oh! how can I thank you," Acte murmured. "What is your name?"

"I am called Rabonia," said the old woman.

"Good Rabonia. What have I done to deserve that you should care for my poor life? I feel as if I had had a long, long dream, oppressive and heartbreaking. And to wake and see such a good, kind face is a blessing. . . ."

"You have lain here in a fever for eight days," said Rabonia. "It began to diminish yesterday. Abyssus will now be able to assure us that you will recover."

"Abyssus? The man who saved me?"

"The same. He is not only a good seaman but learned in medicine; and, as I believe, so skilful that even Caesar's physician scarcely excels him."

Acte gave a start. The name of Caesar filled her heart with a glow of hope and longing. Suddenly she sat up, and fixed her eyes in a rigid stare on the beautiful face of the young woman who still looked down on her in silence.

"Is Satan tormenting me?" she moaned, pointing a trembling finger at the motionless figure. "Octavia! Caesar's wife?"

"I am she," replied Octavia calmly. "Fear nothing. Under this roof you will find shelter from all the tempests of the world."

"But do you know me then?" cried Acte in desperate trouble. "No, you cannot guess—Woe is me! Woe, woe, woe! Why did you save me from the waters only to torture me slowly to death?"

"Compose yourself," said the empress. "You are having a relapse."

"No, indeed no," cried Acte pathetically. "I am clearer than ever." She snatched the cool handkerchief from her head as if she thought to gain energy. "Send away your waiting-woman! I implore you madam, by all you hold sacred, send them out of the room. Indeed, indeed, you do not know me; for if you did you would not be so kind and compassionate."

Rabonia and the girl went away.

"Empress," said Acte with a groan, when they were alone, "swear to me that you will give me a choice of how I will die."

"What can I understand by that? Do you mean to kill yourself when you will have just escaped death?"

"Not I," said Acte despondently. "But you, madam, will have me killed when you have heard my name. Why it is eight days ago. All Rome knows of it. I am astonished that you should have no suspicions! Oh, I am almost suffocating!—I am Acte, Nicodemus' freedwoman. . . . ''

"And Caesar's mistress." Octavia added with a melancholy smile. "I knew it, though I never saw your face till now."

"You knew it? And you did not stab me in my sleep? You did not drop poison into my ears? You did not put out my eyes with hot irons?"

"No, you poor, misled creature. So compose yourself. You are as pale as if you were dying on the spot!"

"Merciful Almighty!" sobbed the girl, wringing her hands. "What sins I have committed! Is it possible that I should ever find forgiveness? Lady, if I could but tell you.— You?—it is you who have sheltered and cherished me? Oh! that I could but sink into the earth this moment, and this overwhelming shame might be buried with me!"

"Do not think me better than I am," said Octavia. "When I first stood by your bed and heard you calling in your delirium on the name I will not speak,—then indeed I felt as if I must have revenge—But afterwards, when you began to cry for him as a child cried for its mother, a strange revulsion came over me. I need only have left you to your fate; fever would have made an end of you without any help from me. But there was a voice in my heart which counselled better things. I took pity on you and Abyssus, my Egyptian physician, sat by your side whole nights through, and his conscientious care has succeeded as we hoped."

"Hoped? How could you hope it, when I was your enemy?"

"Yes, you are Acte; and it is quite possible that in saving you I have saved misery to myself. Ah! I know it well, he loved you—deeply, truly, and with all the strength of his nature. But I could not do otherwise."

"You are beside yourself, Octavia," cried Acte looking up at her in awe. "No mortal woman can do this; no never! if indeed she knows what love is."

Octavia colored to the roots of her hair. "Love him!" she murmured sadly, raising her eyes to heaven. "I would give my very existence if only for one short hour his heart could be mine as wholly as it is yours!"

The womanly pride which had supported so far, now suddenly broke down. Tears poured down her cheeks and she turned away.

"You," she went on presently "are of lowly birth, but I am not ashamed of having envied you. In love rank counts for nothing, nor illustrious birth—nay, perhaps not even law, for all these were against you. The dignity of empire, which I once prized as a grace and gift of immortals, I now contemn as mere wind-blown chaff. I would be the lowest of slaves, if only I could ensure his once looking into my eyes as he has often gazed into yours. Yes, I envy you!—but I do not hate you. It was cruel misery to hear the echo of your infinite happiness in the ravings of a fever-stricken girl; it almost killed me with sorrow. But I lived it down. My love for him is so deep that it can reflect a glow of pardon even on you."

Acte seemed petrified.

"Do you not yet believe me?" said Octavia, smiling through her tears. "Come, give me your hand, I forgive you.—As soon as you are well again you shall go whither you will, no matter where. What good would it do me to banish you, as Agrippina wished? You would be out of his sight, to be sure; but his soul would cling then as now to what he had lost."

Acte sank back on the cushions, utterly exhausted. She had seized with trembling fingers Octavia's slender hand and pressed it passionately to her lips. Now her grasp relaxed; she was as white as wax; and Octavia, mastered by the violence of her struggling feelings, sank on the bed by her side with a deep groan, and both women slept.

CHAPTER III.

WORK is the true panacea. If it had been winter time, and if Caesar, in his anguish, could have flung himself into domestic and foreign politics, who knows how events might have turned out? But the sun was fast mounting to the sign of Leo. State business was at a lull; Rome, in the opinion of the world of fashion was uninhabitable—so there was no alternative but a country life in Campania, with its extravagant and romantic pleasures.

It was a brilliant night at beautiful Baiae. The noisy bustle of the harbor road was dying away. Here and there, from the sailors' taverns, a drinking song rang out across the bay; a repose bred of satiety reigned in the lighted villas. Weary citizens were reclining on their couches with every door wide open, to rest at least though the temperature was too high for sleep.

But on the hill, at a few hundred paces from the shore, there was a blaze of pine torches, and the glowing clouds of smoke rose almost straight up to heaven. Here, in Salvius Otho's rose-garden, a select party sat feasting till a late hour, emptying cup after cup with reckless hilarity. Salvius Otho, the owner of the house, had been appointed master of the revel by his illustrious friend and guest the emperor, and he discharged his genial duties with admirable grace. Richly-dressed slaves incessantly refilled the silver cups; bewitching Hispanians with flowing hair moved lightly about, like winged genii, in closely-fitting garments of sheeny crape of Cos, offering *bellaria,* the spiced dessert with which Roman wine-bibbers were wont to stimulate their drinking-powers. Otho, as king of the feast, occupied the place of honor at the head of the table and reclined side by side with a Greek lady from Epidamnus who had lately been living in the capital. At her right hand was the all-conquering Sophonius Tigellinus, with the wife of a senator. This young lady, Septimia by name, behaved as if she had lost her wits. Her gaze seemed really to pierce her companion's dark eyes. In spite of the length of his name she had vowed to drink it through within an hour; that is, to empty as many cups to the popular favorite's health as there were letters in the word Tigellinus. She was now at the U.

On the master's left was Seneca, drinking too, in obedience to Horace's precept: that it is well sometimes to break the bounds of moderation. In the philosopher's opinion Nero was at this moment on the high-road to rejecting the last remains of his mother's influence. But Caesar needed a certain amount of stupefying to enable him to carry out his opposition. In spite of every disclosure as to Agrippina's past life, a son's feeling for his mother still stirred in his soul. In hours of solitude Caesar would seek excuses for his mother's crimes—"for she had sinned only for his sake;" so the minister judged it favorable to the cause when Caesar, instead of brooding as he had been wont, flung himself gaily into the maddest whirl of life.

Seneca's neighbor was not much quieter than Septimia, but she was a more fashionable fool, and fashion required that, with Seneca, she should talk philosophy. She did not, however, envy her friend, her more brilliant partner, for her conceit was greater than her desire for homage.

Nero had taken his place at the bottom of the table, so that, as Otho flatteringly remarked, the bottom was in fact the top. Caesar's immediate neighbor was Poppaea, Otho's wife. The intervals when the wine ceased to circulate had been amply filled up, in the traditional fashion, by dancers, flute-players, jugglers and reciters. It was now past midnight and Chloris, the most popular of singers, had arrived with an escort of torch-bearers. Following in the track of metropolitan fashion, she had left Rome at the ides of May for Baiae, where she had indefatigably continued to delight audiences in the villas of the wealthy aristocracy. Besides this she had won the devotion of all the men of fashion, who besieged her at every step and called Jupiter Ultor to witness their amorous perjuries.

She now lifted the metal plectrum with infinite grace, and sang a love-song by Melinno. In the light of the unflickering torches she looked like Melpomene.

"The sweet innocent!" murmured Septimia, putting her head close to the Sicilian's shoulder.

There was something ironical in her tone. Tigellinus, not generally a man who would take up the cudgels for a woman's good fame, felt himself aggrieved. But he was annoyed to begin with, by Septimia's love-sick readiness to throw herself blindly into his arms without giving him time to conquer her. So he said: "In point of fact the fair girl is spotless. The mere sight of her refreshes me like fragrant dew."

"Dear me!" said the fair Septimia, somewhat uneasily, "I did not know that you, of all men, thought innocence so engaging."

"And why not?"

"Because you are reputed to be its greatest foe."

"A clever epigram. But gossip slanders me."

"Indeed? So your long list of trophies is a myth? Did you not confess an hour ago that your campaigns under Aphrodite's banner had not been wholly uncrowned with victory?"

"May I remind the fair Septimia that her ruby lips have wandered from the original subject? We were not discussing me or my 'exploits.'"

"True, we were speaking of Chloris. You defend her. Can it be that my friend Tigellinus is so sure of her innocence because he has recently received a rebuff?"

"Not I," replied Tigellinus quietly. "But others have—doughty champions too. For instance—but it is not wise to mention names."

"You can trust me with them."

"Impossible."

"Otho perhaps?" she murmured with a mischievious smile.

"What are you thinking of, Septimia? Otho worships Poppaea!"

"No doubt. But she ill-requites his affection. Did not Poppaea's name glitter on your list of conquests?"

"No, fair Septima. I should have shared the same fate in that quarter as your husband encountered at the hands of the lovely Chloris."

"My husband, Cneius Camillus, the most queer donkey that every jogged in matrimonial harness?"

"Even so."

"I laugh at your inventions."

"I am relating facts—as a just punishment as your sneer at Chloris."

Tigellinus turned away. The woman, young and as fascinating as she was, filled him with loathing.

Septimia tossed off a cup of wine. "There, that stands for S. The name is complete."

She raised herself and proclaimed her achievement to Salvius Otho.

"Clap approval," shouted the master of the revel. "The prize is yours beond a doubt, fair Septimia. Hasdra, our little Phoenician, will hasten to set the crown of victory on your brow."

Hasdra, Poppaea's little companion, came deliberately forth from the grove of plane-trees where she had been crouching, full of bitter disgust, on a stone seat. The tumultuous orgy fanned the passionate grief she kept smothered in her breast to fresh flame. Pharax, who in spite of his awkward style of letter-writing, was still her adored idol—Pharax, with whom she had secretly come to an understanding, had written to tell her that in his new position as military tribune it would not fit him to marry her. He ended, indeed, by assuring her that he should, nevertheless, always think of her with the truest friendship; but of what good was that to poor fragile little Hasdra, to whom her splendid Pharax's friendship was as a menu to a hungry man. She was helpless. Burning hatred lurked behind those drooping lashes. Then the rumors that had reached her ears were true! Agrippina, Caesar's mother—it was too monstrous for belief! Of course a man on whom the Empress of Rome showered favors must have his head turned by his greatness. She, a Phoenician, a mere barbarian, was no longer good enough for him; it was a condescension even to cast his eyes on Acerronia, the daughter of a knight of Corduba. That red-haired vermin, with her venomous eyes and ever-wagging tongue!—But no: Acerronia was but a fool in Agrippina's hand! Acerronia was innocent as compared with the empress-mother. Agrippina! The name was to the Syrian girl synonymous with torture and horrors. By the side of the false tigress on the throne, Acerronia was but a harmless wild-cat.

All this was seeting in the mind of the fiery-eyed girl, unsuspected by the assembled guests. Holding the rose-crown of honor in her right hand, and pressing her left to her heart, she went forward, bowed low to Septimia, who was not feeling the effects of her feat, and gracefully set the elaborately woven high crown of flowers on her head.

Chloris meanwhile had ended her song, heedless of the fact that during the crowning of Septimia she had hardly been listened to. She hesitated as to whether she should go on to another.

But Salvius Otho settled her doubts. Flourishing his vine-wreathed cup high in the air, he said in low but somewhat uncertain accents:

"The long pause!"

Those who were not yet incapable rose to take a turn, alone or in company, in the beautiful wilderness which Otho's father had laid out.

"Excuse me a moment," said the Agrigentine to his partner. "I must speak a word with Chloris."

"The cithara-player? You? Then of course. . . ."

"Purely on business. I want her on the day after tomorrow for an excursion by the sea.—I hope that Caesar and the fair Septimia will be satisfied." She beamed at once with self-importance, while Tigellinus quietly drew the Rhodian singer apart.

"Then you will come?" he asked, holding her hand firmly in his. Chloris trembled and looked down in silence.

"Will you answer me?" he persisted.

"I do not know whether Artemidorus will allow it," she said timidly.

"Artemidorus, the freedman? By Castor, is this Artemidorus your guardian?"

"No,—but he is to be my husband."

"Ridiculous! A childish jest! Do you really believe he will marry you! Chloris to-day—Doris to-morrow. He does not dream of such a thing. In these days men have wings like Tynx, Aphrodite's magic bird."

"He has given me his word."

"And if he has?—Would it bring you happiness? You, freeborn and a divine artist—and Artemidorus, but lately a slave, who has already been in the executioner's hands. . . ."

"My lord," Chloris stammered out with a blush, "he is so noble and good. . . ."

"But you do not love him. If you did, you would not need to praise his merits; you would simply say: 'I adore him!'—I am good, too, sweet Chloris, but no one would be so mad as to assert that I am master of your heart."

"No indeed!"

"Well then, what is the meaning of these difficulties? You promised me to add to the enjoyment of our excursion on the bay; and I know my guests' tastes better than you.—I want to choose the most appropriate from your store of songs. Does that strike you as so strange?''

"No, but I thought. . . ."

"Never think, my pretty bird; you have only to feel and to sing.—So to-morrow, at three hours after sunrise, to the left of the fourth door in the peristyle. But do not come in through the atrium, but from the garden. You must not be seen, or you will spoil the surprise.''

Still she hesitated. Tigellinus patted her on the shoulder with a fatherly air.

"You are made up of false alarms, my little Rhodian. Even supposing that Artemidorus has a right over you—am I asking you to do anything wrong? Or is he angry when you add to the graces of a drinking-bout, for example, with your Alcaic and Alcmanic verse?''

"That is my profession."

"And what I ask of you is your calling too. Nothing can be done to perfection without preparation.—Come, promise me by Apollo, master of the Muses, that you will not keep the most devoted of your adorers waiting.''

He held out his hand.

"Very well, I will come," she said, agreeing doubtfully. "But you on your side must honorably and truly keep the word you have given me.''

"All, everything!" exclaimed the delighted Silician.

"Pyrrhus, your accomplished slave, will be present while you are deciding?''

"Of course. I value his opinion highly."

"Quite positively?"

"Quite positively. And now look me in the face once more; am I so dangerous to look upon? A beast of prey? Smile a little on me, my fair Greek, or are you still thinking of Artemidorus?''

"Alas, only too little!" she sighed. The next instant she repented of what she had said; but it was too late. Tigellinus understood at once that this timid fawn would not now escape him, and a smile of proud satisfaction stole over his lips. This one conquest was worth more to him than twenty among women of senatorial or knightly rank.

Chloris left him. While she hurried away through a side door and down to the valley, Tigellinus returned to his adoring partner at the table and deferentially offered her his hand. She rose and clung to his arm with all her weight.

"I am drunk. Divine Tigellinus, I am quite tipsy!" she repeated laughing. "No, is not it absurd! Everything is going round and round.—You, too, Sophonius—even you!—Mercy, man, hold me up."

Tigellinus was in a merciless mood. He dragged his tipsy burden relentlessly forward, though Septimia constantly stumbled. Almost all the guests were now wandering in couples through the fragrant garden, or mounting the hill-side to seek some comfortable seat where the air was purer and fresher than down by the table under the plane-trees.

Seneca alone remained standing, as if lost in thought, by the side of a huge jar of wine and water, and pushing aside a slave, filled a cup with his own hand.

"A mad world!" he said to himself. "Futile, and yet able to make us forget its futility. Perhaps Bacchus is the best philosopher! Light-hearted god! I pour a libation to thee, for here I have and hold thee!" He shed half the contents of the cup on the ground and drank the remainder with suspicious unsteadiness.

Then he went into the house with a great effort of dignity, threw himself down on a bronze couch in the dimly-lighted exedra and before the echo of his movement, which was strangely like a fall, had fairly died away he was sleeping the dreamless sleep of inebriation.

CHAPTER IV.

IN spite of Septimia's eager devotion in drinking to his· name, Tigellinus had found time during the banquet to observe Poppaea's unusual agitation, and the varying expression of her imperial partner's face.

Caesar seemed to be more and more bewitched by Otho's seductive wife. He had looked in her face two or three times with an expression of secret gratitude. The clouds which often darkened his brow amid the wildest revels this evening appeared at rare intervals, as when Chloris struck the strings of her cithara.

Tigellinus was glad to observe all this. That foolish affair with Acte—though to be sure she was a sweet little thing, almost as pretty and kissable as the bewitching little Rhodian,—was at last fading out of Nero's memory. Poppaea was indeed the very woman to efface it. And what a gain for the whole court if she should entangle the emperor in her snare. Where Poppaea Sabina held sway, joy and all the pleasures of life upheld her throne. If she could achieve this conquest, the home of the Caesars would henceforth become a dwelling for the immortals. It would no longer be necessary to find pretexts and subterfuges to conceal an adventure or a love-affair; millions would be lavished where now only hundreds of thousands were spent; in short, a man might show himself without reserve as the grace of the gods had made him, and trample everything under foot which interfered with his freedom. The gay votary of pleasure would have been only too glad if, in pursuance of this idea, he could have kept an eye on Caesar who at this moment was leaning with Poppaea over the marble parapet of the park-wall, and looking down at the bay. But Septimia, having proclaimed herself tipsy, clung so closely to her amiable cavalier, whispering to him with wine-inspired eloquence, that he could not shake her off without being positively brutal.

Poppaea and Nero were confidentially close to each other. Neither spoke a word. Caesar looked down wide-eyed at the undulating blue-green waters; Poppaea, with engaging coquetry had laid a hand on his shoulder, as much as to say: "Remember that a friend is at your side who has a heart to feel everything that affects you."

For some time they remained silent. Nero's fancies seemed to be wandering sadly and vaguely in some remote world. At length Poppaea asked:

"What are you thinking of, Caesar? Still of the lost one— lost for ever?"

He did not reply.

"I know," she went on, "that a noble soul is slow to forget. Then it shall be my task to help the bleeding wound gradually to heal. Rouse yourself, my friend, or must I really regret the fact that some feature of my face reminds you of the dead? I hoped, on the contrary, that this slight resemblance might make me all the dearer. . . ."

"So, in fact, it does," replied Caesar. "You are every day more indispensable to me.".

"Then, indeed I am happy! Only have patience. By degrees you will look back on the past with less bitter sorrow, and at last will hardly feel the anguish which now racks your soul—Nero! Look me in the face! Yield to the inevitable—that alone in manly and human courage. You were born into a world of perishable joys, and you marvel that a springtide should sink into the grave!"

"Perishable!" echoed Nero. "A terrible word."

"Acte is dead because Fate willed it so," Poppaea said. "But within a century she would have been dead even if the gods had graciously preserved her to the utmost limit of human life. And it is the same with us. The sand in Saturn's glass might run out for us, too, this very day. Would you not then curse with your dying breath every minute you had lost in forlorn regret? To-day we live! Let us enjoy to-day." Poppaea stroked the emperor's head.

Nero drew a deep breath.

"By the Styx, you are right!" he exclaimed, suddenly standing upright. "All is vanity, most of all regret for the 'might have been.' "

She looked up in his face with tearful eyes.

"Tears, Poppaea?"

"Tears of joy—of bliss. . . ."

Nero put his arm round her tenderly.

"Let us enjoy to-day!" he sighed, half-intoxicated by her charms. "How fair you are!"

Poppaea tried to free herself with well-feigned alarm.

"You have roses in your hair again this evening—and roses, roses on your blooming lips."

"Let me go, Caesar," she implored. "Think of Otho."

"Let us enjoy to-day," he repeated, kissing her passionately. "What need we care for the chill stars up there, looking down on men in their scornful eternity, so long as we float blissfully along and the minutes melt away in enjoyment."

Poppaea flung herself on his breast, as if overcome by the fulness of her happiness.

"Nero," she murmured, "I worship you!"

Again he clasped her closely, his hands on her breasts.

"And Otho?" he suddenly said as the bewitching lips met his.

"What do I care for my husband now that I know that Caesar really loves me?"

There was a pause.

"When and where can we meet again?" Caesar suddenly asked. "Alone, of course."

"When and wherever you desire. But be cautious. Otho is as jealous as an old man. . . ." Nero shrugged his shoulders. "But come what may, I am your slave."

"My guide," Nero amended it. "My mistress in the enjoyment of life."

"So be it! And I truly hope that my splendid young pupil will have forgotten by to-morrow that he ever knew a grief."

A loud rattle of drums broke the stillness of the summer night, scaring all sentiment. Poppaea and Nero, hand in hand, turned away from the ivy-grown wall and returned to the banquet in silence.

The young woman's bosom beat high with a sense of triumph: Otho, that sober, vapid, insensible creature, should feel what Poppaea could do when she was sure of Claudius Nero's love.

Nero himself—of that she was as sure of eternal annihilation—would at once urge her to dissolve her hated marriage bond. As soon as he was thoroughly intoxicated by the delights of her love, she would paint the ardor of her husband's devotion in glowing colors. Caesar's jealousy and royal pride must be roused, his feelings must be tantalized, till of his own accord he insisted on her divorce. Then, when once she was free, she would see how far her position could be further assured; and whether in the struggle with his much-dreaded mother—this idea had but just occurred to her—Caesar could be induced to get rid with Octavia, whom she fervently hated.

She could not speak. The excitement of anticipated victory filled her heart, which felt neither love nor even the animal sensuality of such a woman as Septimia. Poppaea loved only herself, and to that selfishness she would have sacrificed everything, even all she held most sacred.

Nero meanwhile scarcely observed her silence. His thoughts chased each other like the clouds of that stormy night when his never-to-be-forgotten Acte had been snatched away from her villa. He felt himself a traitor to the past. Could he, who had loved Acte, find happiness with Poppaea?—And again, was not Otho his best friend next to Tigellinus? And he was betraying that friend on his most vulnerable side. He was digging the ground from under the confiding husband's feet. This was Punic faith, while Otho clung to him with tender devotion.

But presently the old bitter feeling revived; implacable wrath against Fate. Even if he were to alienate his friend's wife, he would only be doing the same as the guilty gods had done to him. The all-merciful Jupiter, as they called him, had robbed him of Acte without asking whether his heart would be broken by the blow. Now Caesar could play the part of Jupiter, and this change of parts he deemed only fair. Nay, looking at the matter in a clearer light, it was Poppaea herself who had assigned it to him. So he was only availing himself of the undeniable right to reap what had been sown for him.

Above all: "To-day alone we live!" her Siren tones had murmured the words in his ears. Hail to the sparkling cup! Drink of it till drunkenness ensues! Never ask if others are thirsty, so long as you may revel in it. Does Fortune ever feel shame? Why in the name of the powers of evil does she favor so few? If Otho should lose Poppaea, what better had he deserved? Scorn and mockery would be his portion on earth! Hapless wretch.—Menelaus, king of the Achaians could wage war against the ravisher of Helen; but Otho—poor fool—what could he do against the omnipotence of Claudius Nero Caesar? The praetorians were a better defence than the walls of Ilion. The betrayed husband must submit; unless, like a frenzied bull, he would rush blindly on the spears.

Nero sighed. The praetorians. This, his first transgression against his sense of right, had made him conscious of his need of that bulwark of brass. Till now he had never thought of it.

The poison-flower of tyranny was swelling apace.

CHAPTER V.

THE summer season at Baiae ended in the same key as it had begun. Banquet followed banquet, thanks to the well-laid plans of Tigellinus and Poppaea; for she now aimed solely at preventing Caesar's having time to think. Refreshing excursions by night on the bay, where not a sound fell on the ear but the dip of the oars, frequently broke the long series of magnificient entertainments, games, and combats. And now that she had caught Caesar in her net Poppaea took good care that his rest was not unduly curtailed. Every revel, though no less extravagant and wild, came to an end by an hour before midnight.

On two evenings in each week Nero—ostensibly at the pressing entreaty of his friends—himself gave an entertainment, reciting verses, playing on the lyre, or performing scenes in pantomime from the old Greek myths—in imitation of the fashionable professional actors: the Sacrifice of Iphegenia, the Sorrows of Philoctetes or the Return of the Laertiades.

Formerly he had done this but very rarely, only in the most intimate circle. But now half Baiae was invited to be present; and though the Roman sense of dignity was offended by this artistic extravagance, the emperor of the world was loudly clapped; and after an elderly senator had, on one occasion, peacefully slumbered through the agonies of Philoctetes, to be waked by a rousing poke in the back from a praetorian lance, they applauded with double vigor. So the early autumn found the court still at Baiae, "unfortunately bereft," as Tigellinus hypocritically lamented, "of Otho's inspiring presence;" for Caesar had graciously appointed him to the rank of propraetor in Lusitania.

What a clasping of hands and embracing, what a waving of flame-colored veils, when the betrayed husband took leave of his wily Poppaea, "for the sake of his duty to his country," and embarked at Misenum! The commander of the fleet, Anicetus, in person took the command of the gaily-dressed vessel which was to convey the superfluous husband through the towering rock-pillars of Hercules to the western side of the Peninsula, for "Honor to whom honor is due!"

Strange to say Otho, once so madly jealous and so vehemently excitable, had for some time been very calm and quiet, so ominously silent indeed that Nero no longer felt quite comfortable in his company. For this reason, if for no other, Caesar had chosen Lusitania as a distant place of honorable exile for his inconvenient friend. As a further precaution he had given the newly-appointed propraetor an adjutant, in the person of a young German officer, who was to keep secret watch on all Otho's proceedings, public or private. This German was Giso, son of Lollarius the prince of the Chatti. Nero believed him to be equally shrewd and trustworthy, never suspecting that Giso, disgusted with the horrible profligacy of Baiae, had long since attached himself to Otho's side.

Poppaea, even, had been somewhat uneasy at her husband's sudden transformation. She had feared some public rupture when she told him that, deeply to her regret, she must remain in Italy, as the physician had assured her that the climate of Lusitania would kill her. But Otho so entirely accepted her statement that she was amazed. Had all his former jealousy been mere feigning? Had he ceased to love her? Or was his increasing conceit so dense that he

280

thought it impossible that she could be unfaithful to him? She almost thought that this was the case—and her husband's parting words confirmed her in the notion.

At the last moment, when stepping into the boat which was to carry him on board, Salvius Otho addressed Caesar with unusual emotion:

"Dearest friend, take charge of my faithful Poppaea, and do not let her find the time too long till my return."

Nero controlled his confusion as best he might.

"Go in peace," he replied waving his hand. "I will not forget your charge."

And the Agrigentine added:

"I know Caesar's immeasurable condescension. I will pledge my head that, if you wish it, he will give your deserted wife an asylum in the Palatium itself."

"That would be beyond my boldest expectations," said Otho smiling.

Not a shade of bitterness or of self-mockery was to be seen on his pale, distinguished features; he nodded once more with winning pleasantness and stepped into the boat, while the bystanders exchanged meaning glances.

The intrigue between Nero and Poppaea was a most obvious fact to all who had eyes to see, though no one would have ventured to allude to it openly. Poppaea had very prudently saved appearances to establish herself all the more securely. Still, that Otho should have failed so entirely to notice anything was more than she could believe for any length of time. As she remembered his smiling contentment as he parted, she was conscious of a sense of danger . . .

Otho was gone. The latter part of September brought cooler nights. In spite of the imperishable beauty of Campania, the pampered citizens of Rome began to wish themselves back at the centre of the inhabited world. By mid-October the travelling chariots were in motion, several hundred in number; Poppaea alone had an enormous train. The crimson vehicles drawn by four and six thoroughbreds in gilt harness; the roomy sleeping chariots; the vans, with elegant mosaic flooring and awnings that unrolled so that they could be converted at any time into dining tents; the lumbering luggage wagons; the *cisia* perched on high wheels and carrying apparatus for the table; the well-filled provision carts—all these, with their lavish abundance and display, were suggestive of the splendor of the old Persian monarchs.

And then there was the formidable and dazzling array of praetorians, who rode foremost in two divisions, mounted on white Cappadocian steeds.

Weird and grotesque among all these came twenty camels, with flowing scarlet housings and bejewelled negroes. This was a whim of Tigellinus', who had once, quite seriously, had a camel-race on the shore at Baiae, and who now wished to repeat the jest in the Circus Maximus.

After these camels, closing the interminable procession, came the famous herd of five hundred she-asses, splendid specimens of their kind from Mauritania, whose milk supplied a bath every morning for Poppaea Sabina; in this she sat for a quarter of an hour to preserve the matchless freshness and youthfulness of her ambrosial person.

The poorer inhabitants stood on each side of the Appian Way, stupidly staring at this amazing chaos of vehicles, men and beasts, till the last gleam reflected from the gold shoes of the asses were lost to sight.

These splendid shoes were already the talk of Hispania and Gaul. They were Caesar's first birthday gift to his mistress and had cost eleven million denarii.

Meanwhile Octavia had returned to the Palatium, never dreaming of Nero's intrigue with Poppaea—for none of the household were so bold or so cruel as to speak to her of such a thing. She was accompanied by Abyssus, the physician, by Rabonia, and by three other freed-servants.

Acte, in Octavia's eyes the most remorseful sinner who ever threw herself at the feet of an injured wife, remained in the villa at Antium under the name of Ismene. No one there

282

knew what her past life had been; only Abyssus and Rabonia had learnt the truth by her sick-bed, and there was no need to tell either of them to keep silence.

Acte-Ismene was to help the old steward, who had lately lost his wife, to keep house, to bring up his orphan grand-children and make herself useful according to her capacity.

This partnership was arranged in accordance with her own earnestly expressed wish. In truth, she took no interest in anything.

She had but one thought: to hide herself from the world, never at any cost to see Caesar again—for now that Octavia had been her benefactress, less than ever could she return to him—and to efface utterly and for ever the memories of her guilty happiness.

Many a time as she thought of the young empress' magnanimity and generosity, and of the sacred griefs which had brought such bitter tears to those lovely eyes, she fancied she had triumphed, and eradicated every selfish desire. But then came hours of longing, when everything which self-abasement, honest effort and fervent prayer had built up crumbled into ruins. Her heart was rent in twain, her whole nature at war with itself. Then she could not comprehend how that could be sin which seemed to her so sweet, so heavenly and pure, which had transmuted empty existence to true life. Oh yes, she loved him, now as ever: ardently, inextinguishably—although she condemned herself for this love more mercilessly than Jesus of Nazareth himself would have done.

Added to all this the news of Poppaea's triumph had reached her ears, though not those of the young empress. The report overwhelmed her with sorrow: not with fierce jealousy, such as a less sincere heart would have felt, but unspeakable pity.

She pitied Octavia, who had lately fanned her hopes into life again, and had returned to the capital with an idea that all might yet be well. She pitied Caesar, who must have been wretched beyond description, if he could seek consolation for his loss with such a woman as Poppaea Sabina. She had heard much from Artemidorus of this "handsome woman of Rome," of her heartless flirtations and malicious egoism. She was sure that this Poppaea could never satisfy Nero's yearning heart. She might bewitch his senses, deaden his grief for a moment; but a complete cure—if indeed there were a cure for the anguish of love—he could find in no one but Octavia. That lovely and innocent creature—aye and fervid too—that empress crowned with thorns—she and none other could pour balm into his bleeding wounds, and bring light to his darkened spirit. She had only to prove to him once that she truly loved him, that her devotion was stronger than her pride, and her cruelly insulted sense of right. Was this yet possible? Or had grief closed the issues of her soul? Alas for her if it were so—and alas for Caesar!

It was Agrippina who opened Octavia's eyes, immediately on her return from Antium—not as a solemn disclosure, but carelessly, in the course of conversation; for the empress-mother supposed that Octavia already knew of all that had occurred at Baiae. "I cannot believe you don't know that your husband has taken Poppaea for a mistress," Agrippina offered.

The look of wild dismay in the young wife's pale face was terrible to see. "Oh, no," she cried. "Not Poppaea." Agrippina herself, though callous to all weak emotions, quite lost her presence of mind. She took the fainting woman in her arms and, carrying her into that room whose wall concealed the tyrant's arsenal of death, laid her gently on a couch. Then, from a closet—close to that secret cupboard where Locusta's horrible poisons stood in rank and file—she fetched a phial of strong waters scented with rose and lemon.

She tended the senseless creature as a mother tends her sick child, calling for no help, not thinking for a moment that any one could do more, or do it better than herself.

At last Octavia opened her eyes; but at once she began to talk deliriously. Her unfathomable woe expressed itself in a frenzied but heartrending natural outcry.

"Poor Octavia!" Agrippina murmured again and again. She kissed her brow, and for the moment the deep instinct of sympathy which always draws a woman to a suffering woman, rose superior to the hard selfishness of her nature. The eyes of this proud scorner of her fellow-creatures, who for years had wept only for wounded vanity or rage, shed a tear of pity on the pillow of this cruelly betrayed wife.

"Acte, Poppaea, Chloris!" Octavia sobbed out, "have you joined in a conspiracy? Do you want to tear him from me? And I loved him so!—You are making him miserable.—Yes— I see it—I see it—there!—How pale his is! What are those ghastly riders at his heels? What do they want?—His blood! merciful gods, his blood! Help, help! save him! Acte, sweet Acte, if you ever loved him, throw yourself on those horrible spears, or they will pierce him! They are rending him! Stop, by Jupiter I bid you stop.—Here! here is my breast; kill me! Oh I cannot live, if you rob me of my all!"

With trembling fingers she tore open her dress in her terrible vision, baring her breasts.

"Here, strike! Here!" she groaned incessantly while she pressed her left hand convulsively to her side as though to relieve herself of some agonizing oppression.

Agrippina flew to the ante-room.

"Run," she said to the first slave girl she saw. "Abyssus, Octavia's physician, must come at once!"

Abyssus appeared and went up to the couch with a look of deep grief in his shrewd, manly face. He felt the sufferer's pulse, raised her half-closed eyelids with the tip of his left thumb, and while with his right hand he alternately shaded her eyes and exposed them to the light, he carefully examined the pupils. He nodded, almost imperceptibly, and then laid his ear against the heart to count its beating.

Octavia all the while was wailing and moaning. Fresh visions seemed to rise before her darkened mind. "Nero; I cannot see your tears. I will do what I can to help you; I will indeed. And I shall find her.—No, no, throw away the dagger; do not kill yourself! You must live; you shall live with her, your own matchless Acte! Believe me, she loves you beyond words. And I know where she is.—Her golden hair, which entangled you so sweetly, is gleaming there among the myrtle bushes!—Oh, that dreadful knife! Phaon! Acte! Hold his arm! Help—Nero—he has done it.—Nero, Nero!—Too late!"

Her voice rose to a shrill scream, like that of a mad thing. Then she lay sobbing in silence for a minute.

Suddenly she sat up. "Let me go!" she cried desperately. "I must, I will go to him! Or else I swear to you he will cut his throat. He vowed he would in the senate. His own mother ordered it! Agrippina! Go and call Agrippina. Do you not hear me? Has every one turned against me?"

"I am here," Agrippina stammered, bending down to her.

Octavia threw her right arm round her neck and repeated imploringly:

"For love of me, go and fetch Agrippina. All the world knows what influence she has over Nero—far more than I.— And so she ought; I am too small a thing for Nero. He could not love such a wretched creature, even if he wished it. Tell Agrippina so. Though he did make love to Acte—I alone was to blame. Even Poppaea is far superior to me. Do not be revenged on her, I beseech you so earnestly! Agrippina must forgive her!—Juno, heavenly mother, of all women, I am the most unblest! Nero can never forgive me, never, never!—No god can redeem the wretched Octavia—not even Jesus of Nazareth, who came to make Acte happy! Happy, happy!— Yes, she was happy. . . . But as for me, nail me to the cross, let me die the death of the outcast! Away!—You are piercing my hands? Oh not yet, not yet! Wait only one single day. I see him coming—Death, merciless, with his hour-glass—the last grain of sand has run! I am dead.—Dead. And Nero never saw his poor Octavia again!"

Her arm dropped from Agrippina's neck, and she fell back exhausted.

Abyssus, down whose cheeks the bright tears were falling, offered his mistress a metal cup with a milky-looking draught in it.

"Here, madam," he murmured with an imploring glance at Octavia's distraught eyes, "take this: it will bring you rest."

She listened to the gentle tones of his voice.

"Who speaks to me?" she asked with a smile. "So gently, with such infinite kindness! It was Nero, my dear husband. Come close; nearer still! I cannot see you. Am I blind?

Abyssus placed his right arm behind her and gently raised her, offering her the cup with his left hand. She swalloed a few drops; then she suddenly threw herself back, and shrieked so loudly that the very walls rang:

"Poison! Poison! You want to kill me!"

"Be calm, madam. It is I—Abyssus, your most faithful servant, who would cherish you as the apple of his eye."

She blinked doubtfully in his face.

"Yes, it is you Nero! The immortals be praised that you are here! Come, my dearest, kiss me. Why do you repulse me? Are you still thinking of Acte? Nay, take me to your heart once more as you used—do you remember—long ago?— Here on my brow is a jewel still hot from the goldsmith's flame—How it throbs and burns! Give me some snow or I shall die!"

"Only drink this," said Abyssus much moved. And she emptied the cup unresistingly.

Meanwhile Acerronia the green-eyed had stolen into the room, followed by Olbia, her slave-girl.

Abyssus, on the strength of his authority as physician, signed to her politely, but emphatically, to withdraw.

"Perfect quiet," he added in a whisper, "is the only chance of allaying by degrees the terrible over-excitement she is suffering from."

The red-haired Hispania obeyed with an ill-grace; under her golden lashes lurked a flame of hatred and aversion.

This was the second time that Abyssus had behaved as though the duties of the physician were paramount to those of respect and courteous consideration! Last winter, when the empress-mother had one day been suddenly seized with violent headache and her own physician was ill, this insolent Abyssus had dared to show her the door in the same way! It was monstrous! A slave took upon himself to give his orders to her, the daughter of a free Roman citizen—a knight? The bastard! The conceited, unblushing fellow!—To be sure, it suited him better no doubt to have no witness at hand when his black curls were so close to his beautiful young patient. She gave vent to her annoyance in some such reflections as those, while Olbia, as usual, smilingly assented.

The flaming Acerronia was certainly unusually irritable. Her union with Pharax seemed to be turning out badly. Hardly were they married when they were forced to live apart: she in the palaces, he in the great praetorian barracks. Agrippina had given him the choice of quitting the legion and remaining as her personal adjutant in the capital. But his short experience of domestic life with Acerronia had been a failure, for, bold as he was—and in his day he had defied the centurion's vine switch—he was not a match for his red-haired tiger-cat's claws. And he had also discovered that Acerronia's previous life was not so absolutely blameless as might have been supposed from the box on the ears she had dealt Tigellinus.

Abyssus, not heeding the Corduban's scowl, now turned to Agrippina. He showed her the remains of the drink, already settling at the bottom of the cup, and said in a low voice:

"It is a sleeping draught, chiefly poppies. If it has the desired effect, this frightful agitation may have vanished by to-morrow morning. Only vouchsafe to give orders that no one shall disturb our patient."

"Thank you," said the empress-mother, giving him her hand to kiss. "No one shall cross the threshold but myself and Rabonia."

Abyssus went away. Octavia's agonizing unrest and sudden starts, with wailing and screaming, went on for nearly an hour; but by degrees she grew calmer. At last a leaden sleep fell upon her, which lasted from one after midnight till noon next day.

When she opened her eyes again, her brain was perfectly clear; only she had not the smallest recollection of anything that had occurred since her conversation with the empress-mother; and she felt tired beyond words.

"We have triumphed," said Abyssus to Agrippina. "Now, all that is needed is the greatest care, suitable nourishment, and strict avoidance of certain allusions.—You understand me, sovereign lady."

For a week Octavia was unable to leave her bed, and yet another week passed before she was strong enough to walk up and down the palace-garden for half an hour.

During this time Caesar had returned, and Poppaea Sabina had made her entry into the imperial palace. She was brought there by Nero, as his friend, left in his charge by his worthy Otho. They had very prudently withheld from him the news of Octavia's illness. The bringer of such a message would not have been safe for an instant from Poppaea's vengeance; and the information would have served no end, for Poppaea was so entirely mistress of Caesar's ardent fancy that one thing only could have supplanted her: Acte's reappearance.

Agrippina tried to guide Nero in the right way. She besought him to send Otho's wife to Lusitania or to her own home, and not to insult the young empress in a way which the humblest wife in Rome would not endure, by harboring his mistress under the same roof with her.

Nero defended his attitude towards Poppaea Sabina, and clung with increased obstinacy to his foolish connection, because he distrusted his mother and suspected her of aspiring to fresh dominion, while in fact she only admonished him from the point of view of a worldly-wise woman.

Octavia, strange to say, affected to believe her husband's false representations. She played the same part as Otho, but from different motives. She was too helpless, too utterly crushed, even to attempt to hold her own against her baser rival. Besides, she knew now more surely than ever, that any contest on this ground was fruitless folly. The reality and fevor of her passion could not lead to victory, nor even to a satisfactory compromise.

At first she doubted whether she should not simply abandon the field to her antagonist, and withdraw once and for all to her villa at Antium. But she cast this thought aside.

"Duty," said she to herself, "bids me stay. If it should please almighty Jupiter, he might fill my husband's heart, to-morrow even, with affection for the wife he has deserted, and whom he now thinks of as a burden and a hindrance. Then I will be here!"

She was gentleness and sweetness itself to Caesar; nay, she was polite to Poppaea, though she bore herself with severe formality, and she even affected blindness when that audacious woman smiled, now and again, in scornful triumph.

This silent resignation soothed her spirit like a miracle. She got well in spite of the presence of the woman who desecrated her hearth. She recovered a feeling of vigor, a sense of freshness such as she had not known since she was a girl. She perceived with secret thrills of delight that she was rounder, more blooming, and more lively than she had ever been.

Now hope began to stir within her; real genuine hope; not that vague day-dreaming which looks for a miracle from the gods. Octavia was startled by the discovery. With all the force of her will she crushed the germ which was budding so temptingly. Had she not suffered enough from disappointments? She would not hope; she would only wait—an indifferent looker-on.

Thus the winter slipped away. Nero revelled and paraded with Poppaea Sabina, troubling himself no further about Octavia than the strictest necessity required. The young empress appeared in public only on the rarest occasions. The gardens of the palace, her conversations with Rabonia,—a woman of wide experience, and the quiet hours when Abyssus would recite the adventures and voyages of Odysseus the son of Laertes—these were the high lights of her lonely life. She had even ceased to keep up any correspondence with the villa at Antium, for the old steward's letters disturbed her peace of mind. He wrote with too much enthusiasm of Acte's domestic virtues, of her kind and lovable ways, which did his heart good and took the place of a mother's natural tenderness to his grandchildren.

Octavia, though incapable of base envy, could not help the recurring feeling: "This Acte is indeed destined by the gods to make him—the only Him—really happy!"

At the beginning of April Octavia, by the advice of Abyssus, took up her residence at Antium. Her meeting with Acte passed without any deep agitation, thanks to the young girl's tender delicacy. In a short time Acte-Ismene's company was as indispensable to Octavia as fresh air and sunshine.

CHAPTER VI.

On the northern slope of Mons Caelius, not far from the Via Sacra, stood the house of Menenius, a young but accomplished jurist who had not long since won the notice of a wide circle in an action brought by a Roman province against the extortionate and tyrannous policy of its governor.

It was early in May, and within an hour of midnight. Lucius Menenius, surrounded by a few slaves, was sitting in the small oecus by the peristyle. He gave them his orders in a subdued tone. He was expecting a large party of men who were to arrive from Gabii at a late hour to discuss an important lawsuit. It was a business requiring close attention, and any kind of interruption was strictly prohibited.

"See that it is so," he said with friendly confidence. "Above all, keep off listeners, prying little simpletons like Leda and Chloe, or that self-important Philemon. They are quite capable of creeping out of bed at the second vigil, merely to pick up a word they were not meant to hear. As a lawyer, in the confidence of strangers, I am bound to keep their secrets, even if Chloe tears her hair.—You understand?

The slaves, men of proved devotion, bowed assent.

"Two of you," Menenius went on presently, "can remain in the atrium close to the doorway. I do not know, but my good ostiarius seems to me absent-minded of late. The other day, when I went up to his seat, he started like Diana bathing.''

''He is in love,'' said one of the slaves.

''Romaeus in love? That is delightful! You shall tell me about it at the next opportunity. Now you may go.''

The slaves withdrew. Lucius Menenius went out into the pillared courtyard, where the moon shone brightly, and sat down in the silence on a bench.

About a quarter of an hour later the side gate clanged. A tall figure came in with a soft footfall, his cape thrown over his shoulder in folds, his head covered with the hood, and his face wrapped in a handkerchief up to the eyes.

''Eos and Thiton!'' he said.

''Come in; you are the first,'' replied Lucius Menenius, who would have recognized his elder brother Didius, even without the pass-word. He at once led the new-comer into the brightly-lighted oecus and bid him be seated. Then he hastened back to the posticum when, almost at that instant two others, equally marked by their hoods and hand-kerchiefs, crossed the threshold. These wore, under their cloaks, the breast-plates of praetorian military tribunes.

When they had divested themselves of their outer wraps the slighter of the two revealed an intelligent and aristocratic face, with flashing eyes and a particularly attractive expression of his lips. This man, still young but yet mature, was Julius Vindex, a scion of one of the most distinguished and respected families of Aquitania. The other, equally tall but brawnier and more robust, came out of his disguise as Pharax, Acerronia's husband, though separated from her in every sense.

Five minutes later and the assembly was complete.

The men who had here met together in secret council differed conspicuously in race, position, and character. Didius Menenius, for instance, who spent nine-tenths of every year on his estates in Eturia, was a perfect contrast to Lucius, vehement, eloquent, and who could never have lived away from the atmosphere of the Roman forum. Flavius

Scaevinus, the grey-headed but hale-looking senator, made Nicodemus, who sat by him, appear more gloomily hollow-eyed and haggard than ever; while the poet Lucanus, a handsome specimen of extreme urbanity, as he took his place next to Marcus Velinus, a bony, square-set Oscan, looked like a royal stag by the side of a buffalo.

In one thing however these men were united: their seething indignation, past all repression, at the revolting deterioration of Caesar, once so nobly promising.

None but Pharax perhaps, Acerronia's husband, had any personal hatred of Nero. Caesar had refused him with contumely when, on his knees, the despairing young officer had besought him to dissolve his marriage with Acerronia; the cuastic taunt flung at him in the presence of a crowd of courtiers still burned in his undisciplined, half-savage soul. And now that Agrippina scarcely noticed her former favorite, but for some time past had entirely taken Acerronia's part and encouraged her to count on her strongest support in the event of Pharax not choosing to submit, the luckless parvenu, mad with rage and indignation, had rushed into an alliance with Julius Vindex, who had cautiously initiated him into the schemes of a daring conspiracy.

This conspiracy was, strictly speaking, no more than the sequel of that originally laid to undermine Agrippina's intolerable ambition. But by degrees circumstances had so far altered that Caesar, in whose favor they were to have defied Agrippina, was now equally, or indeed the first object of their covert hostility. Only Barea Soranus and Thrasea Paetus had lately withdrawn their co-operation, deeming that the moment had not yet come for a successful rising.

Seneca, too, who had taken so zealous a part in their opposition to the empress-mother, had not, for obvious reasons, been invited to join now. His position, even so, was a singular one. He calmly, almost sullenly superintended the business of State. Nero allowed him to have his own way, but forbid any interference in his private concerns on the part of the philosophical monitor. Agrippina seemed to have renounced any kind of influence. In reality she lay in wait for an opportunity of humiliating her son and snatching back the supremacy. The real sovereign was Poppaea Sabina; for Seneca, to whom she exhibited the greatest deference, had persuaded himself that he must succumb to her as far as possible with the hope of winning back Caesar. This crafty and calculating woman had by her flattery crippled his power of judgment. He regarded her as a congenial nature; and as the gulf between Nero and Octavia seemed past bridging over, even his stoically stern conscience was lulled to sleep.

Lucius Menenius opened the meeting with a short and solemn address to his coadjutors. Then he added in lower tones:

"It is now as clear as sunlight that we have been deceived in Claudius Nero Caesar. The Quirites are in the predicament of the man in the fable, who hatched out a bird of prey. At first she took it for a chicken, till at last she perceived with horror that the young vulture's talons were growing."

"A young carrion crow!" snorted Pharax.

Lucius Menenius smiled and shook his head.

"No, alas!" he said bitterly. "He picks the bones, not of the dead, but of the living. We ourselves are his victims. He drinks the heart's blood of Rome to gather fresh strength for his reckless flight. I repeat it; we have been grossly deceived. Seneca, who has studied him from his youth up, ought to have known him better long ago.—Nothing will avail us now but the swiftest and most unflinching energy. Inborn vice is not to be driven out by ingenious philosophical arguments. I almost feel inclined to lay half the blame of all these atrocities to his charge; especially now, when he looks on in silence while that vile Poppaea is getting a firmer foot-hold every day. That wretched woman is the head and fount of everything that is detestable. Agrippina triumphed by crime: Poppaea rules by the arts of a whore. I really hesitate as to whether I would not prefer to have the empress-mother. . . ."

"Oh, oh!" groaned Flavious Scaevinus.

"Pardon me, but as one of Agrippina's victims you may be prejudiced," said the lawyer. "Formerly, when Agrippina held the helm, Nero still kept up appearances. Since Poppaea has held him in her meshes, he treads all that is sacred remorselessly under foot. He carries prodigality to the verge of madness. He openly defies the law in order to fill his perpetually exhausted coffers. He degrades himself by performing as a mime, a wrestler, nay as a charioteer in the circus. . . ."

"Do not recount such small sins, there are plenty of greater ones unfortunately," Flavius Scaevinus broke in, "Though he may act plays or exhibit himself in the ring, some excuse may be found for that. Nero is more Greek than Roman; his youth was fed on Sophocles and the songs of Homer. He lives under the delusion that whatever the Achaians did under the walls of Troy is permissible at Rome. Since Odysseus once wrestled with Ajax for the silver tripod, Agrippina's son thinks that it becomes him to do the same. That I could endure; I can allow for his glowing fancy and his passion for variety and extravagances. But the other, the worst thing. . . . I can tell you, Menenius, with all your eloquence you will never find words strong enough to satisfy me when you speak of that.—You mentioned his shocking contempt of law, his abuse of prerogative, which reduces every citizen to be the sport of malicious informers, and I quiver with rage, though you touched but lightly on these matters. Still, there is one thing which angers me yet more deeply: Caesar's atrocious conduct to Octavia. When I think of it, the blood mounts to my brain in a rush that almost turns me dizzy; my fingers clutch involuntarily as if to grasp the avenging dagger.—And it is to me an unspeakable grief!— My friends, you cannot think how I loved that boy. I would have shed my heart's blood for him; he was as dear to me as my own son. And he loved me, too, with fond and filial affection—I hate him now all the more!—Nay, I am belying myself. Flavius Scaevinus cannot so easily cast out a feeling which has once struck root in his heart. I have not yet learnt to hate him, sincerely as I have tried, But I can be all the more just and impartial. I judge him as Brutus judged his own sons—and my sentence is: He is worthy of death!''

"Not of death," Nicodemus remonstrated. "I, too, am firmly convinced that the State cannot know any prosperity till we have dethroned the hypocritical tyrant. But to kill him would be to arrogate a right which belongs to Almighty God alone."

"I admire your platonic moderation," said Lucanus. "You of all men have reason to hate him, for he has tricked no one of the citizens of Rome more ridiculously than you. I know all about it from Seneca. Your plot was a strange one; as to the merits of your ideas I do not pretend to judge. But there is one thing which in my opinion, must touch you as a special insult: the fact, namely, that at a time when no one troubled his head about the doings of the Nazarenes Claudius Nero published very needless edicts of toleration, while now, in defiance of those edicts, he encourages persecution, if only a simple Christian slave proclaims his crucified Master too publicly. . . ."

Nicodemus turned pale.

"I do not speak here as an adherent of the Nazarene doctrines," he said coldly. "Nor have I any idea as to whether, or how far, your uncle Annaeus Seneca may have thought fit to instruct you.—The matters now under discussion. . . ."

"By Hercules, you may be perfectly easy; we are all friends here!—Then you would spare Caesar's life?"

"I shun bloodshed," replied the Christian. "If we murder a sinner, we are as great criminals as he."

"You are too cowardly," growled Pharax. "Did Nero stop to reflect, when Britannicus was in his way?"

Flavius Scaevinus knit his brows.

"Do not speak so rashly," he said reprovingly to the vehement young soldier. "Britannicus fell a victim to Agrippina."

"But for whose benefit?" asked Lucanus. "If Britannicus had lived, there would have been no place in the Palatium for Nero. Agrippina's son would perhaps have dwelt at Athens and played the title-part in his own tragedy of Jocasta."

They laughed.

"I am quite in earnest," said Lucanus. "Our worthy friend Flavius was observing just now that the extraordinary and fantastic are what Caesar delights in. Lately he has been amusing himself with the sport of nocturnal thrashings."

"That I can affirm of my own experience," cried Velinus, the Oscan. "The rascal, who was accompanied by a few accomplices, fell upon me at the beginning of the second vigil the night before last, as I was coming home from Didius' house. I recognized him, in spite of his hood, and that foul hound Tigellinus. They were five, we were three; but we beat them off. On this his imperial majesty whistled, and we heard the clatter of arms at once. The praetorians came down the Via Curia. I had time to give Tigellinus a swinging blow in the stomach; then we fled round the corner."

"Think it lucky that you are still a stranger here," said the younger Menenius. "If the Agrigentine knew who had served him so, you would be accused at once of high treason.—But time is going on; we must not digress any further. Julius Vindex, inform us of what news you may have."

Julius Vindex rose. Resting his left hand on his gilt sword-knot, he began:

"I was at Luna, on the little river Macra, a few days since. There I met Giso, the son of Lollarius, as we had agreed. He was travelling as a builder; there are large marble quarries at a few miles from the town.—We soon came to an understanding. Salvius Otho could not have sent a better representative than this fair-haired son of the Chatti. And Otho's message is more satisfactory than the account of the feeling rife in the praetorian camp. He has already been joined by several centurions and military tribunes. Giso is of opinion that an outbreak in Lusitania would be possible even now."

"But Lusitania by itself is but a pedestal without a statute," Scaevinus remarked.

"So I think," said Vindex. "Well, to keep strictly to the matter in hand, there is yet another thing: Otho pronounces decisively against the views of the troops who want to proclaim him emperor. He fears that in that case the revolution, which is in fact an act of the strictest justice, would seem to have its origin in reprehensible ambition. I cannot but agree with him entirely. If the purity of our motives is to remain above suspicion, not one of us must aim at sovereignty.

"Not one," was echoed by all the circle. Only Pharax was silent. He had his own thoughts on the subject. No soothsayer had ever prophesied that the haughty and splendid Agrippina should some day call him by tender names! Who should dare to set limits to the soaring flight of this highly-favored eagle? Pharax Caesar—it did not sound so impossible! And when he had reached that summit, when he could distribute thousands daily to the praetorians, and gild all the asses' hoofs in Italy—then he would punish that red-haired tiger-cat and get her out of his way, as Nero had treated his wife Octavia. Pretty Hasdra, whom he had so rashly thrown over, would certainly not refuse to play the part of Poppaea to Pharax, master of the world.

His eye glittered at this dream of the future. A bystander might almost have read the illusive vision in his face.

"Comrades," Vindex went on, "I may tell Giso then that you are of Otho's opinion; that will be enough to quell the obstinacy of his officers. And Rome can boast of a man who would be an ornament to the throne of Augustus: Cneius Calpurnius Piso. . . ."

"Or Galba," Lucanus put in.

"As you may decide. Both are men of honor, and secret but deadly foes of this incredibly disgraceful rule. Nor do I doubt for an instant Piso's readiness; if the path is made easy for him. All that is needed, is that one cohort at least of the body-guard. . . ."

The words suddenly died on his lips. The conspirators started to their feet as if an earthquake had shaken the house. With faces white as death they listened to a noise in the atrium.

CHAPTER VII.

A SERIES of strange sounds indeed had struck pain into the souls of Lucius Menenius and his guests; above all a vehement storm of talk ominously distinct in the silence of the night.

Romaeus, the door-keeper, who had for some little time been on terms of tender intimacy with one of the humblest slave-girls in a neighboring house, had opened the door in response to her familiar timid tap, regardless of the orders that had been specially impressed on him to exercise the utmost caution this night above all others.

The girl, who stole into his little room apparently for love of him alone, was in fact bribed by Agrippina's spies. Before the ostiarius understood that the insinuating serpent had tricked him, Pallas, Agrippina's lieutenant, had forced his way into the entrance with fifteen men-at-arms.

Romaeus desperately strove to repulse the intruders with the help of all the slaves in the atrium. In a voice of thunder he shouted out the words of a recent edict, which strictly protected every Roman citizen, even though he was suspected of crime, against the nocturnal invastion of his home.—In vain.

"Make way!" was Pallas' answer "or I run you through!"
"Push on!" cried the praetorians.

Meanwhile a deep bark rang out; then a furious yelping and fearful howl.

A huge mastiff, lying at the foot of the third column on the left, had broken his chain and seized one of the soldiers by the throat. A sword-thrust in his flank, which quivered with rage, stretched the foaming brute on the pavement. The dying creature's whines mingled with the clatter of bucklers, the threatening shouts of the slaves, their wild assertions that Menenius was not in the house, and the sharp orders of the leader.

The conspirators had not allowed themselves to be altogether panic-stricken.

"Treason!" exclaimed Lucius Menenius, when they had got over their first consternation. "It is the decree of Fate!—Save yourselves, those who can! I will go forward and check the villains!" As his colleagues showed some hesitation, he repeated authoritarilively:

"Fly—for the sake of the cause. You are Rome! If you perish now, the freedom of the fatherland is wrecked for ever. For me there is no hope. The tyrant has discovered us in my house: I am a marked man. He would find me out, even if I took refuge among the Sarmatians."

"I will stand by you," said the elder Menenius. "I, as your brother, am as open to suspicion as you are."

"Go, go," said Julius Vindex to the lingerers. "If you hope to free a nation, you must learn to smother your pride and control the impulses of your hearts. These noble brothers are indeed to be envied! Beloved Lucius, and you, high-hearted Didius, you shall live in our memory so long as we draw breath! Great Jupiter be my witness, I would dare as much in your place!"

The conspirators drew their swords and made for the side door, while Pallas and his mercenaries forced their way in from the atrium.

"What a cursed fate!" muttered Flavius Scaevinus, "to be forced to escape like a thieving fox, instead of flying out like a lion rushing on his prey!—Hallo! but this is indeed a piece of luck!"

His last words were uttered in a tone of startled amazement, and were caused by the sudden appearance of a handful of praetorians, whom Pallas had posted at the back of the house, close to the posticum.

"Stand!" shouted the foremost, extending his sword across the fugitive. A tremendous blow from that of old Flavius was the only reply to this: "Stand!" The soldier's helmet was split in two like a worm-eaten walnut. The blade sank two inches deep in his skull; he fell without a groan. In his fury and giant's strength Flavius felled a second praetorian. The two others met their death from the swords of Pharax, Julius Vindex, and Lucanus, while Velinus, who was short and somewhat awkward, in spite of his courage could not bring his into action.

The whole affair had scarcely lasted two minutes.

The conspirators escaped.

Not one had been wounded excepting Pharax, whose head had been almost severed from his body by a blow from the enemy's sword. When Julius Vindex bent over him, life was already extinct. A disastrous end to the soaring dreams of empire of Pharax Caesar. In spite of every rule and instinct of pious feeling, they were forced to leave him there with the dead praetorians or they must have recklessly risked the very existence of the plot itself.

Lucius and Didius Menenius had meanwhile placed themselves by the outer door of the corridor leading from the peristyle to the atrium.

"If there is another world, love me there as here!" murmured Lucius, giving his brother his left hand.

"And you the same! Here they come! The silent urn has no terrors for me. Under Nero's rule this life is hardly worth a single tear."

The brave brothers neither wavered nor flinched. They covered themselves to the eyes with two enormous shields, which had hitherto hung as useless trophies on the wall. Not in vain had they fought in the campaign against the Parthians: their swords, wielded with a will, dealt death.

At last, however, the attack was too violent. The praetorians, tired of being slaughtered one by one, pressed on them with irresistible force. They drove the brothers backward into the pillared hall, and now could hit freely. In an instand Didius fell, pierced by two swords at once.

"I die for my country! Down with the tyrants!" These were his dying words.

"Halt!" cried Pallas, who saw that the advantages of his discovery would be lost if Lucius, too, were killed. "Spare him!—Lucius Menenius, surrender!"

"Never!"

"A thousand denarii to the man who disarms him!" cried Pallas louder still in his alarm.

There was a pause. Lucius Menenius stood panting three paces away from his assailants, his shield resting on the marble pavement, his bloody sword in his right hand, watching every movement of the foe, and determined to be the death of the first man who should come near him.

Suddenly, perceiving that his position was desperate, he flung away the shield and turned his weapon on his own breast, to throw himself upon it as erewhile Quintilius Varus had done. But at the very instant one of the praetorians rushed upon him with a wild leap. Lucius Menenius tottered back. The blade which had given the soldier a death wound in the right flank snapped short. A minute later he was bound.

"Pallas," he cried, "be reasonable and kill me!"

"Far be it from me! To the rack first—and then you may wait! Caesar and his mother may, perhaps, in their clemency, leave it to you to choose the death you will die."

"All you will ever know I can tell you at once. More than that the worst torture will not drag from me."

"Well, then, speak." said Pallas with a smirk, highly delighted at the prospect of having something exact to report to the empress.

"I will speak, if you will grant me a favor: it is but a small

306

one.—Will you?"

"Let me hear what it is?"

"Unbind my hands. These chains eat into my flesh. You see I am quite unarmed, and with this cord round my knees I cannot possibly escape."

Pallas concented, after the praetorians had searched their captive to make sure that he had not still a dagger hidden in his dress.

"Listen then," said Lucius Menenius, "and repeat it word for word to your omnipotent mistress. I confess myself guilty of being one of the leaders of a conspiracy which extends a thousand ramifications to the uttermost ends of Italy, and whole glorious aim is to make away with a knavish monarch, with his viler mother, and with Poppaea Sabina, whose head is turned with ambition!"

"We have proofs of all that in our hands!"

"That you have not, most mighty Pallas. You know none of the conspirators; if you did, you would have apprehended them by broad daylight at your own convenience. The avowal I have made will strike chill terror to the hearts of those criminals at the capital; for they love this transitory life, which I and my associates despise. I know, only too well, that under that bloodhound's rule a mere suspicion would suffice to ensure my condemnation. For that very reason I deny nothing. A few of my colleagues have been here but now, closely veiled and unrecognized by any slave of mine. You wish to know their names? That would indeed be something!—Perhaps I will accede to your wish—perhaps not.—Where do you propose to take me?"

"To the state prison," replied Pallas, amazed at his prisoner's unexpected tone.

"Very good. Then desire the governor to have a proper bed prepared for me, and to leave me my toga, as an exception to the common rule. Then, if you come to-morrow, and ask me with due respect, I will consider what my answer shall be."

It was with some difficulty that Pallas hid his feeling of

triumph. He could have shouted for joy in the presence of all his men-at-arms. How greatly this would raise him in Agrippina's esteem; and not in hers alone, but above all in Nero's, who had previously underrated him. This Lucius Menenius was indeed an inestimable windfall! If this audacious traitor could be persuaded by him—Pallas—to discover the thousand secret threads of this conspiracy, what an achievement would that be in the service of the throne on the part of Agrippina's favorite!

How well the gods had contrived it all! What incredible good fortune! Till this moment no one had the faintest suspicion. . . . Beyond the fact that Lucius Menenius was a foe to the Palatium and that there was to be a meeting held at his house very late this night, the empress-mother's spies had reported nothing.

"The immortals are spoiling me!" thought Pallas.

Then turning to Lucius, he said with polite dignity: "Very well. I promise you that such a bed shall be made ready as you are accustomed to, and you shall be allowed your toga."

Eight of the soldiers now surrounded the prisoner. Pallas enjoined the most considerate behavior; and he wrote a few words on his tablets to be delivered to the chief warder of the Mamertine prisons. Then, escorted by only three of his soldiers, he hurried away to the Palatium. Agrippina had expressed a wish to be informed as soon as possible of the success of the expedition. Nero, on the other hand, had no suspicion as yet that his mother was thus secretly intriguing to recover her influence.

Leaving the three soldiers in the fore-court, Pallas went forward with the utmost caution to the private rooms where his patroness was impatiently awaiting him. A slave woman in Greek costume admitted him, and at once withdrew, with a curiously meaning smile. Quite unexpectedly, and for the first time at so unusual an hour, Pallas found himself alone with Agrippina. The room, which was furnished with fabulous magnificence, was lighted by a hanging lamp—the famous purple lamp in the form of a flying Phoenix, the work of Anthrax, the Alexandrian artist. It diffused a rose-colored and enchanting twilight. Agrippina was reclining in an easy chair. Her sumptuous beauty was bewitching in this tender light. It seemed as though the ambrosial blood could be seen coursing under the satiny transparent skin.

Pallas, who was familiar with all the subtleties of palace etiquette, knelt at her feet, pressing his hand to his heart with the air of a man who would gladly sacrifice his whole being, and exclaimed in a voice of intense agitation: "Madam, we have succeeded!"

She smiled with exaggerated condescension.

"I knew that the valiant Pallas would return *with* his shield or *on* it!" she said with theatrical emphasis. "Go on. Tell me every detail!"

Pallas, still on his knees, reported all that had happened.

"To-morrow quite early," he ended, in the tone of an omnipotent despot, "the prisoner will give me the names of the leaders. Then: one bold stroke, and the hundred-headed hydra is laid low!" Agrippina gave him her hand.

"You have indeed deserved well of your grateful friend and mistress. Believe me, this hour holds the promise of my renewed rule. I will ask them all—that insolent Tigellinus, the vacuous Poppaea, all, in short, who have enmeshed Caesar—I will throw the question in their teeth: What did you do to unravel this web of treason?—And when they stand mute, the fame of what I have done shall ring out like a trumpet-blast throughout the Roman Empire. Cladius Nero shall declare before all the world: 'Agrippina has saved my life; she alone is able to protect the throne of the Caesars.' Let me embrace you, happy victor!"

Pallas bent over Agrippina's snow-white hand and pressed his lips to it with a slight shudder.

"Nay, that was not my meaning," she murmured tenderly, her dark eyes glowing with an ardent light: "Kiss my lips, Pallas! Do you fear? Oh, you foolish fellow!"

Almost at the same time Lucius Menenius was stretching

himself on his bed in the stone cell of the state prison. The warder's steps died away; the stillness of the grave reigned in the close, lightless dungeon.

The young man shut his eyes. A gentle woman's face appeared to his fancy—a face not young, nor lovely, but so sweet, so indescribably kind—the features of his mother, now dwelling in Rhegium. His heart beat wildly with a sharp pang. Then a smile crept over the lips once so eloquent. Drawing a deep breath he raised his left arm, and with one bite, set his teeth through the vein.

Three hours later the warder came to wake him. Pallas was waiting in the hall to cross-examine him.

But this time old Rome, the Rome of Cato, had triumphed over degenerate Rome. Agrippina's emissary found only a blood-stained corpse.

CHAPTER VIII.

NEXT morning, at two hours after sunrise, Caesar was lingering in his airy sleeping room, cooled by a playing fountain; he was enjoying a luxurious breakfast with Tigellinus, who, by degrees, had become quite indispensable to him. Tigellinus had bribed a great many willing hirelings among Agrippina's slaves of both sexes, who kept him informed with the utmost punctuality of everything that took place, and he had already known for some hours all that had happened at the house of Lucius Menenius. Agrippina's interview with the leader of the expedition had also been reported to him:

"Much-loved Caesar," he began, when he had washed down the last Lucrinian oyster with sweet Falernian, "did I tell you that Agrippina is again stretching forth her hand to seize the sceptre?"

"Indeed; how?"

"For some weeks she has been planning a stroke of genius.—She would like to force you perceive that she alone has the keen insight of the born ruler. You are to be alarmed; to acknowledge her supremacy; in short to be her slave again, as you were before."

"I do not understand you."

"My dear Caesar, you know Agrippina's past, but not her

present. Believe me, the widow of the murdered Claudius has forgotten nothing.—I am your friend, Caesar. I fear lest you should be angry when you hear—grant me this much: when Agrippina speaks with you to-day—and she has sent twice already to ask if you are up—leave me to answer her dissimulation instead of you. You will then discover, by the same opportunity, that in all that concerns the weal and woe of his sovereign Tigellinus is at least as well informed as the empress-mother, who is still and always working against your interests."

"As you will; I trust you entirely. But tell me, by all the gods. . . ."

The Sicilian glanced at him meaningly. Cassius, Caesar's slave, came into the room and announced Agrippina.

"My son," said the empress after a brief greeting, "you know that it has always been far from me to boast of my services before you and the people of Rome. Still, I cannot help saying that if Caesar's mother did not keep her eyes open, you would by this time probably have been a victim to ruthless assassins."

Nero looked doubtfully at her.

"Illustrious lady," said Tigellinus with a smile, "I am afraid you are agitating Caesar quite needlessly. Or am I mistaken in supposing that you refer to the odious conspiracy led by Lucius Menenius?"

Agrippina started back.

"How came you to know. . . . ?"

"It is easy to be almost omniscient, madam, when duty requires it. My soldiers, who were to have apprehended the two Menenii this morning in their own villa, came back empty-handed. Blood had already been shed there during the night, in the name of the Empress Agrippina. Didius was dead, Lucius a captive; and he meanwhile had killed himself in prison. A crowd of events indeed, madam! Pallas has evidently been in too great a hurry. He is too ardent in suing for your favors. At any rate Rome is now the witness of a crying scandal, while the matter might have been carried through legally and without any noise."

The empress-mother had turned pale. She flashed an annihilating glance at the Agrigentine, whose craft she saw through, though she could not confute him. But she collected herself, and said as she turned to Nero again:

"How is it, my dear son, that a third person answers me in your stead?"

"The reason, perhaps, lies in the fact that you have chosen to act when I ought to have led the way. Tigellinus speaks for me."

"Very gracious, but not quite to my taste. When I address the master, I forbid the interference of subordinates."

Tigellinus, secure in his position, leaned against a Corinthian marble pilaster and smiled. He had not taken off his toga, and as he stood, in a self-satisfied attitude, he looked like a Greek orator who had just delighted his grateful audience by the brilliant grace of his antitheses.

"You must know," replied Nero, "that Tigellinus is my friend—my councillor, and in no respect my subordinate."

"By the Styx! He seems to me to be more nearly your master. He has arrogated full influence over all your decisions; and that influence will lead to disastrous issues. Ask of Rome whether it has lately been prouder and happier.—I was not nice in the choice of my means—that I unhesitatingly confess. I insisted on a rule of iron, an absolutely despotic power. Thus alone can tumults be suppressed and order and public prosperity be preserved. But now-a-days what a horrible medley of depravity. You tyrannize, as you order a race, for the mere pleasure of it. Low-born favorites gamble away the property of the people like beggar boys with rusty counters. Men who have a certain skill in organizing magnificient banquets boldly assert that they are statesmen, almost oust tried friends of the Caesars—as Burrus for instance—and make eyes at the troops as if they expected to be commanders-in-chief before night. Even a Seneca must bend to the yoke!—Why, these parasites cannot even take the most essential steps for your safety! I—I must

313

keep watch! And then, when I come and say to you: 'You are saved!' such a fellow as this Tigellinus comes forward and lisps out: 'Be calm; all you have done was quite super-fluous—we had already interfered. . . .' But I tell you plainly, in two words: he lies! and again he lies!''

A flash of intense hatred flamed in Tigellinus' dark eyes; only a flash, it is true, and his handsome, *blase* face at once resumed the smooth equanimity of the courtier.

"Madam," he said with astonishing composure, "I regret that you say: Tigellinus may not reply to Caesar's mother. But that the reproach of lying does not attach to me Nero is well-assured. For the rest I care nothing. He is master. His will alone can uphold or overthrow me. But there is something more. Since you are so well-informed as to the schemes of the conspirators, you know, no doubt, whose name stood at the head of the list of proscribed persons. Shall I help your memory?—You, Empress Agrippina, you had that honor, and you owe it to Pharax, your former favorite. You see, this plot suddenly acquires a quite different aspect! The knife was at your throat, divine Agrippina; and that, and that alone, was the reason why Pallas, with his manly heart beating high, played the part of fate. If the scheme had aimed only at Caesar—with an underplot to place you on the throne—Pallas would not have been so zealous in the cause."

"Miserable scoundrel!" cried Agrippina, furious with passion. Then, turning to Nero, she went on: "My son, do you believe this villain? I—I—oh, it is revolting! Have I not always fondly cherished in you, my idol, all the best and highest hopes I had in life?"

"And you fondly cherished Britannicus," Caesar moaned, "but you murdered him all the same."

"Who says so? Show me the wretch who dares to utter such a shameful lie, that I may kill him!"

"I should be glad to think that Caesar were spared the pain of naming his authority," said Tigellinus with a smile. "But if he should look about him for a man who would confirm the truth of his statement on oath—I am ready."

314

Agrippina was speechless. She clasped her hands and glanced round the room. "Is there no one in the palace," she cried in a half-extinct voice, "who will throw this villain into chains?"

"No one, so long as Nero protects me."

Agrippina folded her arms in despair. She cast a look on the deepest contempt and bitterness at her son.

"This, then, is the reward of my foolish and unbounded mother's love!" she said, quivering. "Head-strong youth, I counsel you: Beware! You may yet live to see what Agrippina is capable of when she steels herself to act."

Nero pressed the palm of his hand to his gloomy brow, and stared at vacancy with the fixed gaze of a visionary.

"If you had but left me *Her!*" he said dully. "Ah, so many things would have turned out better! Acte, dead but never-forgotten, is it then the will of Fate that I should for ever bewail you."

"Just so!" said Agrippina tauntingly. "You carouse till far into the night with riotous men and shameless women, and in the morning you are worn out and wretched! That is worthy of Caesar! Truly divine!" But Nero did not hear. Tigellinus heard, and understood. He stepped forward with eager vehemence.

"What do you mean by shameless women?" he asked with a glare. "Do you speak of the fresh and fair ones who wander from the path of virtue in the intoxication of youth, or of mature matrons—of your own age let us say—when in their autumnal love-sickness they fling themselves into the arms of this and that lover?"

Agrippina's hands trembled with impotent but consuming rage. A hoarse rattle rose from her laboring chest, sounding like the low preliminary roar of a beast of prey. It was some little time before she was able to move.

"Farewell," she said to Nero. "Think over what I have said. Save yourself before it is too late."

Without paying any heed to Tigellinus, she marched out of the room, her head tremulous with fury but still held high.

"What a miserable business!" Nero gasped as the fringed curtain fell over the doorway. "I once loved her truly. 'The best of mothers'—was the pass-word I gave the praetorians on the day when I mounted the throne.—And now!"

"Yes, indeed," sighed the Sicilian. "But is it your fault if your filial piety has by degrees been stultified? She has deserved no better; by all that is sacred, no!"

Nero sighed deeply.

"Send Cassius to me," he said gloomily. "He shall dress me."

"You shall be obeyed. Meanwhile I will go and inform Seneca. The investigation must be begun to-day. The slaves and freedmen of Lucius Menenius must be imprisoned."

"For aught I care. Only do not delay my departure for Baiae on account of this wretched affair.—Oh for Baiae! refreshing and consoling spot! It perennially invites the suffering soul with a thousand soothing voices. Life is easier there, on the shores of the bay, than among the walls of the city of the Seven Hills. In Baiae a man may for a while forget the torment the gods have inflicted on us—the misery of being man."

Tigellinus had merely made a pretext of the interview with Seneca. In fact, he went off to the second cavaedium, where Poppaea Sabina had established herself, in defiance of all the proprieties. He hastened at once to the oecus, pannelled with sky-blue, and smelling deliciously of Athenian violets. Caesar's mistress received him with friendly familiarity. They exchanged a few whispered, but very important words. Then Poppaea signed to Hasdra, who was kneeling on a cushion a little way apart, and praying with eager eyes. Poppaea murmured something in the girl's ear and Hasdra cast down her eyes. She nodded, as though it were something previously agreed upon, and then vanished through a side door.

Caesar meanwhile awaited his body-slaves. At first without impatience; his thoughts were busy with all that had just happened. But suddenly it struck him as strange that he, the Ruler of the World should be kept waiting, like a cook's boy in a barber's shop. He had but to speak and the inattentive slaves would be nailed to the cross before the day was out.—Now in the strength of their youth—and then a senseless mass, a mere heap of bones and muscles that once had life. . . . !

He followed up this train of thought. Not the slaves only were as chattels in his power, but all the freedmen—all the citizens, the knights, the senators—nay, up to the consuls themselves.—What a strange sensation! He clasped his hand over his eyes, as though seized with sudden giddiness.

In point of fact, when seen in the true light not a single head in the immeasurable empire was firm or on it owner's shoulders. At any moment when Caesar might take a fancy to have it severed from the trunk, it must fall. Some feeble pretext was all that was needed, and the sovereign's whim was an act of law. And there could be no lack of such pretexts. The mob of courtiers that crawled at his feet,—pah! the wretches would swear for ten denarii that Rome was but a village and the Pontifex Maximus a woman dressed in men's clothes.

It was a mad world indeed that placed everything in the power of one man. Yes, everything. He could make a beggar of the richest senator by the twinkle of an eye-lash, or a street hussy of the most virtuous wife. Nay more. If he chose, the lowest and foulest corpse-bearer might to-morrow be a propraetor and the most debauched Gaditanian girl might be free to walk by the side of the noblest lady!

Caesar! It sounded as majestic as Jupiter. Or even more majestic?—Nero really wielded the thunder-bolt, while Jupiter was but a myth. Nero Caesar really sat on the throne of his empire; Jupiter existed only in the fancy of the populace.

"Aye, that is the truth," said Nero to himself, speaking as in a dream. "Pray for rain, you miserable and idiotic planters, when the sun has parched the soil to dust! Jupiter can do nothing. But Caesar, if he pleases, can extend the Claudian aqueduct as far as Soracte, and bedew the earth with Olympian nectar! Wail for bread when the corn-ships from Alexandria are delayed, you childish proletariat! Jupiter would have you to starve, if Caesar did not throw open the endless granaries! If you were not all brutalized to the verge of imbecility you could not help seeing that the altars should be raised to me, and to me incense burnt, and flaming sacrifices!"

He threw himself on the couch quite exhausted.

At this instant a supple, small-made man rushed into the room, as swift as an arrow; his head was enveloped in a soft leathern mask, and dealing the blow with a circular movement of the arm he aimed a ringing dagger-stroke at Caesar's throat. The stab must certainly have been fatal if it had not missed; but desperate haste had perhaps diminished the young assassin's accuracy. The knife sank deep into the hard under mattress.

Nero sprang up with a cry of rage.

Was this then the high community of his divinity? He flew at his assailant like a mad creature, trying to seize him by the wrist; but the rascal was as supple as a weasel. He dropped the weapon and escaped through the door. Nero was following him and ran up against Tigellinus. Behind him came the body-slaves.

"You scoundrels!" cried Nero. "Shall I have you sawn asunder alive? While you are loitering in corners, and drinking or throwing dice, you leave your sovereign to be threatened by an assassin."

The men shrank together.

"That may Jupiter forbid!"

"Jupiter! Of what good is Jupiter to protect me against the traitor's dagger? If you had been on the spot, as it was your duty to be, the regicide could not even have attempted the crime."

"My lord," Cassius faltered out. "Do not doubt that we are each and all ready to shed our heart's blood for you. But the empress-mother detained us. She had some message—and then she must have forgotten that we were waiting in the colonnade. . . ."

"A message!" muttered Tigellinus. He stooped and picked up the assassin's three-edged stiletto. His face expressed excessive, almost extravagant horror.

"Caesar, my adored friend. . . ." he murmured in the greatest agitation. Then, turning to the slaves, he said: "Go. Bid the people of Rome offer burnt sacrifices of thanksgiving for the escape of our glorious emperor! Go, fly!—I myself will wait on Caesar."

The men obeyed. Tigellinus fell on his knees in feigned anguish by Caesar's couch and hid his face in the folds of the purple coverlet.

"Claudius Nero," he groaned, solemnly drawing himself up, "this dagger thrust was dealt by Agrippina!"

A cry of horror broke from Nero's lips.

"Sophonius!" he said, raising his fist as if to strike him.

"By Agrippina," the Sicilian repeated.

"Prove it!" groaned Caesar.

"I can; and Poppaea will confirm it. Shall I send for her?"

"Do what you will.—But woe to you, if you deceive me!"

"Does a man deceive his friend? I stake this head on it that Poppaea will say exactly the same. My assertion is simply this: this finely-wrought stiletto comes out of the secret store of weapons which the worthy Agrippina keeps in the wall of her cubiculum. You will find several more there. If they are not as like the dagger which I hold in my hand, as one egg is like another, send me at once to the Gemonian steps."

He went to the door and sent one of the slaves who were waiting now in the middle of the hall, to fetch Otho's scheming wife.

Little Hasdra, who by Poppaea's orders had committed this theatrical attempt on Nero's life, with the marvellous swiftness she always displayed had meanwhile stolen back unperceived to her mistress's side. She had snatched off the mask in the outer passage, and dropped the skirts she had rolled up high.

Poppaea had been waiting in an agony of suspense and

when she learnt that all had succeeded as she wished, she clasped the girl to her heart and kissed her twenty times. Hasdra, however, seemed to require no thanks; her eyes glittered with evil joy. Then she slipped away, sat down on her little cushion, and cried.

Her tears were for Pharax.

The messenger now came in from Tigellinus. Poppaea did not hesitate. What did she care for the rest of the inhabitants of the Palatium, or if they saw her going to Caesar's room. It seemed to her to be high time at last to let the truth stand more plainly confessed than during Octavia's presence on the scene.

"Caesar, I greet you," said she with a smile, as if unsuspicious of ill; and she embraced him fondly.

"Lady," said Tigellinus, "grant me a monent's speech with you."

"What about?" she asked inquisitively.

The Sicilian told his story—first as to the events in Lucius Menenius' villa; then the scene with Agrippina; and finally the horrible crime which some "unknown assassin" had attempted against Caesar's life.

Poppaea Sabina behaved like one frantic.

"Nero, my sweet Nero!" she wailed again and again. "Are you still alive, or is it a dream that I hold your dear head between these hands? Yes, you are indeed here! Oh I am ready to die when I only imagine—Tigellinus, I am falling--oh, my poor, tortured brain!"

Presently she even shed a few tears--genuine, natural tears rolled slowly down her cheeks; and at that moment the Agrigentine held the three-edged stiletto before her eyes, and said quietly: "Look; here is the weapon which the murderer left behind him."

Poppaea gave a loud scream and fell in a well-acted swoon into the arms Tigellinus put out just in time to catch her.

The shock to Caesar was genuine; his blood rushed in a tide to his heart, and he swayed. He clutched with both hands at the heavy bronze table, making the silver cups and dishes ring. But he recovered himself.

"Poppaea," he murmured hoarsely, "do not compel me to believe anything so monstrous. . . . ! It would be my death, Poppaea!"

"Not yours, for you are guiltless! Nero, when Tigellinus told you—it was the truth. This dagger. . . ."

"This dagger?" repeated Nero. "Pause, consider. You are mistaken, Poppaea; you must be mistaken, or the whole universe ought to crumble into ruins!"

Poppaea sakly shook her head.

"It is no mistake; the author of this crime is Agrippina."

She then told him of the singular accident which had made her acquainted with the secret of that concealed niche in the wall, and what she had seen there. The panel which had covered it had at that time evidently not been perfectly fitted; for, on a subsequent occasion, Poppaea had attempted to find it again, but without success. Nero, however, could at any time have the wall torn down. Rigid and speechless, with a glassy stare piercingly fixed on her burning face, Caesar heard her tale.

"Cunning indeed!" he gasped. "So she herself gives the weapon to her hired assassins. Then if the dagger is lost, or breaks off short in the victim's breastbone, it is less easy to track the wretch than if he did the deed with his own weapon.—It is masterly!"

There was an oppressive pause. "Nero Caesar," Tigellinus presently began. "This day is decisive. Two things must be clear to you: First, that in the eyes of the law Agrippina deserves to die: Secondly, that for your safety, if for nothing else, she must perish. To seize her and drag her in fetters before the senate would, strictly speaking, be Caesar's duty; for his illustrious person, above everything else, belongs to his people. But I know that you could never endure this—and to be frank, your aversion seems to me quite intelligible. Even as a criminal she is Caesar's mother. A public prosecution would sully the dignity of the dynasty— nay of the whole Roman Empire. Your divine name must not be disgraced.—Leave it to me to make away with the reprobate woman who could attempt the precious life of her own son to gratify her miserable ambition. I advise—nay I demand this—or I kill myself!''

"Yield to this," Poppaea implored him, falling on her knees. "I cannot breathe till I know that your dear head is safe from her."

She tore her garments, with trembling hands she dishevelled her luxuriant hair, and again she forced up a flow of tears, more ready and abundant than before.

At first Nero resisted. But suddenly, by a truly Titanic outbreak of fury, he threw off the paralyzing torpor which weighed upon him, raising his clenched fists as though holding the gods responsible for this catastrophe.

"Wretched woman!"he cried. "She wades in blood up to her ankles, and still she is insatiable. She must murder her own son to enable her to sleepin peace!—Down with such pitiful weakness, cowardly, timorous heart!— Punish her, Tigellinus! Act.—Kill—murder—what you will."

"Caesar, I thank thee! But one thing more, if I am to succeed."

"Well?"

"From this hour behave to Agrippina as I shall dictate. You have only to give us the support of words, manner, and demeanor. I alone will do the deed—and sooner than you think!"

Nero again hesitated. But there lay the dagger with its gleaming blade. . . .

"It is her own doing!"he muttered between his teeth. Then, with a glare in his eyes, he held out his hand to the Sicilian and said in a hollow voice: "So be it!"

CHAPTER IX.

A WEEK later, and Nero with his splendid court was again at Baiae. Only Seneca, having a multitude of important state matters to settle, had remained in Rome with Burrus, who was engaged in investing the affair at the house of Menenius. Since a military tribune—Pharax—had been concerned in the plot, Tigellinus insisted in the most emphatic terms that the greatest vigilance was necessary and that "no one could efficiently take the place of the distinguished Burrus."

In reality the wily Sicilian's object was to keep the only man who, he thought, might interfere with his audacious machinations against the empress-mother, as far as possible from the scene of their development.

Since the painful scene in her son's cubiculum, Agrippina had not again been seen. She spent two long, miserable days in the solitude of her own apartments, nursing the rage and revenge which almost choked her breathing. On the third day she left Rome precipitately, with a small following. Even Pallas was not allowed to accompany her: she would play the part of a humble, abandoned outcast. To this end she selected a retreat which, though situated on the shore of the gulf of Baiae, was far enough away from the town itself to suggest the idea of obloquy or even of banishment. "What!" she imagined the world would exclaim, "Claudius Nero lords it among the colonnades of his Olympian villa, his life is one endless scene of delicious revelry, while Agrippina, who made him emperor, is living out in dreary Bauli, a deserted fishing hamlet! What a son—and what a mother!"

There was a pretty little country-house at Bauli which Agrippina had but lately given to Acerronia as a wedding present. The red-haired Hispanian was already a widow. Men lived fast in Rome under the Caesars.

Nero and Tigellinus seemed bent on enjoying the far-famed delights of Baiae with more unbridled indulgence than ever. Poppaea Sabina was the confessed high priestess of a worship which consisted of a combination of every conceivable form of earthly enjoyment. There were orgies held with hysterical raptures in honor of Nature; digressions into the region of art; and pauses, preluding excesses of sensuality.

Tigellinus, meanwhile, had completely conquered the fair cithara-player. Forgetful of the past, she leaned on his shoulder in triumph at these mad feasts. Nero, as he noted this, laughed scornfully. He remembered the evening at the house of Flavius Scaevinus when Chloris had made her appearance, an innocent girl, before the expectant guests and had sung that captivating, never-to- be-forgotten song. And what a change was this! Artemidorus' guileless sweetheart— and now! Pooh! The freedman would soon get over it; he would reflect that this was the course of nature and the will of fate. What were these maiden blossoms for, if not to be sacrificed on the altar of imperial omnipotence! Tigellinus with Chloris clinging to him—it was like a pillar of Caesar's shrine wreathed with roses.

As to the song—that song! As he recalled it a sweet, fair face rose before him, a flower-like face with large, deep-blue eyes. Those tearful eyes seemed to say: "I loved you more than anything in Heaven or on earth! But now I am dead,— long ago.Then he would lay his hand with a fevered clutch on Poppaea Sabina, shout a frenzied "Evoe," and empty his winecup at one gulp, to the very dregs.

In this whirl of revelry and pleasure Tigellinus and Poppaea seemed entirely to have forgotten their vengeance on Agrippina. At most would the Agrigentine come in too late now and then to some performance by Syrian dancing girls, or steal away before the noisy debauch was at an end. It might, too, have seemed singular that Anicetus, the commander of the fleet, whose ships of war lay only a few miles away, to the west off Cape Misenum, was to be seen in more frequent and intimate conversation with Tigellinus than of yore. But no one in Baiae had time to take any particular note of other folks' doings, and Nero, who was the only person whom it could concern nearly, was purposely deaf and blind. Thus not a soul suspected that the wily Anicetus had expressed himself willing, for the sum of three million sesterces, to carry out the "sentence" of Agrippina

Early in the third week of their stay, Tigellinus begged of Caesar "the favor of a few minutes of his valuable time."

"What is the matter?" asked Nero, whose brow had all day carried the weight of a painful foreboding.

"If it please your majesty to follow me?" said the Sicillian. "It will save a detailed explanation."

He conducted Caesar into a delightful room decorated in brown, which looked out into the park. A narrow window without panes framed in a view over a perfect sea of roses in bloom. To the right of this window stood a handsome writing-table—the legs of wrought brass, and the top a transverse section of a splendid trunk of cedar. It was here that Tigellinus, who had lately filled the place almost of Caesar's coadjutor, wrote the imperial despatches to Burrus and Seneca. Here, too, he had lately written to Otho in Lusitania, to announce that they had not as yet been able to trace the conspirators implicated with Didius and Lucius Menenius; that they were, however, inclined to suspect that some centurions in Otho's service had been won over to the cause of rebellion; and that he, Otho, was to investigate the matter cautiously but with promptitude.

At this table, too, were those love letters composed—

graced with all the flowers of rhetoric—which Tigellinus threw off, half a dozen at a time, in spite of his immediate preference for the Rhodian singer. All round the Aphrodite-worshipping town of Baiae there was scarcely a lady of distinction with whom Tigellinus would not have corresponded in high-flown Greek: provided always that she were young, agreeable, and pretty. Only on those conditions did his fluent pen pour forth fervent apostrophes and sparkling flattery.

At this moment the beautiful grained cedar-table, which was usually strewn with documents grave and gay, was a pattern of neatness. Only two long strips of papyrus, one quite clean and the other written over, lay in front of the little golden urn containing black ink.

"My lord," Tigellinus began with some solemnity, "I had promised myself and you—and above all Poppaea in her deep anxiety—to wind up the melancholy business which darkened our last days in Rome, without your further intervention;—I mean the empress-mother's crime. It seems impossible, however, to act entirely without your participation. So I would beg of you to copy this letter and send it this very day to the Empress Agrippina. It contains everything which, on mature reflection, I think need be said. Then for one afternoon you will be compelled to play a part, which may indeed be painful, but which cannot be difficult with the distinguished dramatic talent which Apollo has bestowed on you. You have only to behave as you formerly did: a courteous and dutiful son who has never suspected his unnatural mother's purpose."

Caesar took up the papyrus with a slightly trembling hand. The letter was as follows:

"Claudius Nero Caesar to his beloved mother, wishing her happiness and health.

"To my deep regret, I perceive, my dear mother, that the scene with Sophonius Tigellinus is likely to alienate you from me completely.

"I will not pause to enquire how far this man's accusations are true or false; by his own confession he spoke under the influence of great excitement. I only know that all mortals have their faults, so that it would be folly to blame you for what is common to all. Least of all would it beseem me, your son, to judge you; for whatever is charged to your account as evil, you did for my sake. A mother's love is worthy of respect, even when it sins for the sake of a beloved child.

"But to be brief. I feel that I love you as tenderly now as ever, and that all my joy in life is embittered so long as we live in feud and antagonism. I therefore entreat you: let the past be forgotten, and give me again the dear hand which has so often led and guided me—and never to my hurt. If you will, the whole world shall see and know that we are reconciled. I hereby invite you to spend the day to-morrow with the son you have found again. Tigellinus, as a punishment for his insolence, left Baiae yesterday. In all other respects he is an admirable man and sinned only out of faithful affection for me. I have sent him to Rome till further orders; he may, to some extent, lighten the labors of our worthy Seneca.

"Send me your answer by the slave who carries this. I hope you will not reject my supplication. Till we meet, beloved mother, farewell."

Nero looked enquiringly at Tigellinus, who on his part urged him to demand no explanation. With a sigh Caesar set to work.

When he had finished the copy he hastily went out into the *frigidarium*. His head was burning; a cold bath, he hoped would refresh him.

The triumphant Agrigentine meanwhile sent the letter to Bauli by a mounted messenger. The reply came by supper time. The empress-mother wrote as follows:

"Agrippina to her beloved son, Claudius Nero.

327

"I have received your letter, which brought me the comforting news of the long-hoped-for-change that has taken place in you.

"It seems to me equally wise and considerate in you to have sent away Tigellinus. That man has no real friendship for you—would that I could leave you no doubt on that point! He flatters you out of sheer self-interest; he only aims at ruling you to take advantage of you. I, on the contrary, when I endeavor to lead or influence you, have no end in view but those which I have aimed at from the first: your happiness, your greatness, and the permanence of your empire. It is no disgrace to a hero or a demigod even to yield to a mother's guidance—how often have I told you so! Coriolanus, the mighty conqueror, withdrew his army from Rome when his mother appealed to his conscience.

"But enough. I will come; nay—why should I disguise it—I will come with the greatest joy. Only take care that we meet alone: we must understand each other. If the weather remains propitious I will journey by sea. I shall be with you an hour after sunrise. No one will be with me but Acerronia and a few slave-women.

"Farewell."

Tigellinus, who had opened the empress-mother's letter, nodded to himself as he read it; then he carried it to Poppaea's room, where Anicetus was waiting for him.

As he went in, holding the blue-tinted papyrus in his hand, they both started from their seats in anxious curiosity and stared at him as if he were a ghost. Even Hasdra, who was in the fearful secret, gave a start and fixed her black eyes on the Sicilian's face.

"Here!" whispered Tigellinus with a smile, enjoying their excitement.

When Poppaea and Anicetus had mastered the contents, they all agreed that Nero should be kept in ignorance of Agrippina's letter, since the reasonable and trustful tone she had adopted might be dangerous.

328

"When once she is here," said Poppaea, "I will answer for it that even her tenderest persuasiveness will have no lasting effect. But if he were to read what she has so cunningly concocted, he might think it over at leisure and allow himself to doubt."

"Well spoken," said Tigellineus. "The business is only just feasible as it is; even postponement might be fatal to us. Agrippina is indefatigable; if we give the old serpent time, she may very likely succeed in wriggling on the top once more."

"May my lucky star preserve us from that!" sighed Poppaea. "The mere idea fills me with deadly terror."

"For my part," said the Sicilian, "I fear her less than I hate her. My vanity, too, is at stake: I cannot and must not be beaten."

"No, you must not, noble Sophonius," hissed Hasdra, rubbing her hands. "She believes herself a goddess. Show her that she is mortal. Kill her, and I will kiss the very dust your feel have trod, with joy!"

"Do I understand," said Anicetus, "that you are not merely your mistress's faithful tool, but are moved by enmity on your own account?"

"Yes, my lord."

"But why?"

"Did you know Pharax, the military tribune? When he was but a soldier in the guard he loved me.—Do not laugh, Tigellinus. Even ugly little Hasdra, whom you all disdain, was really loved once! And the mightly courtesan beguiled him from me—oh, I could seize her by her foul, lying throat!"

She shook her fist towards Bauli. Her features were knit with rage and her set teeth gleamed between her parted lips, as white and as sharp as a jackal's. The primitive savagery of this outbreak startled Poppaea.

"Control yourself," she said gently. "Agrippina will die without your having a hand in it. For shame! What—tears?"

"Oh no! Not tears. I have long ceased to shed them. My

eyes are only moist with rage; consuming rage!"

Nero meanwhile, after taking a bath, had lain down in the cool solitude of the exedra gazing at the marble statues in the reddish brown niches, or turning over some documents which had just been put into his hand by one of the palace messengers. He had but glanced at the daily reports sent him by Seneca and Burrus, though the general's despatch contained matters which seemed to be of some importance. Burrus announced the successful capture of two tribunes who had plotted to kill Caesar and Poppaea Sabina. When they were asked their motives, they replied defiantly: "Our swords were to avenge Octavia's wrongs!"

For a minute Caesar's attention was arrested. His feelings culminated in the reflection: "Assassination is astir on Octavia's behalf then! She, too, is a source of danger!"

However, he promptly dismissed these thoughts and the vexation they caused him. Far more interesting to him than all that Burrus had to say about this unpleasant incident, was a letter from Phaon, whom he had left in Rome as head steward of the Palatium.

Phaon sent him the plan and estimates for a new and splendid villa, to be erected on the crest of the hills between Cumae and Baiae; a magnificent evidence of Caesar's passion for prodigality and almost Persian love of luxury. This was the fifth monumental structure which Nero had planned for his personal convenience within the last few months. Two of these gorgeous residences were already finished, for a perfect army of slaves and laborers toiled night and day under the command of the architects, painters, and sculptors.

"Enchanting!" murmured Nero once more going over every detail. "By Zeus! that is what I call an intelligent apprehension of the claims and requirements of the Ruler of the World. To be sure—the outlay will be in proportion. Nine hundred million! I doubt if Semiramis had more fitting lodging! Nine hundred million! Enough to redeem Alexandria from taxation and tribute to all eternity."

He rested his brow on his hand.

"For whom to you sow, weary peasant of the Nile delta?

"For whom do you sow, weary peasant of the Nile delta? brawny Mauritanian? For whom do you breed your noble herds, squalid settlers by the blue Danube? And you in Hispania and Cappadocia, your fiery steeds?—For me: Caesar, to whom you may be grateful if he leaves you so much as will save you from dying of hunger, and sow, and hunt, and breed no more! A glorious—an Olympian grasp of power! When this dizzy sense comes over me, the earth sinks before my gaze and leaves no trace behind; then I feel that Caesar is superior to Fate itself. If I am robbed of what I love—that is but as a drop of dew; while what I govern and what I can crush is an inexhaustible sea, a whole ocean of whimpering, miserable creatures."

He lay staring up at the carved ceiling, as though he could look through the elegantly decorated wood-work, up into the infinite sky empty of dethroned gods and ready to receive one guest alone: himself.

Thus he was found by Tigellinus.

"Caesar," said he in the tone of a business communication, "Agrippina will arrive the first thing to-morrow morning."

"I knew it," said Caesar absently. "When Claudius Nero commands, the most defiant of rebels must obey."

"And do you really call that a command which was expressed in such flattering terms?"

Nero passed his hand over his brow.

"To be sure, I remember now," he said, suddenly coming back from remote illusions to practical life. "Yes, I asked her humbly—I, who with a glance of my eye could reduce Rome to ruins! But you were to blame for it. I only wrote exactly what you bid me."

"With the best result, my lord. My messenger tells me that Agrippina was over-joyed, and so excited that she had not time to write you an answer. She sends you a hundred loving greetings, for she supposes that you have returned to your former humble submission."

"Submission!" cried Nero scornfully. "If she could but know.—Submission! I—Caesar!" He started to his feet and walked to and fro, meditating deeply.

"Forgive me," he said at length. "Your hand, Tigellinus. You are one of the few mortals to whom I am gladly and entirely grateful, from the bottom of my heart. I was not thinking of what I was doing. This report from Phaon—I mean from Burrus—here; read it yourself.—So she is coming? And what further am I to do, for I promised you . . . ?"

"We will discuss that presently," the adjutant broke in. "You seem strangely agitated. What Burrus tells you I had already heard from the fair Poppaea. She knows everything, that pearl among women. The two rebel tribunes, whom he has disarmed, were hired by Agrippina."

"Who says so?"

"Poppaea; and she will presently prove it to you. But do not speak of it to her yet. She might be agitated, and for the present we must be bright and gay, so far as possible."

"You are right, Tigellinus. She must be spared. Especially now—when she may so soon be the mother of my child."

"Caesar, my friend!" exclaimed Tigellinus as though he had not long known the secret. "Happy, thrice happy sovereign. Now, indeed, I feel sure that all must go well. Caesar's child is dear to the gods. One day more—and Caesar will be rid of the venomous adder which incessantly threatens his beloved head. Go, my Claudius, sup with Poppaea; let this day be hers alone. Thus may you recover yourself and steel your heart and hers for the last decisive stroke! Be happy, Caesar; Tigellinus will work for you!"

CHAPTER X.

Next morning Agrippina left Bauli, as was agreed, at a very early hour. Nero, surrounded by a splendid suite, met her at the landing-steps, helped her out of her boat with officious politeness, and kissed her hands. Acerronia, too, was graciously welcomed. Agrippina led the way up the steps to the broad terrace hedged round with myrtles, where the litters were waiting. The empress must be spared the fatigue of even those few paces to the vestibulum, so strictly did Anicetus adhere to the rules of etiquette.

One of Caesar's freedmen was charged to see the barge moored in a walled dock and to take proper care of the sweating oarsmen and of Agrippina's slaves.

Poppaea Sabina was waiting at the entrance to the atrium, her head bent in humble homage, and her arms folded in the oriental fashion. Agrippina had by this time been long used to recognize the headstrong woman as her equal in power. Caesar had in fact a genuine passion for his handsome mistress, who was so accomplished in all the arts of flattery; a passion which was but slightly dashed when, now and again, his memory recalled the half-effaced image of Acte, or in those moments of irrepressible license which posessed him most strongly when he had been most deeply studying philosophy. In such hours of extravagance he would wish that all the women on earth were embodied in a single exquisite beauty, that he might clasp in one embrace all that Aphrodite, in her divine folly, had so pitiably squandered. But he always came back to Poppaea with renewed fervor, and she was wise enough to take no notice of the despot's infidelities. Thus he abandoned himself more and more to the sovereignty of her charms.

And now, when it was universally rumored that Poppaea was a mother, when Otho, fully informed of the state of affairs, had calmly announced his consent to a divorce—now at last Agrippina could not but confess: "If I wish to gain the upper hand, I must not betray my hatred of this hussy."

And she was fully capable of acting on this conclusion. The younger woman's humble attitude was splendidly rewarded. Agrippina embraced her, called her her dearest friend, kissed her parted lips, and declared that sweet Poppaea had never looked so bewitching, so lovely, and so ravishing.

They at once sat down to an elegant breakfast, under the awning of a small triclinium. Only five persons shared the meal: Nero, Agrippina, Acerronia, Poppaea, and Anicetus. Tigellinus kept out of sight all day, and every one believed that he had started for Rome. Nor was his name even mentioned during the meal.

The conversation was chiefly sustained by Poppaea and Anicetus. The sailor, particularly, was unwontedly loquacious. Their first point was to keep Caesar and Agrippina from any approach to an understanding. He poured out marvellous adventures by sea, one after another, greatly applauded by Poppaea and Acerronia, now agitating them by tales of danger and suspense, now digressing into the regions of the comic or of romance, now tantalizing their curiosity by unsolved puzzles. Even the empress-mother seemed now and then quite fascinated by the man's vivid manner and powers of description. Any looker-on would have believed that the most genial enjoyment, the most genuine peace of mind, and the brightest good spirits ruled at this board blazing with gold and silver.

But Agrippina at any rate was contending against painful suspicions. Poppaea perceived that she was still distrustful from the covert but unfailing caution with which she refrained from tasting any dish till either Caesar or Poppaea had eaten of it. And once, when Agrippina was looking the other way, Poppaea directed Nero's attention to this by a little sign, intelligible to him alone.

Caesar knit his brows. His mother's fears seemed to him the clearest proof of her guilt. He traced a large B on the table with his forefinger, as if without purpose. A gleam of satisfaction shone in Poppaea's eyes: this B, she knew, meant Britannicus.

The breakfast was choice: fine oysters and tender boneless muraenae; the best ragout that a prince of Roman cooks could prepare; two patties—one of larks' brains, the other of steamed venison with twenty spices; fruit from the most famous gardens of Campania—in short, the rarest delicacies of every description were served by servants in splendid livery, which a sparkling wine from Etna, cooled with snow, exhaled its intoxicating perfume.

But the only member of the party who derived any pleasure from all this luxury was Acerronia. She revelled in it—and drank more than one cheering cup with a fervent wish that the days of exile at Bauli might be at an end. This fleeting life was a different thing indeed under this velarium swelling to the breeze, and away yonder in her "dower-house." Thanks to the immortals she was at any rate rid of her horrible husband; all she now wanted was the gay and brilliant life she had known before, and—a substitute for a husband. She did not mean to marry again—no, not for the world! But a friend—she wished for a friend. Anicetus for instance. His nose was rather broad; but kisses are not given with the nose.—By Hercules! as he talked on, laughing heartily whenever Acerronia did, she could not think how it was that she had hitherto thought so little of him.—And then that ridiculous vision in Scaevinus' park! His eyes, which were now so bright, had then suddenly closed; he had looked like a corpse. . . . ! Of course, she had known at once that it was an illusion—and yet; she could see it now: green water flowing over his face, his lips drawn, pale, horrible! And behind him the statute of Pomona which suddenly assumed the features of the empress-mother. . . . ! Too absurd!

But Epicharis, the wise Egyptian, had interpreted it favorably then and there: She had prophesied that Anicetus would, in the course of the year, convey Acerronia safely to port—to be sure, she saw it all. "To port" could only be a figure of speech, and must stand for a happy love-affair.

Really she was too stupid not to have thought of this sooner. Then she might have spared herself the miserable episode with Pharax, who, in spite of all her most determined scratching and biting, had proved untamable.

Thus her fancy wandered free, and the future painted itself in tempting pictures.

During the heat of noon all the residents of the villa retired to rest.

At about two hours before the chief evening meal they met again in the exedra, the coolest room in the house, and there Chloris sang for their delectation.

"Fair Rhodian," said Caesar, when for the second time she laid down her instrument, "one thing more, which we have not heard for a long time: Pray sing us that sweet, delicious air, '*Glykeia Mater.*' "

Glykeia Mater—Oh, sweet mother—were the first words of a favorite Doric song of the people. All the company, especially Poppaea and Anicetus, clapped agreement.

Agrippina readily yielded to the influence of this delicate attention. She was now quite convinced that Caesar was once more wholly in her power. The fact that his voice had trembled a little as he addressed Chloris, she regarded as of good omen. Much as her pride had suffered, deeply as her love of power had rebelled against the headstrong boy who had so unexpectedly dared to outgrow her management, still he was and must ever be her dearly-loved child. And as the singer began, breathing all the fervor of her impassioned soul into the words *"Glykeia Mater,"* the moving tones sounded so pure, so entrancing, that even Agrippina—the accomplished mistress of sovereign self-control—forgot for an instant the cold demeanor which she considered the first condition of dignity. Her eyes glistened, and two bright tears seemed ready to drop from her lashes, in expiation perhaps of the many dark deeds which no prayer could henceforth undo.

"Glykeia Mater" sang Chloris.

And meanwhile the woman to whom she did honor was hurrying on to her last hour.

At four in the afternoon supper, or dinner, began; all the residents in the villa and several guests were present. At her own particular request, the distribution of garlands had been entrusted to Hasdra. Dressed in a flowing robe of red, with grave and deliberate solemnity, as though she were fulfilling a sacred function, she approached the tables decked for the banquet. Uppermost on her shallow basket lay a wreath of white roses, distinguished from the rest by its thickness and beauty. With sparkling eyes she made her way to the place of honor, where Agrippina reclined on the magnificent cushions with a haughty smile, between Caesar and Anicetus. Poppaea's little attendant raised the fragrant diadem with triumphant grace.

"Roses from Cumae," she said trembling a little. "The finest in all Italy. Claudius Nero, our sovereign lord, ordered them expressly for you. This distinction is yours alone. Roses, a fit bridal-wreath for Proserpine, the queen of death—pale and regal!"

Anicetus, angry at this inopportune address, cast a furious glance at the Syrian. But Hasdra still smiled as if in contempt of the abject man of business, who undertook murder and vengeance for gold, while she would gladly have given millions upon millions only to feel that she might revenge herself. She turned away almost haughtily.

Agrippina had scarcely heard the words uttered by her

secret foe. Carelessly placing the sacrificial garland on her hair, she permitted Anicetus, with a courtier's respectful gallantry, to adjust the sapphire-set pin.

Her eyes had long been fixed thoughtfully on Poppaea Sabina's perpetually-laughing face.

How easily this woman, with her radiant beauty, made Caesar yield to her whims. By Zeus, in any other sphere Agrippina would have felt confident of her power to cope in charm and fascination with any woman—even Poppaea. But in this case, she had the misfortune of being Caesar's mother.

Smiling, she mentioned this idea to Anicetus, adding after a short pause:

"You will admit that the battle was unequal. I could not use my most trustworthy weapon. I'll comfort myself with this recollection."

Anicetus, whose thoughts were busied with his own plans, misunderstood the empress-mother's meaning, and started violently. The horror of the idea he fancied made him shudder. But, with a secret smile of scorn, he raised the goblet to his lips, silently pledging the "prosperous voyage" he desired to arrange for the sovereign decked with the garland of a bride.

It was already dark when Agrippina rose from her couch to return to Bauli. The moon stood high over the distant hills, shedding its soothing light on the broad mirror of the bay, and the numerous temples, theatres, and villas, which stood on the shores.

Nero himself escorted his mother to the quay, and most of the guests followed them. But strange to say her barge had not come round; a loud confusion of voices was audible from the creek where it lay moored.

"What is the meaning of this?" asked the captain of the fleet.

"The boat was sprung a leak," replied an oarsman.

Agrippina scowled.

"How extraordinary! Who could have done such a thing? You, Androchus?"

"Madam, on my life. . . ."

"Silence," said Nero. "To-morrow we will ascertain who is to blame. Cassius, take all these men in charge.—And you, dearest mother, do not let such a trifle disturb your good humor. At a hundred paces from hence lies the splendid boat which this lavish Anicetus but lately presented to me.—Fly, Eurysthenes, get the men on board. Now, mother, rest for a while on this stone bench. In five minutes you will be off, homeward bound."

The words almost choked him; his parched tongue clove to his gums. But he could not now retract. It *must* be done. Justice required it, and his own safety, nay, and the security of Rome; for was not he Rome?

The regular dip and splash of oars announced the approach of the splendidly-fitted barge. Anicetus had manned it with the most reckless of his men-at-arms, and they now sat on the rowers' benches disguised as simple seamen. At a signal from the captain they ceased to ply their oars. A board covered with carpet was pushed out from the quay-wall to the deck. Agrippina embraced Caesar and Poppaea—who was as pale as marble, gave her hand to Anicetus, bowed graciously to the rest of the company, and calmly walked on board, followed by Acerronia and her women.

In the middle of the ship there was a Persian canopy; under it comfortable seats and couches were arranged. Agrippina lay down, and her companions seated themselves round her, blooming girls in rosecolored dresses with cloaks of light-hued woollen stuffs which they allowed to fall about their hips. The group suggested Galatea and her nereids.

A last farewell was shouted from the shore. Then the captain put forth his right hand. Two flute-players began the melting air of "Oh, golden Baiae!" and the soldiers dipped their oars to its rhythm. The bark made a turn to the left, and the gorgeous vessel then went forward out into the silent bay.

CHAPTER XI.

It was a delicious night. The growing moonlight shone broader and brighter every minute on the dancing ripples. Cape Misenum, misty in the distance, the villa-dotted slopes, the climbing pine forests—all looked as if bathed in silver and snow. Silver and snow dripped in gem-like drops from the blades of the oars, glittered on the columns of the canopy, lay on the broad deck, and sank refreshingly into the half-weary souls. Agrippina rested her head on her hand. The soft, pervading blue, the fragrant air, the tuneful piping of the flutes—it was all inexpressibly restful. A gentle smile played on her lips. She was happy again, after so long an interval!

A never-to-be-forgotten day; everything, yes everything was turning out well. Her son had once more found the limit-line where her maternal authority began. He had pledged himself to respect that limit, to trust her implicitly, and to follow her advice as long as she should live.

This was a return to bygone times, to her sense of imperial power and of supremacy over the realm. And power was so delightful, so glorious, so full of promise!

What might she not do as reinstated empress! What decisive measures might she not take! What might she not scheme and carry out, make or mar! Away at once with the rabble rout who were degrading Rome to a mere tavern.

Away with that Sicilian charlatan and his feeble, scurvy crew. Order should be restored in the empire of Augustus—order, at any price: the Parthians should crouch as a dog crouches at the roar of a lion: the Germans beyond the Logana she would tread under foot, once for all, and make a splendid end of the perpetual border warfare. Germania—the terrible yellow giantess—who had killed Varus and drawn vindictive tears from the eyes of the great Augustus—Germania should quail and sink into the dust before Agrippina, Empress of Rome!

Her head sank drowsily on the pillow. Rosy genii floated before her fancy bearing the crown of victory of a Roman triumph, a dense and fantastic dream-cloud. She closed her eyes. A balmy breath fanned her half-smiling mouth, like the kiss of an immortal god. . . .

Suddenly a fearful crash was heard, a splintering rent—and then a wild, piercing cry of terror and anguish. The vessel had fallen asunder, as of its own accord, into three parts, of which the middle portion, supporting the canopy, toppled over headlong into the waves. Before Agrippina was fairly awake, she heard the dark waves gurgling in her ears; the briny flood was in her mouth and nose, her senses had almost forsaken her.

But at last she rose to the surface again. She heard the shrieks of the slave-women in their agonized struggle for life, she heard Acerronia's wailing scream. Agrippina's heart was chill with grief and horror. It was not the fear of death that choked her so mercilessly; it was the certainty of the dreadful truth. Without a cry she clutched one of the Corinthian columns, which had fallen from the canopy and was floating round and round in the eddy.

"Woe is me—I saw Anicetus with closed eyes!" moaned Acerronia, remembering the vision she had interpreted so hopefully. With the energy of despair she swam towards the larger half of the vessel, which remained afloat. The moon was hidden behind a cloud. A strange, ashy hue fell like a dismal shroud over the scene of horror.

"Save me!" broke in a shrill cry from the Hispanian, as she caught at a hanging pole, "Save me!" Then, as no one heeded her, she added in a scream: "I am Caesar's mother!"

Hardly had she spoken the fateful words, when a storm of blows from the oars thrashed up the waters and fell on her head. The gay and pleasure-loving Acerronia sank with a broken skull, and at the same time all of the slave-women shared her fate.

Agrippina alone, hidden from the eyes of the assassins by the pillar she floated with, drifted slowly away to the open sea.

"Acte!" she murmured with quivering lips, "are you come to revenge yourself?"

The death agonies of the blooming girl, who, as she believed, had been miserably drowned, rose before her mind with merciless vividness. Yes, the eternal justice of destiny was now meting out the same fate. She had a dreadful feeling that a ghostly hand from the deep was clutching at her garment. A kind of perverse remorse dawned on her soul. That freed girl had taken her fancy—in spite of everything—she had liked her from the very first. She had acted against her feelings in fostering her aversion and hostility. These thoughts flashed through her brain like lurid lightnings. Then all was dark. She doubted whether to end this hideous torment by letting the beam go and gliding down into the blue depths, cursing her murderer with her dying breath. But one thing still bid her have patience: her wild desire to punish the evil-doer. As Acte's failing strength had been buoyed up by her trustful love, so now Agrippina's deeply-injured soul drew new tenacity from the fount of revengefulness.

As soon as Anicetus' hired tools had, as they believed, finished their task, they got into a small boat which had lain concealed, sank the remaining portions of the pleasure-ship, and returned to Baiae, rejoicing in the deed they had done. Dawn was grey before they reached the shore.

In spite of the loveliness of the weather, Anicetus was

343

audacious enough to spread a report that the vessel had been wrecked on the passage from Baiae to Bauli. Not a creature believed it; every one, however, pretended to be convinced of its truth. Tigellinus had asserted boldly that there were reefs in the bay; the imperial galley perhaps drew more water than ordinary vessels. At any rate the merchant vessels making for Puteoli took a more northerly course. Tigellinus knew what he was saying; and as he had not only inventiveness, but power, no one hazarded any rash criticism.

Nero, to whom Tigellinus reported what had happened immediately on the return of the crew, though not surprised, was greatly shocked.

"Your counsel was evil," he said hoarsely. "Yes, yes; I know all you can say. And I believe what you tell me: she plotted against my life.—And yet, and yet—I would rather have banished her. . . ."

"Banished her?" cried Tigellinus. "My lord, how little you know the character of such women. Walls towering to the sky will not avail to restrain their cruelty. They can break through even the stones of Mamertine prison and the eternal rock-dungeons of Sardinia. I will offer a burnt sacrifice of thanksgiving if that terrible woman does not return, even from the dead, to sow fresh seeds of woe!"

"She *will* return!" said Caesar shuddering. "I see it already! She will stand all night by my pillow, a pallid ghost; she will point to her bosom whence I drew life; she will strangle me gasping in her clutch. . . ."

"Compose yourself," said the adjutant. "How many times must I repeat that she has but met with the fate she deserved. It was not her son merely that she tried to kill, but Caesar. The son might have forgiven her. Caesar could not and ought not."

Nero shivered.

"A chill comes over me," he moaned. "I have no words to describe my feelings—but I am miserable."

"Think of Brutus! How often, beloved Caesar, have I reminded you of him! His sons had sinned only against the

344

State; their parent's life was sacred in their eyes. And yet not for an instant did Brutus hesitate. With heroic dignity he passed the sentence of death. He smothered the instinct which is a thousand times stronger than the love of a child for its parent—the love of a father for his child. No, Claudius Nero; the deed you have permitted was just and praiseworthy; and posterity will not withhold the crown from you for that deed's sake, any more than from the iron-hearted consul.''

"It will stigmatize me as a parricide," groaned Caesar in despair.

"If you love me, compose yourself. Your nerves are painfully excited.—Go and sleep, Caesar; it is not yet broad day, and you need rest."

"I cannot sleep; a thousand thoughts are raging in my brain—old, long-faded memories.—Oh, days of my earliest infancy! When I played at her feet I still was happy; how light and innocent this heart was then! She would look down at me, lost in thought; her features were so gentle, so pure—I felt that I was beloved. . . .''

"My lord, I beseech you. . . .''

"One day—I remember it still, it was in December, just before the Saturnalia—evening was closing in. We were sitting in the oecus, while my father was still at table with his friends. She took me on her knees: 'You will do me honor some day,' she said. There was a laurel branch which I had gathered lying on a little table by the wall; she took it up and twisted it into a wreath for me. And she smiled and called me her darling, her king, and her god—and she kissed me. . . .''

Overpowered with remorse, he threw himself on his couch and hid his tear-stained face in the pillows.

Tigellinus felt every moment more annoyed and more uneasy. After a long pause for reflection he exclaimed dramatically: "It is well. Shed all your tears, glorious Caesar! They are a tribute to past childhood which must ever look like a dream of departed joys, even to the happiest of us. Under the influence of the magic spell of memory, you cannot yet feel that all that has long lain in the grave: that the tender mother who nursed her boy on her knee was drowned in the turbid flood of hateful ambitions and all-absorbing self-seeking, and not, as you would persuade yourself, in the waters of the bay. Weep, Caesar, and if you will, offer an expiatory sacrifice to her Manes. Forget all the vile deeds of which she was guilty and the nubmerless victims she slew. Pardon her fully—and then lift up your head with renewed spirit, to beam, to rule, and to rejoice once more!''

CHAPTER XII.

FOR hours did Agrippina float, wearily clinging to the wooden column which was all that parted her from eternal night. She had been thinking of her own victim, the hapless Acte. And lo! it was as though gods of penitence were fain to have pity on her for those thoughts of ruth. In the same desperate plight as the freedwoman, the same rescue was granted her.

Her limbs were almost rigid from the cold seawater; she was conscious only of her throbbing head and aching arms, which clasped the carved beam with fast-failing strength, when, from the headland of Misenum, a barque approached laden with flowers from Caieta for Puteoli. Agrippina shouted with the shrill energy of despair across the moonlit waters—six, eight times—and a fluttering handkerchief and a loud call of: "Wait—a little longer!" was the response. Five minutes later she was in safety.

Hardly believing their eyes, and dumb with amazement, the honest seafarers bowed before the amazing apparition. Agrippina, the empress-mother! The grave, marked features were known to all; if they had never seen her before, they were at any rate familiar with the numberless busts and statutes which decorated the squares in every town, even the smallest, where the Roman tongue was spoken. No one dared to utter a word. The exhausted woman was carried into the cabin, supplied with clothes and rugs, and even with a dry garment which the gardener's daughter—a strapping girl of nineteen— happened to have brought on board.

Agrippina had but half recovered when her rage, which had been lulled for a time by her struggle with the waves, flared up again with threefold fury.—That villainous assassin! His loving words, warm grasp of her hand, and fond embraces—and the rapturous *"Glykeia Mater"*—in short, every detail of her reception in that reprobate villa was simply a base, false, scoundrelly farce!—And she—Agrippina, who never failed to see through such tricks—she had been taken in! The disgrace weighed upon her almost more than the terrible blow to her feelings as a mother.

But she controlled the storm of her wrath. Full and perfect revenge could only be achieved by compelling her boiling blood to course coolly and evenly through her veins. Her intellect must make itself heard, unimpeded by the turmoil of her feelings. Before long she had made up her mind as to her plan of battle.

"Very good friends," she said, after gathering the ship's company about her, "I thank you all! Yes, it is I: the Empress Agrippina.—We were crossing the bay in a pleasure barge, the moonlit night seemed calm and propitious. A sudden squall wrecked our boat. So uncertain is the life of man! I have but one thing to beg of you. Be as silent about the disaster as if you were yourselves guilty of it. Will you?"

"As your majesty desires."

"Very good. You shall not regret it. Now, carry me as quickly as possible to Bauli. Whatever the gardener may lose shall be made good to him a hundredfold."

The men obeyed.

It was broad daylight when they cast their ropes round the capstans on the beach. Agrippina stepped on shore with majestic dignity.

"Wait here, she said, bowing a farewell. Soon after, her head slave came down to the strand and gave each of the crew a thousand denarii, with five thousand to the captain and the gardener's daughter.

To her household she breathed not a syllable as to what had happened. When the head slave asked how it was that she had come home alone, she gave him a reply which deprived him of all desire to enquire further. She ate a few mouthfuls, drank a cup of fruit syrup and water, and then retired to her cubiculum where she soon sank into death-like sleep.

Towards noon she awoke. She passed her hand across her brow, as though to refresh her memory of what had occurred. Suddenly she burst out into a shrill laugh of scorn.

"It is like a game of draughts," she thought, clenching her fingers convulsively. "We are at the last decisive move—I must be beaten: suddenly the tables are turned in the twinkling of an eye. The very move which was meant to annihilate me places me in a position to win! Wait a while, you cur! You shall learn now what Agrippina is capable of when it is a matter of life and death. My worthy Burrus will at last be startled out of his blissful trustfulness!" She doubled her fist.

"Villain!" she muttered with a grimace. "When I killed Claudius—for your sake—by Styx, I was grieved! I felt something like remorse.—And yet Claudius was a fool, and I hated him!—But as for you! was ever such a thing heard of? If there were indeed gods, they would surely torture you throughout eternity!"

Scalding tears flowed down her cheeks. Then she controlled herself. "A curse on the weakness of this mother's heart!" she thought, grinding her teeth. "I, after being half-murdered, already, can weep over the cowardly miscreant instead of smiling and chastising him. But I will cure myself of tears! I will strike him—inevitably—when the hour is come."

She threw her palla round her, hastened into the next room, and with a firm, determined hand, wrote as follows:

"The Empress Agrippina to her omnipotent son Claudius

Nero, greeting:

"The gods are envious, my beloved son. When they see happiness in the greatest perfection, they send the children of Latona with their deadly arrows.

"Nero Caesar, your mother craves vengeance for an atrocious crime. You are surrounded by traitors, by base hypocrites who are plotting against my life, and perhaps against yours. The vessel which the villain Anicetus presented to you was a mere trap. Half way across the bay it broke asunder like a badly-joined toy made to frighten children at the feast of the Saturnalia. I escaped death by a miracle. Avenge me, Nero! Look about you, and try to distinguish between your true and tried friends and those self-seeking villains, aiming only at pelf and power, who abuse the sacred name of friend only to drag you and the Roman Empire more surely to ruin.

"Out of shame, I have concealed from my household all I have suffered; but the sailors who saved me seem to have suspected that there had been foul play. The facts will soon be known all over Italy. Make it your care that the news of the punishment of the criminal does not follow too long after.

"I am well, in spite of the fearful agitation of the past night. So, I hope, are you."

She entrusted this letter to a peasant, with instructions to deliver it into Caesar's hand and not to be deterred by any difficulties which might be put in his way.

Total darkness reigned in Nero's closely-curtained cubiculum, and yet he could not get a moment's sleep after Tigellinus had left him.

"Matricide!" range incessantly in his ears. Now it was his wretched victim's voice, and now his own, that he fancied he heard, mingled with the roar of the towering waves, while hideous demons and nightmares lengthily rose from the abyss of waters, in blood-stained garments, and with ghastly grimaces. He tried to shake himself free of them; he struggled and fought like a desperate creature; but all in vain. Faces as pale as death came out of the bubbling foam—in thousands, in millions. The whole universe was full of them—a grim and endless chaos. Now and again, when this horrible state of things had reached a pitch beyond which madness lay, Acte's flower-like form appeared in the midst of the horrible confusion, and looked at him with pale reproach as she murmured with a sigh: "Nero, my joy, my idol! Ah! how differently you were wont to look me in the face, when your hands were unstained with blood. Those hands have stroked my hair, have caressed my cheeks, have clasped me in rapturous embrace. . . . And I gave my heart to you, as Io gave hers to Zeus. But now—woe is me! I would not touch your fingers for all the treasure on earth."

He buried his burning face in the pillow.

Hark! That was a despairing cry for help. Did he not see the gleam of the doomed woman's white palla?

Now, now—the weight was dragging her under—she threw up her arms.—"Nero, my son. . . . !" And the waters closed with a sullen gurgle over the drowning head.

The sun rose higher and poured its life-giving light in broader splendor on the crowded town. Down near the strand, all along the fine quay road, there was the usual traffic of a motley throng. Hundreds of singing birds were piping among the trees in the park. A refreshing air blew in from the sea, filling a multitude of shining sails. It was indeed a scene made for earthly enjoyment. But Caesar, as he stepped out into the peristyle, felt nothing of the reviving effects of day; his eyes ached, and the hot blood throbbed and burned in the veins of his forehead. He walked up and down two or three times, and then withdrew to the exedra where he lay down on a bronze couch. At last a heavy, unrefreshing slumber fell upon him.

When Agrippina's messenger reached the villa Caesar was still sleeping. Cassius and the other bodyslaves refused to disturb him. The brawny peasant was about to make short work of forcing his way in when Tigellinus came out, and enquired what was going forward.

"My lord," Cassius exclaimed, "a stranger says he has a pressing letter to deliver to Caesar."

"Give it to me."

"Impossible! The message I bear is intended for Caesar alone."

"I will give it to him."

"That I am forbidden to allow."

"By whom?"

"A friend of his majesty, who will give no name. Do not prevent me. Caesar will be wroth with you if you detain me any longer."

The Sicilian felt a sudden pang of uneasiness which seemed quite inexplicable.

"Very well," he said indifferently, "come into the oecus. I will go and awake Caesar."

The worthy native went forward in high contentment. Tigellinus gave the slaves a signal. They followed the messenger, flung themselves upon him and snatched the letter out of his tunic. Tigellinus also had entered the oecus.

"Silence!" he whispered to the man, who began to make an outcry. "I will have you hewn in pieces if you utter another sound."

He took the letter and glanced at the contents. For two seconds he seemed at his wits' end; then he said coldly: "Bind this fellow with cords and carry him off at once to the underground vaults. There keep him a prisoner till you hear from me. If he resists, pierce him to the heart without more ado.—Not you, Cassius; Caesar would miss you. But you others. Well done, hold him fast by the middle.—And now, not a word to any one, not even to Caesar. The man who fails to hold his tongue had better drown himself at once in the fish-pond, for I promise him a dreadful death."

As soon as this was done Tigellinus, escorted by two soldiers, went off to Anicetus.

"Read this," he said, holding the letter under his eyes. The sailor turned pale.

"Take your choice," said Sophonius Tigellinus in Greek.

"Either you must now fall a victim to your own wily scheme, or you must this very day, by some means, finish the job you failed in yesterday."

"Curse it!" muttered Anicetus. "The lioness has a tougher vitality than we imagined. In a few hours I am a lost man—for you, worthy Sophonius, will, of course, leave me in the lurch." The Sicilian shrugged his shoulders.

"Every man for himself," said he with cold-blooded diplomacy. "If it comes to a public scandal I must let you go, that is self-evident. But if you get out of the scrape with success, well and good: your reward shall be doubled."

Anicetus sat thinking for a moment.

"Is the messenger gone again?" he asked.

"No. I have him in custody in case of accident."

"Capital! If you help me half way, I hope to finish the job off neatly yet. But we must fight shoulder to shoulder.—For at any rate you will not escape all suspicion, since we have been seen lately in constant intercourse. Besides, the polite note in which you so kindly invited me to the banquet is still in my possession, and is all too cogent evidence of the connection of our common efforts."

"Do not flatter yourself!" replied Tigellinus. "If I speak the word, in two minutes you are a dead man. I would have your head off, and then tell Agrippina that your attempt on her life was avenged. Do you think that then any one would suspect me—the judge who condemned you—of making common cause with you?"

Anicetus forced himself to remain calm.

"They might, nevertheless," he said with a chill smile. He felt that he was copying his illustrious model to perfection. "Nevertheless! But jesting apart; I am, of course, fully determined to carry my work to the end. That the sum agreed on should be increased seems to me only fair; the danger, too, is double. Listen to what I propose. Have the messenger whom you so wisely took into custody killed at once. Spread a report that he was commissioned by Agrippina to assassinate Caesar. You will take care to have

353

trustworthy witnesses who will testify to his confession. You are not altogether inexperienced in such matters."

"Very good. And what then?"

"The rest you may leave to me. Before sunset the odious task will be done."

"You excite my curiosity," said the adjutant.

"Trust me! You have only to send at once to my triremes. I want fifty men added to the twenty who rowed the royal barge. Fifty of the picked men I call 'the sea-gulls.' Perhaps one of these men-at-arms can carry the message?"

Tigellinus agreed. Anicetus wrote a few words on his wax tablets. The swift-footed praetorian flew down to the bay where the two triremes, the "Samos" and "Herakleia," were lying at anchor.

"There!" muttered Anicetus. "I hope my prompt decisiveness will be a thorough surprise to you! Nay, nay, I will tell you nothing."

"By Zeus, do not be so mysterious! Indeed, my worthy friend, in naval matters you may be a god, but on land you seem to me as clumsy as an awk, that seabird of the north. Do you really hope—as I imagine—That you will drill your seamen here in the atrium? Or that you will get me and Caesar out of the saddle?"

"Only listen to me. You do not see through me yet. I will really make an end of the empress-mother. This very day she must sup in Tartarus or my head, and probably yours too, is not worth a denarius. Thus much you have guessed. What further I purpose you certainly cannot suspect.—Well, it will be better after all to let you into the secret. . . ."

"Speak."

"I have observed," said Anicetus, "what anguish it occasioned Caesar to pronounce sentence of death on his own mother. I shall tell him that I myself, overcome by compunction, saved her from drowning, meaning to crave forgiveness for her from you and Caesar. But Agrippina has made an ill-return for my compassion. So now I am setting out to seize the criminal and imprison her for her fresh attempt on Caesar's life;—not to kill her, for the idea of killing the empress-mother revolts my tender soul. I shall, of course, kill her nevertheless, but Caesar will be told on the best authority that she has committed suicide in prison. . . .''

Tigellinus drew back a step. "Anicetus," he said, "I withdraw my insulting comparison. You are not an awk on dry land. By great Epona! Your ingenuity amazes me. It is perfectly contrived to restore our Nero to his former light-heartedness. And indeed, the pangs of conscience, as they are called, are quite out of place on the throne."

"Poppaea too will be in a better position if the death bears the aspect of suicide," Anicetus went on. "Or do you suppose that Poppaea has never thought. . . . ?" He broke off.

"Has never thought. . . . Proceed!" said the Sicilian.

"Great Tigellinus, I am afraid. Here, in Baiae, a man is never sure that he is not cutting his own throat."

"Pooh! To me, at any rate, you may be as frank as a drunken man. You suppose that Poppaea cherishes the hope of being empress and sharing in the government of the Empire?"

"Such an idea is sufficiently obvious.—Then you will allow that if Agrippina's death could be traced to her as the third party to the plot, Caesar, in his extraordinary changes of mood, might so turn against her. . . .''

"Admirable!" cried Tigellinus. "I cannot think how it is that we never devised this suicide before.—Hark! What is that?"

"The tramp of my men-at-arms," replied the seaman. "Yes—the 'sea-gulls' are prompt to obey when Anicetus holds the time-keeper's hammer. Farewell, Tigellinus, and let the prisoner die without delay."

"Do not be uneasy. He will be a corpse before you can reach the highway. Good luck go with you! If you throw the dog instead of the Venus this time, the only thing you can do is to use your sword to cut your own throat."

CHAPTER XIII.

THE soldiers were waiting in the vestibule; bronzed, sturdy fellows, whose brows bore the impress of the most dogged resolution; most of them had swords at their girdles; a few were armed with spears or clubs. Anicetus did not take long in reviewing them. They set out, at a double quick march, along the high-road leading to Bauli.

"Soldiers," said Anicetus when they had left the town behind them, "Rome relies on you. Your pay shall be trebled for seven years if you carry out the task I charge you with. Are you ready?"

The 'sea-gulls' declared themselves devoted; Anicetus briefly explained the matter in hand, and that out of regard for Caesar's excitable feelings the truth must on no account get abroad.

"Long live Caesar! Long live our glorious Anicetus!" the men shouted.

As their captain looked about him he perceived, at about a hundred paces behind his men, a slender, girlish figure in a fluttering white tunic. It was Hasdra, the Phoenician girl. Anicetus, supposing that she brought a message from Poppaea or from Tigellinus, halted for a moment.

"What is it?" he asked, as the girl reached him quite out of breath.

"Nothing of importance. I am going with you to Bauli. I know everything. I must be there—when she is killed."

"Has Poppaea given you leave?"

"No. But I heard Tigellinus telling her what you were about to do. You are going to make an end of that atrocious Agrippina."

"Silence, I beseech you! Or do you want to chatter your head off?"

"Not in the least. I will hold my tongue, I promise you. But I must go with you—at any cost!"

"Folly! What business has a frail girl with such deadly deeds? Go home again without more ado. Do you hear?—I will not allow it."

"Don't be so harsh, my lord! When I say: 'I will,' I do as I say."

"Crazy girl, you are putting me into a terrible dilemma. It will excite the attention of those men coming down the road; you are as well known in Baiae as a lame riding-horse. Let us go in peace.—I command you!"

"My lord, I am going with you. That is as certain as the sky above our heads. Don't roll your eyes so angrily, it is useless. And if you prevent me, I will raise such an outcry that all the inhabitants on the shore will come rushing up headlong. Then I will tell them what you are going to do, I will betray that it is all a sham; I will say that Poppaea. . . ."

"Not another word!" said Anicetus furiously, laying his hand on his sword-hilt. Then controlling his wrath he added: "And if your heart is set on it, march at our heels, through the blazing heat! But I should like to know what can prompt you to such folly. If you are so bloodthirsty, go to the arena."

"I am not bloodthirsty, but I thirst for *her* blood."

"But why?"

"That is my concern."

The girl was so pale and so agitated that Anicetus judged it best to leave her to herself. She humbly retired behind the file of men, and the party proceeded at a rapid pace towards the villa at Bauli.

Delicate, dainty Hasdra seemed tireless. Not one of the seamen surpassed her in speed, endurance, or silent tenacity of purpose. She did not drink once, though her tongue was cleaving to her parched palate. She appeared to have vowed to the god of vengeance of her native land not to appease the torture of her thirst until the spring of more delicious refreshment had gushed forth from the opened veins of her hated foe.

In fact the little Phoenician's lips moved constantly as if in prayer.

"Melkarth, Incomprehensible One," she doubtless murmured in her despairing soul, "grant me one more boon. Terrible God, whose footstool is the earth, whose breath is the heaven, grant, oh grant, that I may have a share in this work of vengeance. My wounded heart cries out to thee; my limbs are failing, I have been like a land laid waste since he abandoned me. Thou thyself has commanded: 'Do not suffer like dogs who allow themselves to be trampled under foot by the insolence of their tormentors!' Thou thyself hast admonished us: 'Both eyes for one, and a life for both.' Melkarth, dear god, annihilator of falsehood, guardian of justice and loyalty, do not desert me."

She moved forward with eyes bent on the ground, like a mystic wholly entranced by the grandeur of a vision.

They reached their destination by four in the afternoon. Anicetus surrounded the house with men. Then, with a handful of the strongest, he rushed into the ostium.

A few praetorians, on guard there, were easily cut down. Not a man was spared. But immediately after, the rustle of a palla was heard over the marble flags. Agrippina came proudly forward.

She saw at once that her hour was come. The sight before her was more than eloquent. Anicetus' broad sensual face would have been enough.

Yet this royal woman, spite of all the vices and crimes that burdened her soul, showed that she possessed far more of the half-forgotten heroism of the ancient Roman republic than most of the men of her time. A defiant light flamed in her eyes.

"What do you want here?" she asked in a firm voice.

"You.—Miserable hag!" shouted a brutal Celt, rushing up to her and dealing her a heavy blow on the forehead with a bludgeon. The empress staggered. A groan of despair broke from her. Then, with sovereign dignity, she bared her bosom and said with intense bitterness: "Spare my head: its brain has always thought for the greatness of Rome! But pierce my heart—the heart that once beat above the murderer of his mother!"

Anicetus, not unmoved in spite of his sordid nature, thrust back the men who were rushing upon her in a mass. He turned to whisper to a fair-haired young giant at his side: "Do it, Gelo—but do not miss your stroke." The man raised his sword.

Meanwhile Hasdra, pale and trembling, had crept into the room unobserved to seize Agrippina from behind. She flew at the unhappy woman like a mad she-wolf, and set her sharp teeth deep in the back of her neck, while her fingers, quivering with frenzy, clutched like poisoned talons at that white throat.

"Take that for your treachery," the raging Phoenician hissed out as she sprang on her victim. "I am Hasdra, and was plighted to Pharax!" For an instant the empress-mother tottered under this attack. Then, with her right hand—for the left still held her bosom bare—she gripped the mad girl's fingers, and clenched them so tightly as to break them.

But at that moment the brawny Celt leaped forward and gave the empress her death-blow. He drove the sharp steel into her panting breast with such terrific force that it pierced her through to the back, and wounded the savage little monster who still clung on, with her teeth set in Agrippina's neck, making a deep gash in her side.

Agrippina fell without a sound.

Filled with loathing, the stalwart soldier seized Hasdra by

the head and flung her still foaming with murderous fury, three ells away.

"Can you hear me still, vile Agrippina," shrieked the girl, dragging herself back: "That was revenge for Pharax! Why did you steal him from me, foul and shameless vermin!"

Then Hasdra became unconscious. Her arm was broken, her hand crushed; blood flowed in a stream from the gaping sword cut.

"Carry her away," said Anicetus, and two of the men carefully lifted her up.

"Curse it all," he muttered between his teeth. "Poppaea Sabina will be furious with us. She was bewitched by that girl. . . ."

The two soldiers had laid her on a bench in the adjoining library. They returned almost immediately. "She is dead, my lord," they said indifferently.

"And this one?" asked Anicetus glancing at the empress.

Gelo, the Hun, bent over his victim.

"It is all over," he said presently. Then standing up and gazing at the magnificent figure, and the face, imperious even in death: "A splendid woman by Heaven! and a born ruler. If she were but fair, she would be a match for Gudbara, the Queen of the Chatti!"

Anicetus left half of his following in the villa, with instructions to have the two bodies burnt in the course of the day, and to do it as quietly as possible. The few slaves in attendance at the retired country villa had fled at the entrance of the fighting-men, so that the tale of the empress-mother's suicide could hardly be disproved. Hasdra had been stabbed as a punishment for speaking so insolently of Agrippina.

Anicetus returned to Baiae rejoicing in the deed he had committed. By next morning the murderers' lie had spread over all Campania, from the noisy streets of Caieta to the silent rose-gardens of Paestum. But was it believed?

CHAPTER XIV.

It was November again. The withered leaves were already falling from the elms. The hapless Octavia had prolonged her summer stay in the villa at Antium later than usual.

The gleam of the evening sun fell on the young empress as she reclined, under the shelter of a laurel hedge in the park, on a stone bench piled with cushions, and looked out across the flaming, dazzling sea. Her face, usually so pale, seemed to have recovered its bloom under the glow of departing day, but her heavy eyes, eloquent of unspoken griefs and weariful anxiety, plainly betrayed the true reason of her lingering here so long. It was not the unusually mild weather, not the magic of these glorious sunsets, but her secret dread of not being able to bear another meeting with Poppaea in her triumph.

At Octavia's feet sat Acte, now known as Ismene, looking up into her mistress' face with grateful and sacred veneration; not one of the inhabitants of the villa, excepting only Abyssus and the faithful Rabonia, knew or even suspected that she was Caesar's former mistress.

"If only you were right," sighed Octavia after a long pause, "I would wait patiently indeed, even if it should be for years. But I cannot think so—I cannot!"

"Lady. . . ."

"Spare yourself the trouble," she went on, shaking her

head. "By degrees I have learnt wisdom. I understand now that it is madness to regard constancy as a duty. It is a free gift, a grace. Those who love are faithful without effort, without a struggle. All the laws in the world of gods or men will never bind the truant who is not tied by affection—much less bring him back."

"But affection has its birth where enchantment ends. Only let him once know the heart that beats in your bosom, know how noble and single-minded you are, and how fondly you worship him. Oh! I could fly to him myself and clasp his knees and cry to him with joy: 'See, Octavia alone of the women on earth is worthy to share your lot!'—But that cannot be; that would be a desecration of your divine purity. For I myself have sinned against Octavia—not less than that Poppaea, whose hatred and ambition are all that distinguish her from me."

"Silence; you have amply atoned," said Octavia. "What have I to forgive in you? That you accepted him when he offered himself with ardent devotion?—Or do you pretend to say that you laid a snare for him as Poppaea Sabina did?" The empress propped her head on her hand. "Fair child," she presently went on, "it is a bitter confession to make—but I cannot help saying it: Acte, I envy you."

"You overwhelm me, you annihilate me! It was sin and betrayal, not happiness. True happiness lies in virtue, which I have so shamefully trodden under foot. You, a saint, can wish to change places with a reprobate? What madness!"

"I envy you," Octavia repeated.

"Then you still love him!" cried Acte triumphantly. "Not ten minutes since you denied it; but I see you do still love him, in spite of his faithlessness, in spite of the monstrous things which rumor brings to your ears."

"Spare me. All this breaks my heart—I am ready to die of shame. And yet—it would seem that love cannot die."

"After a long pause Acte began again:

"May I ask you one question, madam, which I have suppressed day after day with the utmost difficulty?"

"Speak."

"Did you ever answer Poppaea's insolent letter?"

"Never."

"Then you intend. . . ."

"To maintain my rights. You see, child, one thing still remains to me. When he has played himself out, when he is weary of wild orgies with this rabble company, perhaps he will one day feel suddenly and miserably alone; then he will long for one true heart on which he may rest. Then, dear Ismene, I shall have a right to offer him a quiet and peaceful refuge. If, on the contrary, I were to accept his paramour's proposal, whether from cowardice or sweariness, and consent to a divorce all, all would be lost. Poppaea would be his wife before men and gods; and if he then were to wake from his frenzied dream nothing is left to him but despair."

Acte rose. Tears stood in her eyes.

"How fervently," she exclaimed, "how devoutly will I pray that all may turn out well!"

"Good soul!" said Octavia smiling. "And yet I know that you—you cannot pray thus without a struggle."

Acte colored.

"Nay, lady, you are mistaken,' she murmured bashfully. "Believe me, I look back on those days as penitently as Paul, our beloved Apostle, on the follies of Saul."

"Then why those tears?—Sit down again here, and tell me more about that glorious man. Yesterday you were saying that he was in Rome."

Acte dried her eyes and cheeks. A bright glow of enthusiasm lighted up her sweet, rosy face.

"I heard of it from Abyssus," she said, sitting down again on the grassy bank. "Paul arrived about the kalends. The priests and scribes in Judaea had accused him of something, and Felix, the procurator, wanted to bring him to judgment. Paul, however, protested. 'I am a Roman citizen,' said he, 'and I appeal to Caesar.' So Felix sent him to Rome under escort. But he was set at large without trial. Tigellinus, who hates the Jewish priests simply because Poppaea protects them, is supposed to have persuaded Caesar; but I think it is more likely that they could find nothing agianst the great Apostle. Now he is living in the heart of the empire, preaching the doctrine of the Nazarene and giving the weary and heavy-laden that peace of God which passeth all understanding.''

"I should very much like to hear the man," said Octavia. "Much of what you have told me about the crucified Jesus is, to be sure, quite incomprehensible. But His love and His powers of endurance have struck me greatly. He has been an example to me, when I have sometimes thought that I could bear my misery no longer; and often your gentle way of telling me of Him has given me a sense of unearthly peace. Then I ask myself: 'What if all this were no pious fable, but salvation found at last?' ''

"Madam, it is no fable," whispered Acte, "but God Almighty's perfect truth. But for our Heavenly Father's grace, and the Son's atoning intercession.—Ah! how could I ever forget all this and lose my soul. . . . !''

She broke off and gazed at the ground in the deepest confusion. She wanted Octavia to believe that the sinful delusions of the past were all forgotten—and now the penitent betrayed with terrible distinctness how deeply and firmly that past was rooted in her heart. Octavia, with a faint sigh, looked down on the shining hair which waved like spun gold over the girl's brow.

They heard steps approaching from the peristyle. A stately and aristocratic figure was seen, a man who paused at the door of the posticum and glanced carelessly about the park. Octavia at once recognized Tigellinus. He had not yet caught sight of Octavia and her companion.

"Hide, child," said Octavia in alarm. "If he sees you, you are lost. His friend Poppaea will never rest till you are put out of the way."

Acte slipped away into the bushes.

Almost at the same instant the Sicilian perceived the young empress, who pretended to be lost in thought and scanning the purple fire of the sea.

He came towards her with a leisurely step and greeted her more politely than he had intended.

"Madam," said he, "I have to inform you that you are unmasked."

Octavia rose. Her eyes rested with unconcealed contempt on the man whom she had long since learnt to hate and fear as Caesar's evil genius.

"What is your meaning?" she said coldly.

"Any affectation of innocence is useless," said Tigellinus. "You are accused—to put it briefly and plainly—of adultery with your slave Abyssus."

A flaming blush mounted to Octavia's face.

"You are mad!" she said. "I—accused!"

"You- Octavia, Caesar's wife."

"And by whom?" she enquired, quivering with rage.

"By Caesar, of course."

"You lie! Nero has not yet sunk so deep in the foul bog of infamy. It is you and Poppaea—a pair!—who have hatched out this preposterous calumny!"

Tigellinus shrugged his shoulders. "I only repeat that everything is known. It had long been strongly suspected—so long ago as at the beginning of your illness, when Abyssus felt you so tenderly, and—held you so fondly in his arms."

"You contemptible wretches!" cried the young empress beside herself; the shameless audacity of this misinterpretation was too much for her. Clasping her hands over her face, she could only repeat: "Wretches! Reprobates!"

"By Hercules! make no fuss. If you are wise, you will at once confess everything. You will thus spare Caesar a most cruel scandal, and save your freed servants from the rack."

"The rack!" cried Octavia in horror. "Has that disgraceful folly not yet been done away with?"

"The law is sacred," said the Sicilian with a smile.

The young empress fought a hard battle; she knew now that she was hopelessly lost. Very few could resist the horrors of torture. The most improbable statements could be wrung from the witness when his limbs were being crushed by the hideous instruments of the executioner. The senate would then pronounce the accused guilty; that she could not doubt. Should she then, for no good whatever, bring such suffering on her household, who were almost without exception bound to her by ties of affectionate gratitude? And yet she could not say she was guilty. Never could she stain her womanly honor by a false confession, even from the noblest impulse of her nature.

"I do not believe you," she said deliberately. "Even if you spoke the truth, even if you really came from Claudius Nero, he would retract at the last moment. It is simply impossible that he should seriously doubt my fidelity. Impossible!—go and tell him so."

"You have not chosen the wiser course. If you had quietly confessed what will now be proved by public trial—by Hercules, you would have fared better. The supreme court would have decreed your divorce, but you yourself would have been pardoned by Caesar. As it is. . . . Well, you will see."

"I see one thing only: that villainy is probably mightier than virtue."

"Mere words!—Now, I command you in Caesar's name: call together all the free born or freed slaves of the villa, in the peristylium. The slaves cannot, by law, bear witness against you."

"You—command Me!"

"By virtue of my commission."

"And I refuse to obey."

"For aught I care!" said the Sicilian with a laugh. "Then I will do it myself. I have walked so far in this dirty business that a few steps more or less will not count."

With a shrug, he went through the posticum into the colonnade, where the fifteen men-at-arms who had escorted him had begun a flirtation with the women of the household. None of these men knew what the object of this unexpected excursion might be.

"Fly!" The sobbing empress whispered to Acte. The girl crept trembling and pale as death out of the shrubbery.

"Fly?" That would be base cowardice indeed! I will bear witness in your favor."

"What good will that do? Do you think that any living soul will believe that I am guilty? But they will condemn me, whether you speak or are silent, for the senate crawls before Tigellinus.—Fly, I entreat you."

"Madam. . . . !"

"Do you want to be put to the torture, mad girl?"

"To stand by you—yes!"

"But I, Octavia, forbid it. Acte, Acte, spare me the last, worst humiliation. Do you not see. . . . ? You, his—his former love—to appear before him—and me. . . ."

Acte shivered.

"Yes, you are right," she said despairingly. "Forgive my vehemence, forgive me for daring—I, Acte, the sinner, must hide myself.—But when it is all over, when you have triumphed, then let me return. I have not home on earth but this spot at your feet!"

"Come what may, never doubt my friendship. But, as no one can tell how the gods may have decreed that it shall end, take some money. I will go into the peristyle where the vile Sicilian is assembling the household; I can contrive to delay him. Steal away through the pines, and in at a window. There is a chest in my cubiculum—here is the key. Take as much as you need. Quick, quick! I should be too miserable if they caught you. . . ."

Acte slipped among the laurels again.

"Farewell," sighed Octavia. "There is a deadly weight about my heart. I fear all that is most horrible."

"Try to pray," Acte whispered; "not to Jupiter, but to Jesus Christ the Lord."

"I will try."

"And give me your hand once more. Beloved Octavia, tell me, have you forgiven me wholly, from the bottom of your heart?"

"From the bottom of my heart."

"Then I am comforted. Our Father in Heaven cannot leave such goodness unrewarded."

CHAPTER XV.

Two days later saw the beginning of a trial so scandalous that the history of the world can hardly show such another.

Sophonius Tigellinus prosecuted in Caesar's name. His indictment, put forth in an elaborately worked-up speech overloaded with disgusting details and lasting half an hour, plainly suggested to Octavia's servants the line their depositions must take if they wished to escape "waking up" by the tortures. After concluding with a few phrases of hypocritical regret Tigellinus once more appealed to Octavia to confess without reserve.

"You see before you," said he, "an assembly of learned and venerable men whose brows are crimson with shame at the scandalous publicity of your disgrace. They have seen much to shock them, but nothing so basely, so thoroughly and shamelessly foul. Nevertheless this high assembly will recommend you to Caesar's clemency, out of regard for your illustrious birth,—and if you confess."

"I am innocent," said Octavia with unexpected composure. "Everything brought forward against me is a fabrication of calumny, a despicable tissue of lies which cannot deceive the assembled Fathers."

"Certainly not," said a deep bass voice.

It was that of Soranus the worthy stoic.

"No, by Jupiter!" added Thrasea Paetus. "And to prove my words I will add, before we go any further, that I should think myself happy if the illustrious Octavia would do me the favor to take my daughter, a girl of fourteen, to be her companion.

A murmur of surprise ran through the hall. The senator's strict morality was well known, and the almost excessive care with which he had brought up his children, who were conspicuous for their beauty.

"Do not provoke him," whispered Flavius Scaevinus, who was sitting at Thrasea's right hand. "A single glance at these anxious and depressed faces will show you that we cannot intercept Fate. It seems incredible, but it will be done: the purest and most virtuous woman who ever entered the Palatium will be pronounced guilty by the cowardly, sneaking majority."

"But shall I consent in silence?"

"No, Thrasea, when the votes are taken we will say: 'Not guilty,' loudly, and in the face of all the people. But open hostility now is premature. Do you wish that he should have all who cherish the idea of freedom basely assassinated? I thought we had a higher mission to fulfil. Believe me, the blood boils in my veins—as hotly as in yours. But I control myself. The hour of reckoning has not yet struck."

"You are right.—But silence, Flavius. That bald-headed rascal in the corner seems interested in our whispering."

"A relation of the Sicilian?"

"Yes; that odious Cossuthianus. Since the squabble with the Cilicians he is as irrepressible as a fiend?"

Sophonius Tigellinus had vouchsafed no reply but a shrug of the shoulders, to Thrasea's outbreak. Without troubling himself any further about the sensation in the senatorial benches, he proceeded to examine the witnesses.

Octavia's freed servants were called one by one.

First came a beautiful lad named Alcinous, whose ashy paleness betrayed extreme anguish of mind. By the kindness of the young empress he had saved enough money to buy a little land in the Sabine province and to marry his adored Lalage, a maiden of thirteen. And now—on the very eve of so much happiness—he must be broken in every limb if he should testify to Octavia's innocence, a witness which would probably be nullified by the word "Guilty" wrung by torture from the rest. He shuddered visibly from head to foot, when Tigellinus shouted out the question:

"Freedman, what has come within your knowledge concerning the adulterous connection between Caesar's wife and that foul dog of an Egyptian?"

"My lord—" said the lad with an anxious glance at the torturer who stood waiting. ". . . . I . . . . it may be. . . . I heard say. . . ." But a sort of pious shame came over him.

"Tear me in pieces," he said, clenching his fist. "My mistress is as pure as sunlight! Assembled Fathers, you who have wives and daughters of your own, can you doubt if you look but once in that noble and innocent face? The Egyptian Abyssus has always been faithfully attached to her, like all who ever entered her service—but how should he have dared. . . . ? The thought cannot be put into words."

"Let us see if Alcinous, the freedman, will adhere to this declaration," said the Sicilian, signing to the executioners. The slaves stepped forward, seized their victim, and with wonderfully noiseless celerity, tied him on to a long iron machine known as 'the bed of Procrustes.'

"She is innocent!" Alcinous repeated incessantly. The screws were turned.

"Harder," said Tigellinus.

And now, as the horrible pain almost bereft him of his senses, the youth cried out in desperation: "Mercy, mercy, I will reveal all!"

"Ease him," said Tigellinus. And the screws were turned back a little way.

"Let me go!" he still cried in heartrending shrieks. At a sign he was released.

"Then you will confess?" said the Sicilian.

"Yes."

"You discovered the guilty woman in the fact?"

"Yes."

"And she tried to bribe you?"

"Yes."

"She gave you money?"

"Yes."

"How much?"

"I do not know.—A hundred thousand denarii."

"Very good. These are important disclosures. Now you may go."

The lad turned away, hanging his head. Suddenly he looked back and solemnly raised his hand, still trembling from the rack.

"But she is innocent!" he shouted in a voice of thunder.

"You recant?" laughed Tigellinus. "Well, we will discuss that again. Seize him, men!—But we will hear the others first."

The next to be called was a fine tall man of forty, who had a wife and child.

"Spare yourselves the trouble," he said coolly to the torturers. "My lady is innocent. Whether you tear me limb from limb or not, it will make no difference: I shall stick to it. It would be a pretty kind of truth which could be turned to lying by a little pain. Athenaeus fears not those who can only kill the body."

In the hands of the torturers he did not wink an eyelash.

"She is innocent," was the only thing to be got out of him.

Tigellinus, enraged by the Nazarene's constancy, wanted to aggravate his sufferings. But Thrasea Paetus protested.

"What!" he exclaimed with stirring fire. "You admire Regulus for defying the scorching sun of Africa; and Murius, famous in song, for letting his hand burn in the flame with a smile on his face, and yet you would fain punish such steadfastness as this with death? Are you still Romans, or must Judaea send us teachers to show us what honor is, and heroic manhood?"

The old magical tale of Roman heroism had its effect.

Three senators, out of the usually subservient majority, with all due respect implored the "judicious and benevolent" Tigellinus to reprieve the freedman from any further examination. So Athenaeus, the immovable, was released.

Two-thirds of the witnesses contradicted the calumny with no less determined constancy;—as heroic as Mucius Scaevola, as unshaken as Regulus. It appeared that the old Roman spirit, which found no more than half a dozen representatives in the senate, had taken refuge in these humble and simple hearts, that mankind, though degenerate, might not despair of itself. The rest of Octavia's household, who failed under torture and supported her accusers, did not count in comparison.

Tigellinus was boiling with rage, although he pretended to the senate that he regarded the prisoner as convicted beyond a doubt.

The last witness exposed to the rack was Rabonia, for even women and girls were not spared this hideous ordeal.

As Rabonia was known to be Octavia's closest confidante, and her evidence was therefore the most important and weighty, the Sicilian had saved her till the end, and had signified to the torturers that they might set to work with a will from the very first. But the faithful soul fully understood the responsibility that lay on her, and determined that she would die before she would allow the smallest stain to attach to her mistress. She answered every question put to her by Tigellinus with a defiant: "No, you villain!"

The executioners strained the bed of torture more and more. The hapless woman's right arm was broken; her head fell on one side in a death-like swoon. As soon as she recovered consciousness Tigellinus shouted at her: "Now, at last, will you confess?" and she answered with the same irrepressible words: "No, you villain," as undaunted as ever.

"Away with the old harridan!" hissed the Sicilian, forgetting his usual aristocratic demeanor.

"To my house, with your permission," said Thrasea. "My physician shall take care of the sufferer, for I admire her, assembled Fathers, though I admit that she was not exactly polite to his excellency, Caesar's representative.''

Tigellinus made no reply.

When the horrors of this loathsome inquisition were ended, Octavia's defenders rose. First Barea Soranus and after him Thrasea Paetus. They both confined themselves to insisting on the fact that no one—literally no one in their distinguished assembly believed in Octavia's guilt.

"By all the gods," said Thrasea in conclusion of a short speech, "this trial was not needed to prove the empress's spotless virtue. Still, if any one ever entertained a doubt of the loftiness of her mind, the immaculateness of her life, the unclouded purity of her nature, the evidence of these witnesses has demonstrated that such a doubt is blasphemy. Tigellinus, in his praiseworthy eagerness to serve Caesar, has plainly gone too far. He has attached greater weight than he ought to the reports of abject spies; he must now be convinced that he has been impudently deceived. An accused person never came out of the ordeal of a trial more triumphantly than Octavia, the sister of the noble Britannicus. A new and brighter radiance shines on that ambrosial head. Hitherto we have known her as the most gracious sovereign lady, the best and most perfect of women; but henceforth she is as one of the immortals! Assembled Fathers, I appeal to you for mercy.''

In fact, not one of the senators believed her to be guilty, but they all knew what the meaning of the farce was. Caesar—or, at any rate Poppaea Sabina and Tigellinus—desired to see Octavia and Nero divorced. To know this was enough for a body of men which, for a long period of years, had thought more of the safety of their own privileges than of maintaining justice and public morality.

Consequently, and in spite of all rational judgment, the empress was pronounced guilty by an overwhelming majority, and sentence was passed, condemning Abyssus to death and Octavia to banishment. Her villa at Antium was to be her prison for life; and, that she should not repeat her disgraceful misdeameanor, the censors were instructed to appoint a special civic guard over her morals, whose orders she was to obey without appeal. Quite spirit-broken, the unhappy woman heard her doom without a word or a sign— incapable even of shedding a tear.

Thrasea Paetus went up to her solemnly, bowed before her, and reverently kissed the hem of her palla.

"Once more," he said with deep emotion and pain, "I crave your permission to send my daughter with you. Would that she could ever become like you!—even though the resemblance should cost her greater suffering than you have to endure."

Octavia could not speak. She gave him a grateful look which sank into his very soul. Then she was led away by the praetorians. The carriage which was to carry her to Antium was standing ready.

"Do not be too rash!" a vengeful voice whispered loudly close behind Thrasea Paetus. The stoic looked round. It was Cossuthianus, whom he had accused of embezzlement in the settlement of Cilicia, some years since.

"I understand you," said Thrasea with a smile. "But I do not fear you—neither you nor your relation who could then sue to the emperor for pardon for a criminal.—There are misdeeds which raise up indignant champions of insulted justice from the very stones in the highway. You are as crafty as a vulture, but, take my word for it, this sentence is a foolish blunder. If evil befalls you, think of me!"

CHAPTER XVI.

THRASEA's warning seemed to be verified that same day. The atrocious result of this unheard-of trial fell on the populace like a tremendous blow making each man's face to tingle.

Octavia condemned! This was too much. The Roman people, who looked on in resigned silence at so many excesses of the Imperial Court, rose as though in sudden concert to give expression to its indignation at this base and cowardly insult offered to a beautiful and magnanimous victim. For the moment it might have been thought that the contemporaries of the hapless Virginia had come to life again and gathered on all sides to breathe out curses, accusations, and threats, and finally to shout with the unanimity of the rallying cry of a long fostered rebellion: "Long live Octavia! Down with Poppaea Sabina!"

The women of Rome, more especially, led the van in this spontaneous but fierce revolt. From the furthest fishing huts at the foot of the Aventine as far as to the villas of the Pincian Hill and the Milvian Bridge, women everywhere formed the nucleus of excited groups: women in the dress of humblest citizens, passionate and caustic in their wild eloquence, and ladies too, in snowy flowing mantles, with the scarlet flammeum over their elaborately-dressed hair, dignified and graceful in every movement. The wives of the contemptible senators protested against their husbands' perjured verdict; and the wives of the torturers against the foul service of the rack. Thus urged on by a hundred thousand women, who felt themselves aggrieved in their most sacred feelings, the boldest among the men at last collected in a surging mob outside the Palatium, and demanded in a thunderous roar that Octavia should be brought back. Fresh recruits arrived in masses.

A division of the town-guard, mounting the steps of the Capitoline, attacked the rioters.

"Stand!" cried the captain. "Not a step farther, or I will have you cut down."

"For shame!" cried a slim, dark-eyed youth, raising his fist. It was Artemidorus.—"For shame" he repeated in loud tones. "Would you defend dishonor against virtue? Are you a Roman or a Memphite pander?"

"Make way" cried the officer wrathfully. "Hark! There is a howl like a German battle-song.—Forward, men! I must do my duty. Fix your spears!"

"Pooh!" cried one of the soldiers. "The truth is the truth for ever! The empress is innocent, and Poppaea has flung dirt at her."

"I am a Roman citizen," said another, "I will not fight for the prostitute Sabina!"

"Long live Octavia!" shouted a third.

"That's right!" cried Artemidorus in triumph. "One shout for the city-cohort!"

"The city cohort!" shrieked the mob. "Octavia's brave defenders!"

The captain looked about him in despair. All his hundred men refused to obey him. The clamor in the Forum Romanorum increased every instant. Artemidorus suddenly seized him by the arm.

"Do you still hesitate?" he cried in the voice of an inspired seer. "This dishonor and disgrace must be avenged or the universe will go to ruin."

With a powerful clutch he snatched the broadsword out of the astonished soldier's hand.

"On, to the Capitol!" he cried, brandishing the weapon over his head. "Come on, spearmen, your appearance on the scene will, I hope, turn the scale."

"The city guard are on Octavia's side!" said one and another. "Make way there. Here come your leaders to storm the palace.—Caesar, come forth to the ostium. Swear by the gods that you will restore Octavia to her sovereign rights! Away with that shameless jade, Poppaea! She has dragged Rome down to the dunghill."

And then a voice was heard above all the rest—a voice as loud as a trumpet-call, shouting: "Down with Claudius Nero if he refuses."

Every one turned round. But Nicodemus the Nazarene, who, thirsting for revenge, had raised this startling threat, had hidden himself again. He seemed to have vanished into the earth and left no trace, like a ghost.

In the Palatium no one knew what to do, all was in the greatest confusion. About fifty praetorians, sent by Tigellinus, at Poppaea's desire, to check the rioters, were defeated after a bloody skirmish, some disarmed and some beaten to death; and now, when the town cohort turned their spears against them, they could only feel their way in the dark. Tigellinus sent out one messenger after another to the headquarters of the praetorian guard, but no reply came. In anxious haste he tried to think of some plan of attack and defence, but without coming to any decision. Everything depended on how soon he could count on the arrival of the guards from their barracks; nay, indeed, on whether they would be ready and willing at all to fight against Rome in its present angry mood.

He expressed this doubt to Caesar. A pang of terror seized the agitated despot and almost choked him. It was not cowardice that was tormenting him with tremulous distress, but an evil conscience. Yes; the people were right: it was a crime to believe all this false witness, convincingly as the cunning informers had concocted their story.

Tigellinus had allowed himself to be deceived; that mattered little. Poppaea, too, had been deceived: that, indeed, was harder to bear, for she, of all people, she from whom the much-to-be-pitied Octavia had suffered so much, ought to have made every effort to detect the weak points of the indictment.

But that *he* should have believed that Octavia was guilty was an unpardonable crime, a blindness for which he could never atone. How was it that all Rome knew that the illustrious lady was blameless?

He, Caesar, knew his Octavia even better. Ah! he saw through it all now. The villainous informers had hoped to do Poppaea Sabina good service, which she was to repay with Persian generosity! Perhaps she herself had given the hint that Octavia stood in her way. Was that the origin of this atrocious crime, this desecration of innocence? Had he really been blind? Or was this the horrible doom with which Agrippina had threatened him: that so long as she was his protector he would be all-powerful, but that without her he must sooner or later come to ruin. . . . ?

Aye, that was it! His splendor, his divine authority was crumbling into dust. The town guard had already deserted; the praetorians, who had also shown some degree of reverence and sympathy for the gentle and defenceless victim of this monstrous insult, would presently join the rebels—in fancy he already heard the tramp of their columns—the lava-pavement trembling under their tread—the ringing shout: "Down with Claudius Nero!"—soldiers crowding into the ostium—Burrus and Julius Vindex forcing their way into his presence, swords flashing in their hands—: "To avenge Agrippina!"—"And Octavia, crushed and broken. . . . !"

He cried aloud in horror, as though he already felt their blades in his panting breast.

"Why do you kill me, when I wanted to spare her?" he groaned in the anguish of that vision. And he sank with his face on the table.

At this moment Poppaea came in and laid her white, velvety hand on his shoulder.

"Be comforted," she said coaxingly. "At last we have an answer from the praetorium. Burrus has been suddenly taken ill. But a trustworthy young tribune is coming through the Subura with two thousand men."

"Silence!" he said wrathfully. "Send Tigellinus to me."

"What is the meaning of this?" she asked in amazement.

"That you will hear. Call Tigellinus!"

"Send one of your slaves."

"No. Go yourself," he exclaimed, and starting to his feet, he seized her by the throat.

"Are you out of your mind?" She freed herself and stood confronting him like a Bellona, her beauty enhanced by the flaming color which mounted to her face.

"Forgive me," muttered Nero. "I do not know what has turned my brain.—Cassius!"

The slave appeared through the curtain.

"By all that's vile! Fetch Tigellinus," said Caesar in a tone of fury, as though it had been Cassius to whom he had twice given the order in vain.

"What are your commands, my friend and sovereign lord?" asked the Sicilian as he came in.

"Take a herald with you; go at once to the vestibule, and proclaim to Rome that the senate has judged wrongly."

"How?"

"That the senate consists of mere brainless oxen,—if you prefer that formula. Octavia is innocent. Claudius Nero Caesar returns thanks to his beloved Romans for discerning the truth, while the assembled oxen were bellowing out 'guilty.' Do you not yet understand?"

"Yes—but. . . ."

"There is no but in the case.—And you will moreover have the goodness to send a dozen of mounted praetorians in pursuit of my illustrious wife, to escort her, with all due respect, back to the Palatium. . . ."

"Do you really mean it?" asked Poppaea, turning pale.

383

"Caesar, do not act rashly. The highest assembly has pronounced sentence. Its verdict is beyond appeal."

"I nullify the sentence in virtue of my sovereign power! The trial is as though it had never been. Octavia is as she ever was: my imperial consort.—And you. . . ."

"Well? I—I. . . . ?

"And you—quit the Palatium.—Decency and public sense of right demand it.—Go, Tigellinus. You will answer for it with your life, if my orders are not immediately carried out. Tell the multitude that Poppaea Sabina is in the very act of setting out for her villa on the Esquiline.—Well, why do you delay?"

The Sicilian bowed low.

"For aught I care!" said he to himself. "A sudden freak!— Or is he afraid of the roaring mob outside! How long will it last?—And after all, even if Octavia returns for good, I am too safe in the saddle to have anything to fear."

Poppaea Sabina was beside herself. All she had striven for through years of fevered ambition was overthrown by one weak moment in Caesar's life, her bark upset just as she hoped to land! Why need Tigellinus behave with such an aggravation of brutality? Less zeal would have had more success.

"Nero!" she cried, falling at Caesar's feet. "I will not leave you. I will die rather than depart an outcast! Have you forgotten, ungrateful man, the hour that awaits me? Am I not the mother of the child you have so often seen in fancy clinging to your knees and calling you 'Father' in lisping tones?"

She tore her hair and struck her forehead on the floor.

"Stop, stop!" said Caesar; and stricken by the sight of her wild agitation, he raised her up. "Do not lament so vehemently," he added, "and bring my divided heart to utter despair. No, Poppaea, I do not forget you; I remember those day-dreams. . . . I love you alone, Poppaea."

He clasped her fondly, and she clung to his neck and pressed her burning cheek to his.

Outside they heard the noisy blast of the herald's trumpet. The terrific hubbub which had been raging, from the Forum as far as the slopes of Caelius, now gave way to expectant silence. The Sicilian's ringing voice was heard addressing the crowd in short, broken phrases. The words were inaudible here in Caesar's apartment, but the effects of the brief address almost shook the Capitol to its foundations. The mighty shout of gladness that went up from the people was louder than the roar of the storm which had hardly died away. Again and again from a thousand throats rose the cry: "Long live Octavia! Long live Caesar!" A few even shouted: "Long live Tigellinus!"

Poppaea clung to Nero, pressing her lips to his while she trembled with rage and indignation; kissing him indeed more tenderly and fervently than ever, for she had been quick to perceive that she had not lost her old power over him.

"Farewell," she said in heart-broken tones. "I thought my name was more deeply graven in your heart. I am going, Caesar! Be happy with your Octavia!"

He held her clasped in both arms. "We shall meet again," he said, quiet bewitched by her. "Be reasonable, Poppaea. Do you not hear them shouting with joy for Octavia? If the people demand it.... Answer Poppaea—What is Caesar without the people?"

"The people!" she echoed scornfully. "You hold your sovereignty, not from the people, but from Fate, and the bulwarks which resist the attacks of the mob are the troops. Do you not hear the long-drawn blare of the tuba? Those are Burrus' men, coming to our rescue. But now, indeed, now that Tigellinus has proclaimed your decision, it is too late. Oh! I see through you! Your sudden love of justice is only a mask for satiety. Octavia, too, is a beauty, and Caesar longs for a change."

"Woman, you are mad!"

"Yes, I am mad! Do not heed me; my brain is in a whirl. Brands of fire are scorching it up. I could strangle you this moment, with these hands, I love you so madly!—I cannot bear to think of your loving another—not even the pure and spotless Octavia!"

This farce of passion was played to admiration. She seized Nero by the shoulders and looked up at him with all the art of a coquette; so fascinating, so seductive, that he succumbed entirely. He felt, as Paris felt in a famous passage in the Iliad, that Helen, the ravished wife of the hapless Menelaus, had never seemed so lovely before—and, like Paris, he clasped her to his heart.

An hour and a half later the carriage which was to have carried the empress to her country retreat was rolling back along the Via Sacra. Endless shouts of rejoicing rose on all sides.

"Long live Octavia" was shrieked by every living soul in Rome, and an ominous echo was heard at intervals: "Down with Poppaea!"

Invisible hands wreathed the statues of Octavia which had been erected in the time of the empress-mother in the Argiletum, in front of the Temple of Saturn, on the top of the Capitol, and in various parts of the Field of Mars. Those of Poppaea Sabina, set up by Nero, were, on the contrary, overthrown from their pedestals, broken, mutilated, insulted with dust and dirt, or dragged, like the bodies of criminals, to the Gaemonian steps.

Octavia, as pale as death, was welcomed by Claudius Nero as she entered the hall of the Palatium.

"Hail to Caesar! Hail to the Empress!" shouted the populace as they witnessed their greeting, strange as it was, painful and speechless.

The mob crowded in endless multitudes to the public altars to offer thanks to the gods for the termination at last of the division in the imperial household, and for the reinstatement of Octavia in her inalienable rights. Almost at the moment when Octavia set foot in the palace, Poppaea Sabina, thickly veiled, stole through the palace gardens to the gate by the Circus Maximus. Here a litter was waiting for her. She cast a last indignant scowl at the splendid residence where of late she had ruled as sovereign. Then she set her lips tightly and resolutely, pressed her hand to her heart, and got into the litter.

Caesar at once convened the senate to declare that the sentence which had but just been pronounced by an overwhelming majority of themselves, was null and void in consequence of the pretended oversight of some formality.

Thrasea Paetus and Barea Soranus contemptuously expressed their acknowledgment to the assembled Fathers, and concluded by saying, each in his own way, that for the future they must renounce the honor of belonging to a body which could overlook indispensable formalities in a case of such importance. Every one felt the bitter scorn and angry contempt which found utterance under the guise of biting irony. Cossuthianus, Thrasea's old opponent, foamed with rage, for the brave stoic dealt him a specially crushing blow. Nevertheless, no one ventured to reply.

CHAPTER XVII.

DURING the first few days of his reconciliation with Octavia Nero was full of genuine and heartfelt repentance. His young wife's sufferings had touched him deeply. He vehemently reproached himself for having so rashly believed in appearances. That spoiled and broken life was a grief to him.

"Octavia," he said, as she reclined, quite worn out, on the couch in her room. "You shall henceforth see how everything turns out for the best. I never knew how sweet and lovely a creature you were. Nay, do not weep, poor Octavia! Yes—these are tears, running down your cheeks in a silent stream, as though of their own accord. You are ill, Octavia! Listen, I swear by all the gods I would give this hand to be crushed by the executioner if I could but atone for all the griefs I have caused you! And so far as that is possible it shall be done. Tigellinus has already cast four of your infamous traducers into prison. They will suffer on the cross. Octavia, forgive me. I cannot bear to live if you are severe with me."

She forgave him freely and fully. But the memory of all that had occurred still gnawed too cruelly at her heart for her to be able at once to get over the impressions of this year of sorrow, winding up with the fearful climax of the trial.

"Let us wait," she said, "and see if you do not change your mind. The sacrifice you propose to make is perhaps beyond your strength. I would not have you feel as a burthensome duty what has come to me as a grace from the gods. Try whether you are indeed able to forego a happiness which, in spite of everything—was happiness."

Claudius Nero poured out the warmest protestations. The unselfishness of his young wife and the sorrow in her sweet face, which appealed to his very soul, shocked him deeply. With the timidity of a criminal who is unworthy of such a privilege he clasped her slender fingers and kissed them. Then he sank into brooding throught, till the *tricliniarch* came to announce that supper was ready.

Caesar rose and looked at Octavia; she had fallen asleep. A faint flush tinged her cheeck, and on her lashes sparkled the last dews of a tear. He woke her and gazed ardently into her eyes, as though once more imploring pardon. She smiled; then she smoothed her hair, draped her palla about her with a few touches, and followed her husband to a small private dining-room. Even he, who usually changed his extravagant attire three times a day, forgot to go to dress.

He dined with her tete-a-tete, served by only a few slaves, like an ordinary citizen. Neither he nor Octavia spoke more than was absolutely necessary; she from extreme exhaustion, he from a painful timidity and awkwardness in the presence of the woman against whom he had sinned so deeply—the gods alone knew why.

Octavia ate only a few mouthfuls. Even Caesar, to whom as a rule the pleasures of the table were as great a temptation as any other enjoyment in life, found no savor in the delicious guinea-fowls and the luscious Capuan fruit.

They separated at an early hour. Octavia withdrew at once to her sleeping-room. In spite of the conspicuous change in Nero's demeanor, her heart was so heavy within her that she would gladly have welcomed death. She felt that her spirit would have been calmer, clearer, and stronger if, even under the stigma of that shameful sentence, her carruca had conveyed her back to Antium. She foresaw no good end to this unexpected reconciliation; Caesar's decision had not been freely taken, whether it were his fear of the raging multitude, or his conscience, or pity for her that had led him to it. Love—which alone could have brought balm to her heart—Love, it too surely was not. Still, the Nazarene sage of whom Acte had spoken to her, taught the beautiful motto: "Endure to the end." She would endure; she would neglect no means that lay in her power. Then all must work out as the supreme Will should order it.

Nero, left to himself, was at once aware of a vague sense of emptiness which presently took a more definite form. He wanted Poppaea Sabina. No sense of decency, no diversion of thought that he could command availed to disguise the one great fact: that his passion for that fascinating witch amounted to insanity.

A faint resemblance in her eyes and lips to those of his never-forgotten Acte lay, unconfessed, at the root of this possession. The idea of losing Poppaea—for on one point he was quite clear: such a woman as Octavia would endure no half-measures—the bare idea almost maddened him. Only a few hours since he had implored Octavia's forgiveness, and now to the inmost core he quailed before the outcome. Reason and justice alike failed to release him from the spell of this influence. His wife was beautiful, young, noble, the very ideal of a high-souled woman; but, to him, all this was as nought in comparison with the one indescribable charm which Acte in her childlike innocence had had in common with the profligate Poppaea, and which was lacking in Octavia's beauty. This was to him the very essence of sweet, yielding, fervid womanhood; everything else seemed rigid, and cold—a tuneless, voiceless monotony; and he felt at this moment, after his reunion with Octavia, as though he were standing on the summit between youth and age.

For four long days did Caesar fight this desperate battle between inclination and duty. He seemed incapable of any effort. None of his friends were admitted to see him.

Tigellinus, and even Phaon—who wanted to report progress from the new Campanian villa—were forced to retire unsatisfied. Caesar's sole companion was Octavia. It was as though he wanted to accustom himself as quickly as possible to the inevitable, and to learn to endure this sunless life without Poppaea.

Octavia saw through it. On the fifth day, as she met him, she looked tearlessly into his face and said, in a firm voice:

"I know that you are lost to me for ever. I am not wroth with you: the gods have willed it so. Allow me—it is all I ask—allow me to return in peace to my villa at Antium, and there to end my days as best I may. I only pray that Poppaea may love you as truly as I have loved you." She longed to add: "Do not trust her too far. All she loves is power, and the magnificence of a palace. . . ." but the was silent.

In spite of the emotion that stirred him, and his admiration for the heroic magnanimity of this grief-stricken victim, Caesar could scarcely conceal his joy at this unhoped-for proposal. She had put into words what he had indeed long been aware of: she understood that love could not be coerced. However, for form's sake, he resisted. He called in Seneca, and his confidential servant Phaon, to help him to mollify her. But Octavia was firm.

Without any fuss or parade she returned to Antium, bereft for ever of her last timid hope—hardly, indeed, ever to be called a hope. All was now forever at an end;—such was the language of her mute farewell, her mournful smile, which expressed no rebuke, only infinite sorrow.

Slowly, as if it bore a corpse, her carraige rolled over the dewy road. Withered leaves rustled from the terraces of the villas; the chill December wind moaned through the deserted colonnades. Once she looked back. Rome lay behind her, a dark shapeless mass, the sepulchre of the happiness of which she had once cherished such roseate dreams. Dark clouds rested threateningly on Mt. Janiculum. One sigh, one secret groan, and the young empress turned her thoughts toward the desolate future. It was useless to struggle against the crushing decrees of fate. This was her pre-ordained destiny; she must endure it, without hate or rancor, according to the will of the gods.

The torches of her attendants blazed more and more brightly, a shower of sparks glittered around her carriage. She felt as if it were her funeral pyre, whose flames were consuming her enfeebled body. Ah, if one could die so easily, so calmly. . . . Suddenly as she thought of death, a wild terror, a horrible anxiety overpowered her. It was like a reflection of that fearful shock which had clouded her brain with such hideous visions. Closing her eyes, she forced herself by an almost superhuman effort to be calm, and at last the threatening attack passed away. Lulled by the monotonous rolling of the wheels, she fell asleep. And equally demurely, Poppaea Sabina came to her old place in the Palatium, welcomed with overflowing joy by the man who, a few days since, had sworn, as he looked on Octavia's pale features, that he would gladly suffer a thousand deaths if he could but atone for the past.

Octavia herself had taken care to make it known that she was leaving the capital by her own desire.

At the same time Tigellinus took the opportunity of attaching the body-guard by lavishing millions on them, so that the greater number of the officers vociferously clamored to have him appointed commander-in-chief—for Burrus, after a short illness, was now dead. Thus everything had settled down peacefully once more.

The guard in the palace was considerably strengthened. Tigellinus, in his new command, explained that it would be a mere trifle to rout the mob, however loudly it might roar, if it should ever again dare to lay down the law to Caesar. New maniples, consisting for the most part of German mercenaries, were immediately put into training.

Nero, who could now say truthfully that Octavia had quitted his roof of her own free-will, had settled with the last twinges of his conscience.

The people, too, seemed to have calmed down; for the

chief end they had aimed at—atonement for that monstrous sentence—had been achieved in spite of the overbearing Sicilian. As to Poppaea, in the opinion of any impartial observer, she had every reason to be satisfied with the upshot of affairs. It was no very serious matter that, after nullifying the sentence of divorce between Nero and Octavia, she could not actually be empress; Caesar had been almost starving for her flattery and devotion, and she ruled him now more absolutely than before. The business could be taken in hand again later. Perhaps Octavia, who was evidently quite crushed, might be induced by gentle means to abdicate her rights in every sense.

Meanwhile those persons who attributed to Poppaea such a cool head and practical calculations were altogether deceived. Poppaea did not calculate, she only felt. Every fibre of her body throbbed for vengeance. She had never dreamed that such a poor creature as Octavia could, under any circumstances, prove dangerous to her; but the impossible had come true, and Octavia had triumphed, though only for a few days, over the handsomest woman in the City of the Seven Hills. This had sealed the unhappy woman's fate: she must die, if Poppaea herself should have to thrust the dagger into her heart.

To begin with, Poppaea tried to win the confidence of the populace. Tigellinus sent his mercenaries to tear down the garlands from the statues of the fugitive empress, and to restore the broken images of Poppaea, which they covered with flowers or did homage to with sacrifices. All the sculptors of Rome were commissioned to produce busts of her in marble or bronze—a defiant retort on the insolence of the mob. Large bodies of praetorians paraded through the city, and with each company there was a party of three dozen imperial slaves, carrying short swords and heavy, knotted whips. Thus assemblies and rebellions were nipped in the bud.

The senate, to whom Caesar announced the young empress's resolve three days later, now simulated deep regret; as though lamenting the nullification of their verdict as slavishly as they had previously repented of their decision. This amazing behavior on the part of the supreme council suggested to Poppaea the possibility of making use of them again to assist her in making away with the rival she hated so fiercely: perhaps, if she set to work in the right way, the minions at the senate house might once more be over-ridden, and pronounce a third sentence by which, in spite of everything, the empress would be held guilty of any conceivable treachery.

But no. It was doing such a crew too much honor to demand their co-operation in any such important business. She rejected the idea. She would act for herself, she alone.

This time Tigellinus should not cross her path with his foolish caution. From the very first she had pointed out to him that his fiction of the empress's intrigue with Abyssus was a blunder—in the first place because it bore no great semblance of probability, and also because, by the laws of Rome, no slave could bear witness in the trial of a free-born citizen. Tigellinus, to be sure, had represented to her that she would more effectually degrade her rival by accusing her of a love-affair with a slave than if her paramour were supposed to be a member of the order of knights or of noble senatorial rank.

This, of course, was a fact beyond dispute; but by selecting a slave, whose confession had no legal weight, the Sicilian had made the use of torture necessary, and the results of that detestable method had been conspicuously in favor of Octavia's innocence. The failure had almost annihilated Poppaea, accustomed as she was to triumph.

She would have no more of such a counsellor. The plot she was now hatching would be fatal, annihilating, like a flash from Jove's thunder-bolts.

CHAPTER XVIII.

IT was a dull day in December; a melancholy downpour of rain fell from the gloomy grey clouds. Nero was lying on the lion-pawed couch in his writing-room. One slave had spread a handsomely-marked antelope-skin over his feet, while another was carefully tending the glowing charcoal which burnt‑ in a brazier placed in the middle of the room on a silver tripod, blowing it with a fan of ostrich and peacock feathers.

Early in the morning Caesar had given audience, as usual, to the senate; then he had exchanged a few words on business with Seneca and the Sicilian, and afterwards devoted some time to Phaon, whose architectural schemes lay much nearer his heart than the news of the suppression of an unexpected revolt in Gallia Narboniensis, or proposals for a large equestrian statue to be erected by "the grateful praetorians in memory of the adored Burrus." Now, when it was near dinner-time, Caesar was somewhat exhausted, particularly as an orgy given last night by Cossuthianus had not ended till a late hour. The dripping of the rain-spouts and the lead-colored sky made him melancholy; an uncomfortable shiver ran over his relaxed limbs. He felt indisposed to talk, and Cassius knew his master's habits well enough not to proffer a syllable when Caesar was in this depressed state of mind.

"You all lie to me," thought the despot, as he gazed through the half-open door into the drenched court-yard beyond. "The fair Poppaea calls me 'a god'; the smooth-tonged Agrigentine says I am the 'Will of the universe.' I myself fancied I had strength enough, if I exerted it, to raise humanity to heaven or sink it in ruin. And now I must submit when Jupiter Pluvius casts this dismal shroud—not merely over the bright firmament, but over my own miserable mind and person! Nero the omnipotent is chilled, not only in limb but in spirit." Suddenly he pressed his hand over his eye: "Take the charcoal out of the room, Cassius. My senses are clouded and my head aches. And you know, Cassius, that when Caesar's head aches the effects are felt in the remotest regions of the Empire."

Cassius obeyed.

"Aye—so I used to fancy," Nero went on in speechless bitterness of soul. "But I know now that mankind—curses on it—cares not for an instant whether I am well or ill at ease. So much the worse for them. I will repay them in kind. The more deeply anguish eats into their quivering marrow, the greater my contentment!—The base and vile mob rejoiced and shouted when I dismissed Poppaea—Poppaea, the only delight of my life! My heart was breaking, but the beasts outside bellowed with joy—just because they felt, perhaps, how wretched I was.—Poppaea Sabina! How sweet the name is to my heart. I owe my very life to her. If it had not been for her, the loss of that other one would have bereft me of my senses. As I could not have Acte, it was a boon from Fate that Poppaea could live for me. Often when she puts her arm round my neck and I close my eyes, I fancy I am with Acte—as on that first evening in Scaevinus' park. . . ."

"Caesar," said Cassius entering from the peristyle and interrupting these meditations, "the lady Poppaea begs to be admitted."

"At last," said Nero. "Now there will be some sunshine in this dreary room! Tell her I have been expecting her for a long time."

Then, turning to the other slave who sat on the floor in one corner: "Light the lamps," he said. "The clouds grow darker every moment. This corpselike twilight gives me the shivers."

The lad ran off and returned with a hand-lamp. In a minute the wicks of the marble standing-lamps shed their golden light, and immediately after Poppaea Sabina appeared in the doorway.

"Are you at leisure to listen to me, my darling?" she said in Greek.

"I was pining for you. Come, sit down here on the couch. You look so grave, sweet Poppaea. What is the matter?"

"Unheard-of things!" replied Poppaea calmly. "And yet, as I look you in the face, I think it will be better to say nothing, and speak to Seneca, or Tigellinus. . . ."

"What?" Caesar broke in. "Is there anything you would rather discuss with Seneca or Tigellinus than with me?"

Poppaea stared absently at the floor.

"Once already it has been my misfortune to be doubted by you for a moment, when my intentions were noble. To be thus misunderstood a second time—by all the gods! I could not bear it."

"Are you alluding to Octavia?" asked Nero with a frown. She hesitated.

"Partly to her," she said at length with an affectation of reluctance. "But in the first instance, of an audacious criminal who is, happily, in my power. Forgive me, Caesar, for keeping faithful and indefatigable watch lest harm should befall you."

Claudius Nero seized her hand. "Come to the point," he said, kissing the rosy fingers. "What misdeeds have you uncloaked?"

"Revolt, bloody rebellion,—and alas, alas!—But to keep to the main facts. Anicetus, who has for a long time been on terms of friendship with Octavia. . . ."

"You speak in a strange tone."

"I feared your wrath; for you, like the Roman people,

believe your Octavia to be as spotless as newly-fallen snow. Because her freedmen knew nothing against her you believed that there was nothing—a piece of astounding logic; and the few witnesses who spoke against her you supposed had been influenced by torture. As if one might not sin for years without being found out."

"Do you mean to assert that that wretched Abyssus, who swore that he was innocent with his dying breath, was a liar?"

Poppaea shrugged her shoulders.

"So far as the Egyptian is concerned I assert nothing. It is possible that the Sicilian's spies may have been deceived—in directing their search. When a loving couple are discovered at night in a vine-covered bower, it is conceivable that Lucius should be taken for Sempronius, or vice versa. This time, however, all error is excluded. Anicetus has boasted to one of the officers of being Octavia's lover, and two soldiers, as free-born as you or I, both heard him. Utterly overwhelmed by their testimony, he does not deny it. I questioned him myself, yesterday; and when I promised him that his miserable life should be spared if he would confess publicly. . . . But I see you are exciting yourself, Nero; your face is quite pale, and you are trembling. Can you take it so ill that she should retaliate. . . ."

"Retaliate?" cried Caesar in a voice of thunder. "Do you, even you, take the view of the contemptible creatures known as 'the women of Rome?' I am Caesar; and, above all, I am a husband. It may hurt her feelings, when I bestow the favors due to my wife on one who has no claim to them. I hurt her feelings, but by Hercules I do her no dishonor! No one will laugh at her; no one will think her ridiculous. The world has nothing but pity and passionate sympathy for the abandoned wife, even now when the separation was her own doing. But I, if it is true—if Anicetus. . . . But it is a lie, Poppaea; it is inconceivable."

"I pardon you," she replied coolly, "for I understand you. The idea of being mocked at by the mob robs the wisest of reason. A betrayed husband, a Caesar whose wife carries on an intrigue, in defiance of all probability, with Caesar's most confidential servant, and, to crown all, concocts schemes with him to overthrow the monarch and place her sweet paramour on the throne—it is an unenviable position, to be sure.''

"And Octavia has done all this?" asked Caesar.

"Convince yourself.—Without informing any one I got Anicetus and three of his accomplices to land, placed them under a guard, and made a centurion write down word for word the statement they made to me. Here is the result of the whole business. Read, and then try to doubt.—Happily the stupid conspiracy has had no time to gather allies. Almost all the officers are loyal. A letter from Octavia, whose writing you know, is here with the other papers."

She placed the fateful documents in his hands. Nero read, looking paler, more ghastly, and more corpse-like at every line.

"The viper!" he snarled through his teeth. "Indeed! So the fleet would rise in a body, with the peasantry of Campania. The blow was to fall from Cape Misenum—a blow that was to dethrone Caesar and raise that base scoundrel Anicetus from the mire of his low birth! Horrible! Atrocious! Is it to be believed of the chaste Octavia, who is too coy to speak a word that might not be uttered at the altar of Vesta? But it is just like her, a hypocrite—a hussy! The more innocent her face, the more reprobate her soul! By her side Chloris, the Rhodian, shines as radiant as Artemis.—And that wretch has dared to boast—to brag of Caesar's dishonor? They both deserve to die."

"I promised the villain to obtain his pardon as the reward of his full and free confession," said Poppaea. "Banish him for life to Sardinia. Do you not know that a Roman dreads Sardinia more than death?"

"Never mind, never mind! We will discuss that latter," said Caesar, still absorbed in the centurion's report. He knew the man; he was one of his most faithful soldiers; his name was a sufficient guarantee that nothing in this document had been falsified. Besides, as Poppaea had suggested, he had only to question the accused officers to enable him to discover at once the smallest deviation from the truth.

In fact, nothing was falsified by the short note from Octavia, which was so clever a forgery that Caesar himself would have staked his head on its genuineness.

"She must die!" he cried, crushing up the crackling sheets in his fist. Then, drawing a deep breath, he asked: "Where have you placed the villain?"

"In the fourth court-yard, in one of the slaves' rooms."

"Then have him brought to me. Hark, how the wind is rising! The right weather for such horrible deeds. How it wails and howls. I could fancy I heard Agrippina's death cries."

This time Poppaea was victorious. Anicetus, whom she had bribed with untold millions, humbly bowed to a blow of Caesar's fist, swallowed down three broken teeth, and then, thanking his imperial clemency, submitted to be led away to the trireme which set sail the same day in spite of the storm. His accomplices departed with him; Poppaea had signified to Nero that, if he desired to be just, he would not punish the criminal's tools more severely than their leader.

When he refused she murmured in his ear that if he loved her he must observe this fundamental principle of justice.

But she exacted a sentence of death on Octavia. Half-granting and half-promising, she flattered and coaxed him with shameless coquetry, till, inflamed by her charms and stung to the quick by her mockery at his hesitancy—"a second Otho," she called him—he signed the death-warrant she had long since held in readiness.

CHAPTER XIX.

OCTAVIA was sitting in the oecus with a slave and listening to the letter written some years since by the mysterious Aspostle Paul, from Philippi in Thracia, to the congregation of Nazarenes at Corinth. This venerable epistle, which was more highly esteemed for its simple and moving fervency than many others written by the great Christian teacher, had been copied and recopied many times, and was in the hands of every Nazarene who could read. The reader, a girl of twenty and a native of Argolis, who had been baptised a year and a half since, lent the touching words all the unction of a melodious voice, and the ardor of faith. Octavia had hitherto watched the deeds and words of the great Apostle with half-recalcitrant astonishment and curiosity; in spite of her sympathy with the doctrines of the Nazarene, she still clung in her heart to the solemn, ancient worship of Jupiter; and it was for the first time that she was conscious of the inspiration of an irresistible Spirit, as the slave girl read on:

"Though I speak with the tongues of men and of angels and have not charity, I am become as sounding brass or a tinkling cymbal; and though I have the gift of prophecy, and understand all mysteries and all knowledge; and though I have all faith, so that I could remove mountains, and have no charity, I am nothing; and though I bestow all my goods to feed the poor, and though I give my body to be burned, and have not charity, it profiteth me nothing.

"Charity suffereth long and is kind; charity envieth not; charity vaunteth not itself, is not puffed up, doth not behave itself unseemly, seeketh not her own, is not easily provoked, thinketh no evil, rejoiceth not in iniquity, but rejoiceth in the truth; beareth all things, believeth all things, hopeth all things, endureth all things. Charity never faileth. . . ."

"Phoebe," said Octavia interrupting her, "one minute—give me a moment. . . ." The young empress had covered her eyes with her hand. "Faileth not," she repeated slowly. "Seeketh not her own, endureth all things—again, Phoebe. Read that passage once more."

Phoebe obeyed; Octavia listened, her eyes fixed on the gentle, candid face of the reader. And again the words sounded like music from another world: "Charity never faileth. . . ."

But suddenly what an ominous bustle and stir! Hasty steps in the atrium, terrified mutterings, and then a low clatter as of armed men advancing cautiously on tip-toe.

Octavia sprang to her feet. As she went to the door, she ran up against the two praetorian officers to whom Poppaea had entrusted the execution of the sentence of death.

"Lady," said one of them, "we are here by Caesar's commands. Spare us the explanation we could hardly bear to utter. Here—read this. . . ." And he held out the document to the trembling woman.

She glanced at it timidly, almost incredulously, and then with a rigid stare, like that of a bird who sees into the jaws of a serpent.

At last she understood. With a loud cry she dropped on her knees. With burning tears she pleaded for life—she, unhappy as she was, to whom life and sorrow were one. Perhaps some spark of hope still glimmered among the ashes of her ruined life—or had the terrible struggle of contending feelings so utterly exhausted her young powers that Fate refused her the comfort of the desperate: the dignity of a brave and steadfast death?

"Mercy!" she cried, wringing her trembling hands. "I am still so young, and have known nothing in this life but its misery! Let me fly—far, far away—beyond the Pillars of Hercules! I only ask to see the sun, to breathe the air, the heavenly air—the sweet, heavenly breath of life."

The centurions wavered; it was a hard task for honest soldiers to be the executioners of this tenderly-delicate creature who, by right, was entitled to share all the honors of sovereignty. But their dread of Poppaea, and a care for their own safety, won the day.

"Lady, it cannot be," said the elder: "Caesar commands, and centurions can only obey."

He drew his sword, but the weapon dropped from his hand at the sight of such heatrending anguish.

"Come on!" he said to his younger companion; but as he, too, could not deal the fatal blow, the leader signed to his men and ordered them to bind the empress, but with all possible respect.

"Forgive me," he said with moist eyes, while the praetorians tied her hands and feet with soft woollen scarfs. "It is a crime—but I must do it. If, indeed, there be a God, and a future life, and you enter into that glory, pray for me that this deed may be forgiven me!"

They carried the half-senseless creature to a warm bath, and a vein was opened with a sharp stiletto.

"Lady, it is not painful," said the elder centurion. "You will die away gradually, exactly as though you were falling asleep."

But life fought hard and with desperate tenacity against the eternal night in which it was to be so early extinguished, against all the laws of nature. The blood flowed but slowly from the wound, and less by degrees. Terrible convulsions came on, and a moan of indescribable agony broke from the drawn lips. The veteran shuddered with horror; with a deep groan he grasped her abundant light-brown hair and held her head under water. Soon all was over.

The centurion who had drowned her gave vent to a fearful curse on Caesar and Poppaea Sabina, drew his sword, and pierced his own heart.

His younger comrade lifted up the body of the murdered empress and laid it, with that of his ill-starred leader, in the atrium, each on a bier and covered with sheets in readiness for burning on the funeral pile. In obedience to Poppaea's commands, he carried Octavia's head to Rome and delivered it over to the lady herself.

This time Poppaea had woven the web of falsehood with so much skill that even honest folks were half-disposed to believe it. The various documents, including Octavia's forged letter, were read before the senate. The only voices that might have been heard in behalf of the victim so ruthlessly made away with, were now silent; for Flavius Scaevinus was at Mediolanum, while Thrasea Paetus and Barea Soranus were safe within the walls of the state prison, charged with high treason and criminal plots against Caesar's person. The few others who still cherished a spark of noble feeling—Piso, for instance, the light-hearted Epicurean—had of late kept quite aloof from affairs so as not to appear cowardly and base on one hand, or on the other to risk their heads. Thus it came about that the assembly of the Fathers hailed the murder of Octavia as a political achievement, and passed a resolution to offer thanks and sacrifice in all the temples of the Capitol for Caesar's safety and the escape of the Roman Empire from her conspiracies.

"Wretched curs, those wearers of the purple!" said Poppaea with a laugh, when she heard of this vote. "The head-cook's scullion-slaves are heroes as compared with the lick-spittles of the senate-house! They shall be treated as they deserve for the future."

A month later Claudius Nero and Poppaea Sabina solemnized their marriage. During the interval the facile and impressionable populace had quieted down. Poppaea's enemies, who had secretly exerted themselves, even in the Palatium, to hinder Caesar's union with her, seemed to have been silenced. The new empress, by her personal affability and lavish bounty, soon found means to win over the mob who not long since had overthrown her statues and left them in the dust. Her triumph reached its climax when, in the following February, she gave birth to a daughter. The festival held for several days by the two million souls throughout the city, from Janiculus to the Labicanian Way, was as far beyond description as Caesar's delight.

But Nero's passionate devotion to Poppaea was shown even more conspicuously in the sorrow which followed too soon on these uproarious rejoicings. The young mother had not yet left her couch, when the infant which had been hailed as a divinity throughout Italy, died suddenly—in consequence, probably, of the excitement Poppaea had lived through during the last few months. An attempt was made to conceal the disaster from her. But as she insisted impatiently on seeing her little daughter, whom she had had in her arms only a few hours before, Nero himself timidly went to her and whispered: "Sweet Poppaea—try to bear it.—Our flower is dead!" And with a shriek of despair she fell back on her pillows, unconscious.

For three days she was delirious. Once she was on the point of dashing out her brains, but Nero seized her in time.

"Octavia!" she screamed, "Octavia, childless! Look! She rises from the dead. She takes her revenge—she is drinking my heart's blood!"

Nero soothed her; he sat by her couch with the tenderest affection, day after day, week after week, till the sufferer was restored to health.

Toward the end of March, leaning on her husband's arm, she crossed the threshold of her sick-chamber for the first time. The spring sun was shining in the courtyard; the soft air fanned the brow of the convalescent. A smile flitted over her beautiful face, a smile that shimmered like the water in the fountain. Its meaning was: "I suffered—but as an Empress!"

Poppaea Sabina had reached the goal. By degrees she learnt to view the loss of her child as a tribute which she must be content to pay to the gods, if she hoped to be safe from their envy. She now made every effort to secure her footing in the high place she had won. She had seen from Octavia's example how little the position of empress had to give unless Caesar's affection were permanently hers. She proved herself mistress of the art of keeping her husband's love on the alert, and his pleasure in her society; of flinging him into a whirl of the maddest amusement, and then drawing him lovingly to her side so as to make him feel that there alone was his true home. She bent to his every change of mood without hesitation, without fear, without a pang of remorse. Thus she gave him what he gratefully acknowledged to be perfect happiness, but she contributed more than any one to foster his unbridled folly, his scorn of all justice, in short, his insane autocratic depotism, and to develop the terrible nature of the man which to this day glares from the yawning void of the past—one of the mysterious demons of history.

CHAPTER XX.

It was midsummer. The rank and fashion of Rome had long since fled to the mountain valleys or to the sea-shore. Caesar and his court were residing at Antium where Tigellinus had built a new and splendid villa on his imperial master's account.

Rome was like a city of the dead all day; not till an hour after sunset did the taverns begin to fill with half-naked revellers, or the Campus Martius—where in the cooler season the men played foot-ball and threw the discus—wake up to life again. Then it was crowded with citizens, seeking fresh air, who lounged on the half-parched grass eating bread and fruit, or stood in thirsty groups round the public fountains. An hour or two later and the steps of every public building, the marble flags in front of the Temple of Saturn, the far-famed slope to the Capitol, the Colonnade of Agrippina—in short, every imaginable spot, was covered with deeply-breathing sleepers, who found it impossible to rest even for a minute in the oppressive atmosphere of a lodging-house. Among them were many sick, for the malaria of Rome, the immemorial curse of the City of the Seven Hills, claimed its numerous victims year by year. Thousands of parched creatures, too much disturbed for sleep, were seeking refreshment in the scanty waters of the Tiber. From the

Aelian Bridge down the stream as far as the quay under the Aventine, heads on heads were to be seen—men, women, and children, while the boats' crews, in spite of the exhaustion which ennervated them also, were straining every sinew to discharge their freight and get back to Ostia, the healtheir sea-port, before day-break.

Along the shore at this spot, and parallel to the Circus Maximus, lay extensive warehouses and stores, particularly granaries and oil-stores.

July the 24th, and the sun had been slowly lost in blood-red mist. An ominous sultriness, heavier than ever, brooded over the metropolis. Not a breath stirred the dense atmosphere, which was as thick as the coarse wool of Southern Italy. Pale flames of harmless lightning flashed now and again above the Quirinal.

Suddenly, two hours before midnight, the startled populace saw a more vivid glare rising, as it seemed, from the light timber roof of one of the granaries on the Aventine.

"Fire!"—The shout of terror flew through the terrified throng. A spark even, in that neighborhood, in such terrific drought!—There was not a man among them who did not understand the magnitude of the danger. Before the cry could spread through even the nearest groups, the flames were soaring high up to heaven.

The town cohorts, whose duty it was to act as a fire brigade, as well as to preserve order, were later in arriving than could have been wished. The conflagration had spread with raging swiftness. The soldiers, seconded by the populace, set to work to pull down the houses and sheds which were most immediately threatened, hoping to isolate the centre of mischief. The oil merchants' store-houses were already in a blaze, and the burning fluid carried ruin away to the south-east, like a lava-stream down Etna. Sparks and blazing splinters flew in all directions to a great distance, now crackling and hissing among the crowd, and now flung up in a fountain of destructive fury—up to the silent stars, which looked down on such a scene as they never had looked upon before since men had dwelt on the earth: the burning of a city of two million souls.

Every one toiled like mad; but their strength presently failed. At the end of a few hours the fearful certainly forced itself on their conviction that no struggle with the raging element, on the present basis of operations, could be of any avail. There were not hands enough to remove the debris of the buildings they pulled down, and these consisted chiefly of beams, rafters, boards, and wooden furniture. There was no help for it: if they hoped to save the rest of Rome, not this region only, but the two adjoining ones must be sacrificed, and the line of isolation be carried through those quarters of the city where the massive stone-work would oppose a more effectual resistance to the hail of sparks.

At the end of the third vigil the town prefect sent a mounted messenger to Antium.

"Mighty Caesar," he wrote in despair, "I curse the fate that has let me live to see this day. Rome is burning. We have rushed to combat the raging flames as a lion rushes on the dogs; but are fain to yield to superior strength. Come, Caesar! Help us in the struggle. Vouchsafe your encouraging presence. You alone can yet be able to check the hand of Destiny!"

Nero at once set out, accompanied by Poppaea Sabina and a numerous escort. The disastrous state of things in Rome was far worse than his most anxious fears had painted it. By the time he arrived an eighth of the city was in flames. He was visibly shocked. And the catastrophe had an even deeper effect on Poppaea Sabina. With her acumen and knowledge of the world, she knew that she had no stronger ally in her antagonism with the aristocracy and the middle classes than the people, who cried for bread and the Circus, and who were ready to shout: "Ave Caesar" when a horse-race had been nobly won. And now it was precisely the homes of the poorest of them that had fallen a prey to the fire. This seemed to the empress most disquieting. The mob, though loyal to the dynasty, were not to be reckoned on. It was characteristic of the populace to rejoice effusively when full and amused, but to grumble loudly or fall upon the military if, by chance, the corn-ships from Egypt were delayed. Omnipotent Caesar, to whom they owed their welfare, they held no less responsible for their woes; finding in his sublime and mystical personality the first cause of all that befell them. And how naturally it might occur to the half-frantic creatures to take the same unreasonable view of the terrible catastrophe which had left unnumbered thousands without a roof to shelter them.

Poppaea communicated her thoughts to Caesar.

"That is the very reason why I have come," replied Nero. "They shall see that I am in fact their god and preserver." And he looked gravely round at his followers. "There is no time to lose; we cannot even change our dress.—We must divide into two parties. I, Caesar, will lead one; you, Tigellinus, the other. Each man must do exactly as he is bid, without remonstrance, be he a consul or a charioteer. Every man who distinguishes himself by bravery or presence of mind I will reward splendidly; if he is a slave, he shall be freed and have a knight's allowances. Tigellinus, you must stay here in the southern quarters of the city, I and my men will proceed to the Subura!—Forward! The Eternal City shall be preserved this day; for Caesar speaks the word!"

The two divisions separated to organise the work of subduing the fire.

"Caesar! In the storm of sparks!" the astonished crowd cried out. "Poppaea among the falling ruins! Hail! Hail!— The flames must yield now! Rome has triumphed over their fury!"

And the Eternal City would indeed have triumphed, had it not been for that refuse of the people which always and everywhere takes ruthless advantage of a common misfortune.

In the midst of the hideous confusion, which was aggravated by the fact that there was no police in most of the northern and eastern regions of the city, a hundred-headed

412

thievish mob suddenly came to the surface. Under the pretext of carrying off the portable property in the endangered buildings to a place of safety, these beasts of prey plundered with unblushing boldness, committed every conceivable deed of violence, and finally—finding the horrible tragedy so profitable to themselves—set fire to many parts of the city which had hitherto been spared. When Claudius Nero, tired to death, threw himself on his bed that evening in the hill-villa of Maecenas, the city was burning at four different points. The Palatium was a heap of ruins and ashes, though the imperial guard had succeeded in saving some of the most precious of its treasures of art.

And now, as a climax of woes, bad weather came to aid the cunning of the incendiaries and robbers. Early next morning a storm arose which, within a few hours, spread the conflagration in a way which seemed to nullify every effort to intercept its progress. The flames flew on like torch-bearing furies, attacking temples and theatres, the splendid buildings in the Via Lata, and the merchants' halls in the Argiletum. The fever-haunted Subura, the villas of the ruling consuls in the midst of their gardens, and the solemn splendor of the palace of the Pontifex Maximus alike went up in smoke. So far as the eye could see, there was nothing but fulvous red glare, leaping white flames, and lurid smoke-wreaths rolling eastward before the driving wind. An incessant flash and roar came up from the hundred thousand craters which had once been Rome. The atmosphere quivered and surged as with subterranean thunders, and the consuming heat instantly destroyed every living thing that felt the breath of that immense furnace.

The despair of the unhappy inhabitants had reached a climax. Wild yells and howls, as of men suddenly demented, rang through the quarters which were as yet unconsumed, and furious roars and threats were mingled with shrieks of terror and anguish.

The human victims amounted to thousands; fearful details were on every lip. A whole block of houses had been so suddenly surrounded by the flames that every inhabitant—the children, the sick, and the aged—had been burnt alive. In the Subura the badly-built lodging-houses had in many cases crumbled into ruins as soon as the adjoining dwelling began to give way, and dozens of the poorer citizens, while trying to save their belongings, had been killed by falling beams and brick-work, or, which was worse, lingered, crushed and in frightful torments, till they were suffocated by the scorching vapor or till the brands and cinders slowly burnt their shattered limbs.

The immensity of the danger and abject terror of the most agonising form of death had given rise to scenes which, for sheer horror, cast into the shade everything which Rome, the blood-stained and guilty city, had ever before known. Sons trod their wailing fathers under foot if but they might so reach the smoke-filled window which seemed to offer a chance of escape. Mothers snatched their screaming infants from their breasts and threw them into the flames to have their arms free to fend off a burning wall. In short, every tie of love, of nature, and of law was sundered before the maddening power of the raging element. The end of the world seemed at hand. Many of the citizens flung themselves into the fire, either under the influence of that mysterious spell which drags the horror-stricken traveller into the abyss, or with conscious determination to die and so escape seeing the destruction of the Rome they loved so well.

CHAPTER XXI.

WHO, who had brought this visiation on the Queen of Cities? Was all this accident? Was it conceivable that ruin should take so well-directed a course? First the conflagration by the Aventine, and then the three fires at three different spots, which had seconded the greater one till everything was one blazing chaos, flaming to the skies!—Was such a systematic destruction of the "Daughter of Ares" conceivable unless some far-reaching and guiding will had been at work? But who could be the man to spoil her, crush her, leave her in ruins? And who were his foul and malignant accomplices? One man there was who must know: one who had thousands of eyes and ears in every place—the eyes and ears of his officials, his police, his soldiers, and his spies: Caesar.

And as evening fell the populace gathered in denser and denser crowds round the house of Maecenas, which, by its situation, afforded a screen from the intolerable heat of the burning city. The praetorians kept the uproarious and desperate mob at a distance with the greatest difficulty.

"Claudius Nero must tell us!" bellowed one of the proletariat. "He is our lord and master; he must protect us. Is there no talk of apprehending any one? Is no one to be castigated, blinded, crucified? We demand justice! Villains and incendiaries are not to be allowed to go unpunished. Where are the lictors? The axes? The executioners?''

"Fool!'' whispered a young aristocrat, laying his hand on the eloquent artisan's shoulder.

"What do you mean?''

"I mean that you are talking nonsense or you would not have said "Catiline—punish Catiline!''

The man stared at his unknown adviser. "Who are you?'' he asked with a scowl.

"One of those who will not submit to be deceived. At any rate I have good eyes. And with those eyes I saw the town soldiers set fire to the house of Lucanus the poet. . . .''

"And so did I,'' another threw in, a knight with a broad gold ring. "All the citizens know it quite well; Caesar, himself. . . .''

"What, what?'' was creid in chorus.

"Well; it was all a farce—the excitement at his arrival, the rewards he offered. . . . It was he, himself, he alone. . . .''

"Silence! It is as much as your life is worth. . . !''

"Better to die,'' said the young noble, "than to live under the rule of that bloodhound. See how his miserable subjects were housed. Whole regions were plundered by the praetorian body-guard; but for the fire, they could not have had the sport.—You seek the incendiary, you want to crucify him? In there, behind the hedge of spears, behind the walls of this accursed house, he is wallowing in Caecubina wine, while our glorious city is perishing in ashes!''

"Nero!'' was muttered from one to another. "Nero is the originator of all this ruin. . . .''

"But why?—What object can he have in view?''

"Nothing but wickedness! None of the crimes he had as yet committed were great enough to satisfy him. If the earth could burn, he would have set all Europe in flames.''

"And only think of his vanity! Herostratus destroyed the temple at Ephesus; Nero reduces eight centuries of historical glory to ashes. So much greater is he than Herostratus!''

"Do not you know that so long ago as last autumn he said

to Poppaea: 'When you are Empress, I will sweep away the old city in your honor and build a new one, finer, more magnificent, and more worthy of you?' "

"To be sure. And the newly-founded city was to be called Neronia, that this aper of Romulus should be remembered to all posterity. . . ."

"Was such a thing ever heard of?" cried ten, twenty, thirty voices at once. "An incendiary on the throne? Curses on the devastator! Down with the wretch! He deserves to die!"

The young aristocrat and the eques had vanished in the crowd, to spread the horrible report of Nero's guilt still further in other spots. They both were concerned in the conspiracy which Agrippina had so nearly discovered at the time when her favorite Pallas had attacked the house of Lucius Menenius. They had reached that pitch of bitter despair in which a man thinks all means justified by the end, and the members of the secret society now seized every opportunity of casting odium on the tyrant and his tools. No moment could be more favorable than the present for applying the lever. The praetorian and town-cohorts had, in fact, committed some excesses; nor was it impossible that Nero, in his amorous folly, should have declared that the Rome of Augustus was unworthy of such an empress as Poppaea. All this was volubly poured forth, details were amassed, invented, and falsified, wherever they seemed to serve the end in view,—and thus, by degrees, the rumor took form, which, in spite of its obvious absurdity, obtained credence for many centuries, namely: that Nero was the destroyer of his capital, and that merely to procure for himself and his Poppaea a vast and fearfully splendid spectacle.

Caesar, unconscious of the calumny, was standing with Poppaea Sabina on the roof of the tower, and looking down at the roaring, surging, raging sea of fire. Red-gold fire on every side—millions of quivering flame-shapes soaring heavenward, serpents of fire, writhing in a thousand blazing coils, infernal dragons with bloated bodies and volcanic

417

bursts from innumerable, inexhaustible craters.

The terrible splendor of the scene excited him to the highest pitch. The sacred thrill of inspiration ran through his highly-strung nerves. He forgot the weight of anxiety which had oppressed his heart like a load of lead. He forgot his palace in ashes and the desolate waste which ere long would greet his eyes on every hill. He even forgot the presence of his Poppaea Sabina, whose head lay fondly on his shoulder. He turned round and signed to one of his body-slaves to bring him his cithara, which was carried with him wherever he travelled.

Gazing still on burning Rome, he hung the scarlet ribbon round his neck, tuned the instrument, and raising the plectrum, struck a loud chord from the metal strings, while from his blooming young lips broke a heroic song. The verses were in the metre of the poetess Sappho, and the fourth line of each was a refrain accompanied by the fullest tone of the lyre: "Heaven-kissing fires!"

"You sing like a god!" cried Poppaea as he ended, and she clapped her hands like a playful child.

But he did not hear her. A vision floated before his gaze, strangely near and vivid; a fair maiden-form, which rose up mysteriously from the flaming gulf, as the goddess of Love rose from the waves of the ocean—Acte—sweet, lovely, never-forgotten. Her deep blue eyes, fixed on his face, seemed to be asking: "Has she altogether supplanted me? Or do you still feel at the bottom of your heart something which turns to me, a dim yearning which no other than I can ever satisfy?"

"Acte!" he groaned with a deep sigh. The cithara dropped from his hand, and slipped down the folds of his toga to the ground.

Thus had he seen her in that golden, blissful hour when he had first sung those verses,—to her—one evening when the crests of the remote Alban hills had glowed, flame-colored, in the last rays of the setting sun. It was all gone—lost for ever, like the city at his feet now breathing its last in gasping agonies.

"Aye! Perish!" he cried, raising his hands. "Die, Rome, imperial city! Burn, expire! I can raise you from your ashes, new and more magnificent than ever. But no god can give her back to me nor fill her place! Acte dead, what right had you to enjoy this transitory life? Soaring flames! Aye, let them soar; and though they blazed a thousand times more splendidly, they would seem too poor a sacrifice to the dead. She deserved a nobler one! Sempiternal night might well have fallen on the world at the moment when her thrice blessed life was ended."

His voice rose as if in solemn prayer. The rapturous tones were even audible to the crowd below, who had also heard the mysterious song and the music of the lyre.

"Do you hear him—glorying in it?" cried a Ligurian sailor. "The city may burn: he rejoices in it—and the nine regions that lie in flames are not enough to satisfy him."

"He can sing and be glad," roared a dealer from the Argiletum, "while despair is raging around him!"

"Caesar shall answer us! Make way, praetorians there! The people of Rome want Caesar. The Romans insist on knowing what is the meaning of this farce. Down with the incendiaries! Caesar must know who has reduced Rome to ashes!"

The praetorians calmly kept the mob back at the point of the lance, and they gave way once more. Still, the tumult having been once set going, spread every instant. The military tribune in command of the guard sent a soldier up to the top of the tower to report to Caesar the gravity of the situation.

"What fools!" cried Nero with a laugh.

"Do not take these fools too lightly," Proppaea said. "They are maddened, like dogs when the sun is near the sign of the Lion."

A fearful howl of rage checked the reply on Caesar's lips. Five or six of the foremost had fallen victims to the soldiers. The rest pressed on with redoubled fury. In a moment there would be a pitched battle.

"Do you hear?" said Poppaea in warning. "The populace insist on a criminal to punish. Do you wish to be he? The cry that comes up to us seems to me ominous enough!"

"This is the work of my deadliest foes," said Caesar bitterly. "I do not know them, for they hide behind the mask of friendship. But I know of a body of men who have stabbed me more deeply and filled my soul with more cruel torture than the senators who plot to overthrow me: the Nazarenes."

"By Zeus!" cried Poppaea, grasping his hand, "that is a grand idea! Ever since those edicts were forced from you, the whole kith and kin of the Nazarenes have made themselves thoroughly hateful. The more I think of it, the more happy the notion seems. I am almost inclined to believe it true. Yes, Caesar, you have solved the riddle. The Nazarenes are the criminals; they desire to see the fulfilment of the prophecies they have so long uttered."

"Do you think so?" said Nero with an incredulous smile.

"I am sure of it. Did you never hear that one of the principal promulgators of the Nazarene doctrine, named Paul, tells the populace that the God of the Christians will soon reduce the world to ashes and then judge all mankind. 'Everlasting fire,' is a catchword of the Christian faith. Paul has prophecied it hundreds of times to the rich and great of this earth. Does it surprise you that the impatient rabble, who have long ceased to offer sacrifices to the gods of Rome, at last desire to see the prediction realized and aid in the work themselves?"

"Are the common people aware of this attempt of the Nazarenes?"

"No doubt they are. Their utterances, laughed at in the first instance, and then criticised and condemned for their monstrous audacity, are repeated from mouth to mouth! You have only to give the hint, and the mob will jump at it as a long-expected fact!"

"Well, then. . . ." Caesar began thoughtfully. Poppaea anticipated him; she went towards the stairs, while he stood gazing down into the surging furnace.

The Nazarenes! Once on a time the name had been a familiar one; he had associated many ideas with it, soaring, world-moving schemes—till he learnt to hate the disciples of the Carpenter's Son, not only because he perceived that, under their influence and that of the fanatical Nicodemus, he was becoming a slave to the duties of the State, and learning to contemn his own natural impulses but, even more, because Nicodemus, in his pursuit of an impossible end, had robbed him of the delight of his life. Acte would never have disappeared if Nicodemus in his bigotry had not degraded her to the instrument of his mad projects.—How different would his life have been but for the flight of the maiden whose mere image still had so irresistible an influence over him. He would never have been Octavia's husband, and thus would never have become such a half-hearted man, torn asunder to the very depths of his nature.—Yes, he hated the Nazarenes; and their type and image in his tortured fancy was that lean, restless, glaring Nicodemus. They were all just like him, all; and they would suffer no more than they deserved if he now were to abandon them to the mob as the destroyers of the Queen of Cities.

He, too, hastened down the stairs. Wrapping his toga majestically about him, he went into the vestibule.

"What is your will?" he asked defiantly, as silence fell on the multitude at his approach.

"Revenge—revenge on the rascally incendiaries!"

"Do you know who they are?" asked Caesar. As the red glare lighted up his youthful beauty he looked like a demigod.

"Nay, you must tell us!" was shouted in chorus.

"Well, I will name them. They shall atone for it, as never criminals atoned before since our forefather Aeneas trod the soil of Latium.—The Christians have caused our misfortune. Go and seize the Christians."

"The Christians!" was roared and taken up by thousands of voices on the burning hills. "Drag them out of their hiding-places. Go and seek them in the catacombs where they blaspheme against the gods and the throne of the Caesars. Pick them out among the throng—here—there, and there again!—There is Phlegon, the flower-seller;—did you not just see Epenaetus, the friend of Paul of Cilicia whom they call the Apostle?—And that slight fellow is Artemidorus, the freedman of Flavius Scaevinus! Yonder are Tryphena and her sister.—Trample them to the ground! Fling them into the fire! Take them as they come—men, women, and children!"

"Stop!" said Caesar, raising his right hand. "Let no man do the misled creatures an injury! First get this conflagration under; then I will give the Romans a feast in my gardens yonder, where I will now have huts and tents erected to shelter the roofless, and I will distribute money enough to enable you build up again all that has been destroyed. At that feast the miscreants shall be punished! You shall see sights such as no sovereign has ever yet shown you! The bloodiest combats with wild beasts, the maddest fights between gladiators, are mere child'a play in comparison with what I promise you.—Do not lose heart; do no listen to the voice of the traitors who would fain sow division between Caesar and his beloved Roman subjects! Work, struggle, and entreat Jupiter that he may set a limit to the flames!"

"Ave Caesar!" cried the roaring multitude. "Hail, the divine ruler who bestows blessings and refuge, and who invites his Quirites to be his guests!"

CHAPTER XXII.

The fire was extinct. For ten days it had raged like a devouring beast in the vast metropolis of two million souls and consumed two-thirds of it. At last it only lurked smouldering under heaps of ruins. Pale wreaths of smoke still rose straight into the glowing summer air, the last efforts of the element's dying power.

On the morning of the eleventh day Nero went up, as he had done so often during the conflagration, to the roof of the tower of Maecenas' house. He remembered the evening when, inspired by the sight of the burning city, he had played his cithara up there. The splendor of the fire in its all-consuming rage, driven on by the storm in surges of flame, over the endless stretch of houses, had turned his brain. He had fancied himself playing the part of Zeus, the thunderbolt in his right hand, and setting the whole world in a blaze with a lightning flash, up to the very heights of Olympus. The city was burning for him; it showed that Rome might sink in ruins and that the world would still have lost nothing, so long as he, the omnipotent Caesar, stood firm on the pedestal of his divinity.

But now, when, having left his hot bed, he leaned over the parapet and saw what had but lately been the scene of a light-hearted and pleasure-seeking population reduced to smoking rubbish, a feeling came over him of wrath against the gods—in whom he did not believe—of hatred against unconquerable fate. The implacable Inevitable, in its terrible vagaries, was as irresponsible as a mischievous boy, who tramples down a flower-bed, defaces a painting, or mutilates a statue.

What then! What if Fate had presumed to run riot like a drunken wretch, what if she had placed a thousand hindrances in his way when he had meant so well; should he, Caesar, who held imperial sway, yield to Fate in the scope and audacity of his arbitrary schemes? The great catastrophe had overtaken the guilty and the innocent alike: then he, too, would now be a scourge to humanity; but with this difference: that his feelings were nobler than those of the power which Seneca had once ventured to speak of by the incomprehensible name of "Providence." Nero's victims should not be blindly sacrified like those of Fate; they should perish for deliberately-weighed reasons. He would slaughter them in the first place to gratify his hatred, and in the second, as he reluctantly confessed to himself, to secure his safety.

The populace, notwithstanding all Caesar's endeavors to mitigate the public calamity,—more particularly · by an admirably organized distribution of food, were still fuming with unappeased rage at the fearful catastrophe, and clamoring loudly for an atoning sacrifice on a scale commensurable with the ruin wrought. If Nero should grudge them the satisfaction of their vengeance, there was some danger that the indignation of the unruly mob should reach the sovereign himself. And that very indignation would be a manifestation of Fate—of that Ananke, hateful to gods and men, which had laid Rome in ashes.

But there was no resisting Ananke. He could but treat her with scorn, or evade her perhaps by some master stroke of cunning, or else—and this was the more worthy issue for the ruler of the world—outdo her in astounding and dazzling brutality.

The Christians who were to be tortured that evening for the delectation of the people in Caesar's gardens on the

Vatican hill, might, when their torments had reached a climax, show their tyrant Caesar whether he were not indeed a match for Fate.

Ay, he hated the Christians. Their doctrine now seemed to him as foolish, senseless, and purposeless as the stoical philosophy of Seneca. This pitiful world, which from the ruins of the daughter of Ares uttered so loud a verdict against its own lack of reason, rewarded neither earnestness nor self-mastery. Pleasure was tolerably tangible and genuine; philosophically mystical speculations, which never succeeded in penetrating the horrible enigma to its depths, could do naught save lessen the area of what was tangible and real. Nicodemus and Seneca seemed to Caesar to blend into a single haggard, boding figure. How ceaselessly Seneca had dinned into his ears high-sounding phrases about the free moral development of mankind, abstract duty, and the grandeur of renunciation. It was positively insufferable.

"Witless folls!" muttered Nero, gazing eatward, where a yellow streak announced the approach of dawn. "What is virtue! To leave a tempting goblet untouched, though the soul is thirsting for the draught. To act Tantalus of one's own free will! Who will thank me for it, you crazy hypocrites? If I should really obey your teachings, should I be less under the evil spell of life? Should I have less cause to dread illness and the all-destroying might of death?"

He sighed heavily.

"True, death is not the most terrible fate! The curse of growing old seems to me far worse. Greedy age, which feasts upon our blood until we dwindle into mere ridiculous shadows—what fiend devised that doom? Time will draw the strength and vigor from the veins of all things bright and blooming, joyous and gay, leaving only a remnant as pitiful as these ruins. To grow old! To feel that the round arm clasping my neck no longer thrills in harmony with my own pulses! To perceive that tenderness is but hyposcrisy, and kisses, languishing glances, are only a farce! It is not I, Claudius Nero, who will then be loved, but my imperial

425

power, my purple robes of royalty, my scepter, my boundless wealth! Like yonder proud Palatium, I shall be but the pale shadow of my former self—hollow-eyed, wrinkled, lean, a horror even to the hussies of the Tullian Wall."

He covered his eyes with his hands, as if he beheld the vision of his future.

"And they all know this!" he thought wrathfully: "Seneca is experiencing it himself. He feels spark after spark of his vital fire slowly dying, and yet he set to work with Nicodemus to blind me to the simple, unmistakable truth. I was to squander the fleeting hours of youthful vigor in ascetic philosophy instead of devoting myself to the present, and enjoying the light while day still lingered! I was to become a Caesar to the followers of the Crucified One!"

He leaned over the marble parapet and rested his brow on his hand. A sorrowful expression hovered around his lips, as he gazed with dilated eyes into the broadening dawn.

"Yes, I, too, see in your prophet a symbol of the truth—his thorn-crowned figure embodies the mournful fate of all earthly things. We are nailed by the curse of destiny to that terrible cross called the world. We all, sooner or later, bleed on this implement of torture, crying out to Heaven, like the dying Nazarene: 'Hope, thou deceiver of every living creature and thou, immortal courage, why have you abandoned me?' Jesus in his sorrowful death is the type of suffering humanity. But, because this death is certain, shall I increase the tortures of my pilgrimage? No, ye ascetics! Rather would I perish at once! A leap over this parapet seems to me more logical than the delusions of your cheerless self-denial."

Gazing downward, he saw a long line of his slaves, bearing heavy burdens of all kinds toward the Vatican gardens.

Caesar's eyes suddenly blazed with a savage fire, and he looked after them until they disappeared behind the walls of a ruined theatre.

"Aye, it is true," he muttered through his set teeth. "If every sun that rises over the mountains does not bring us fresh pleasure and excitement, life is torture. I will revel till

426

the last drop of blood stagnates in my veins; feast my eyes and ears; lose my last ray of reason in the intoxicating Caecubian vintage and, like Hellenic Jove, clasp blooming matrons and budding maids. I should not be Nero were I faithful to Poppaea alone. But, ah, the wildest revelry only fills a few fleeting moments. It does not quell the raging fires within. Nazarenes, ye shall tell me whether there is any means of quenching Caesar's thirst to live. I feel an eager impulse urging me to the scne of your horrible death agonies. Perhaps I need your indescribable tortures for a background to the happiness I am pursuing. When every nerve of your bodies writhes with pain like a crushed serpent, pleasure must seem twofold bliss. Our forefathers built their *triclinia* in view of tombs and monuments—the sight heightened the joys of the banquet. I will surpass them. I will behold men slowly dying, so slowly that madness seizes them under the torture of delay, while thrills of rapturous enjoyment raise me to the height of a god. I must make good what I have lost.''

Folding his arms across his breast, he paced several times up and down the gallery. A strange smile curled his lips.

''The worthy Quirites! Should they suspect that their emperor had been on the point of calling that wretched Nicodemus brother. Had he been less knavish—by Styx, who can say what might now be the state of Rome. . . . ?''

He sighed, then shrugged his shoulders.

''Scarcely better! I can see before me every line of that stern, rigid face, with its deep-set eyes. His watchful manner, half-proud, half-humble, seemed to say: 'Come down from the throne of the Caesars: I, Nicodemus, hope to take my seat there!' Had that happened, had reverence for Nicodemus destroyed every vestige of independence in the sovereign's soul and substituted the Nazarene's intolerance—in sooth, the terrible catastrophe now drawing to a close would have been a jest compared to the bloody revolutions throughout the whole vast empire! He would have persecuted the foes of Christianity with fire and sword, and erected funeral pyres whose flames and smoke would have surpassed the blaze of Rome."

Nero bent his eyes on the ground.

"Strange!" he murmured softy. "The same religion produces fruit so diverse. Nicodemus and Acte! what a contrast, what a yawning gulf lies between them!"

Higher and higher rose the crimson light of dawn above the crest of the Sabine mountains. Pale rose-hued clouds floated like flakes in the zenith. The first sunbeam quivered over the burned city, announcing the advent of a day which was to be forever memorable in the annals of Roman imperial history.

Two hours later Nero received Tigellinus, who had come to inform him of the progress of the preparations for the gigantic festival arranged to take place in the evening. Everything was going on as they desired.

"I will guarantee," said Tigellinus, smiling, "that even you, my lord, whose eyes are almost satiated with shows and skilfully-devised pageants, will be surprised and admit that my work is masterly."

"And what is this masterly programme?"

"Let me reserve the details, I bessech you. You are artist enough to understand that it is better to reveal too little than too much. The entertainment of the people is entrusted to the worthy Phaon, whose talents daily rouse my admiration more and more. The store-houses of Capua are half emptied to supply the lights, the flowers, the flags, the hangings. Everything else will blend harmoniously with the general spectacle. When I add that I have had the festal music prepared especially for this purpose by our most famous composer, I have said enough. In short—the whole scene will be glorious."

"Well—and the people? What say the people of the emperor's magnificent hospitality?"

"They are rejoicing."

"You said that yesterday. Are there any who have doubts about the Nazarenes?"

"Scarcely. The prisoners, it is true, deny their crime; but one, named Paul, cried out to the judges in tones of thunder that he beheld in this conflagration the judgment of the omnipotent God, and the fulfilment of the ancient prophecy which runs:

"I will blot out their names forever, and make their land a wilderness."

"Paul? I have heard the name."

"I spoke of him myself," replied the Sicilian. "A person of irresistible power. The supernatural vigor of his words carried away—at least for the moment—all who were within reach of his voice. That is why I hesitated to iclude this dangerous man in the programme. His mere aspect would have won adherents—especially if, in his dying hour, he had opened his lips to testify in behalf of the faith of the Nazarenes."

Claudius Nero nodded silently, then cast a look of inquiry at the Sicilian.

"I had him crucified secretly," replied Tigellinus.

A long pause ensued. Nero gazed mutely at the many-colored mosaic floor, where an exquisitely-executed figure was piercing a lion's throat with his sword.

"A pity!" he said at last, drawing a long breath. "I would fain have learned what answer this fanatic, who inspired even you with secret dread, would have replied to my exclamation: 'You are raving.' "

CHAPTER XXIII.

At the sixth hour of the afternoon Nero went with Poppaea and their whole train of attendants to the Vatican gardens, whose elms and pines, centuries old, offered even now, in midsummer, a refreshing shade. Numberless fountains tossed their silvery jets upward from alabaster basins. Artificial streams, fed by the Claudian aqueduct, flowed through grottos and mossy ravines, or scattered their spray over fern-grown cliffs. Here and there were bushes as high as a man, hedges of box, and gay beds of flowers—in short, it was a bit of Campania close to the capital.

Phaon, by Tigellinus' orders, had laid three long tables in the superb avenue that ran straight through the park from north to south. Mixing vessels, goblets, garlands of flowers, plates, and dishes gleamed as far as the eye could reach. It had been impossible to procure a sufficient number of couches—but the common people of Rome were accustomed to sit at table, not recline, like the higher classes. The smoothly planed benches, covered with Galatian carpets, seemed sufficiently luxurious for these guests.

Claudius Nero had invited nearly eighty thousand persons, and the spectacle was one to baffle description.

Eight thousand slaves had been toiling an hour and a half to provide the immense throng with viands and liquors.

The imperial pair, Tigellinus, the military tribunes, about twenty senators of noble birth, and the whole court—except Seneca, who had pleaded sudden illness—attended this gigantic feast. Among those immediately surrounding Nero his youngest and latest favorite, Helius, was espeically conspicuous. This youth, a slave by birth, understood how to flatter Caesar's whims scarcely less skilfully than Tigellinus, lauding every act of weakness as a deed of heroism, every crime as the manifest right of royalty. The cruel, sensual face of the freedman Helius had a touch of the swinish nature, though without being repulsive by extraordinary ugliness.

The praetorians had been quietly stationed in all directions. Countless spies listened to every conversation, seeking to discover the persons who were disseminating the report that Caesar had been the author of the catastrophe. A knight from Nola and two members of the Menenius family— cousins of Lucius and Didius Menenius who had fallen victims to their hostility to the imperial rule—had been arrested just before the commencement of the banquet.

To avoid inflaming the passions of the populace, Caesar had taken care that only the light Vesuvian wine, mixed with an equal portion of water, should be served. Yet, spite of this precaution, the reckless gayety of the revellers reached so perilous a height that Phaon constantly urged his cohorts of slaves to greater haste.

At last the so-called *bellaria* was consumed. One last drink, a libation, a cheer for Caesar and the charming Poppaea!

Then a loud blare of trumpets, rousing the echoes of all the hills, rang out above the heads of the eighty thousand guests. With wonderful rapidity the tables were deserted and the people, eager for the spectacle, flocked through the side-avenues to the spot where a large amphitheatre had been erected.

This magnificent arena, with its rows of turf-covered seats rising one above another, and the superb royal tribune in the centre, was a masterpiece of the greater purveyor of pleasure,

Sophonius Tigellinus. There was no sign of hasty preparation. The lofty poplars and maples, which had covered the space a few days before, had vanished as completely as the marble temple and flower-adorned hill on which it stood. Fresh sand covered the sepulchre of these beauties of nature and art—as clean and smooth as if the fantastic disarray of a luxuriant wilderness of bloom had never existed here.

Iron torch-holders, candelabra as high as houses with huge pitch-pans, and silver lanterns with panes of horn or mica were provided in such countless numbers that the whole arena could not help being as bright as day.

Directly in front of the imperial tribune, on the long line extending from one end of the semi-circle of spectators to the other, stretched a row of holes about two feet apart, numbering perhaps three hundred. The mass of earth which had been shovelled out still lay behind them.

Just as the emperor and Poppaea Sabina took their places beneath the canopy on the *pulvinar*—where the courtiers had assembled long before—the slaves from the Palatium, advancing in groups of four, brought in posts of irregular form, whose pointed ends they thrust into the holes, put the earth around them, and packed it firmly.

Each of the broad tops supported a human form, wrapped to the shoulders in tow. Stout iron wires fastened their bodies and limbs to the beams, and the whole covering was saturated with wax, pitch, tar, and oil.

These three hundred human beings were to be lighted like torches by the slaves—as a sort of preliminary illumination— as soon as darkness closed in.

The people had heard the day before of the spectacle to be enacted here. Yet the sight of the horrible procession so surprised them that they fairly howled with delight. The old, pitiless, blood-thirsty longing of the spectators in the amphitheatre, who could never be sated with the hacking and mutilating of the gladiatorial conflicts, stirred with redoubled power in the hearts of the well-fed throngs.

433

"The Nazarenes!" shouted the multitude. "The Nazarenes in their robes of pitch! How do they like these tunics! Curses on the incendiaries! Curses on the fanatics who assailed Rome! Now test in your own persons how delightful an element is consuming fire!"

At the end of five minutes all the posts were firmly set in the earth. The bearers swiftly withdrew, and from the neighboring shrubbery a throng of dancing girls flitted like a hovering cloud, strewing roses and violets over the earth around the posts so that, as Tigellinus expressed it, even the tortures of death might wear a festal aspect in Caesar's blessed realm.

There stood the Christians, in an endless chain, like the mulberry-trees whose boughs are clipped by the gardener in the early spring.

Some uttered loud lamentations; others fixed their glassy eyes on vacancy; three or four had already died of fright. Most of them, however, not only bold youths and men, but fair girls in the first bloom of youth, gazed heavenward with rapt ecstasy, murmuring almost inaudible prayers.

At the right of Caesar's *pulvinar*, but a little lower down, stood a broad, luxurious couch with soft cushions, also covered with a canopy—the place assigned to Tigellinus. The Agrigentine fairly beamed with self-importance; his aristocratic face, slightly flushed with wine, looked far younger to-day than usual.

Beside him, leaning her head, whose locks were interwoven with pearls, against his breast, reclined the charming Rhodian, Chloris, attired in a transparent robe from the Isle of Cos, fair and bewitching still, spite of her fall, and filled with admiration of the hero of the hour, who tenderly clasped her slender figure. Poppaea Sabina, mindful of her dignity as Caesar's wife, had at first protested against their appearance in public together; but how could she answer the bold Agrigentine's retort that she herself, though not a Greek, but an aristocratic Roman, had openly accompanied her royal lover in the same way, even while his wife was still alive.

Chloris perhaps gazed all the more intently into Tigellinus' eyes because she had no fondness for the cruel spectacles, which were the Romans' daily bread. As a Hellene and an artist, she possessed a highly-developed perception of beauty—and from this standpoint her heart shrank from the sight of suffering. It was only in obedience to the wish of her idolized Tigellinus that she shared his purple couch, but her lashes involuntarily drooped and she fixed her eyes more intently on her beloved conqueror, whenever a post with its human burden was carried by.

Suddenly, while all were silent in breathless expectation, and even the wailings of the Nazarenes seemed to die away, a shriek pierced the gathering twilight, a shriek as wild and awful as the death-cry of a madman falling from a dizzy height into a gulf below.

Chloris looked up in terror.

A well-known face, horribly distorted by agony,—the face of Artemidorus—looked forth from the wrappings of tow on one of the two posts that stood near the foot of her couch.

Until now the Nazarene had borne his fate calmly and resolutely. His heroic courage had conquered every impulse of weakness, but when, from the terrible height where he was to suffer a martyr's death, he beheld the girl who had once loved and then so basely deserted him, he lost all self-control.

The longing for the fleeting joys of earth, which he believed had long been vanquished, once more thrilled him with the mingled bliss and grief of yore.

So this was the fulfilment of the dream cherished for years in the inmost depths of his heart.

He recalled that never-to-be-forgotten evening in Flavius' house when, on his knees, he had offered her the garland. Chloris had been his sole thought night and day. He believed in her as he did in Jesus of Nazareth. At the first rumor that she was receiving the homage of the great, he had rushed to her in bitter grief. She had kissed him tenderly, laughing at his fears, and earnestly assured him that she would be his alone. Yet afterwards she vanished from his side entirely and became more and more absorbed in the society of the court. Artemidorus' suffering was beyond description. He suspected, knew the truth, long before his own eyes verified it. Then he tore himself away from his love with all the might of his will, struggling desperately until the words of the Saviour, who had said: "Whosoever will come after me, let him deny himself, and take up his cross and follow me," at last gave him peace.

He had hoped that the divine power of this peace would abide with him till his last moments.

Then, almost at the instant the executioners approached with their torches, he was forced to behold his faithless love, alas! and to behold her thus—clasped in another's embrace—an idle spectator of his torments. It was too much anguish.

"Parted from her!" he had wailed, on the day when, under sentence of death, he had been dragged a prisoner along the Cyprian Way. "Parted from her!" This thought had been his greatest sorrow during that terrible walk. That "Parted from her!" now flashed through his memory like a scoff at his unutterable misery at the moment when Fate had condemned him to die, unloved, before her eyes, so near her that he was almost fanned by her breath.

Again he shrieked—in a tone yet more piercing, terrible, heart-rending, than the first cry of anguish. He was suffering superhuman tortures. Now, ere they were lighted, he felt the fierce flames that were to slowly consume him.

Chloris trembled from head to foot.

"What is the matter?" asked Tigellinus.

She was unable to reply.

He drew her closer to his side and kissed her snowy throat.

"Did yonder coward's death-yell frighten you?"

"Perhaps so," she whispered.

Every feature of her face was convulsed, her eyes looked lustreless.

"You Greeks are too soft-hearted," said Tigellinus consolingly. "You must make yourself familiar, like the descendants of Romulus, with the sight of death and its horrors. It bestows vivacity and courage. It strengthens the power of enjoyment and steels the nerves. But, am I right? Surely I recognize the fellow. It is Artemidorus, Flavius Scaevinus' freedman. Speak, dearest, does a sorrowful memory steal over you? In those days you were the unapproachable cithara player—and now. . . . ! But have you lost anything by the exchange? Sophonius Tigellinus is second to Caesar in imperial Rome. Fannius Rufus, who shares the chief command with me, is my colleague in name alone, in reality my subordinate. Caesar loves me, Poppaea hardly draws a breath without asking the shrewd Agrigentine's counsel. As for Artemidorus—well, you see to what end his fanaticism about the legend of the Galilean has led him.''

"He is so young," sighed the trembling Chloris, "ah, and so good!"

"So good," replied Tigellinus, "that he helped to baffle Nero's first mad passion. You have heard of Acte. . . . ? Caesar had only once spoken to her of love, then she suddenly vanished and, eagerly as he searched, he could find no trace of her. Artemidorus was questioned and replied: 'I know nothing.' It was a lie. He did know the place where Acte had concealed herself. And he is now attoning, in addition to his other crimes, for the sin of withholding the truth from the emperor. That is why the scoundrel was placed near the imperial *pulvinar*. His agonizing death must pour balm into the emperor's still bleeding wound. I am revealing more than I ought to say. Poppaea Sabina must not learn it on any account. Do you hear, bewitching Chloris?"

"Yes," she murmured in a hollow tone.

After this disclosure there was no hope for Artemidorus.

To implore mercy for the man whom Claudius Nero hated, seemed to the Rhodian like risking her own existence. So she summoned her unconquerable levity to her aid, and resolved to let everything proceed as Tigellinus had arranged. Yet she offered a silent prayer to the death-god of her Hellenic home, Hermes Phsychopompos, beseeching him to convey the soul of the dying man gently to the dim realm of Hades.

Meanwhile Artemidorus had raised his dilated eyes tearlessly to the blue sky, in whose azure vault the first pale stars were shining.

"Oh, my God," he pleaded fervently, "aid me in this boundless torture. Merciful Father, let me once more experience Thy grace, let my soul be filled solely with Three and the Saviour who died to redeem the world! Ah, how bewitchingly her hair waves! How her eyes sparkle! How blooming are her fragrant lips! Alas, she does not stir! She does not start up to utter one soothing word to comfort me in this last horrible parting! She can look on calmly, indifferently, while Artemidorus dies in torture. I loved her ardently; she would have constituted my entire happiness, nay I love her still, spite of her fall. Ah, Caesar, why did you pardon me, when I might have died in the possession of her love? Father in Heaven, deliver me from these thoughts! Into Thy hands I commit my spirit, receive me among the elect, for Jesus' sake, and efface the memory of this hour, or my soul can find no rest through thousands of years."

He bent his head and closed his eyes to avoid meeting the glance of the Rhodian, who had now shaken off her horror and become absorbed in admiration of her idolized Tigellinus.

The venerable Nicodemus had been placed next to the freedman by the slaves who had brought in his senseless form. His post had on the top a huge cross-beam, to which the sufferer's arms were fastened by means of two iron spikes driven through the palms of the hands. Tigellinus had used this means of distinguishing the bold mouth-piece of the Nazarenes, whom Nero so heartily detested.

Artemidorus' shriek recalled the hapless man's senses.

Filled with frantic horror, he beheld the agony at his right and left hand and the splendid orgy at his feet—Caesar in the arms of the proud Poppaea; Tigellinus and Chloris; the favorite Helius with the bold Septimia, and reclining on the imperial tribune ten or twelve other pairs.

He saw dozens of fair female slaves, holding in the right hand an artistically-chased wine-jar and in the left a goblet, pass among the emperor's guests.

He beheld garlands on heads reeking with ointment, the wreaths of grape leaves, the crimson roses, the panther skins on the shoulders of half-nude boys, waving their thyrsus staves above their heads; he noted their reckless gestures, their bold jests, their unbridled laughter.

Horror overwhelmed him as he inhaled the whole indescribable atmosphere of revelry and cruelty, which rose from the confusion like the stupefying fumes from sinful Gomorrah.

All at once, the full magnitude and extent of the error he had so carefully cherished burst upon him.

No, this repulsive, evil, thoroughly corrupt world must utterly decay, ere the soil would be sufficiently manured to receive the seeds of the gospel of Jesus Christ. Meantime, Christianity could find shelter only beneath the roofs of the poor and miserable, in the hovels of the corpse-bearers, among the sailors beyond the Tiber, in the houses of the laborers and slave-drivers.

The lowest stratum of humanity must be new-born, transformed, and made capable of receiving the Word, instead of commencing the work at the throne, which merely formed the apex of a heartless, brainless, dreary society.

And as this suddenly became clear to him, Nicodemus also distinguished, with startling clearness, what portion of his aspirations had been really genuine and noble, and what had been suggested by selfishness and the desire to rule.

"It was Satan who tempted me," he murmured, grinding his teeth. "To him, the destroyer of the world, have I sacrificed my rest, my peace, the harmony of my nature. Woe betide me, I have slain you, too, lovely Acte, whom the Creator entrusted to my charge as the lamb is given to the shepherd. All-merciful Father, in so far as it is possible, grant me Thy pardon. I have sinned against Thee and Thy laws. I am not worthy of suffering death here with my believing brothers and sisters in the faith."

Burning tears streamed down his face.

Then his brow suddenly contracted.

"If I have lived my life in vain, I will at least in dying bear witness to the divine truth! Perhaps, perhaps, I may yet find favor with the all-merciful God."

He raised his head defiantly, and shouted in a voice of thunder:

"Claudius Nero Caesar, have you courage to hear one last word from the dying lips of Nicodemus?"

A somewhat oppressive stillness followed the menacing cry of the martyr.

The praetorians looked at their lord, as if expecting the command: "Thrust a sword into his breast." But Nero, raising himself, said scornfully:

"Speak, my friend, but hasten."

"I well know, Nero," replied Nicodemus, "that it would be futile to hope for mercy, either from you or the cowards who fawn upon you like curs. Not God, but his eternal antagonist fashioned your souls from mire and blood. This world is still in Satan's clutch; that is why you are emperor, for you stand nearest to him in diabolical baseness and bestial cunning. But I warn you. God is not to be mocked. He, the Omnipotent One, who lends us courage to die fearlessly for the amusement of your shameless courtiers, will blot out forever, this pitiful race which to-day decks itself in gold and purple. In truth, your end is near. I already hear the distant roll of thunder; I already see the lightning which is to blast you. All your power will vanish like chaff before the wind. The new deluge will soon flood the earth, and the only thing which will tower victoriously above the ruins of your magnificence is the cross of Jesus Christ! Your face has blanched, Claudius Nero, and now impatience seizes you. But we, faithful to the example of our Saviour, pray God's mercy even for you, our foe. Comrades in death: Control your righteous hate. Raise your eyes to Heaven, and say with

440

the most unworthy of your community: 'Father, forgive them, for they know not what they do.' "

A low murmur ran through the ranks of the Christians.

An instant after the long-drawn note of a tuba gave a signal.

Several hundred slaves, provided with small torches, rushed upon the victims.

The next instant the wrappings of tow, saturated with tar and wax, were in a bright blaze from one end of the row of posts to the other. Shrill, frantic shrieks rang through the gathering dusk, but louder yet rose the wild roar of the spectators, who clapped their hands as if at a circus, and gave expression to their delight by shouts and exclamations.

"Ave Caesar! What an Olympic festival! What a flood of light! Applaud, Quirites! Applaud Nero's magnificent flaming torches."

Tigellinus raised his brimming goblet, and seizing the catch-word of the populace, cried with icy scorn:

"Nero's torches, Tigellinus, the accused, salutes you!"

"And so does Nero, who will efface the delusion of the Galilean as the fire consumes your bodies," shouted Caesar, swinging his rose-wreathed beaker like a radiant young Dionysus. Draining half the contents, he handed it to the "divinely beautiful" Poppaea, who bent her snowy neck backward until the last drops of Falernian had been swallowed. Then, with a cry of exultation, she flung the heavy drinking-vessel at Nicodemus' flame-circled head, striking him full on the brow.

"That's right!" said the Agrigentine. "It was the most fitting answer to his babble."

Poppaea, as if desiring to banish the recollection of her coarse brutality, nestled closer to Caesar with bewitching grace, laughed gaily, and whispered tenderly:

"Nero, Nero, how I love you! I feel as though yon blazing pillars were our hymeneal torches."

Nero clasped her in an embrace as impetuous as those the comrades of Romulus, in days of yore, had bestowed on the

Sabine women.

Tigellinus, too, seemed incited by the Christians' death-cries to devote himself to Chloris with still more lover-like ardor.

Musicians, stationed at a distance, played festal melodies. The burning bodies of the martyrs sent forth whitish-grey clouds of smoke, which mounted skyward. Here and there the terrible shrieks of agony sank into low moans and sighs—then ceased utterly. In other parts of the arena esctatic voices were heard issuing from the soaring flames, the voices of devotees so rapt by their belief as to conquer all earthly torture and joyfully praise the infinite mercy of God and the world's Redeemer.

"Raging flames, consume my perishable body," cried a girl of fifteen, "my soul will rise from its ashes to the radiant heights. Halleluia!"

Nicodemus, who had been half-stunned by the blow of the heavy metal goblet, once more recovered his senses.

"Listen, ye blinded ones!" he shouted in a resonant voice. "Here, amid the fire that is consuming me, I acknowledge as a most insignificant witness of His infinite Majesty, that the Lord Jesus Christ is the only true God, and all salvation cometh through Him alone. Father in Heaven, have mercy on me! I repent with all my heart and all my mind! Amen!"

A light gust of wind swept the flames aside, and Artemidorus beheld Chloris for the last time, just as Tigellinus stroked her cheek caressingly.

"Chloris!" he shrieked, throwing his head back as if seized with an epileptic convulsion—"Chloris!"

His agonized cry rang out so loudly that, drowning every other sound, it reached the farther rows of seats occupied by the shouting spectators.

"Chloris!"—once more his voice pierced the crackling flames that now mounted straight upward to heaven—"woe betide me, I am dying!"

"Praised be Jesus, the conqueror of death!" murmured Nicodemus, then his voice, too, sank into silence.

The posts burned slowly down. Pools of blood trickled into the earth; for the wrappings of tow had not entirely absorbed it. Flowing from the burned veins, it had quenched the flames, and in many cases extinguished the fire in the lower half of the "robe of torture." Here and there a post broke and fell, carrying with it a half-consumed human form. The air was filled with the sickly, repulsive odor of burning flesh, as if priests had sacrificed to Pluto on a hundred altars.

Then at the sound of the popular Gaditanian melody, "Swell, ye roses;" all the lights in the arena flashed upward, as if touched by an enchanter's wand, and a scene of revelry never before equalled, even in the crime-stained annals of imperial Rome, began in Nero's gardens. The eternal city, so late the prey of the devouring flames, now seemed on the verge of destruction by a still more terrible foe.

CHAPTER XXIV.

A TWELVEMONTH passed away and with the tropical heat of midsummer recurred the anniversary of the conflagration of Rome, but in the meantime whole districts had risen from their ruins in far more beautiful and splendid guise than before.

Wide, regular streets, bordered with colonnades, had taken the places of the narrow alleys in many a secluded district of ill-repute.

The rubbish left by the fire had been removed in huge ships to Ostia, to help fill up the marshy lowlands near the port.

Thanks to the rewards Nero offered for new buildings completed by a certain time, the industry of the private citizens surpassed all expectation. Labor continued night and day, even the terrible heat of July did not wholly interrupt it.

A new spirit had animated the Romans, so that the anniversary of the terrible catastrophe was greeted with grave, but by no means sad or disheartened feelings.

The provinces, especially Asia Minor and Greece had been forced to fill the treasure-houses of Caesar, who lavished the funds thus obtained upon the capital.

A sort of private ministry—Helius, "the pig-eyed man," at its head—had been instituted to devise means of finding fresh sources of revenue for the imperial purse, and the methods of extortion practised mocked all ideas of justice.

About the middle of September, the activity in building received a fresh impulse. Thousands of Gallic and Hispanian laborers arrived. If this continued, the completion of the last house might be expected by the end of the year—with the exception of a few details concerning the interior decorations, especially the paintings, for the Roman knights and senators were extremely exacting in this respect.

The court had again spent the summer in Baiae, in the magnificent new villa, erected by the freedman Phaon at the cost of nine hundred millions, while its art-treasures and costly furniture had devoured at least two and a half millions more. On its roof were groves of trees, shrubberies, fountains, and a beautiful lake thirty ells in extent, framed wholly in onyx. A boat of cedar-wood, just large enough to hold two persons and a rower, lay moored to the trunk of a fan-palm.

Poppaea called this wonderful solarium "my hanging garden."

Yet this masterpiece of unprecedented extravagance did not fully satisfy Nero. He dreamed of something still more magnificent—a dream afterwards realized on the Esquiline Hill in Rome—the Oriental fairy palace, to which the amazed populace gave the name of the "Golden House."

Toward the end of October the imperial pair were reclining under the trees of the roof-garden, gazing out upon the Gulf of Baiae, where the imperial trireme, Ichthys, was rounding Cape Misenum on her way from Ostia. Beside the emperor stood Tigellinus, and Phaon, who had arrived from Rome only a few hours before, sat in a cushioned chair a few paces away. Cassius, Nero's body-servant, and several of Poppaea's maids were crouching in the background.

"See how exactly the commander calculated the time of transit," said Phaon, waving his hand toward the trireme. "He was to cast anchor opposite to the temple of Hercules two hours before sunset."

"I thank you," replied the emperor. "We will go this very

evening. After all that you have said, I may expect at last to have a house really fit to live in."

"A home of pure gold, adorned with jewels, many of which are equal in value to this villa."

"You hear, Poppaea. Glittering gold plates cover the walls. Your lovely image will be reflected a thousand times from the royal metal. Your foot will tread on acanthus-hued malachite. Rubies, emeralds, and diamonds will vie in lustre with the sunlight falling through panes of Phoenician glass into the sparkling hall. All that art and wealth, creative genius and the foil of panting slaves can accomplish has been embodied in the golden house. Now we will enter upon an era of revelry, of death-scorning riot, of rapturous bliss, such as the world has never witnessed since the days of Ninus and Sardanapalus."

"My lord, you are indeed fortunate," said Tigellinus, with a semblance of deep emotion. "Hail, Poppaea Sabina, empress of the realm, fairest and most enviable of sovereigns! You have conquered every foe: calumny, hatred, prejudice, the fury of the elements. Everything lives and breathes for you alone. You stand at the apex of existence, and the earth is but your footstool."

"Avert it, ye gods!" murmured Phaon.

"What are you saying?" asked Caesar with a slight frown.

"I mean—if Tigellinus' words should rouse the Immortals' wrath. . . ."

"How?"

"My lord, you know the popular belief that praise like that of the illustrious Tigellinus bodes evil. So I prayed the gods to avert it."

"Folly!" replied Caesar sadly. "We ourselves are the gods. So long as I hurl thunderbolts like Jupiter Zeus, I shall fear neither Olympic Jove, nor blind, simple, foolish fate. Have I not tested, hundreds of times, my power to cope with the boldest assaults of destiny? Let the roaring surges men term Anake rush on; they will part and break against this breast as the sea vainly foams against a stone dyke. Rome sank in ashes; I have restored her to still greater magnificence. The mob raved over the misfortune, and flung its slaver even to the height of the throne; I tamed the fury of the populace. The aristocrats, who from the beginning rebelled against my supremacy because it crushed their power, conspired under the leadership of crafty scoundrels and planned the most terrible revolution: I stretched out my hand—and Piso, with the thousands he commanded, lay crushed upon the ground."

"Yet. . . ." Phaon murmured, then hastily interrupting himself, gazed timidly into Caesar's face.

But Nero was so fully absorbed by the idea of his own unexampled greatness that he felt no anger against the freedman.

"Speak, if you have anything on your mind," he said laughing.

"I fear I may seem irreverent and bold."

"Impossible. If any man possesses my entire confidence, it is you. You have rendered me service—but so have many others. Yet no one save my worthy Tigellinus has devoted himself to me with the same fidelity. I see that in your eyes, whose clear, glad glance sparkles with secret sympathy. Ay, at the risk of rousing your jealousy, Sophonius, I must confess it—Phaon would perchance have won my love, had I been a beggar, while only a prince's friendship would suit your nature."

"My lord," said the Agrigentine, pressing his hand upon his heart.

"Let it pass," replied Nero. "It was but a caprice that flitted through my brain. So, what were you going to say, Phaon?"

"I desired to beseech Caesar not to lull himself into too great security. Piso's conspiracy still makes me quake to my inmost soul; and I am surprised to find how quickly my lord and sovereign has conquered the hurt. Was not Piso your friend?"

"He called himself so, but was far from being one. His

448

feigned affection was a cloak for malice."

"Yet—you had no suspicion of him, nor of many others, Fannius Rufus, for instance, who jointly with Tigellinus commanded the praetorians, and Flavius Scaevinus, who named his son for you and yet besought his fellow-conspirators to grant him the privilege of dealing the first blow."

"What?"

"It is true, my lord. The fact was concealed from you, but it *is* a fact, and the others bore witness to it. 'I ask as a special favor permission to deal the first blow.' Those were the very words he uttered at their last meeting."

"He has atoned for them," replied Nero.

"And the poet Lucan. . . ." Phaon continued.

"Pshaw! Envy tortured him. His verses were not half so good as mine."

"But Epicharis! Had you any suspicion of the Egyptian's plans? She and Piso were the soul of the rebellion. Even Seneca, your trusted teacher, allowed himself to be ensnared by the conspirators! They must have been wonderful masters of the art of deluding others, if he succumbed to their wiles."

"He was enfeebled by age," said Caesar.

Phaon shook his head thoughtfully.

"His death proves the contrary," he answered gravely. "Like Socrates, he drank the poisoned cup calmly, indifferently, as though the step were merely the departure from a gay banquet. I confess that Seneca made me very anxious."

"I don't understand you," remarked Poppaea. "Were he still alive—you might have cause to fear him. But now that he has reaped the reward of his treachery, the remembrance, as well as the death of the heroic Thrasea, and the hypocritical Soranus can only heighten our pride."

"Thrasea, too, died like a hero. Full often have I heard men repeat the dangerous words he uttered as, raising his hand with its severed veins toward Heaven, he shouted: 'To thee, Zeus, the liberator, I offer this blood!' It sounded heroic, by all the gods, terribly heroic! I would give ten years of my life, had he been a coward. But I am digressing. What I desired to urge is something quite different. Will you permit me to go on, my lord?''

"Certainly," replied Nero, smiling.

"Piso's conspiracy has been successfully baffled. In this instance you have conquered fate. But how did this happen? Had Flavius Scaevinus been calmer, behaved in a less theatrical fashion—who knows, who knows. . . . Milichus, the crafty freedman, to whom he gave the dagger to be sharpened, Milichus, to whom he cried: 'This weapon is sacred,' Milichus, with whom he placed his will—you see, my lord, this was really the source whence deliverance came. Had not Milichus discovered the affair at the twelfth hour. . . .''

"That is just it," the emperor interrupted. "My genius, infinitely mightier than fate, gains me these allies. Nay, Phaon, you are a prophet of evil. But I thank you. You have gained two points. I now feel doubly assured of your love—and also of the height at which I stand above the changes of destiny.''

With these words he rose and went to the parapet. Poppaea followed, while the Agrigentine lingered behind with Phaon to privately reproach him for the gloomy views he had advanced.

"My lord," said Phaon, with a despairing glance into the eyes of his censor, "this matter has long weighed on my mind, and I could not help giving it utterance. I love Caesar, he has always been gracious to me, and besides—as he himself said—it seems as if some secret tie bound me to him. A frank monitor, I think, will be of more service than an enthusiastic rhapsodist, who paints everything sky-blue and rose-color.''

"You are aiming that shaft at me. But I do not paint, I merely let him see the truth. Nero's realm really does shine in the ambrosial hues of the sky; he actually does stand upon the pedestal of godlike grandeur. I believe in the infallibility of his good fortune, which is also mine. Go! You have never been a foolish croaker. Eat your fill, and seek the intoxication of Cyprian wine. Your blood is getting too thick; you need refreshment. For the rest—everything is ready. We start at sunset."

Poppaes talked to Nero in the same strain as Tigellinus had used to Phaon. She, too, had been carried away by the delusion that he could vanquish destiny. Her eyes, usually so shrewd, flashed with something akin to the frenzied excitement of a prophetess.

"Yes," she whispered, pressing her glowing face against Nero's shoulder, "we are and shall ever be victors over fate. No prince of the earth has ever withstood such perils, nor smiled at them with such Olympian indifference. Your fortune is peerless. The future belongs to you and to your race."

Her eyes drooped in mock modesty. "Poppaea," Nero murmured tenderly.

"Yes," she went on, "I feel the most absolute certainty that our next child will be a boy and the living image of his father. Long after we have wandered among the shades, the race of Nero will govern a wider and wider realm. The Parthians and Indians will bow beneath their scepter, and so, too, will the defiant descendants of Giso. I can see in imagination the gigantic army rolling northward and eastward, subduing Germany to the banks of the Vistula; vanquishing the land of the Sarmatii, Rugia, and ice-clad Scandia. And everywhere that the standard of Nero's race is planted, the laurel-decked Apollo-head of their ancestor will be displayed in temples of gold and marble as the only true god, to whom all nations will raise the same prayer, exclaiming: 'Nero, omnipotnet father above the clouds, have mercy upon us?' "

"So be it!" cried Caesar with sparkling eyes, and embracing her, he kissed her on the forehead, saying in a solemn tone:

"Hail, blessed among women, who will be the source of the welfare and future of the whole world."

CHAPTER XXV.

Just as night was falling Nero and Poppaea, with a portion of their train, put out to sea.

The passage was safely made. On the morning of the third day the ship anchored in Ostia, where a long train of traveling-chariots received the royal party and in a few hours conveyed them to Rome.

Nero, to whom nothing seemed too grand nor splendid, nevertheless was secretly surprised—though he showed no sign of it—at the sight of the newly-built gigantic city.

He felt as if the huts of Romulus had been replaced by palaces, so greatly did this new Rome surpass the Rome of Augustus, who had boasted that he had inherited a city of brick and left one of marble.

Several fashionable streets were changed beyond recognition by superb colannades. Nay, even the districts occupied by the poor formed, by their superior regularity, an avantageous contrast to their former condition, though the numerous wooden stories bore witness that now, as before, the cupidity of avaricious builders had played a larger part than was desirable in the interest of the populace or with regard to security against future conflagrations.

At last the chariot stopped before the wonderful vestibule of the new palace. Court officials, slaves, and a part of the body-guard with their banners, were waiting in festal array.

After the formal greeting from the courtiers and praetorians, Nero and Poppaea entered his Persian litter and were borne from room to room, to show the empress the various details with which Caesar had long been familiar from the building plans and from Phaon's descriptions. The freedman acted as guide.

The vast structure extended far beyond the Esquiline Hill. The main entrance, with its towering Corinthian columns, faced the south. A triple colonnade four thousand feet in length surrounded the palace. Phaon had not exaggerated the truth, when he said that no royal palace had ever surpassed the magnificence of this "Golden House." Every detail displayed the wildest extravagance, the most lavish luxury,— unfortunately frequently to the detriment of genuine artistic beauty.

All the ceilings were ivory, of the most exquisite work-manship, set with jewls; many were so arranged that a single slave could push them asunder in the center to afford a view of the blue sky.

The furniture, made principally in Alexandria, though some had been ordered from Mediolanum, displayed in each apartment a certain plainly marked, yet varying character. Here one was reminded of the sea-washed cliffs of Capri, anon of flowery meadows steeped in sunlight, and again of the marble majesty of a temple in Paestum. The materials used were the noble metals, silk, and Tyrian purple, with here and there fragrant woods from distant Taprobana or the southern shore of Arabia.

The mosaic floors, copied from the designs and pictures of the most famous artists, represented scenes renowned in the world's history, such as the battle of Arbela, and the death of the three hundred Fabii, or incidents and idyls of mythology. Here Aphrodite stretched her white arms tenderly towards the beautiful Adonis; there Danae, with half-closed eyes, reclined on a glittering couch. And the whole was executed with such delicate, artistically-arranged pieces that it might have easily been mistaken for the production of the most careful strokes of the brush instead of that of a mosaic-worker.

One room in the gigantic palace was so arranged that, by means of skilfully-planned machinery, it moved on its axis, thus following the motion of the heavens, so that the sun did not appear to change its position, but only to ascend and descend perpendicularly.

"Look, Poppaea," said Caesar, while explaining to his wife the peculiarity of this apartment, "I will enthrone myself here, when I reflect upon the destiny of the empire. Then I shall be released from the thrall of earthly things. I shall float—perceiving my divine counterpart, the orb of day, always in the same direction,—freely above the earth, and thus circle around the world my sceptre enslaves."

The main-building was connected with numerous courtyards, enclosed gardens, meadows, groves, and artificial mounds affording beautiful views, the whole united by paths, arcades, and bridges, which gave the impression of a single architectural whole. There were even several ponds with skiffs and sail-boats.

"By Zeus," cried Poppaea, "we might have a real pleasure voyage from one glittering marble shore to another, not a mere rocking to and fro on the water, such as we had in the onyx basin of the new villa at Baiae."

"Everything here shall be as you desire," replied Nero. "At last, at last we have reached our goal. Caesar, as beseems his majesty, dwells in a city of his own, a city which shall bear the name of Roma till, in the passage of the centuries, it crumbles into ruin. This will sufficiently per-petuate the name of Romulus, the founder of the state. His portion of Rome was not half as large as this house. But yonder Rome outside, which I raised anew from the ashes of the conflagration, shall be called Neronia, for it is *my* work, not that of Romulus. Do you wonder that I here utter an idea which my foes imputed to me ere I could cherish it? That is the very reason! I will thus prove that all the evil malice devises against me is transformed into laurel and roses. On the day we give to the son whose birth we are joyously anticipating the glorious name of Claudius Nero Sabinus, the city shall also receive its new title by a decree of the senate, which I will solemnly acknowledge before the assembled Quirites."

"Long live Claudius Nero Sabinus," murmured Poppaea rapturously. "Long live Neronia."

At that instant one of the litter-bearers stumbled over the malachite threshold leading into the largest of the five banqueting-halls.

Falling on his knees, he jerked the pole so violently that the man behind staggered.

The efforts of the two other bearers saved the litter from being entirely upset, but Poppaea Sabina had been so near the edge that she was hurled with great violence against one of the pillars.

Every one rushed shrieking to the spot. Nero, who had clung to the side in time to save himself, sprang lightly to the floor and bent over the death-like form which Phaon carefully supported and one of the slave-women sprinkled with essences, while the Agrigentine ordered the hapless bearer to be instantly led away.

"Poppaea!" cried Nero despairingly.

She raised her lashes and tried to smile, but the expression of the contracted forehead and brows showed that she was suffering violent pain.

"It is nothing," she sighed, closing her eyes again. "The terrible fright—Have the scoundrel hewn in pieces. Phaon, I thank you. No, no, you are lifting me too high. Let me lie down. . . . there. . . . there. . . ."

"Call the doctors!" cried Nero in terror. "Quick! Carry the empress to her chamber! Curses on this day of misfortune! A delightful arrival, and a cheering welcome! Gently, if you value your lives! Calm yourself, sweet Poppaea! Here comes Aristodemus and the clever Eurotas."

Poppaea was borne with the utmost care to her luxurious

sleeping-room, where her attendants disrobed her and the physicians carefully examined every limb. As there was no sign of any external injury, both agreed that the sudden faintness and violent pain were due to the condition of their august patient's health, and at the worst. . . .

Aristodemus whispered his suggestion into Nero's ear.

"It would be your death, scoundrel!" cried Nero furiously. "Shall my hopes be blighted a second time? And now, when she was sure a son. . . ."

"My lord," faltered Aristodemus, "how can our illustrious mistress be sure. . . ."

"Miserable slave! Whatever Caesar and his wife desire is a certainty! So I command you—avert the misfortune or you die."

"Then kill me," he said, bowing his head. "I cannot battle against the might of destiny and nature."

"What? You dare?"

"I do. I dare to point out to you the decrees of the gods and the omnipotence of fate, to which we are all subject, you, the mighty ruler of the world, as well as the condemned slave. Strike off my head, since you can wreak no vengeance on the gods and fate."

Nero made no reply. He was rigid with horror.

At last, grasping the slave's right hand, he said almost imploringly:

"Try! I will reward you! I take back all my threats. Consider what is at stake—the future of the world, Claudius Nero Sabinus, the ruler of the earth to the Vistula and the island of Rugia."

"Grief has turned his brain," muttered Aristodemus, approaching the couch. "How do you feel, my gracious mistress?"

"Oh, my heart is bursting," moaned Poppaea. "That scoundrel! I believe he did it intentionally. He was paid. . . . by. . . . the secret friends. . . . of. . . . the dead Octavia."

"No, no," replied Aristodemus. "It was an accident,

sovereign lady. All who witnessed it agree on that point."

"Silence! I know better. . . . It was. . . . it was. . . . Octavia. Go! Go! Leave me! Oh, how I suffer! As if I wore the oil-soaked tow of the Nazarenes! Flames are scorching me! I am dying in torture!"

Nero was obliged to be removed from the room almost by force.

Accompanied by Tigellinus, Phaon, and several slaves, he went to the wonderful apartment which imitated the motion of the vault of heaven.

Its machinery had been put in motion at the arrival of the imperial pair.

Here Caesar now sat throned, the ruler of the universe, keeping pace with the all-illuminating sun, while only a few hundred paces distant, his dream of a Neronian dynasty was crumbling into ruin.

Cassius offered his master Samian wine and fruit.

Nero drank eargerly, but found it impossible to eat a mouthful, even of the juicy figs. He was trembling in every limb.

At the end of two hours news came that he was the father of a dead child—a son, as Poppaea had always predicted.

The slave who brought the tidings spoke with downcast eyes, as if he feared a dagger-thrust. Then his lips moved gain, but the words would not come.

"Go on!" shouted Nero, approaching him.

"My lord, I dare not. . . ."

Tears were streaming down his face.

"Speak!" said Caesar imploringly, thrilled with sudden emotion. "Do you not see how your foolish silence is racking my heart? Speak, though it were the worst news possible."

"My lord, your illustrious wife—some internal injury— Aristodemus says she can scarcely live an hour."

"Then may ye all wander in madness where Cocythus howls in primeval gloom. Let me go, Tigellinus! Hence, Phaon, or I'll strangle you! Malice has called me tyrant, corrupter of my people, incendiary. Ye gods above, if ye are aught save figments of the brain,—I'll show ye henceforth how Nero, the god on earth, avenges your spite. Ye and your accursed decrees have conspired to drive me mad. Now ye shall shrink in horror at the inhumanity of my rage."

He sank exhausted into a chair, then suddenly starting up, exclaimed:

"I must go to her! I must see her! I must clasp once more the dear caressing hands that smoothed my brow when all earth's woes assailed me! Phaon, go with me! Your arm! Phaon, Phaon, I believe you, too, are a scoundrel."

"I am faithful, my lord, faithful unto death. See, my tears are falling, too, for as surely as I believe in the gods, I cannot see you suffer."

Nero was unable to thank him. Only a slight pressure of his fingers showed the freedman that his master believed in the sincerity of his grief.

When Nero entered the room where Poppaea lay a convulsive tremor shook his whole frame. She did not stir, save when, ever and anon, her limbs writhed in violent convulsions.

"Poppaea!" he shrieked, wringing his hands.

A bitter mile flickered around her lips, a distortion which wore an aspect of contempt. Then she again lay motionless and expressionless. Consciousness seemed to have deserted her.

Suddenly she started up in bed and her voice rang shrill as the shriek of a maniac:

"Octavia! Have you sated yourself with my blood?"

Her eyes seemed starting from their sockets, and her fingers were clenched like a vulture's claws as she struck two or three blows at the empty air. Then she sank back, her head drooped toward her right shoulder. Once she ground her teeth as if in impotent fury at the frustration of all her hopes. Poppaea Sabina was lifeless.

CHAPTER XXVI.

A YEAR had passed. . . .

What tumult filled the streets of Rome! What shouting and cheering, blended with shrill jeers and fierce curses, rent the air! Everywhere, from the tomb of Scipio to the Milvian bridge, excited groups were rushing to and fro, questions and answers were hurriedly interchanged—and a thundering "Hail to the liberator" greeted each new message from without.

At last, at last the revolution had conquered. The populace, ever demanding bread and games, on whom the terrible despot had relied, looked on indifferently at the destruction of his authority. Tigellinus, the commander of the body-guard, cowardly and faithless, as Phaon had predicted, had gone over to the rebels. But his destiny was already sealed. Galba, the future emperor, who, with his legions, had arrived within a few miles of Rome, would inevitably exile him at once, for the hated Agrigentine's co-operation was the one dark spot in the brilliant picture of this honorable revolt against the mad insolence of absolution.

Julius Vindex, the heroic champion of ancient Roman liberty and manly dignity, had taken up Piso's work—baffled at the twelfth hour by the treachery of Milichus—and by the iron self-control which had enabled him to bear the tyrant's yoke until the decisive moment, had won for himself a laurel wreath more glorious than the garlands of the divine Africanus. True, the laurel was a death-garland, for he did not survive the victory of the good cause. Nero, who beheld in Vindex only the loyal soldier, not the wrathful patriot, had made the noble Aquitanian Propraetor of Northern Gaul—and on the banks of the Sequana he matured the plan which ended Caesar's mad career. It was not for himself that Julius Vindex sought the mastery. A second Cincinnatus, his desire was merely to serve his native land, which was slowly bleeding to death under the claws of the Caesarian lion. The upright, venerable Galba, who had ruled Northern Hispania and other provinces with the strictest justice, ever striving, so far as lay in his power, to mitigate the fierce onslaughts of the imperial tyrant, seemed to the enthusiastic Vindex the person best fitted to unite the shattered state, restore the respect due to the sovereign, and secure to the nation the blessings of internal peace. So he proclaimed Galba emperor. The war-loving Gauls flocked in throngs to Vindex's standard. Ere a month had passed he had collected a well-armed force, eager for the fray. Meantime the governor of Roman Germanica, Virginius Rufus, had been won over to Galba's cause. Vindex's troops were to join those of Rufus. Then occurred the event which cost the life of the creator of the gigantic insurrection. When both armies were on the eve of uniting, a misunderstanding happened, Rufus' soldiers imagined that Vindex was about to attack them. A hand to hand conflict began between the foremost ranks. Julius Vindex, terribly excited, supposed himself to be betrayed by his fellow-conspirators. Despairing of the success of the work planned with so much toil, he flung himself on his sword, ere Virginius Rufus could explain the truth to him.

But the hundred-thousand headed revolution did not die with Julius Vindex—on the contrary, it imbibed resistless power from the heroic blood of its idolized leader.

Nearer and nearer the enthusiastic troops approached the capital, and Galba had already sent couriers to the senate.

In the train of the newly-proclaimed emperor was a tall, slender man, with a pale face surrounded by dark waving locks, and lips, once wont to smile joyously or pout for tender caresses, now firmly set—Otho, the governor of Lusitania.

He had come to take a cruel revenge on Nero for the unspeakable shame, the mute sacrifice, the terrible anguish of so many weary years.

The whole tortured land longed for vengeance on the destroyer of the state, who held all the world in scorn, who since Poppaea's death had shattered the last barriers of self-control and become what Piso's followers had formerly termed him—the curse of the human race.

The promoters of this crushing insurrection did not ask the condition of the heart and brain of the man who had performed such reckless deeds of cruelty. They judged only the acts, not the dreary, hopeless mood which gave them birth. And, in sooth, they had a right to do so.

Down with the criminal who thought of naught save his own desires and agony, and would fain pulverize the whole universe to make a balm to soothe the torture burning in his soul.

Down with the fiend, odious to the gods, who had trampled on mankind.

Rome was in a wild uproar. The praetorians had long since retreated from the Golden House, and were now roving in large bodies through the city, where Nero's statues, amid jeering laughter and curses, were flung from their pedestals, insulted, and mutilated. Even the usually faithful Germans had slipped quietly away. No one desired to perish with the sinking Caesar. The vast palace was deserted. Nero, deadly pale, waited in the revolving chamber, whose machinery that day was not in motion. In his hand he held a sword, irresolute whether to turn its point against his own breast or rush down and slay one more victim to soothe his burning rage.

All had deserted him, save Cassius, his body-slave, and the

freedman Phaon, who still remained in the terrible solitude. The superb building which, but a short time before, had been the scene of bloody conflicts between gladiators, riotous drinking-bouts, and shameless orgies, was like a tomb. The outer gates were locked.

Phaon pondered deeply, forming plan after plan to save his master, and rushing in despair from one courtyard to another.

Vain. How should he, known to every one in Rome, venture to fly with Claudius Nero through the swarming throngs?

Utterly disheartened, he sank on a marble bench and clasped his hands in his lap.

The main entrance on the southern side was open. Brave Cassius, spear in hand, stood there with glassy eyes, ready to slay the first person who approached.

Strangely enough, not one of the rebels dared to enter the vestibule. In his stupor Cassius had not even attempted to push the bolt through the iron sockets. He did not know that the flying praetorians, as if ashamed of their noiseless retreat, had shattered the door. Yet no one came. Nero's name still possessed the power of paralyzing the two millions of excited people outside. The fear of him was so deeply rooted, that even the news of the desertion of all the troops did not efface it.

Suddenly Cassius started. One of the furious mob was an exception to the rest. His steps echoed in the ostium.

"What do you want?" asked Cassius levelling his spear.

"Caesar," was the reply.

Now the slave reocgnized him.

It was Pallas, Agrippina's former confidant. He had secretly aided in the emperor's downfall. Far away in distant Lusitania, he had poured venom into the desperate Otho's wounds, told honest Galba of the empress-mother's death, and branded Nero, the murdered woman's son, with the deed. He lingered, too, in Gaul to fan the flames of rebellion against the man whom he hated more than any other human being, not for the sake of the slain Agrippina, but from his burning memory of the fair girl, whom he had loved with fervent longing—and lost for Caesar's whim. So he believed, for this was Agrippina's account of Nero's relation to Acte.

"Let me pass, Cassius! I mean the fallen emperor no harm. I seek to save him."

"You?" asked Cassius doubtfully.

He had lowered his lance.

"Yes, I," the other repeated. "The senators are already ascending the steps of the Capitol to sit in judgment upon the state-criminal. Time presses."

Cassius followed.

"Speak, what do you intend to do?" he asked.

"You shall see. Only let me know where the illustrious Caesar is, you can stay here."

At that moment Cassius perceived that Pallas was carrying a naked sword under his tunic."

"Halt!" he shouted. "What is the meaning of that blade?" He had seized the intruder by the shoulder.

Pallas tried to shake him off, but failing in the effort, suddenly flung aside the mask of hypocrisy and grasped his concealed weapon, piercing the breast of the faithful slave, while Cassius buried his dagger in his shoulder. Both fell groaning on the ground together.

"Cowardly dog!" gasped Cassius. "You would not trust yourself in the lion's presence till malice had treacherously cut his sinews. There, take this, ere you descend to the horrors of the nether world."

In falling he had snatched the dagger from the wound and now thrust its blood-stained blade into the groin of his master's foe. Pallas, with the last energy of despair, clutched him by the throat, but Cassius struck the weapon to its hilt, as if he could not do enough in punishment of the crime.

Directly after, the limbs of both dying men relaxed. Pallas writhed in terrible convulsions, then lay stark and stiff as a bronze statue. Cassius slipped from the corpse, opened his eyes once more, then with his head resting against the foot of the Corinthian column, lay calm and dignified as a warrior who has died a glorious death amid the rage of battle.

Meanwhile Caesar had been listening to the uproar in the streets, which echoed ominously through the opening in the vaulted ceiling.

Did not he hear the noise of battle?

Surely Tigellinus, his old and faithful friend, would collect at least a cohort to defend him.

Nero did not suspect that Tigellinus had been the first to desert, as quickly as possible, the sinking ship of Caesar's sovereignty.

Yet if he still had friends, if there was any one to wield the sword for him, why was the vast palace so lifeless, so silent?

Had the runaway slaves lost all fear of the master who would crush them for their disobedience?

Where were the countless court-officials, the Atrienses in their gold-broidered garments, the men who announced the passage of the hours, the body-slaves, the stewards, the physicians—all the miserable wretches who had shared his splendor and his greatness?

Where, too, were the Sicambrian body-guard, on whom he had lavished thousands, who had vowed fidelity to him by the raven-attended god of their native land.

Raising his sword, he went to the door. A long suite of apartments stretched silently before his searching gaze.

"Cassius," he called—and "Cassius" echoed back as if in mockery from the golden wainscot of the walls.

All was empty, desolate as a necropolis. He walked on, his knees tottering as he moved. At the right and left he saw his own pale face mirrored a hundred times in the shining metal. Going to the nearest wall he stared like a madman straight into the eyes which seemed to him so large, so terror-stricken, so vacant. Seized with sudden horror, he hurried on, trembling at the echo of his own footsteps.

"Cassius!" he called again, then paused to listen.

All was still.

Despair such as he had never before experienced seized

him, and when he again beheld in the golden plates the reflection of his own distorted visage, he rushed at it with uplifted sword, striking the shining metal like a maniac till the blade broke and the hilt fell rattling on the floor from his wearied hand.

Hark, what was that?

He distinctly heard the threatening shout which robbed him of the last vestige of hope.

"Bring him out!" The words seemed instinct with the malice of fiends. "Drag the villain before the Senate! Or will you give him time to drink poison?"

An icy chill ran through the betrayed ruler's form from head to foot. It was Tigellinus' voice. For an instant Caesar felt as if a dark veil had been thrown over his head. Staggering backward, he sank moaning on the nearest couch.

Steps—steps close at his side. He started up, while his trembling fingers sought a weapon. Ay—there was a Syrian dagger in the girdle of his tunic. With the speed of lightning his hand clutched its hilt—to fall paralyzed again.

Between the draped pillars of the entrance stood a girl, a dream of the night, a bewitching vision.

Claudius Nero fell upon his knees.

"Acte!" he cried, covering his bloodless face. "The dead rise from their graves! The end of all things earthly is at hand, and the world dies with Caesar."

"Nero!" said the girl, "it is my living self, the happy and hapless Acte who once rested on your heart. I have been dead—to you. But in secret and unsuspected, I have watched your life as though it were my own and shed tears for you, tears. . . ."

Nero had slowly risen ,and stood gazing timidly at the lovely face over which years of solitude, renunciation, and grief at the terrible degeneracy of her idol had passed leaving no trace save that she was paler than of yore and the sweet deep-blue eyes seemed larger. Yes, she had wept and prayed as a mother prays for her lost child. Each fresh misdeed of Caesar had wrung her heart and uttered to her soul the admonition: "you must hate the man who could sink to such shameful degradation." Yet—she was still radiant with the magical charm of her early youth, still the bewitching fair-haired Acte who, at their first meeting, had shed such light and fragrance into the stainless soul of the youthful Caesar.

"Acte!" he cried, shrinking from the sight of the blissful vision of his early manhood. "What do you seek? Alas, you come too late! Am I raving? So the sea did not swallow you? It was all a deception, a shameful lie? And you could live alone for years, leaving my soul to pine in agony?"

"I was forced to do so. God's law commanded it. Alas, and afterward—Nero, Nero, I trembled when I heard your name from afar."

"Then you will scorn me? At this terrible moment? Ah, had you but come forth from your hiding-place, the past would have been far different, Acte. I became a criminal, a scourge to the human race, because there was a void in my breast which nothing, nothing in this wide world could fill."

"Faith in God would have filled it. Do not gaze at me so despairingly. I have come to save you."

"You? You, my lofty, glorious love? You desire to save the tyrant who has trampled everything under foot, who has sucked the very marrow out of the empire, the bloodhound, whom thousands pursue with curses?"

"Yes," replied Acte, clasping his hand. "In the days of your happiness, you called me your all: now that the whole world turns against you, I will deserve the name. No, no, say no more. I do not ask what you have done, or whether God, in His infinite mercy, can ever forgive you! I know one thing only—that I love you!"

"Then some divine power must have steeled your soul!" cried Caesar, deeply moved. "Acte, Acte, my ever-lamented happiness!"

"Come," she said, sobbing. "A leather paenula, like those worn by workmen, will disguise you, and Rome forgot me long ago. Walk with bowed shoulders, and lean on a staff. Rest your hand firmly on my arm. There! I have chosen the right moment. Where is Phaon? Has Phaon, too, been faithless?"

"Here, here!" said the freedman, who had just entered and now stood rigid with amazement. "What are you planning? Speak, Acte! I will obey blindly."

"Do you hear the noise in the vestibule?" replied the girl. "The last fear of invading these rooms is vanishing. The mob is rushing from the Cyrian Way into the first courtyard! But on the other side, where the clumps of myrtle border the pond, I found the streets deserted. Two of my friends, Nazarenes—do you hear, Caesar?—are waiting there with the necessary garments and a rope ladder. We will climb the wall. My companions are strong. Should chance lead any one to pass that way, they will detain him till we have time to escape. Hasten on before us, Phaon. Your villa will furnish us a refuge till the tumult in Rome has subsided. Then it will be an easy matter to fly by way of the sea, first to Hispania and thence to the distant strand of Germany."

While speaking she passed swiftly from room to room, followed by Nero and Phaon.

"And then?" asked Caesar.

"Then I will help you pray that God may forgive you, as He once pardoned me."

CHAPTER XXVII.

A GLIMMERING moonlight night spread its dim silvery veil over the Roman plains. The Sabine mountains towered aloft in blue-black masses against the sky, and on the other side appeared the long spectral outlines of the gigantic aqueducts.

The road was deserted.

Every creature who possessed life and motion had flocked to Rome, where Galba's entry was expected early the next morning.

Two figures, clinging closely to one another, were walking over the lava slabs of the military road—Nero and his trembling preserver. Phaon and Caesar's private secretary, Epaphroditus, the only one among the throng of courtiers who had also thought of saving his master, had ridden on in advance to make all necessary preparations. Acte had deemed it wiser for Claudius Nero to go on foot, in the guise of a wandering artist. Whoever met him would say: "Impossible! No ruler, with a frantic mob at his heels, flies in that way." Suspicion would then vanish.

What thoughts were passing through the fugitive's brain?

He held in his left hand the kerchief with which he had concealed his face until he reached the limits of the city, and with his right convulsively clutched his companion's slender fingers.

At a bend in the road, the moon shone full into the young girl's face and Nero, for the first time during their flight, gazed deep into her eyes—the same faithful, loving eyes which had met his in the Egyptian's tent with a look so gentle, so tender, so prophetic of future bliss.

What a gulf yawned between that day and this! A torrent of blood rolled through it; wild jeering laughter resounded in the multitudinous echoes above the steaming abyss.

And yet—those eyes smiled as before, nay with a lustre still more divine and tender, for they smiled through tears.

Was there perhaps comfort for the hopeless—mercy for him who had known no mercy, either on himself or mankind?

Exhausted by the emotions of the day, full of hate, wrath, remorse, despair, he stopped and leaned on his companion's arm—like Zeus on the arm of the exslave—then sank down upon the ruins of a forgotten tomb.

"I greet you, pious souls," he read on the dark piece of basalt which had crumbled from the masonry.

Suddenly he started up. He dared not say. The spot was consecrated and he a despised criminal, from whom the most horrible sinners in Oreus would avert their eyes that they might not be turned to stone, as men and gods were at the sight of Medusa's head with its serpent locks.

Acte drew him gently down again.

"Rest!" she whispered, passed her loving hand soothingly across his brow. "My heart tells me that no danger threatens us. Come! Lay your head in my lap! Sleep! I will watch for you."

At the sound of her voice infinite grief overcame the wretched Nero. Hiding his face on her breast, he clasped her in his arms and, sobbing aloud, burst into a flood of burning tears.

"Acte! Acte!" he cried in a voice that rent her heart. Then he sobbed on till his head sank into her lap. She lovingly stroked his waving hair, and he fell asleep—asleep on his flight from the rebellion which menaced him with ruin and death.

Acte gazed at his face which, in the moonlight, looked as pallid and spectral as a dead man's. The last tears were still clinging to his lashes. His lips, once so sweetly eloquent, so ardent, were slightly parted. A flitting smile, scarcely perceptible, yet bewitching, glided over them.

"I know one thing only: that I love you!" she murmured, repeating the words she had uttered in the Golden House. "Now that you are alone and wretched, I can dare to say so. No one, not even the Omnipotent Father Himself, can condemn me for it. Ay, I love you, spite of all your crimes. Love is stronger than death! says the apostle. But it is more, it is stronger than disgrace and sin."

Stooping, she pressed a light kiss on his forehead, and again a smile flitted over his face, a smile as gentle and peaceful as if the dissolute, blood-stained past were effaced and naught remained save the youth's ardent, yearning heart, with its radiant dreams.

Stirred by a strange emotion, she rested her head on her hand.

Suddenly the words she had uttered to the wrathful Pallas on the terrible night when Agrippina's confidant had dragged her away, came back to her memory. Every syllable was still impressed upon her mind. "The hand of God Almighty, in punishing me, shall absolve me" and: "A foreboding that cannot deceive me, tells me that my lips shall still tenderly kiss his brow when the hapless Octavia shall have long quitted this earth, and Agrippina, and you yourself, her crafty, contemptible tool." Was this the fulfilment of her prophecy, a complete and entire fulfilment, so that nothing remained. Or was there still a future?

"Jesus, Saviour of the World," she murmured, looking heavenward, "grant him the sacred strength that leads to atonement! He has not always been wicked; fate, too, is partly in fault—and Thy love is infinite. Aid me to save him— thus shall he learn to believe that Thou didst die on the cross for his redemption also!"

473

Steps were heard approaching from the direction of the Alban Hills.

Nero awoke.

"Do not move, love!" she murmured softly.

But he had already started up—and laid his hand on the dagger hidden under his cloak.

"No," he said, "let us go and meet the men."

They were peasants who, urged by curiosity concerning recent events, were on their way to the city.

"Have you come from Rome?" asked one. "What is the news there? Has the emperor been imprisoned?"

"There was a rumor of it," replied Acte, "but we have no definite tidings."

Her heart was in her throat.

The men passed on.

"Long live Galba!" said the one who had first spoken. "To the cross with Nero the corrupter of the people. I would give you two measures of the best Cyprian to learn that the scoundrel had been dragged to the Gemonian Steps."

"He'll be flogged to death," said the second. "That is the ancient punishment for treason to the country."

Nero shuddered and grasped the hilt of his weapon still more firmly as he hurried on.

Acte walked by his side in silence. She had a thousand different things to say to his suffering soul. She longed so eagerly to question him, search his heart, that she could scarcely resist the impulse. She ardently desired to explain one thing and another; in a word, to obtain light for him and herself. But she controlled the yearning. It was impossible to do this now. He must be spared and comforted.

Again steps rang on the road. A soldier, who had doubtless obtained leave of absence, passed them.

Nero looked him full in the face.

The warrior recognized him.

"Ave Caesar!" fell from his lips.

"I thank you," replied Nero, his eyes flashing with bitter scorn. Then he felt Acte's hand slip gently into his, and the bitterness of his mood vanished.

At the end of an hour they reached the spot where they were obliged to turn from the main road and force a passage through shrubs and thorny bushes to reach Phaon's villa from the rear instead of entering the vestibule. The fugitives found the utmost difficulty in making their way through the tangled undergrowth, but at last succeeded in reaching the appointed spot, where Phaon and Epaphroditus stood waiting to receive them. By dint of great exertion they had made an opening in the wall, through which Caesar, unseen by the slaves, could enter the house.

A pool of water glimmered in the moonlight at the foot of a pine-tree, for rain had fallen the day before.

Nero, torn by the thorns, wearied, and almost dead with thirst, stooped, dipped some of the water in the hollow of his hand and eagerly drank it.

"This is my reviving-cordial now!" he sighed sadly, then turned suddenly to Phaon.

"Hark! What is that? Doesn't it sound like the trampling of hoofs on the highway?"

Epaphroditus hurried to the vestibule and almost instantly returned.

"My lord," he faltered, scarcely able to speak, "you are betrayed. The men are Tigellinus' soldiers sent to seize you. The senate, at the instance of the freedman Icelus, had declared you an enemy of Rome—and pronounced the sentence that you are to be punished according to the custom of our forefathers."

"What *is* 'the custom of our forefathers.'"

"My lord, the doom is horrible," replied Epaphroditus. "The condemned criminal is stripped of his clothing, pilloried, and flogged to death."

"Then tell Icelus, whom I do not know, that I pardon his malice. Whoever has suffered through me is a thousand times avenged by this freedman. Announce to the senate my supreme contempt. I hold the knaves, who while I was sovereign, slavishly licked my sandals, unworthy to crimson my brow with the flush of anger during the last moments of

my life. Phaon, I thank you! And you, too, Epaphroditus!
Guard my corpse. Ask the new Caesar not to forget that all
human affairs are subject to change, and that it does not
beseem the ruler of Rome to insult his conquered enemy in
death.''

His dagger quivered against his heart.

''Acte, my first and last happiness, my all, farewell.''

With a despairing shriek of love, longing, and mortal
terror, she rushed to him to avert the blow, and with a faint
sigh sank on her lover's breast. The keen stiletto had pierced
deep into her bosom.

An expression of indescribable anguish convulsed Nero's
features.

''Acte! Acte! What have you done!'' he gasped, kneeling
beside the dying girl. ''Am I doomed by fate to deal woe and
murder with my latest breath?''

''There is no pain,'' she whispered with a happy smile.
''What would this world be without you? I have lived alone—
alone and desolate—far too long. Now I shall be. . . . with
you. . . . forever. . . . forever.''

Nero flung himself beside her, and again kissed the sweet
lips, then clasping her trembling fingers with his left hand,
raised his right, and buried the dagger in his heart.

The praetorians' swords were clanking behind the hedge.
The centurion, who had stooped and touched Nero on the
shoulder, heard him breathe.

''Bring ropes!'' he shouted to his soldiers.

The dying emperor raised his head.

''Too late!'' fell from his lips.

Then he sank on the faithful heart which, to the last
moment of existence, had throbbed for him alone. He felt the
pressure of a loving hand, and as of yore a whisper reached
his ear, blissful even in this hour of anguish, a whisper of
infinite love and, almost too faint to hear, the fervent
pleading: ''May God be merciful to us!''

Then all was over.

Phaon took his cloak and laid it gently over the lifeless
forms.